Alexander Wilson was a writer, spy and secret service officer. He served in the First World War before moving to India to teach as a Professor of English Literature and eventually became Principal of Islamia College at the University of Punjab in Lahore. He began writing spy novels whilst in India and he enjoyed great success in the 1930s with reviews in the *Telegraph*, *Observer* and the *Times Literary Supplement* amongst others. Wilson also worked as an intelligence agent and his characters are based on his own fascinating and largely unknown career in the Secret Intelligence Service. He passed away in 1963.

By Alexander Wilson

The Mystery of Tunnel 51
The Devil's Cocktail
Wallace of the Secret Service
Get Wallace!
His Excellency, Governor Wallace
Microbes of Power
Wallace at Bay
Wallace Intervenes
Chronicles of the Secret Service

a&b

Wallace of the Secret Service

ALEXANDER WILSON

Allison & Busby Limited
12 Fitzroy Mews
London W1T 6DW
allisonandbusby.com

First published in 1933.
This edition published by Allison & Busby in 2015.

A CIP catalogue record for this book is available from the British Library.

10 9 8 7 6 5 4 3 2 1

Paperback ISBN 978-0-7490-1815-3
Hardback ISBN 978-0-7490-1900-6

Typeset in 10.5/15.5 pt Adobe Garamond Pro by
Allison & Busby Ltd.

The paper used for this Allison & Busby publication has been produced from trees that have been legally sourced from well-managed and credibly certified forests.

Printed and bound by
CPI Group (UK) Ltd, Croydon, CR0 4YY

CONTENTS

FOREWORD

In accepting the invitation to write an introduction to certain records of the career of Sir Leonard Wallace, I was actuated not so much by the friendship and admiration I feel for the famous Chief of the Intelligence Corps, as by the fact that I was luckily instrumental in obtaining his services for the department. At the time of which I write, I was Secretary of State for Home Affairs, and Sir Leonard was recuperating, after being discharged from hospital, at the tiny seaside village of Kimmeridge in Dorset. He had been badly wounded in the left arm, and, with his great friend, William Brien, also on sick leave, and his charming wife, Molly, had originally gone to Kimmeridge merely to laze about, as he himself puts it. But that astuteness of his, which since has proved of such great value to the country, enabled him to ferret out a German submarine base actually on the Dorset coast. He immediately travelled up to London, and got into communication with me through his father, the Earl of Westcliff.

The story he told was astounding, and I found the utmost difficulty in crediting it. I was in favour of putting the matter in the hands of the Intelligence Department, and also making arrangements for a force of troops and a squadron of destroyers to proceed to the spot, but Sir Leonard – he was Major Wallace then – pointed out that the Germans would be certain to get wind of the operations against them, and decamp before there was time to invest their headquarters. He declared that he believed it to be not only a submarine base but also a distributing centre from where spies were sent to all parts of Great Britain. In reply to my question concerning what he himself proposed, he put before me a plan that for sheer ingenuity and daring almost took my breath away. He asked to be given charge of the affair, with full authority to call in the aid of the coastguards and troops from Wareham, if necessary. Naturally I was very reluctant, but he had impressed me so much by his obvious ability and sagacity that eventually I agreed, not without a great deal of misgiving, however.

The result was stupendous, and reads, even in the cold, official report, like a page from the chronicles of the old Greek and Trojan heroes. It is too long a story to tell here; perhaps some day it may be given to the public – I hope so, for it is quite one of his greatest exploits. Suffice it to say that, with Brien, Cecil Kendal, his brother-in-law, half a dozen troops from the camp at Wareham, and a few coastguards, he actually entered the large cave which the Germans had so ingeniously turned into a secret base and, effecting a complete surprise, captured five submarines and killed or captured their crews. Not only that, but he also apprehended several spies. Unfortunately he was shot again in his damaged arm during the fight, with the result that it was later found imperative to amputate it.

In a sense his triumph was one of the greatest feats of the War, for it not only badly interfered with Germany's submarine campaign but supplied us with a mass of information that was priceless. Major Wallace richly deserved the KCB which was conferred on him and the full rank of colonel to which he was promoted. Brien received his majority and the CMG while others, who took part in the historic exploit, were adequately rewarded.

Without an arm, Sir Leonard's active military career received a set-back, but it was impossible for such a man to be shelved. I suggested his being attached to the Intelligence Service, a suggestion received with enthusiasm by my colleagues, and immediately acted upon. It was not long before he became head of the bureau, and his work since then has been remarkably successful, bearing always the hall-mark of that astuteness, ingenuity, coolness, and wit which have always placed him above his fellows. Major Brien returned to the front, but after the War, at Sir Leonard's special request, was transferred to his department.

I am delighted that certain deeds are now to be chronicled and given to the public. They should prove most absorbing to people who are interested in the workings of the Secret Service. Sir Leonard himself, though not actually objecting to the publication of his achievements, would much prefer, I think, that they were lost in obscurity. He is not the man to desire fame or notoriety; rather he prefers seclusion and privacy. His chronicler has, therefore, been forced to fall back on office records and information supplied by various members of the service who, once they understood there was no objection to their divulging certain happenings, eagerly prepared the way for the publication of a few of the exploits of the chief to whom they are all devoted.

Romance and adventure are not dead while there exist men

of the type of Sir Leonard Wallace. He proves that fact is stranger than fiction, and into the cold, matter-of-fact atmosphere of the twentieth century brings a flavour of daring enterprise that is reminiscent of more adventurous times. Yet to look at him you would not imagine that there were even the elements of romance and adventure in him, unless he gave you the opportunity of gazing deep into his expressive, steel-grey eyes. He is a slightly-built man of about five feet eight in height with an attractive but by no means handsome face, the curves of which show that he possesses a great sense of humour. He has an easy-going disposition, and rather gives the impression of being a man who loves to loiter his way through life. He has a cool, calculating mind, behind an unruffled exterior, which provides him with the imagination and quick perception that make him so successful in detective work. Perhaps his greatest asset is his unexcitable temperament and perfect self-control. I have known ministers of State exasperated at his nonchalance but, being no respecter of persons, that worries him not at all. I must confess to a sneaking fear that he does not always regard His Majesty's statesmen with the respect they invariably think is their due.

Sir Leonard himself would be the first to admit that he owes a great deal to those assistants of his of whom the names of Major Brien, Cousins, Maddison, Carter and Shannon come most readily to mind. They have shared dangers and difficulties with him, or undertaken duties at his behest, which would cause the ordinary man to blench. Then there are the others of both sexes distributed throughout the world who, often carrying their lives in their hands, supply him with the information which enables Great Britain to deal with the delicate international situations which constantly arise, and combat the still frequent foreign plots. The agents, who live abroad, generally follow some harmless profession in order to cloak their real activities, but their lives are full of danger, and they know well that once unmasked their chances of avoiding long terms of imprisonment, sometimes even death, are small indeed. Then there is the enormous office staff which deals with the many documents relative to foreign intrigue and international diplomacy. This staff nowadays is directly under the orders of Major Brien, an arrangement that saves Sir Leonard Wallace a considerable amount of routine work.

It is remarkable the degree of proficiency which the Intelligence Department has attained. Every branch dovetails into the others with meticulous exactitude, and the work proceeds day and night, quietly, silently, efficiently. Few people realise what the country owes to the gallant men of this silent service. To them fame and glory seldom come, riches never. Often they die shameful, inglorious deaths, honoured only by their colleagues, who mourn them mutely, unable to make public their devotion, or acknowledge them as associates. Theirs is the ideal patriotism, the love of country which takes no account of self, but is prepared to sacrifice home, family, everything for the sake of the land that gave them birth.

I do not feel that I can deal adequately with such a subject. The Secret Service has naturally far more to do with the Foreign Office than any other government department, and my political activities were mostly confined to the Home Office and law departments. However, as I have stated, I was associated with Sir Leonard Wallace in his first adventure, and I am honoured now to be associated, even though so insignificantly, with a volume narrating a few of his exploits.

C.

CHAPTER ONE

Out of the Land of Egypt

'I'm worried, Bill, and there's no use disguising it. It's over a week now since we heard from Henderson.'

The speaker strolled to one of the two large windows, and eyed the busy stream of traffic passing in Whitehall almost as though he hoped to gain inspiration from it. The tall, fair man, whose upright carriage and small moustache suggested a soldier, remained standing by the large oak desk thoughtfully tapping his fingers on its polished surface.

'It isn't often you admit feeling worried,' he commented. 'Surely a week without news is not very disquieting. Perhaps circumstances have caused a delay, or Henderson has no news to send.'

'He was ordered to keep in communication with us,' retorted the other without turning round, 'and he would have done so – if he could.'

The significance of the last three words was not lost upon Major Brien. The lids half-closed over his twinkling blue eyes, banishing their humour, and rendering them very nearly sinister.

'Are you suspecting foul play?'

There was no answer, and he helped himself to a cigarette from a large silver box on the desk, apparently quite content to wait until his chief came out of the brown study into which he appeared to have fallen. Sir Leonard Wallace remained at the window for some minutes longer, then walked slowly back to the desk.

'I am going out to Egypt myself,' he announced quietly.

His companion looked sharply at him.

'You really think it is serious then?'

'Very serious,' was the reply. 'I believe that Henderson's object has been discovered, and he himself imprisoned, or perhaps even assassinated.'

Brien's lips pursed in a low whistle, but he smiled.

'You're imaginative this morning, Leonard,' he observed.

'Have you ever known me allow my imagination to run away with me?' demanded the other sharply. 'No, you haven't!' replying to his own question. 'You possibly have not studied affairs in Egypt as I have. The country is seething with intrigue, and the extreme Nationalists under that impracticable fanatic, Zaghlul Pasha, are going to make a lot of trouble before very long.'

'But, dash it all! The independence of Egypt has been recognised. What more do they want?'

'My son, they want full control. They resent the powers which the British Government retain, particularly with regard to the Sudan. Henderson's job, as you know, was to find out exactly what is happening; if possible to unmask any plot that might be brewing, and bring us details. All we've had from him was his code message a week ago saying that he was on the track of something big. Since then there hasn't been a word. It's all wrong, Bill and I'm going to find out what has happened.'

He took a pipe from the desk, filled it from a large tobacco bowl, and lit it carefully. An onlooker would never have suspected that one of his arms was artificial, so cleverly did he use it. The only noticeable peculiarity was that his left hand was covered by a glove, which was seldom removed.

'When are you leaving?'

'Tonight. I thought at first of taking you with me, but it's not necessary. Besides I may want you here.'

He walked to the fireplace, and stood with his back leaning against the high mantelpiece. He hardly gave one the impression that his mind was full of great issues; in fact he looked thoroughly indolent as he stood placidly puffing at his briar, and gazing round his comfortable office with an air of proprietorship.

It was a large room unusually well-furnished for a government office. The carpet which covered the floor was an Axminster; a warm-looking thick pile rug lay in front of the fireplace, which was deep and surmounted by a massive mantelpiece. A large, beautifully carved clock stood on the latter with heavy brass ornaments, reminiscent of the War, on each flank. Against the opposite wall of the room were bookshelves, containing practically every known reference book as well as voluminous reports from all the government departments. On one side of the great oak desk was Sir Leonard's swing chair, on the other, two leather armchairs, another standing close to the fire. The desk itself was covered with official-looking documents and books, while from most of the available wall space hung maps. Obviously the office of a busy man, it was just as obviously the room of a man who liked comfort.

'I think I'd better come with you,' observed Brien. 'If there's likely to be trouble, I might come in useful.'

'You might be very much in the way,' was the blunt retort. 'No, Bill, I'd much rather you remained at headquarters. I'll go alone – I don't think I'll even take Batty with me.'

It was so unusual for Wallace to go abroad without his manservant that the frown on Brien's face grew deeper, and his forehead became wrinkled with perplexity.

'What is the game?' he demanded.

'Deck tennis and quoits on boardship,' was the joking reply, 'and possibly a round or two of golf in Cairo.'

Brien, muttering something that sounded uncomplimentary, threw himself into one of the armchairs.

'What are the orders?' he asked.

Wallace strolled back to the desk, sat himself in his chair, and leant towards his companion. All the flippancy was gone now from his face and manner, his whole attitude denoting grave purposefulness. For the next quarter of an hour he spoke rapidly, Brien listening to him intently and occasionally making notes in a small book that he had drawn from his pocket.

A few days later Sir Leonard arrived in Port Said on board an Italian mail boat from Brindisi. The pontoon had hardly connected the liner to the shore, when he was walking rapidly along it, followed by a man carrying his meagre luggage consisting of two large suitcases. He went direct to the Eastern Exchange Hotel, booked a room under the name of Collins, then choosing a secluded table, under the awning in front of the hotel, sat down and ordered coffee. He was pestered by the usual crowd of street vendors, conjurers and the like but chased them all away until a tall, good-looking native approached, carrying upon his head a tray full of boxes of Turkish delight. Sir Leonard at first ignored him as he had done the rest, but presently, as though allowing himself to be persuaded, took a gaudily decorated box in his hand and asked the price. They were alone for the moment, and the seller of the sticky sweetmeat spoke in a low voice, but his reply had nothing to do with the question asked.

'I received your cable, Excellency, and am here as you see. What is it you wish of me?'

'Have you any news of Mr Henderson?' asked Sir Leonard also in a low voice.

'No; he was here two weeks ago, then left for Cairo.'

'You have seen nothing of him since?'

'Nothing.'

'He had not communicated with us for over a week before I left England. I think his mission must have been discovered. I want you to trace him to Cairo, Achmet, and, if possible, find out what has happened to him there. I'll wait here until I hear from you. But hurry; there may be no time to lose.'

'I understand, effendi.' Then, in a louder voice, for people had approached and several other vendors were nearby, he added: 'I know you, Mr Macpherson; my name Macpherson too. Buy my Turkish delight – ver-ry good!'

Sir Leonard laughingly bought a couple of boxes, thinking of his little son's glee when they were presented to him. The sight of their compatriot's success caused a horde of the chattering Arabs to descend on Wallace with their goods and, to escape them, he was forced to retire into the hotel. In the meantime Achmet, one of the most astute members of the rank and file of the Secret Service, who cloaked his real identity under the guise of a purveyor of Turkish delight, had slipped away and before long, through channels known only to himself, was commencing his task of tracing Henderson.

Three days passed slowly by, and Sir Leonard, having exhausted the diversions that Port Said presented for his amusement or delectation, impatiently awaited news from his assistant. It came in the form of a cryptic telegram regarding the despatch of curios to Europe. It did not take him long to decipher the message, and he frowned deeply at the news it contained. It told him, as he had feared, that Henderson was a prisoner in the hands of the people whose doings he had come to Egypt to study. Achmet was waiting in Cairo, and would watch at Shepheard's Hotel for Sir Leonard's advent.

That same afternoon the latter left for the capital, and on arrival was driven to the hotel. He still retained the name of Collins and let it be known that he was a retired army officer travelling for his health.

It was the wrong time of the year for tourists. The trouble in Egypt, too, was keeping a lot of visitors away. The hotel, therefore, was not overburdened with guests, a state of affairs which did not altogether please Sir Leonard. Inquisitiveness and speculation concerning him were more likely to be rife than if the hotel were crowded. However, it could not be helped; it behoved him to take extra precautions, that was all.

Achmet came to him before he had been long installed in the hotel. He wore now the dress of a dragoman, and had told the servant, who announced him to the Englishman, that he had been ordered to attend, as the white lord had need of his services on the various excursions he contemplated making to the pyramids and other places of interest. When they were together, even though there was apparently no one within hearing of their conversation, little of a private nature passed between Wallace and his subordinate. The former merely detailed his plans for a trip up the Nile and asked Achmet to engage a *dahabeeyah* to be ready for him early the following morning. The spy stood obsequiously before the languid-looking Englishman, listening carefully to the instructions he was receiving, and appearing for all the world the typical dragoman.

Wallace had no intention of travelling up the Nile at all, but he was careful to give the appearance of complete innocence to his meeting with the Arab, knowing perfectly well that the main lounge of Shepheard's was hardly the place, under any circumstances, in which to discuss confidential matters. Apart from that, Achmet on arrival had uttered a warning.

'This place is full of spies,' he had said, as he bowed low before the other. 'Command me to engage a small *dahabeeyah*. Tomorrow we will go a few miles beyond Cairo for a little trip. It will be safer to speak then.'

Thus it was arranged, and Achmet departed. A little later Sir Leonard left the hotel for a stroll. It had been an intolerably hot day, but now, with the setting of the sun, a breeze had sprung up which materially cooled the atmosphere. He walked as far as the bridge, guarded so strikingly by the two bronze lions, and watched the heterogeneous crowd that was crossing over the Nile. Several years had passed since he had looked on that scene with its riot of gaudy colouring and its confused uproar, but nothing appeared to have altered. Motor cars, donkey carts, carriages, asses, and camels were mixed up in apparently hopeless disorder, but somehow managed to move and be content with the slowness of their pace. An ancient vehicle, drawn by a donkey almost as ancient, and containing two veiled women, did manage to cause a stoppage by becoming entangled with a stylish carriage. The driver of the latter belaboured the donkey boy unmercifully, while the women added their shrill voices to the general din, but a policeman succeeded in separating the two vehicles and, with a final hearty cuff to the old donkey, sent the creaking cart on its way.

Wallace had watched the scene with amusement, indeed had even added his efforts to the process of extrication. At first he thought the carriage empty, but as it moved by he caught a glimpse of a pair of dark eyes, flashing seductively under thick black eyelashes. The woman, whoever she was, wore the thinnest of *yashmaks*, and it seemed to Sir Leonard that he could faintly discern a mocking smile lurking at the corners of her lips as she glanced at him. He wondered idly who she was, as he walked slowly back to the hotel, but soon forgot her existence.

After dinner that night, a note was brought to him and, feeling perplexed and a trifle concerned, he took it from the tray which the *soffraghi* held towards him. His mystification was further increased as he caught the elusive scent of some perfume and, for a moment, he balanced the note in his hand frowning thoughtfully. The waiter remained standing by and, on being told to go, informed Sir Leonard that an answer was awaited.

The Englishman then tore the envelope open, and extracted the half sheet of dainty notepaper which it contained. His bewilderment, instead of being diminished by what he read, increased to a state of sheer astonishment. There were only two sentences, and neither superscription nor signature. The writing was obviously that of a female.

The lady in the carriage on the bridge would like to meet Mr Collins. If he follows the bearer of this note, he will learn something to his advantage.

For several moments Wallace sat staring at the paper in his hand, and he was doing the hardest thinking he had engaged in for some time. He was by no means a ladies' man, his wife, Molly, being all in all to him, and not for one moment did he imagine that the dark-haired woman, of whom he had caught such a fleeting glance, had been attracted by him, and desired his acquaintance, merely for the sake of coquetry. There was something deeper underlying her motive in sending him such an extraordinary invitation. Of that he was assured. What could she have to tell him that would be to his advantage? And how did she know his spurious name? So many possibilities hinged on the note that a feeling of intense disquiet troubled him, and he came to the conclusion that speculation was useless.

'Where is the messenger?' he asked suddenly.

In the foyer, he was informed, and directed the waiter to lead him to the man. A gigantic Ethiopian stood stiffly at the entrance like a picturesque statue, but to all Sir Leonard's questions he shook his head, either indicating that he could not answer them or did not understand. The situation was growing momentarily more perplexing, but, although anxious to solve the problem, he had no intention of accepting the invitation of the letter, and following the lady's sable messenger. Bidding the *soffraghi*, who still remained in attendance, to tell the man to wait, he walked off to the writing room. Some instinct caused him to glance round after he had gone a few paces, and he saw the two in earnest conversation – much more earnest than

Wallace's instruction to the waiter would appear to warrant. It looked as though the latter was in collusion with the other or, at least, knew more about the affair than a disinterested member of the hotel staff should know.

Sir Leonard sat for some minutes at a writing-table idly tapping, with a pen, the notepaper he had drawn towards him. He remembered Achmet's words: 'This place is full of spies,' and wondered if the *soffraghi* and the eunuch were connected with the people he had come to Cairo to unmask. If so, it would mean that he and his purpose were known, and that a plot was on foot to get him into their power. It seemed impossible that such could be the case, but nobody knew better than Wallace himself how often the seemingly impossible happened in life, especially in his profession. A smile curled his lips for an instant as he reflected on the nature of the attempt. It was crude and gave him a poor opinion of the craftiness of those in opposition to him. Did they actually expect him to go blindly into the zenana of a private house, there to be killed or captured, or found by a professedly scandalised husband, reported to the government and sent back to England in disgrace? To use a woman as a decoy in a country where women are segregated from men was, in his opinion, a clumsy sort of ruse. The very banality of it gave his thoughts pause. Surely if he were actually known, and a conspiracy in operation to seize his person, there were dozens of ways of accomplishing their designs without causing suspicion to their proposed victim by the very puerility of the venture. Perhaps, after all, the message was genuine, and the lady was actually in possession of information which would be of use to him. Then he remembered the mocking smile which he could have sworn he had perceived beneath the gossamer veil, when she had passed him on the bridge, and he slowly shook his head. But whichever way he contemplated the matter, it appeared evident that he was known to a certain party in Cairo, a contingency which caused him to look very grave. With a slight shrug of the shoulders he commenced to write.

> *Mr Collins is honoured by the invitation of the lady in the carriage. He feels, however, that a visit to her might be misconstrued, and regrets, therefore, his inability to accept. The information which the lady desires to impart may be sent by letter, but Mr Collins is certain that a mistake of some kind has been made.*

Sir Leonard smiled grimly as he read over what he had written, then folding the paper he placed it in an envelope, which he sealed. He found the Ethiopian and *soffraghi* still together, but now they were apparently ignoring each other. He caught a fleeting expression of surprise on the latter's face, which roused his suspicions more than ever. The man knew the contents of the letter, he surmised, and had expected him to be dressed to go out. Handing his note to the messenger, Wallace directed him to take it to the person who had sent him. At once the tall eunuch broke into a string of voluble Arabic, which the waiter translated to mean that the fellow had received instructions to take the English Lord with him.

'Tell him that the letter explains,' Wallace ordered curtly and, without further ado, turned and walked away.

He was tempted to question the *soffraghi* in an effort to learn how much the man knew, but decided that such an essay would be injudicious and certainly unsuccessful. He went to his room, locked himself in and, filling and lighting a pipe, threw himself into a cane chair and thought things over. But he failed to come to any definite conclusion, and eventually prepared himself for bed, reflecting that perhaps Achmet would be able to give him a clue on the morrow.

Selecting a novel from a pile on the table, he lay reading until close on midnight when, with a yawn, he put the book down and, switching off the light, composed himself for sleep. But, try as he would, he was unable to entice the requisite drowsiness, his mind persisting in dwelling upon the woman with the dark eyes and her extraordinary message to him. At last, with an impatient grunt, he reached out and turned on the light again, having decided to resume reading, when there came a gentle rap on the door. It was so soft that, at first, he thought he had imagined it, but a few seconds later it was repeated. Wondering who could want him at that time of night, Wallace slipped out of bed, and hastily donned a dressing-gown. He strode towards the door, but stopped half-way to return and rummage in a suitcase, from which he extracted a revolver. Smiling a trifle grimly to himself, he put it into his pocket. The knock came again and, a moment later, he unlocked the door to stand almost bereft of movement as his eyes took in the dim outlines of the person standing on the threshold. It was a woman.

With an effort he pulled himself together, and was about to ask her business, when she pushed him aside and quickly entered the room.

'Shut the door, Monsieur,' she commanded, speaking in French.

'Pardon me,' he retorted, also in that language, 'but I think some sort of explanation is necessary before I—'

'Please! Please!' she interrupted urgently. 'I will explain when you have done what I ask.'

He still hesitated and, with an exclamation that sounded very much like a cry of fear, she swept past him and closed the door herself. Then, returning to the centre of the apartment, she threw herself into a chair, and gave a sigh of relief. She was clothed in Egyptian dress, and a suspicion in Sir Leonard's mind that she was the lady of the bridge was turned into fact, when she deftly removed the Spanish shawl, which had enveloped her head and shoulders, and turned her uncovered face to him. Its beauty almost caused him to gasp, but he restrained himself and looked at her as though unaware of the flawless complexion, the allure of those perfectly shaped scarlet lips and large, dark eyes surmounted by long black lashes and delicately pencilled brows. It seemed to him that her face was familiar, but he could not remember on what previous occasion he had seen it.

'I am waiting, Madame,' he reminded her, 'for the explanation you promised me.'

She smiled, but the shadow of fear lurked in her wonderful eyes.

'I have come to you,' she told him, 'because you would not come to me.'

'But why? Do you realise that you have compromised yourself by forcing your way into this room?'

She nodded.

'Of course I realise it,' she returned in subdued tones. 'Oh, why did you compel me to come here?'

'I compel you!' he exclaimed. 'I did nothing of the sort.'

'But you did, by declining my invitation. That made it necessary for me to come to you.'

'I am afraid I don't understand.'

'It was to warn you that I took the risk of writing to you, and now of coming here.'

Sir Leonard frowned at her.

'Warn me of what?' he demanded.

'You are known, and there is a plot to murder you.'

For a few seconds he stood gazing at her, then took a chair opposite hers and leant forward.

'May I ask you to be more explicit?' he requested quietly.

'Listen then, Monsieur,' she complied. 'My husband is one of the leaders of the extreme Nationalist party, whose object is the entire freedom of Egypt, recognition of the Sudan as part of the Egyptian Kingdom, control of the Suez Canal, and other matters not so important. Perhaps you are already aware of that?'

Wallace nodded.

'The party has spies everywhere,' she went on, 'and when you stepped ashore at Port Said it was known here almost at once. You have been watched ever since, and it has been decided to murder you as the safest means of preventing you from prying into the secrets of the extremists.'

'But this is absurd,' protested Sir Leonard. 'Why should these people be interested in a retired officer spending a well-earned holiday in Egypt? And as for prying into their secrets, I—'

She interrupted him with a little exclamation of impatience.

'Monsieur,' she pleaded, 'let us be frank with each other. I have come here at great danger to my reputation, perhaps my life, and there is no time to lose in this pretence. The extremists know you are not Monsieur Collins – they know your real name is Sir Leonard Wallace, and that you are the Chief of the British Intelligence Department; so do I!'

'This is most interesting,' commented Wallace. 'And how do they know that?'

'Yours is not the only secret service in the world, Monsieur Wallace,' she retorted. 'Apart from that, you are well known in London, are you not? Many Egyptians go to your country in the season and attend your functions. My husband and I go frequently, and both of us know you well by sight.'

Sir Leonard remembered then that it was in London where he had seen her before. She had been in European dress, of course, which explained why he had not readily recognised her. He decided that it was useless to continue to pose as Collins.

'Since I am known so well, Madame,' he observed regretfully, 'I suppose I must admit my identity. I still don't quite understand, however, why I should be watched and suspected of ulterior motives. My object in coming to Egypt may be quite innocent.'

She smiled mockingly.

'Is it likely that Sir Leonard Wallace would leave his beautiful wife and come to Egypt for a holiday during the wrong season of the year? Nobody with sense would believe that, Monsieur. My husband's party was expecting you to send out a man to investigate, and every Englishman landing in Alexandria, Port Said, and Suez has been subjected to the keenest scrutiny for a long time. The arrival of the great Sir Leonard himself made things for them so much the easier.'

Again came that mocking smile. Despite the fact that he was beginning to feel that she was really actuated by a desire to save him from her husband and his party, that smile prevented him from dismissing his suspicions altogether. He was about to ask her if she knew of Henderson's fate, but instinct restrained him, instead:

'How do you know all this, Madame,' he asked; 'and why are you telling me?'

'Because I do not wish you to be murdered,' she replied earnestly, answering his second question first. 'Also I am not in sympathy with the extremists, although I am a Nationalist. As for my knowledge of these things, it is easily explained. My husband thinks my ideas are the same as his and, in consequence, he does not keep anything from me.'

'You recognised me on the bridge today?' he questioned.

'Yes. It was then that I made up my mind to warn you.'

He rose and stood looking down at her.

'It is extremely good of you, Madame. I appreciate the service you are doing me, and your risking so much to come here.'

'And you will leave Egypt at once, will you not?' she pleaded earnestly.

He smiled at her.

'If I am here for the reason you suspect,' he observed, 'I can hardly let a little danger deter me from my purpose, can I?'

'Oh, but, Monsieur, you must! You are in deadly peril.'

'If I am, then that shows me very clearly that there must be something going on which requires my attention.'

He caught a gleam very much like antipathy in her eyes, but it was gone almost before it had come. It sufficed to put him immediately on his guard, however, and to cause his suspicions to return in force. He thanked her once again for her warning, and urged her to depart. At once she was on her feet entreating him to leave Cairo. She came so close to him that he felt her breath on his cheek, and drew back involuntarily. All the time his thoughts were busy, trying desperately to guess the real reason for her presence in his room, for he had suddenly become convinced that her motives were detrimental to him. Continuing her pleas, she persistently drew near him, while he as persistently stepped back. Then, turning from her, he walked towards the door.

'I dare not let you stay longer, Madame,' he observed. 'The risk to you is too great.'

Before he quite realised what she was doing, she flung her arms round him, as though in a paroxysm of fear.

'You must go! You must!' she implored.

He was commencing gently to disengage her hands, when she cried out something in Turkish. Immediately the door opened, three men slid quickly into the room, and closed the door behind them. One, a dark, refined-looking fellow in evening dress, held a revolver in his hand; the others, low class Arabs, carried long, sharp knives. They advanced on Wallace, while the woman held him tightly, pressing convulsively on his arms, but with that steel-like strength of his, upon which she had not reckoned, he suddenly flung her aside and stepped quickly back, placing the bed between him and his would-be assailants. For a few moments they stood eyeing him malevolently, then he laughed quietly.

'So, Madame,' he remarked, bowing coolly to her, 'your job was to get me to unlock the door, and lull me into a state of trusting innocence. You nearly succeeded, too.'

The woman, who had stumbled to her knees when flung aside, rose to her feet, in her eyes a look of undisguised hatred.

'What are you hesitating for?' she demanded harshly of the three newcomers, still speaking in French.

The man in evening dress lifted his left hand in peremptory command for her to be quiet. He smiled sardonically at Wallace.

'There is little use your attempting to resist,' he remarked in perfect English. 'We have you in our power.'

'Not quite,' retorted Sir Leonard quietly. 'You probably expected to be able to enter quickly and stab me while the lady held me for you. However, reluctant as I was to tear myself away from the arms of such a beautiful woman, I did not quite see eye to eye with you concerning the stabbing part of the business. I rather imagine the tables are turned.'

He stood, his hands in the pockets of his dressing-gown, and smiled triumphantly at the other. Despite his peril, he actually appeared to be enjoying himself.

'The tables are certainly not turned,' retorted the Egyptian. 'As you perceive, I am covering you with a revolver, which, after all, is more effective than a knife.'

Wallace, still smiling, shook his head.

'You daren't fire,' he commented, 'for you have no desire to rouse the hotel. Your only hope was to enter and stab me before I had time to cry out. That hope has gone and, I think, as it is very late, you had better go also.'

The man in dress clothes nodded almost imperceptibly to the two Arabs, who immediately sprang on the bed and made a dive for the Englishman, their knives glittering balefully in the light, but, almost like a conjuring trick, a revolver appeared in his hand, and drew a steady bead on them. The presence of a weapon, where they had expected none, nonplussed the scoundrels, and they halted in their onrush, balancing themselves on the bed, and uncertain what course to pursue.

As they looked into the cold, steel grey eyes of the man they had expected to murder with such ease, they saw death there, and involuntarily retreated until they stood once again on the floor at the other side of the bed.

'Your hired bravoes are sensible men,' observed Sir Leonard to the Egyptian. 'Although you dare not shoot, I shall do so with pleasure, if you give me any necessity. In fact,' he went on with the air of a man discussing the fluctuations of the money market or some other commonplace topic, 'it would be just as well if I shot the lot of you. Nobody could blame me, and such an act would do Egypt quite a lot of good.'

A look of baffled fury disfigured the beautiful face of the woman. Her husband, for such Wallace presumed the man in evening dress to be, showed no emotion at all.

'What do you think I should be doing while you were shooting us?' he sneered. 'You appear to have overlooked the fact that I also have a revolver.'

'I'd fire at you first,' retorted the Englishman, 'and I bet you'd be disabled before you could press the trigger. Shall we try it?' he added pleasantly. 'If not, throw your revolver, and tell your men to throw their knives on the bed.'

After a momentary hesitation, his orders were complied with, and the four stood sullenly looking at him, the two Arabs with fear shining out of their dark eyes, wondering what would be his next move. Wallace was rather puzzled what to do with them himself. If he roused the hotel, and caused them to be handed over to justice, it would mean that his own identity would be made public, and, although he was known apparently to the people he had hoped to deceive, he still had no desire to be mixed up in a trial. After all, Egypt was now an independent kingdom, and he might as well go back to England as allow his name and profession to be broadcast throughout Cairo. He decided to find out what he could about Henderson, then let his four adversaries go. As he made up his mind, the composure of the Egyptian broke.

'You may have obtained the upper hand this time,' he snarled, 'but you won't win again. You can do what you like with us, but there are others – hundreds of them – and they will get you.'

'Thanks for the information,' acknowledged Wallace cheerfully. 'But my private opinion of you is that you are the world's worst bunglers. First you try to get me into your power by means of an expedient that a child would have suspected, then you come to a hotel, where the slightest noise would have meant your discovery, with the intention of murdering me. A pretty lot of conspirators you are, to be sure. Why wasn't Madame entrusted with a dagger? She would have had a fairly good chance of stabbing me when I was almost persuaded into believing in her.'

'Our women are incapable of that sort of thing,' declared the fellow, a note almost of pride in his voice.

'So are the rest of you from the look of it,' retorted Sir Leonard. 'Sit down, Madame, and you also, Mr – er – Conspirator, and tell that pair of beauties to squat in the corner over there so that I can keep my eye on them.' His orders were obeyed. 'I want to ask you a few questions,' he went on.

'You will get no information from me,' began the Egyptian.

Wallace waved his hand airily.

'I am not going to ask you anything about the secret plans and intrigues of your party,' he observed. 'I know all I want to know about them already.' Both the man and woman started violently, and exchanged dismayed glances. 'I simply wish you to tell me,' went on Sir Leonard, 'what you have done with Mr Henderson.'

'Henderson!' exclaimed the Egyptian. 'I do not know any one of that name.'

'Try again!' encouraged the Englishman. 'A little reflection may help you to remember.'

But the fellow persisted in maintaining a pretence of ignorance, and at last Wallace desisted from attempting to obtain information. A better idea had occurred to him. Still covering them with his revolver, he strode round the bed, and stood looking down at them.

'Listen to me carefully,' he enjoined sternly. 'I know very well that Mr Henderson is in your power, or perhaps I should say, in the power of the political party of which you are a member. You and your wife and those two cut-throats over there are, on the other hand, in my power. I am going to make a bargain with you. Obtain the release of Henderson before sunrise, and you all go free. If he is not in this room by then, you will be handed over to the authorities, and will have to stand your trial for attempted murder.'

'How is it possible for me to obtain the release of this man, if I am detained here as your prisoner?'

'So you admit that you do know where Henderson is?'

'I admit nothing.'

'You'd better. Your liberty and that of the lady with you depend upon your obtaining Henderson's release.'

'You do not mean to say you would allow my wife to be arrested?'

'Most certainly. She is a party to the conspiracy and, though I regret that the whole story would be made public including the fact that she, an Egyptian lady of high degree, spent over half an hour in a man's bedroom after midnight, nevertheless there is no option unless, as I have already stated, you obtain Mr Henderson's release.'

The face of the woman had gone deadly pale, the man's sickly yellow. Apparently the honour of his wife was the strongest argument in favour of his agreeing to the proposal, for he looked at Sir Leonard almost eagerly.

'Tell me what you wish me to do,' he solicited.

Wallace pointed to the table.

'There are pens, paper and ink there,' he said. 'Write a letter to whomsoever is concerned, explain the predicament you are in, and the conditions of your release. One of those Arabs can take the note, and I suppose, as you have apparently entered the hotel without being seen, Mr Henderson can be brought up in the same manner.'

'Suppose my – friends refuse to send him?'

Sir Leonard shrugged his shoulders.

'Then you go to prison. It depends entirely upon you now whether you are released, and your wife saved not only imprisonment but a most embarrassing disclosure. But I warn you; no treachery! On the entry into this room of any unauthorised persons, whom in your simplicity you may ask to come to your rescue, I will shoot you and at the same moment press that bell over there. I hope you thoroughly understand me.'

'I will write in French, then you can read the letter yourself,' muttered the man hoarsely.

For quite ten minutes he wrote and, from the intent expression on his face, Wallace gathered that he was addressing an earnest appeal to the person concerned. At length he laid down his pen, and handed the letter to his captor. It stated matters bluntly and concisely. Having read it, and found nothing in it of an objectionable nature, Wallace called one of the Arabs to him. The man, his eyes alight with suspicion, approached warily, and was given his instructions. The Englishman then let him out of the room, and locked the door after him, taking care to keep his eyes on the three who remained. As he walked back towards them the woman smiled.

'You are a brave man, Monsieur,' she observed, a note of admiration in her voice. 'Do you realise that you have sentenced yourself to death? You will never leave Cairo alive.'

'We shall see, Madame,' he rejoined. 'I don't think I have much to fear from people who are so clumsy in their intrigues.'

'They are not usually clumsy,' she retorted, 'and this will be a lesson to them not to underestimate Sir Leonard Wallace in the future.'

He bowed mockingly.

'I thank you for the implied compliment, Madame. Can I offer either of you any refreshment? I am afraid I have only whisky and soda handy.'

They declined, and Sir Leonard helped himself. The time passed wearily by. The little travelling clock on the mantelpiece pointed to the hour of three, and still Henderson did not come. The Egyptian began to look perturbed, and spoke to his wife who had fallen into a gentle doze. She roused, and the two held a whispered conversation. Wallace, who had been half-sitting, half-reclining on the bed, had never for a moment relaxed his vigilance, and appeared as fresh as though he had slept all the previous day. The Arab in the corner had gone frankly to sleep, and was snoring gently, his mouth wide open.

At last came a soft knock. Wallace sat up alertly, and the other two looked at him with eyes in which suspense struggled with hope. He considered them in silence for a moment, then took the bell push, which hung above the bed, into the hand that held the revolver and pointed to the door. He addressed the woman.

'Will you be good enough to let my friend in?' he requested. 'And Madame will remember that, if there are others who enter in the hope of effecting a rescue, I will shoot her husband and, at the same time, ring this bell.'

She darted a look of detestation at him, rose, and walked slowly across the room, cloaking her head in her shawl as she did so. Before turning the key she hesitated, and there came another rap, whereupon she opened the door and stepped back. Into the room stumbled a man, to all appearances in the last stages of exhaustion. His clothing was unkempt and filthy, his eyes were sunken and lacked lustre, several days' growth of beard disfigured his jowl, while the rest of his haggard face was incredibly grimy. He looked questioningly at the occupants of the room, his eyes resting at last on Wallace, while a horrible travesty of a smile curved his cracked lips. He was followed in by the Arab who had been sent to fetch him.

'Good – good morning, sir,' he croaked.

A look of pity filled the glorious eyes of the Egyptian woman, and involuntarily she led the newcomer to the seat she had vacated. Then she mixed him a weak whisky and water, and bade him drink it. Wallace watched her with a smile of appreciation, but when he presently turned his eyes on her husband, the latter was appalled by the cold fury he recognised in their grey depths.

'So this is how you treat a prisoner,' snapped Sir Leonard. 'You and your companions will pay bitterly for such wanton cruelty.'

'He is a spy,' muttered the other hoarsely. 'He is lucky to have escaped death.'

'Death would have been merciful compared with what it is

obvious he must have suffered. You can go now and, if you take my advice, you will get out of the country as soon as possible. It will be safer – much safer for you.'

The fellow rose to his feet, a sneering smile on his lips.

'You had better follow your own advice,' he snarled, 'that is, if you can.'

He called to his wife, spoke curtly to the Arabs, and they all left the room. The woman was the last to go, and she looked through the folds of her shawl at Sir Leonard. The mocking smile was once again on her face.

'I hope they will be kinder to you, Monsieur,' she murmured. 'It would be a pity to see you brought to such a pass.'

He locked the door behind them, and hastened to the assistance of Henderson. Gently he helped him to undress, refused to allow him to talk, and insisted on his getting into bed. It was not long before the poor fellow dropped off into a deep sleep. Sir Leonard sat in an armchair, put his feet on another, and dozed in that position until a knock on the door roused him. It was broad daylight. Henderson still lay in a heavy slumber, and Wallace crossed the room quietly to avoid disturbing him. Outside stood a servant, who carried a tray on which was tea and toast.

'A dragoman requests an interview with your Excellency,' the man told him.

'Send him up!' directed Wallace and took the tray.

A few minutes later Achmet entered the room, and closed the door behind him. His astonishment was great when he recognised the man lying on the bed. In as few words as possible he was told of the events of the previous evening and night. When Wallace had concluded the recital, Achmet was looking very grave.

'It is very unfortunate that your identity is known, Excellency,' he murmured. 'Every movement of yours will be watched, and neither you nor Mr Henderson will be allowed to leave this hotel alive, unless we are able, by some means, to trick the people who will be on the look-out for you.'

'What about you, Achmet? Probably by now you are suspect.'

The man shrugged his shoulders with true Oriental fatalism.

'It is possible,' he admitted, 'but I do not think so. There is nothing suspicious in your meeting a dragoman in the lounge or even having him up here.'

'Still you must be careful. Now that Henderson has come, there is no need for us to hire a *dahabeeyah*.'

'Why not, effendi? His arrival does not make it any the less risky to talk in this hotel. Even now ears may be listening.'

Wallace smiled.

'They would not hear much since our conversation is carried on in such low voices. Also you fear that an attempt will be made to murder us if we leave the hotel.'

'True. What does your Excellency propose?'

'First we must ascertain what Henderson has discovered. Perhaps he has all the information I require. If so he and I must get back with all speed to England. How did you trace him?'

Achmet tiptoed to the door, and suddenly pulled it open. To his relief there was nobody outside, nor indeed within sight. Closing it once again, and locking it, he returned to Sir Leonard and, speaking in a low voice, told his story. In Port Said seventeen days before he had, as Sir Leonard already knew, met Henderson by arrangement, and had assisted him to disguise himself as a well-to-do Egyptian. He had given him the address of a compatriot in Cairo, who would afford him shelter and ask no questions, and where he would meet him if required. When Wallace had directed Achmet to trace Henderson, he had gone to the house of his friend. From the latter he had obtained the names of certain men, well known as leaders of the extreme party. Keeping a close watch on one of them, he had been lucky enough to be able to worm his way into the man's house, and there overhear a conversation, which informed him that Henderson was alive and a prisoner. Where his captors were keeping him did not transpire. He learnt, however, that they were starving him, hoping thus to force him to reveal his knowledge of their activities, after which he would be killed. When Achmet had discovered this he sent a telegram in code to Sir Leonard, and had awaited his arrival.

'It is a wonder you are not under suspicion, Achmet,' commented Wallace. 'From what I was told last night, I understand that a close watch was being kept on all Englishmen landing in Port Said, as the Nationalists expected men from my department to come out. Probably Henderson was under surveillance from the time he arrived, and he must have been seen to meet you, go with you to your house, and emerge disguised.'

The Arab shook his head.

'Not so, effendi,' he replied. 'Mr Henderson awaited me on the ship whither I went in my capacity as a seller of Turkish delight. It was not difficult to slip down to his cabin, the number of which he had included in the code wireless I had received from him when he was at sea. There I handed him the clothing he had requested, helped to darken his face and hands and afix a moustache, received his instructions, and returned to my goods. He went ashore by himself, and left for Cairo immediately. He had already given instructions for his luggage to be sent to the office of the steamship's agents, there to await him.'

'I see.' Sir Leonard rubbed his chin thoughtfully. 'That sounds as though he took precautions enough. I am afraid I did him the injustice of thinking he had been careless.'

A sound from the bed caused them both to turn in that direction. Henderson was awake and, although his face was terribly emaciated, he looked better than he had done on his arrival. Wallace hastened to his side, and fed him with toast soaked in tea until he could eat no more. Already a little colour was stealing through the mixture of grime and stain on his cheeks.

'Had a bad time, old chap?' asked Sir Leonard.

'Pretty bad, sir,' was the whispered reply. 'They were starving me to – to force me to tell them what I knew.'

'So Achmet has told me,' nodded his chief. 'Do you feel strong enough to tell me what happened?'

Henderson slowly nodded his head.

'When I came to Cairo,' he began in such a low voice that Wallace had to lean towards him to hear what he said, 'I went straight to the house of Achmet's friend. There by careful inquiries I learnt the names of the ruling spirits of the extreme Nationalist party, and was able to get in touch with one of them. I posed as a merchant from Wady Halfa who had come to Cairo on business, and pretended that I had a deep hatred of the British. I was invited to my new friend's house, and there was subjected to a thorough cross-examination. My knowledge of the country, and the fluency with which I speak the language, enabled me to answer all questions with ease, and I am convinced I lulled any suspicions he may have had. He refused to discuss the political situation with me, however, but another man called while I was there, and the two of them held a whispered conversation in a corner of the room remote from me. That is where my ability to lip-read came in useful, sir. I saw that they were arranging a big meeting for the following night in that house, and I made up my mind to be present.'

He paused, and Wallace held a cup of tea to his lips. When he had drunk a few drops he pushed the cup away, and continued.

'The following afternoon I called at the house with the intention of secreting myself there if possible, for I knew that I would stand no chance at night of getting anywhere near it. I was admitted, but told that my friend was out. After waiting for some time I pretended to leave but hid myself in the garden, and re-entered the house as soon as I felt sure that I could do so safely. In the room where the meeting was to be held was a large carved chest, and in it I concealed myself and awaited events.

'It was a most uncomfortable ordeal. I was in that box for nearly six hours before the meeting took place, and by that time my limbs were so cramped that practically all feeling had left them. But I forgot my disabilities when the conspirators arrived. There must have been twenty or thirty of them, and they discussed plans for a great demonstration against the British, including the mutiny of Egyptian troops in the Sudan and the massacre of all British officials and advisers. The owner of the house was apparently the leading spirit, and in his possession I learnt was a book containing the names of every important member of the extreme party with a description of the duty allotted to him when the uprising occurs.

'The book was kept in a safe in that room I heard and at the suggestion of somebody, was brought out, and the names and duties read over. It was then returned to its receptacle, a date was fixed for the demonstration, and the meeting broke up.'

'What is the date?' asked Wallace sharply.

'The first of September, sir.'

'Three weeks from today,' calculated Sir Leonard quickly. 'Go on!'

'I made up my mind to obtain the book,' continued Henderson, 'and waited in that awful chest for another half hour. Then I tried to get out, but I was so numbed that I could hardly move. After some time I managed, with much effort, and by gradual stages, to push up the heavy lid, but my arms were almost nerveless, and it crashed down again with noise enough to rouse the dead. Almost at once I heard two or three people running into the room, the chest was opened, and I was discovered. There is not much more to tell, sir. They hauled me out; I could not stand, and was unable to make a fight for it. At first they were inclined to kill me, but the owner of the house decided to keep me alive, and force me to tell what I knew. It was useless to keep up the pretence that I was an Egyptian myself. Indeed he immediately guessed I was an Englishman, for he tore off the false moustache I was wearing, and rubbed some of the stain from my face. I was thrown into an underground, evil-smelling cellar full of rubbish, and without an article of furniture. Every day I was brought up and questioned, either by the fellow himself, or his friends. They occasionally gave me water, but nothing to eat. Then at last, I was released and brought here. I don't know how you managed it, sir, but I owe you my life.'

Sir Leonard explained how he had been able to obtain Henderson's freedom, then ordered the latter to try and sleep again.

'I will look after you myself until you can get about,' he declared. 'You must stay here for today. Tomorrow, if you are better, I'll engage another room close by. It's beef-tea and sleep for you, Henderson, for today anyway. Now, Achmet,' he turned to the Arab, who had followed Henderson's story with deep interest, 'you and I are going to find our way into that house, and obtain the book – the sooner the better.'

A gleam came into Achmet's eyes, but Henderson looked alarmed.

'Don't you think they'll expect something like that, and be waiting for you?' he asked.

'We'll have to risk it,' was the calm reply.

'I wish I could come with you, sir.'

'My dear chap, you've done your share. Achmet and I will manage all right. Will you describe to him the house, and the way to get to it?'

Henderson did so; then Sir Leonard told the Arab to go, and meet him at ten that night by the bridge. Achmet seemed to think that the hour was too early, but Wallace explained that he wanted to inspect the place before attempting to enter it.

'When you go down now,' he added, 'look as disgruntled as you like, call me the worst names you can think of, and let it be known that, after ordering your attendance and arranging for a *dahabeeyah*, I have changed my mind and dismissed you. That ought to keep suspicion from you. Do you think you can find the house from Mr Henderson's description?'

The grinning man declared that he could, and departed. Sir Leonard shaved, bathed, and dressed, then interviewed the manager, as a result of which no servants went near his room all day, except to hand in bowls of beef-tea. No doubt this caused a certain amount of mystification – the manager himself was puzzled, for he had been told very little – but

Wallace did not mind very much. By evening Henderson's condition had greatly improved, and he was able to have a bath and shave, which made an extraordinary difference to his appearance.

After dinner Wallace took some garments from a suitcase, changed into them, then stained his face, neck and right arm a deep brown. He smiled rather ruefully at the other – an artificial arm does not require any stain to make it brown, especially when the hand is covered by a glove of that colour. He had completed the transformation, and was examining himself critically in a mirror, when Henderson, who had been sleeping, awoke. The latter, to his astonishment and dismay, saw a typical fellah standing before him and demanded to know what he was doing there. Sir Leonard laughed and announced himself, whereupon the other whistled with amazement.

'It's a great disguise, Sir Leonard,' he remarked.

'Glad you like it,' returned his chief shortly. 'Now, as soon as I've gone, lock yourself in, and open the door for no one until you hear my voice. I've bolted both the windows, though I doubt if anybody could get in that way; and here is a revolver. Put it under your pillow.'

He handed his subordinate the weapon, and secreted another in his clothing in handy proximity to the wicked-looking knife already stuck in his girdle, then went quietly to the door.

'Good luck, Sir Leonard,' said Henderson.

Wallace nodded his thanks, and the next moment was looking cautiously up and down the corridor. Nobody was about, and he slipped out, made his way to the service stairs, and quietly descended. Twice he was compelled to hide to avoid running into servants, but eventually was out of the hotel walking swiftly to the bridge. He heard a clock strike ten just as he reached it to find Achmet leaning on the parapet gazing down at the *feluccas* riding at anchor below. He tapped him on the shoulder, but Achmet looked him up and down without recognition until Wallace quietly announced himself, then a similar look of surprise came on the Arab's face to that which had been on Henderson's.

'It is wonderful,' he breathed.

'Not very appropriate, I'm afraid,' muttered Sir Leonard, 'but a good disguise.'

He chuckled to himself as he remembered that the last time he had worn it had been at a Covent Garden ball.

Without another word Achmet set off, with the other in close attendance. Before long they had plunged into a district of narrow streets and labyrinthine alleys, where the old buildings huddled together, and the latticed windows above appeared to lean over and almost touch each other. Although late, the tortuous streets were crowded with water carriers, merchants, peddlers, closely-veiled women, beggars, donkeys, horses, goats and, here and there, camels. After walking for some time they reached a slightly wider, almost deserted, thoroughfare containing houses of a better class. Before one, surrounded by a high wall, Achmet stopped.

'This is the place, Excellency,' he announced simply.

Walking on a dozen yards, Sir Leonard squatted down in the deeper shadows on the opposite side of the road with his companion beside him. For a long time he contemplated the building in silence, then whistled softly to himself.

'It is going to be a bigger job to enter that place than I imagined,' he murmured at last. 'I thought we might have been able to climb the wall and get into the garden easily enough, but it's too high.

There is only one thing for it, and that is to knock at the gate, overcome the man who opens it, and truss him up somewhere where he won't be discovered until we have finished our job. Once in the garden, the rest shouldn't be too difficult.'

Achmet nodded but made no comment, and the two continued to squat where they were for another half hour. Then Wallace rose. Ten minutes before, a belated string of camels had passed, moving with stately deliberation towards the bazaar. Since then not a human being, or an animal of any sort, had been seen, and it seemed safe enough to make the attempt.

'As soon as the gate opens,' he whispered, 'push your way in with me, and shut it directly we arc inside. Don't bother about the gatekeeper, I'll deal with him.'

In response to his knock a little grill opened, and he could dimly see the outlines of a dark face beyond.

'What dost thou require?' a voice asked.

'We have a message for the Lord,' replied Achmet promptly.

The heavy wooden door swung open, and Wallace entered immediately, pushing back the man who stood before him. Achmet followed, and closed the barrier. The gatekeeper commenced to utter protests, but Wallace produced his revolver, and brought down the butt on his head. He collapsed without a sound, the Englishman catching him as he fell, and lowering him to the ground. Looking round the small garden, Wallace noticed the dim outlines of a well, and thither he and his companion conveyed the unconscious form of their victim. Once there, they tore strips from his own clothing, and gagged and bound him, leaving him lying well hidden behind the wheel. The first part of their task had been easy, now it remained for them to get into the house, which was in complete darkness, as though the inmates had gone to bed. Henderson's description of the interior had left a picture in Sir Leonard's mind, and once inside he felt he could not go wrong.

It was a peculiar building, half ancient, half modern, part of it having obviously been pulled down and rebuilt. Wallace studied it in silence for some minutes, endeavouring to calculate where the room, which was his objective, could be. He was not long making up his mind, and crept towards a low balcony followed by his assistant. He could just reach it, and with remarkable agility, considering he was only able to use one arm, which brought a low grunt of admiration from Achmet, swung himself up. The Arab was soon standing by his side, and they found their further progress barred by two French windows. But to a man who had studied the intricacies of safe-breaking, the opening of a locked window presented little difficulty. He produced a bunch of small steel instruments from somewhere among the folds of his clothing, and worked silently at top and bottom where the bolts were sheathed. In five minutes they were in the room, listening intently. No sound disturbed the silence, and presently a thin ray of light shot out, circled quickly round, and was gone. Sir Leonard Wallace had taken his bearings, found also that his calculations had been correct; he and Achmet had undoubtedly come to the right apartment. In his rapid survey he had glimpsed the chest in which Henderson had crouched for so long, the table round which the conspirators must have sat, the safe remote in a corner which probably contained the precious book. He had noticed also that there was only one entrance apart from the windows.

'Go and stand close to that door,' he directed Achmet, 'and warn me if you hear the slightest sound.'

Again the brilliant but narrow beam of light stabbed the darkness, indicating to Achmet where to go, and was extinguished as soon as he arrived there. Moving softly, without aid from his torch, Sir Leonard reached the safe. Once more the flashlight came into play as he studied it. Although small it was an essentially modern article, and he drew a deep breath as he eyed the dial. Then he was down on his knees before it, had extinguished the light, and was rubbing the tips of his fingers on the carpet until they glowed and tingled. He had made a study of opening safes soon after joining the Secret Service. It was an art that he had learnt more as a whim than anything else, but it had come in useful more than once. Presently, with his ear pressed against the face of the safe, he was twirling the dial with those sensitive fingers of his.

The minutes went by, but nothing happened. He felt a bead of perspiration break out upon his forehead, and paused for a moment to wipe it away, smiling grimly to himself when he found that his hand was trembling. Once again set himself to his task; then, at last, he gave vent to a low exclamation. The handle was flung over with a metallic click, and the door opened. Immediately the inquisitive ray of his torch was searching among the masses of papers and cash boxes within, to hold steadily on a small volume bound in red leather. Taking it out he opened it, and eagerly examined the pages. For a moment a sense of disappointment came over him, then he smiled. He could hardly expect to find what he was seeking written in English or French. A whispered command brought Achmet to his side, and the Arab carefully studied page after page.

'It is the book, effendi,' he declared at last. 'There are many names here and much information.'

A deep sigh escaped from Sir Leonard.

'It isn't written in Arabic, is it?'

'No, Excellency. That is Turkish.'

'I thought so.'

A moment later the safe was closed and locked, and the two men crept across the room to the window, the book clasped tightly under Wallace's arm. They were quickly over the balcony, and back in the garden, hurrying towards the gate. Then they stood stockstill, as though rooted to the spot, as a thunderous knocking suddenly broke the stillness.

'Damn!' swore Sir Leonard softly but fervently.

Again came the noisy hammering, and he drew Achmet into the deeper darkness of a group of trees.

'Whoever they are, they'll have the whole household about our ears presently,' he muttered. 'Go and let them in, Achmet. You may not rouse their suspicion.'

He had come to the conclusion that it was better to risk opening the door than to be caught between two fires, with the certainty of a search being made for the gatekeeper.

The banging had now developed into a continuous rat-a-tat. Achmet hurried to the gate and, hastily unbolting it, threw it open. At once a tall figure strode in, followed by two others. He subjected Achmet to a loud tirade, which Wallace rightly guessed to mean that he was censuring the Arab for his sluggishness. Then, as he was about to pass on, he bent and looked closely into the latter's face, calling out something sharply to his followers as he did so. Another man appeared with a lamp, which illumined the scene, and threw Achmet's face into sharp relief. Exclamations of astonishment and wrath broke from all four newcomers, and Wallace, observing that the game was up, broke cover and ran to his subordinate's assistance, the precious book tucked safely away in his clothing. As he did so two other men came out of the house, making the odds six to two; perhaps even greater if there were others outside.

His sudden appearance took the Egyptians by surprise, and he was on them, had brought down his revolver butt on two heads, laying their owners low, before any attempt at defence was made by the others.

'Run for it Achmet,' he shouted and, sweeping another man aside, was out in the street with the Arab in close attendance.

There, however, they found their passage barred by two gigantic Ethiopians, who swooped upon them with long knives, and matters began to look ominous. Sir Leonard did not want to shoot for fear of rousing the whole neighbourhood. He sidestepped the onrush of one man, cleverly tripping him as he stumbled by. When the fellow measured his length on the ground he dropped his knife, and Wallace kicked it away. At the same time Achmet was engaged with the second, who drove his knife down with such force that it would have almost split the Arab in two, if it had taken effect, instead of which it proved the Ethiopian's downfall. Missing his object he overbalanced, and was an easy prey to the upward lunge of Achmet's weapon. But the others were on them by now, and they were forced to turn and meet them, to find themselves fighting desperately not with four, but with six or seven adversaries. Wallace no longer hesitated to fire; it was obvious that he and his companion would quickly be overcome if he did not. Shooting with deadly purpose at their legs, he brought down three. None of their assailants had firearms, and they were at a big disadvantage. Seeing their comrades fall, the rest drew back in confusion, whereupon Wallace and Achmet seized the opportunity and ran. Several people roused by the firing had appeared, but the two had dashed by them before they understood what the trouble was about. There was a stern pursuit, but, chiefly owing to

Achmet's cleverness in doubling and twisting in among the narrow alleys, they eventually got clear away.

Sir Leonard went straight to the residence of the Sirdar. He had a great deal of difficulty in obtaining admittance, but eventually prevailed, his English voice and commanding manner overcoming the distrust caused by his disguise. The Sirdar was awakened and, when told the name of his visitor, immediately descended from his bedroom. Wallace put all the facts of the conspiracy before him including the proposed date of the demonstration, the plans for the mutiny of Egyptian troops, and the massacre of British officials and advisers, and showed him the red book. The Sirdar, who was greatly impressed and perturbed by all he had been told, sent for a secretary who understood Turkish. The latter was instructed to copy out the names and make a précis of the information contained in the book.

It was a long task and took over two hours. At last it was done, and Wallace wearily returned to his hotel, satisfied that the duty which had brought him to Egypt was accomplished. It remained now for him to get out of the country safely, and he smiled grimly as he remembered the threats of his unwelcome visitors of the previous night. Achmet left him at the entrance to Shepheard's.

It was rather a puzzle to get in without being seen especially as the servants' way was closed to him at that hour, but he managed to dodge the night watchman and reached his bedroom without rousing suspicion. He knocked gently, but there was no reply. Apparently Henderson was sleeping very soundly. Again he rapped, this time a little louder, then took hold of the handle to rattle the door. To his astonishment it opened, and a horrible foreboding took possession of him. For a moment he stood deep in thought, drawing his revolver as he did so; then, suddenly flinging the door wide, he stepped quickly to one side. But nothing happened to indicate the presence of an intruder, and, after waiting a few minutes, Wallace stepped into the room, and switched on the lights. A bitter oath broke from his lips at what he saw, and he stood aghast. Henderson was lying dead, had been stabbed in half a dozen places, and the bedclothes were soaking with his blood.

For some minutes Sir Leonard remained immovable, his teeth clenched, his eyes expressing the agony of his thoughts. He had not the slightest doubt that Henderson had been murdered in mistake for him. Somehow the assassins had forced an entry without rousing the poor fellow and, probably seeing the dim form on the bed, had stabbed without risking a light. It was a ghastly crime, and proved, in no uncertain fashion, that their intentions were desperate indeed. Then enlightenment came to him, and he felt sure that the men with whom he and Achmet had fought were the murderers returning after having completed their foul work.

Quickly Wallace changed into his own clothes, and removed the stain from his face and arm. Then, dashing down to the office, he despatched one of the surprised watchmen for the manager, and telephoned the Sirdar. It took him some time to get through, but at last he had the satisfaction of hearing the Governor-General's voice, and told him what had happened including his suspicion of the identity of the assassins. He was listened to in silence, then:

'You must get away from Egypt at once,' came the urgent command. 'I'll give orders for an aeroplane to be at your disposal at dawn, and send an escort to see you safely to the flying ground. Tell the manager a representative of mine will interview him shortly, that I'll take full charge of the body, and inquiries concerning the murder. We shall have to hush up a good deal on account of Henderson's business in Cairo, but you can trust me to see justice done. The most important thing at the moment is for you to get away.'

Sir Leonard saw the force of his argument and, though reluctant to leave Cairo without avenging in some measure the death of his assistant, his first duty was to his government. The manager arrived as he replaced the receiver, and was terribly shocked when informed of the tragedy. He accompanied Wallace to the room and stood by, his face as white as a sheet, while the Chief of the Secret Service examined the lock of the door. It had obviously been forced and by an expert, who had probably made little or no noise.

No doubt the assassins had bribed a locksmith to accompany them, or already had a man of that trade in their pay. Two officers of the Sirdar's household and a high official of the Egyptian police arrived before long, and took charge of affairs. Sir Leonard made a statement which was taken down, left instructions for Achmet to return to Port Said; then hurriedly packed his bags. Before leaving the room he took a last sad look at the face of the man who had given his life for him.

A closed car with a small escort of armed soldiers awaited him below. He at once drove to the aerodrome, and arrived there without incident. Dawn had broken when the aeroplane rose into the sky and headed for Alexandria. A Royal Air Force flying-boat took him from there to Brindisi and two days later, he was in London once again.

The British Government was immediately put in possession of the whole facts, while the red book contained enough evidence to force the Egyptian Government to take severe and immediate steps against the extremists, with the result that there was peace in Egypt for some time. Unfortunately the return to parliament of

Zaghlul Pasha and the Nationalist extremists a year later caused fresh disturbances culminating in the murder of the Sirdar, Sir Lee Stack, in 1925. But the mass of information in the possession of the British Government which had been obtained by Sir Leonard Wallace and men he sent out after his return, enabled the British to take firm action. The murderers were tried and executed, the Egyptian demand of sovereignty over the Sudan was definitely refused, and a separate Sudanese Defence Force organised, while all Egyptian officials and troops were expelled from that province.

Henderson's murderers escaped through lack of evidence until the outrages of 1925, when they were arrested for their participation in the assassination of the Sirdar, and confessed to the crime they had committed nearly two years previously. They were sentenced to death and hanged. Thus was Henderson avenged.

CHAPTER TWO

Bound in Morocco

Although his duties kept Sir Leonard Wallace in London most of the year, he spent every available moment at his estate close to Lyndhurst in the New Forest. In fact during certain summer months he lived there, travelling daily to the metropolis by car, and returning in the evening.

His country residence is a small but beautiful Tudor house set in an old world garden, with a farm attached, and encircled by the majestic trees of England's most noble forest. Both Sir Leonard and Lady Wallace loved the place, and if it had been possible would have resided permanently there. London held little attraction for them and, though they were to be seen at most functions during the season, and entertained liberally themselves, their hearts were in the New Forest.

Lady Wallace loves flowers, and is never happier than when pottering about the garden herself, while her little son Adrian has inherited her love for beautiful things and, if possible, will always escape from his governess whenever he catches sight of his mother wearing her old gardening gloves, and preparing to assist the gardener in his daily warfare against slugs, green flies, and all the other pests sent to try the horticulturist. Sir Leonard is also very fond of flowers but, as he admits himself, cultivating them does not appeal to him. He prefers to see other people doing the work, and admire the result.

'You see, Molly,' he observed one day a few weeks after his return from Egypt, as they lounged on the terrace, 'gardening is all very well for the young and innocent. What do you think your precious flowers would feel like if a hoary old sinner like myself messed them about? Besides, the real art of gardening is to sit and watch things grow.'

She laughed.

'How would you expect them to grow,' she asked, 'if they were not cultivated?'

'Of course someone must do the cultivating,' he admitted, 'but the real artist is he who sits and appreciates.'

'Thank you,' she murmured sarcastically, her eyes twinkling with merriment. 'You're a fraud, Leonard,' she went on; 'a lazy old fraud.'

'I confess it, but it's humiliating to be unmasked by one's wife.'

She laughed again in that attractive way of hers, and lay back in her chair, her hands behind her head, in an attitude he loved. Never tired of admiring her, he watched her now. Lady Wallace is as clever as she is sweet, as accomplished as she is charming. Her beauty is not only physical, it is mental as well, and that is perhaps why she is as popular with her own sex as with the other. It would be impossible to dislike her, impossible to think lightly of her. Her glorious chestnut hair, falling in natural waves round her head, her deep blue eyes, *retroussé* nose, perfectly shaped scarlet lips, and clear complexion are too well known to require description. She and her husband adore each other and jointly worship Adrian. In this twentieth century of broken marriages, divorce, unrequited love, Sir Leonard and Lady Wallace have proved that the perfect state of connubial happiness is still possible.

Wallace had given himself a well-earned holiday and, for a week, had been engaged in proving, at least so he said, that it is possible to reach an ideal state of indolence. For the time being a deep, blissful peace had entered Molly's heart, a glad relief from that feeling of anxiety which always pervaded her when he was actively engaged on those dangerous duties which so often took him away from her. Though often she felt that he undertook ventures which might have been left to others, nevertheless she would not have thought of attempting to dissuade him from them. But she dreaded the necessity which so often compelled him to risk his life. Proud of him, as she was, and of his position as the head of a department upon which the well-being and welfare of the British Empire so greatly depended, she yet prayed for the time to come, when she would have him entirely to herself, and no longer be subject to the heartache and trepidation she felt when he was away from her.

It was a glorious day in September, and the sun was sinking gradually behind the great trees that stood like sentinels to the west of their domain, as they sat on the terrace of their beautiful home. They had been playing tennis together, and were resting after their exertions. Everything was peaceful and quiet with that languid stillness which is the country's greatest charm. A feeling of contentment was in Molly's heart; she had entirely forgotten for the time being the existence of a Secret Service; was, in fact, living in the present and treasuring up every moment of the delight she felt at having her husband with her.

'Visitors,' grunted Sir Leonard suddenly.

In the distance could be seen a motor car coming rapidly along the winding drive towards the house, and they watched it casually as it approached.

'It's old Humphrey's car from the station,' decided Sir Leonard presently. 'Now who can have come by train to visit us?'

As he spoke a premonition that her happiness was about to be interrupted came over Molly, and she sighed. Somehow the beauty seemed to have gone out of the day, she even felt a little chilly, and involuntarily shivered. Sir Leonard glanced at her, but asked no questions. He understood quite well what she was thinking.

The car swung round the last bend, and drew up in front of the terrace. A small keen-eyed man stepped briskly from it, and approached the two who now awaited him with the certain knowledge that their idyll was to be shattered. He raised his hat and bowed to Molly, disclosing the fact that his hair was grey.

'As a rule,' remarked Sir Leonard by way of greeting, 'I rather like you, Maddison, but just now I think you're a most unpleasant person to know.'

The visitor smiled slightly. He had noted the strained look in Molly's face, and addressed himself to her.

'My apologies are due to you, Lady Wallace, I'm afraid,' he said.

'You mean,' she responded quietly, 'that you are going to take my husband away?'

'That, of course, is for Sir Leonard to decide himself.'

'I understand.' She rose. 'I will leave you to discuss your business here.'

Wallace, who had risen with her, hastily interposed.

'Not on your life, Molly,' he protested. 'My study is the only place possible for the proper consideration of whatever Maddison has to tell me. I couldn't be serious with all those flowers round me.'

'Go along then,' she smiled, sinking back into her chair. 'You'll stay the night, Mr Maddison?'

'I'm afraid I cannot,' he murmured regretfully.

Her eyebrows were slightly raised.

'As urgent as all that? At least you'll dine with us?'

He thanked her, and followed Sir Leonard into the house. Molly sat for some time staring straight before her and occasionally a sigh escaped from her. The appearance of Adrian, who had been out to tea, relieved her mind temporarily, and she played with him until his bed time. But her heart was heavy as she went to dress for dinner.

In the meantime Sir Leonard had taken Maddison into his comfortably appointed study and, closing the door, he nodded towards one of the large leather upholstered armchairs, dropping himself into another. His demeanour had changed entirely. No longer indolent or perfunctory in his manner, he had the alert air one would expect in the head of such a department as his. Maddison had a feeling that the clear grey eyes were delving into the inner recesses of his brain.

'Serious?' was Wallace's pithy question.

'The Prince has disappeared,' replied Maddison almost as tersely.

'You mean the Prince of Emilia?'

The Secret Service man nodded.

'Yes, sir,' he assented. 'We received information from the Foreign Office at half past three this afternoon, and Major Brien ordered me to come to you at once. He thought it more satisfactory than telephoning.'

'What are the details?' demanded Wallace.

Maddison consulted a notebook which he had taken from his pocket.

'The Prince with his escort arrived at Gibraltar on the destroyer *Lapwing* yesterday afternoon. He was received by the Governor, and a dinner and ball were given in his honour. Towards the end of the ball he mentioned that he was very warm, and went for a stroll in the grounds of Government House. He has not been seen since.'

'But, dash it all man! Was he alone?'

'No, sir. One of his equerries and our man were with him.'

'You mean Cousins?'

'Yes, sir.'

'What has he to say about it? Has his report come in?'

'Both Cousins and the equerry disappeared with the Prince,' Maddison informed him quietly.

'Good Lord!' Sir Leonard was on his feet now, standing in his favourite attitude on the hearthrug. 'Is there anything to go on at all, Maddison?'

'Not a thing, sir. The Governor's cable simply states that the Prince was last seen walking in the garden with his companions, and asks for expert help. There is nothing whatever to suggest or even hint at the reason for the disappearance. The Foreign Office is in a regular stew.'

'It would be,' commented Wallace drily.

'It's a nasty business, sir. A most critical international situation may arise through it.'

'It's possible, especially in the present state of tension between Italy and Britain. But the Italian Government is hardly likely to take an unreasonable attitude. Let me see: the invitation to the Prince to visit our Mediterranean possessions on board a British destroyer dated from the time of his call at Malta, didn't it?' Maddison nodded, and Sir Leonard went on: 'Since then, he has been to Cyprus and Palestine, back to Malta, and was to conclude his tour at Gibraltar, where an Italian warship was due to pick him up and take him back to Italy. I haven't taken a great deal of interest in the affair, but I believe I am right, am I not?'

'Quite, sir.'

'Well, during that time, has any report arrived from Cousins that all was not as it should have been?'

'Nothing at all, sir. We've heard from Cousins twice since you sent him out to keep an eye on the Prince at Malta, and there was certainly nothing in his letters to suggest that there was anything wrong. In fact, he seemed to regard the affair as a holiday, and spoke of enjoying himself immensely.'

'I expected it to be a change for him,' observed Sir Leonard. 'This has dished his holiday – and mine,' he added a trifle ruefully. 'Is there anything else you can tell me about the affair?'

'Nothing, sir. I hope it doesn't mean foul play.'

'I hope not. Personally, I believe it is a move by a foreign power either to cause trouble between Britain and Italy, or to use the safety of the Prince as a lever to force the Italian Government to agree to something of advantage to that power.'

Maddison looked sharply at him.

'Surely no power would allow itself to be party to the kidnapping of a royal person of another nation,' he objected. 'Why, sir, it is sheer brigandage.'

'It is,' agreed Sir Leonard, and added significantly: 'But there is one country that would dare. Of course, it would be done under the cloak of innocence. The devil of it is that it should take place on British territory. I'll leave for Gib tonight, and see what I can do to pick up the threads.'

'The Foreign Secretary expressed a wish to see you at the earliest possible moment, sir.'

'Oh, did he? I've no time to go to Town. Get him on the phone, Maddison. Ring up the Southampton post office first, and order them to give us a clear line.' He looked at the ormolu clock ticking on the mantelpiece. 'He'll be at home now, I should imagine, but get him wherever he is.'

Maddison crossed to the desk, and set to work to get the necessary connection. Sir Leonard thoughtfully filled and lit his pipe. Certain words spoken softly into the instrument set the telephone service working at lightning speed, and in three minutes the call was through. The Foreign Secretary proved to be at home, and Maddison handed the receiver to his chief.

'That you, Wallace?' came the Minister's agitated voice.

'Thank God!'

Sir Leonard quickly repeated to him what he had been told by Maddison.

'Is there anything else?' he concluded.

'No; except that the Italian Ambassador has been to see me once, and telephoned three times. Apparently the Embassy is receiving frantic telegrams from Italy every half hour.'

'I don't wonder,' commented Wallace coolly. 'There was bound to be a spot of bother.'

'Spot of bother!' gasped the excited statesman at the other end. 'Don't you realise the serious nature of the affair?'

'Of course I do, but what's the use of getting agitated.'

'What are you going to do about it? You'd better come up to London at once; we'll talk it over and see what can be done.'

'There's nothing to talk over,' objected Wallace. 'I know all there is to be known apparently, and it would be only a waste of time coming to Town. I've decided to go to Gibraltar myself.'

There was a distinct sigh of relief.

'When do you propose to leave?'

'Tonight. Will you get in touch with the Air Ministry, and ask them to order Calshot to put a flying-boat at my disposal?'

'Certainly. But do you really intend to fly at night?'

'Yes. Why not? It's going to be an ideal night for flying. A harvest moon and all the rest of it should make it a glorious trip. I'll be at Calshot just after ten and, if all goes well should be in Gib tomorrow morning somewhere between eight and nine.'

'Splendid. You've relieved my mind tremendously.'

'Please get on to the Air Ministry at once.'

'Very well. You can rely upon me. Good luck, Wallace.'

Sir Leonard put down the receiver, and smiled at Maddison.

'You are quite right,' he remarked. 'The Foreign Secretary is certainly in a stew.'

After dinner Maddison returned to London and, soon after his departure, Sir Leonard took leave of Molly and, accompanied by his manservant, Batty, was driven to the Royal Air Force station at Calshot. It was a beautiful night, as he had predicted, making the countryside look even more fascinating than by day, especially at Beaulieu, where the ruins of the famous Abbey had assumed a witchery never theirs by daylight.

A wing commander met him, and introduced him to the two young flight-lieutenants who had been told to pilot him. He was informed that there had been a certain amount of difficulty in getting the flying-boat ready in time, as, when the message came through, work had ceased for the day, and most of the men had gone to Southampton or Portsmouth for their evening's amusement. However, with the keenness for which the Air Force is noted, those remaining on duty had set to work, with the result that the boat was then at the slips ready for her long flight.

The two pilots were as keen as mustard on the trip. Though naturally they knew nothing of Sir Leonard's object in going to Gibraltar, they sensed mystery, and were rather thrilled at being called upon to convey the Chief of the Intelligence Department to the Rock. A certain amount of discussion took place regarding the route, but Wallace left it entirely to their discretion, and it was decided to go by way of Ushant, Cape Ortegal, Finisterre, down the coast of Portugal, and round by Cape St Vincent to Gibraltar.

Batty had already stowed the scanty baggage on board, and stood by listening critically to the discussion, nodding his head now and again, as though in approval. He was a short, stout man with a round, red face, which a snub nose and twinkling blue eyes made delightfully cheerful. An ex-naval seaman, Batty had entered Sir Leonard's service on discharge, and had proved himself the very handiest of handy men. His employer had grown to put entire reliance on him, and treated him always as a confidential servant.

'These 'ere craft are all very well,' he commented, as he watched his master climb aboard, 'but a tidy bit o' deck space and the sea all around is good enough for me.'

It was nearly half past ten when the great aeroplane rose into the air, and commenced her flight. Sir Leonard sat up, alternately reading and looking out of the window by his side, for a couple of hours until, as they were passing over Brest, he went to bed. He slept soundly and woke early. There was hardly a tremor as the great flying machine flew rapidly on her way. Wallace could see the coast of Portugal far below, glittering in the morning sunshine, and before long the Tagus, like a silvery streak, with Lisbon nestling on the estuary, burst into view. An air mechanic brought him an appetising breakfast, to which he did full justice, after which he sat and watched the scenes unfolding rapidly below with a sense of fascination. Sir Leonard felt a keen delight in flying, and was wont to declare that the beauty of nature was at its best when viewed from above.

It was nearly ten o'clock when the grim rock of Gibraltar was sighted, and a quarter of an hour later the flying-boat descended, skimmed the water, and eventually came to anchor close inshore. A long, lean destroyer lay a few cables' length away on the port side and, beyond her, a cruiser flying the Italian flag. Farther away still were anchored three grim-looking battle cruisers belonging to the Mediterranean fleet, while merchant ships of all nations and tonnage lay in various parts of the harbour. A crowd of idlers watched their arrival from the Mole, indulging probably in interested speculation concerning the business which had brought the great seaplane to Gibraltar.

Their arrival was expected, for hardly was the machine stationary before a beautifully appointed pinnace glided alongside.

'Sir Leonard Wallace?' inquired a smart-looking military officer standing in the stern sheets.

'I am he,' replied Wallace from the open door of the saloon.

The officer saluted.

'I am from the Governor, sir. Will you come aboard?' Sir Leonard first thanked his pilots for the celerity with which they had brought him to Gibraltar; then stepped aboard the pinnace, followed by Batty with the bags. An RAF launch arrived, and took the flying-boat in tow. A berth had been prepared for her in the inner harbour, where she would wait until required for the return trip.

Twenty minutes later Sir Leonard was closeted with the Governor. The famous soldier had welcomed the equally famous Secret Service man almost with open arms.

'I can't tell you what a relief it is to have you here,' he confessed. 'When I heard you were on your way, I felt as though a load were about to be removed from my shoulders.'

'Don't be too optimistic, sir,' returned Wallace. 'From the little information I possess and to which I doubt if you can add, there doesn't appear to be a great deal of hope.'

The bronzed face of the white-haired Governor paled.

'For God's sake don't say that,' he protested. 'My career is rapidly drawing to a close. I have held the highest military commands and, up to date, have flattered myself that my administration here has been fairly successful. I have even exterminated the monkeys,' he added with a faint smile. 'To finish up with a blot like this against my name would—' He shrugged his shoulders with a sigh, and did not finish the sentence.

'I can quite understand how you feel about it,' sympathised Wallace, 'but you can't be held blameworthy. At any rate, sir, you may be sure I'll do my best to clear up the mystery, and find out where the Prince is. Now, can you tell me anything which I do not already know?'

'What do you know?'

Wallace told him, and the Governor shook his head.

'You know as much as I do,' he observed. 'All I can do is to show you where the Prince and his escort were walking.'

'Would you mind sending someone with me to show me the

place and describe to me exactly what they were doing?'

'I'll come with you myself. But, in my anxiety, I am afraid I am forgetting the duties of a host. You must need a rest and refreshment after your rapid journey?'

'No, thanks,' was Wallace's quick reply. 'I slept wonderfully well and had an excellent breakfast. The sooner I can get my teeth into this business the better I shall be pleased.'

'Come along then.'

They went into the grounds, and the Governor pointed out to his companion where the Prince and the two men with him were last seen. From the ballroom a flight of wide marble steps led down to a spacious lawn dotted with flower-beds, and lined on two sides by thick shrubs and trees. The lawn, his Excellency explained, had been lit by fairy lamps, and had contained an open-air buffet. It was beyond the buffet close to the trees where the Prince had chosen to walk.

'Do you mean to say,' asked Wallace, 'that he and his companions were merely pacing backwards and forwards?'

'They were when I saw them,' returned the Governor. 'From the steps, where I was standing at the time, I could only see them dimly, for they were beyond the lights, but they were certainly walking up and down.'

'Were they in your view all the time you were standing there?'

'No. As you will notice, at the end of the lawn is a dense mass of tall shrubs.' He pointed. 'They disappeared behind there every now and then, but always emerged while I was watching them.'

'Were they all walking together?'

'No; the Prince and his equerry were together. Your man, Cousins, was a yard or two behind.'

Wallace nodded thoughtfully.

'I won't bother your Excellency further,' he remarked. 'I want to have a look at those bushes over there.'

The Governor, sensing that he wished to be alone, left him. Wallace strolled across to the place that had been indicated, and began to look about him. He discovered at once that when the Prince and his companions had reached that end of the lawn they must have been completely out of sight of all the other guests.

'It must have been here that the dirty work took place, whatever it was,' he muttered. 'Of course, the Prince may have suddenly decided to take a stroll round the grounds, but I don't think so. Cousins was a yard or two behind. Now, I wonder—'

His gaze suddenly became riveted on the ground at his feet. The grass all round him looked as though something heavy had been trampling determinedly on it, in places it was even uprooted. Obviously there had been a struggle, unless the police, when searching, had trodden the ground into that condition, and that was hardly likely. He went on his knees and made a careful examination over a wide area, rising to his feet at last and wiping the perspiration from his brow, for it was broiling hot.

'No blood,' he murmured. 'That's one relief.'

'Is it?' demanded a harsh voice behind him. 'And who the devil may you be?'

Sir Leonard turned casually and eyed the speaker. He was a tall, thin man with a prominent jaw and fierce eyes overshadowed by beetling brows. Behind him was a sergeant of police.

'Are you the Superintendent of Police?' inquired Wallace.

'I am,' was the reply, 'but you haven't answered my question.'

His manner had become less aggressive, and he was now regarding his *vis-à-vis* with a mixture of interest and resentment.

'My name is Wallace,' Sir Leonard informed him quietly. 'I have come from England to – er – help in the search for the Prince of Emilia.'

An involuntary whistle of astonishment broke from the lips of the other. The truculent air disappeared completely and, in its place, came a look of embarrassment.

'Sir Leonard Wallace?' he asked uneasily.

Wallace nodded, and smiled at him.

'Glad to meet you,' he said cordially, and held out his hand.

The superintendent grasped it rather awkwardly, and commenced to apologise for his rudeness, but Sir Leonard interrupted him.

'That's nothing,' he remarked pleasantly. 'Have you discovered anything of importance?'

'Not a thing, sir. We found a notebook lying on the grass here, but it tells us nothing.'

Wallace's eyes glittered.

'May I see it?' he asked.

The sergeant, who had been regarding him with awe, took a little volume from his pocket, and handed it over. Sir Leonard took it almost eagerly from him, and examined it carefully. It was the usual type of thing except that its binding was of a more superior kind of leather than is customary with notebooks. On the fly leaf, written in a neat hand, was the name, 'G. Cousins', and a feeling of elation began to take possession of him. Here, he felt sure, was a clue. But the book contained nothing at all to substantiate his sudden optimism. It was a private diary in which Cousins had jotted down certain thoughts and quotations – he had an inordinate fondness for the latter – and occasional appointments. There was nothing, of course, to give a clue to his profession, or any of the duties upon which he had been engaged; he was too good a Secret Service man to make a mistake of that nature.

Sir Leonard examined it from cover to cover, smiling a little at the excerpts, then he stood balancing it in his hand, his brain working at high pressure in an effort to solve the riddle which he felt sure it contained. He was certain that Cousins had dropped it purposely, hoping thereby to lead those who would search for the Prince on to the right track. Wallace knew his man, knew the wonderful subtlety of his brain. He had been unable to write a message, or leave something more obvious as a clue, and his mind had hit on the expedient of leaving the little book. What did it indicate? What was its message? The superintendent broke the silence.

'As you see, sir,' he observed, 'that book leads us nowhere. It was probably dropped in the struggle.'

'I don't agree with you,' replied Wallace softly. 'I think it is going to tell us quite a lot. It belongs to Cousins who as perhaps you know, is in my department, and was attached temporarily to the Prince. Now I happen to be aware that Cousins kept this book in his hip pocket, and hip pockets invariably button. Even if his did not, it is unlikely that a struggle would have caused the book to fall out.'

'Perhaps he was searched by his captors and, when they found that the book was of no importance, they threw it away.'

'That's very likely, isn't it?' returned Sir Leonard sarcastically. 'People who set out to kidnap princes would be sure to throw a few clues about wouldn't they?'

The superintendent bit his lip. He looked as though he would have liked to have made an angry retort. Wallace guessed his thoughts, and smiled disarmingly.

'You see,' he observed, 'even if those people, whoever they were, had discovered this little volume and considered it worthless, either to themselves or to us, they would certainly not have flung it away in case it contained something which they could not find but we might. There must have been other things, to their minds, even more innocuous in Cousins' pockets than this. If they searched him, why should they throw the book away, and not the other things? No; I am convinced that this book was dropped by Cousins on purpose. His hands might have been tied behind his back, but he could reach his hip pocket easily enough, while he certainly could not reach his other pockets, and leave what might have been a more obvious clue.'

He sat on an old tree stump still balancing the book in his hand, his brow puckered in a frown of deep thought. Presently he put it down on the ground before him, and filled his pipe, which he lit with the greatest care. He was doing his best to imagine himself in the place of Cousins, and reason with that astute individual's mind. For long minutes he sat there, puffing away furiously, while the two police officers watched him in silence. Suddenly he removed the pipe from his mouth, and gave vent to a low whistle; then spoke quickly, incisively to the superintendent.

'Find out for me,' he instructed, 'what Moroccan dhows sailed between midnight and dawn on the night of the ball, either from here or Algeciras and, as far as possible, their destination and business. Leave no stone unturned to discover if any left, or appeared to leave, secretly. You'll find me awaiting your report in Government House.'

The two officers hurried away and, left alone, Wallace indulged in a chuckle. He picked up the book, and examined the covers carefully, rising to his feet as he did so.

'There is not a doubt about it,' he murmured, 'it is bound in morocco leather, and they are *bound – in Morocco*. I believe I am right, in fact I'm sure I am. It was clever of you, Cousins – very clever.'

Slipping the book into his pocket, and not bothering to make any further investigations in the grounds, he strolled back to the house. His Excellency was in the library, he was told, and thither he bent his steps. The Governor looked up eagerly as he entered.

'Well?' he demanded.

'I have an idea,' remarked Sir Leonard quietly, 'but, as it's only an idea, I think I'll keep it to myself for the present. Can you tell me what time approximately the Prince disappeared?'

'His secretary will do that better than I can. It was he who discovered that the Prince was missing.' He rang a bell and gave instructions for the Italian to be sent for. 'It was nearly half past one when he left me,' he went on, 'and I should think I stood on the steps for about five minutes.'

'He was walking up and down all the time you stood there?'

'Yes,' nodded the Governor.

There was a knock on the door and, in response to the invitation to enter, a young man came quickly across the room and bowing politely, stood looking at them anxiously.

'This gentleman,' the Governor told him, 'has come from England to investigate the disappearance of the Prince. He wishes to ask you a few questions.'

'Oh, signor,' burst from the lips of the agitated young fellow in perfectly good English. 'What can I do? What can I say? This is a terrible calamity, is it not? I cannot eat; I cannot sleep. All the time my brain seems to be on fire, and my heart full of anguish that—'

'Yes, yes,' interrupted Wallace. 'It is natural for you to feel like that, but it won't help either you or us. Tell me: did the Prince ever have reason to suspect that there would be an attempt made to kidnap him?'

'Not as far as I know.'

'You have never had cause to think that there was a plot against him?'

'Most certainly not.'

'Has any unauthorised person endeavoured to seek an audience during your tour through the Mediterranean?'

'No.'

'On the night of the unfortunate affair, everything was, to your knowledge, perfectly normal?'

'Quite, signor.'

'The Prince was as usual? I mean to say; he was not excited or emotional, uneasy or anxious? In fact nothing about his bearing gave you reason to think that he was troubled?'

'He was as he always is, signor; charming, and happy, and gay.'

'H'm. When did you see him last?'

'It was about one o'clock. He was then dancing.'

'How did you discover that His Highness was missing?'

'I went to seek him because I had not seen him for some time, and thought he might require me. I was told he was walking in the garden.'

'And you were unable to find him?'

'There was not a sign of him anywhere.'

'What time was it when you went into the garden to look for him?'

'Ten minutes after two, signor.'

'Ah!' He glanced at the Governor. 'Then the Prince was actually kidnapped, that is if he was kidnapped, between half past one and two.'

'What do you mean by saying, "if he was kidnapped", signor?' cried the secretary. 'Surely you do not think that His Highness was murdered, and – and his body taken away?'

'No, I don't think that,' replied Wallace to the young man's evident relief. 'I might have been disposed to think that he had gone away of his own accord, if the equerry and Cousins had not been with him.'

'Why should he do that?' demanded the secretary indignantly. 'His Highness would not think of behaving in such a manner.'

Sir Leonard smiled.

'I don't suppose he would,' he admitted. 'You must not be annoyed, if I ask you a question touching the private life of the Prince. Has he ever had any clandestine love affairs?'

The young man shrugged his shoulders.

'One or two, signor,' he answered, 'but they were a very long time ago. Since he has been married His Highness has proved himself a model husband.'

'Were the ladies Italians?'

'Yes, signor. At least those with whom I was acquainted were.'

'Thank you,' said Wallace. 'That will do, I think.'

The secretary clasped his hands together imploringly.

'For the love of the Virgin, signor, find him,' he cried. 'Italy will always be grateful to you, if you do.'

'I will do my utmost,' promised Sir Leonard.

Alone with the Governor he showed little inclination to discuss the affair, but the famous soldier's repeated questions drew from him the statement, which he had already made to Maddison, that he believed a nation, jealous of Italy, was behind the abduction.

'But,' protested his amazed companion, 'surely no country would stoop to such a crime, especially on British territory?'

'The country I have in mind would,' retorted Sir Leonard. 'She would be delighted if Italy and Great Britain quarrelled. Naturally she would not show her hand in the affair, but it is quite likely that her idea is to "discover" the Prince, hand him over to his people, and accept the thanks and, later on, certain concessions of a grateful Italy. Britain, in the meantime, having proved herself incapable of protecting her royal guests, receives the opprobrium and distrust of all good Italians.'

'Good Heavens! You don't really think that?'

'I do. We've got to discover His Highness very quickly, or you will find he has been rescued, and returned to his own country by—'

He stopped and smiled.

'By?' prompted the Governor eagerly.

Sir Leonard shook his head.

'Even the walls of Government House, Gibraltar may have ears,' he observed quietly. 'If I mention the name of the country I suspect, I may cause international complications.'

'I cannot understand,' remarked his Excellency after a silence lasting for some minutes, 'how the Prince and his companions were taken away. The walls round the grounds are very high, and—'

'You forget, sir,' interrupted Wallace, 'that probably at that time several of your guests were leaving. Nobody, therefore, on duty at the gates, would have taken much notice of a car or cars going out. It would not have been difficult to have concealed the three inside a large limousine. There may have been more than one.'

'But, my dear fellow, nobody was permitted in the grounds that night without a card of invitation. If what you say is correct, then the car, or cars, used must have belonged to a guest.'

'Quite so! It is obvious.'

'I never thought of that. Would you like to see a list of the guests?'

Wallace shook his head.

'It wouldn't help,' he declared. 'If my present theory is wrong, then I'll go through the list, for it will mean recommencing the inquiry from a different angle.'

A few minutes before lunch the superintendent of police arrived and was taken to a small room, where Sir Leonard was awaiting him.

'Three dhows only sailed from Gibraltar on the night of the ball, sir,' he announced, 'and one from Algeciras. There was nothing suspicious about any of them.'

'Their destination?'

'All for Tangier.'

'What was their trade?'

Before the superintendent could reply, there came a knock on the door. A servant entered to inform the police officer that a sergeant wished to see him urgently.

'Show him in here,' directed Wallace.

In a few minutes the man arrived and, from his face, it was easy to see that he had news of importance to impart.

'What is it?' asked the superintendent.

'A dhow without any lights was seen to slip away about half past two on the morning of the ball, sir,' was the quick reply. 'My informant, a Spanish fisherman, told me he was working towards the east of the bay when he saw her coming out. She passed quite close, and there appeared to be an unusual number of men on her deck. He yelled at her about the absence of lights, but received no reply. Apparently that roused his suspicions, for he kept his eyes on her until she was out of sight. She seemed to be steering for Ceuta, he said.'

'Ah! That sounds interesting. I'd like to see the fisherman.'

'Shall I go and fetch him, sir?'

'No; it would take too long. I'll go to him, if you'll show me the way.'

Without bothering about lunch, Wallace set off immediately in one of the Governor's cars. Half an hour later he was cross-examining the fisherman, and discovered that the dhow in question was painted white, had white sails, and was much larger and altogether cleaner than the usual Moorish craft.

'It looked to me, señor, as though she were the property of a wealthy man,' stated the Spaniard.

'A kind of pleasure yacht?' asked Wallace. Like most European languages he speaks Spanish well.

The man nodded.

'There was a large deckhouse astern,' he said, 'which is most unusual on a dhow. It looked to me as though it had been built there as a cabin or saloon for the owner.'

'Have you ever seen the boat before?'

'No, señor.'

Two hours later, leaving the mystified Governor to puzzle out things as best he could, Wallace was on his way across the Straits in a large motor-launch, borrowed for the occasion, with a small skiff in tow. With him was Batty and a crew of three British sailors detailed from HMS *Lapwing*. He would have liked to have taken a couple of policemen as well, but mindful of the fact that he was about to enter foreign territory, and of the necessity of secrecy, he had decided to take Batty only.

The launch was headed for Ceuta, but Wallace had no intention of entering that port. If the dhow had had on board the Prince, it is certain that he would not have been landed in a seaport belonging to Spain. In fact it was unlikely that he would have been taken to any town at all. It is impossible to land prisoners, even in a Moroccan port, without causing comment, and comment was the very last thing the captors would desire. It was Sir Leonard's belief that the dhow would have entered one of the many inlets on the coast between Ceuta and Tangier where it would be possible to land its prisoners without fear of observation. His intention was, therefore, to search the coast between those two towns.

He did not lose sight of the possibility that he was on a wild goose chase. Actually he had nothing to go on but the finding of a morocco-bound notebook and the suspicious behaviour of a white dhow, precious little to lead him to the whereabouts of a kidnapped prince. But he knew Cousins well, and felt sure he had read the message of the notebook aright. Certain, then, that the captives had been taken to Morocco, it did not require a great deal of intelligence to connect the dhow with the abduction, when she was known to have slipped away with such an evident desire for secrecy so soon after the Prince had disappeared. Another thought struck Wallace. The dhow was apparently privately owned, according to the fisherman. A man who kept a dhow for his own pleasure would probably live near the sea. It did not seem too much to expect, therefore, that once the dhow was found, it would not be difficult to find the house. The question was: would the captives be kept there, or sent inland to some more inaccessible spot? Then again, the owner may have merely lent his boat; he may even have been unaware of the purpose for which it was borrowed. Wallace made a grimace as the numerous possibilities paraded one after another through his mind.

When within two miles of Ceuta, he gave orders for the pair of powerful binoculars; he studied the coast as the boat moved gently along. There was hardly a ripple on the sea, and not a cloud in the sky, the powerful sun streaming down on the unprotected deck, and causing the perspiration to run down Wallace's face. But he took no notice of the discomfort, examining every mile of the shore with meticulous thoroughness. Tiny little bays were disclosed to his view, sometimes with villages, gleaming white in the sunshine, above them. Several dhows were seen, but not one answering to the description of that for which they were searching. The thought occurred to Sir Leonard that by then it may have been painted another colour, but the owner surely had no reason to think that his boat would be sought. Still there was no telling, and the thought was not pleasant. The search would be rendered far more difficult if the colour of the dhow had been altered.

It took nearly three hours, at their rate of progress, to traverse the thirty or so miles to Tangier, and the sun was setting as they came in sight of the city. With a keen sense of disappointment Wallace gave orders to turn. A little cove was chosen for their night's harbourage, and running close inshore, the launch dropped her anchor. An ample supply of provisions had been brought, and Batty soon had a meal ready for them all. A watch was set, the ex-sailor taking his turn with the rest.

Soon after dawn the following morning they breakfasted, and the sun had barely risen before the boat was again under way, running now towards Ceuta and closer to the shore. But once more Wallace had to face disappointment. None of the dhows they saw bore much resemblance to the one they were after. At ten o'clock they passed Ceuta, two miles out at sea, and turning in to within a mile of the shore, when that city was out of sight, continued on their way east. At noon the launch was anchored in a small bay, while Batty served lunch. By this time Wallace had almost given up hope of coming across the white dhow, but doggedly he ordered the boat's nose to be kept east and, through the heat of the afternoon they ran, ever searching.

It was half past four, and the launch was sixty miles from Ceuta, when Sir Leonard, through his glasses, caught sight of a narrow opening between two hills. Trees grew down nearly to the water's edge on both sides, and the gap was almost hidden from view. If it went in far, it was an ideal spot in which to hide. It was certain that, if he had not been searching so carefully through binoculars, he would not have espied the entrance.

Running in close to the shore, the engine was shut off, and the launch glided along quietly until about twenty yards from the gap, where she was anchored. Wallace and one of the sailors dropped into the skiff, and he was rowed to the land. There was no beach to speak of, but they found a spit of sand in between the rocks, and ran the small boat ashore there. Bidding his companion await his return, Sir Leonard set off to ascend the hill. It took him twenty minutes' stiff climbing to reach the top, but his exertion was well repaid. Where he stood he could see perfectly down into the gap between the hill on which he was standing and the other. The narrow entrance continued as it was for about fifty yards, then opened into a basin large enough to hold half a dozen fairly large boats. A Moorish building stood close to the water, where a landing-stage had been built. But what interested Wallace most, and caused him to utter an exclamation of satisfaction, was the beautiful white dhow with sails furled that lay alongside the wharf. The search was ended.

Unslinging his binoculars, he now gazed long and earnestly

first at the boat, then at the house, but there was not a sign of movement from either. He felt fairly certain that, if the dhow had brought the Prince across from Gibraltar, he had been taken to some island retreat, and probably most of the men from the dhow had gone as an escort. But surely there would have been someone left. Yet both the boat and the house had a deserted appearance.

For half an hour he stayed where he was, but, during that time, nobody appeared, and he had reached the conclusion that the place was indeed abandoned, when a man came through the gate from the courtyard carrying a small wicker table, which he placed on the lawn between the house and the landing-stage. He was followed by two others carrying chairs. The three returned, and a few minutes later brought out food, which was put on the table. Then, as though at some signal, an atmosphere of activity prevailed where before everything had looked so desolate. Several men appeared on the deck of the dhow, four tribesmen armed with rifles emerged from the narrow archway leading to the courtyard of the building. Then came a tall Moor wrapped in a spotless white burnous, accompanied by a young, slight man in European dress. Sir Leonard stiffened, and stared without movement through his glasses for quite five minutes. The Moor bowed ceremoniously to the other, who, with a shrug of his shoulders, took one of the chairs. He appeared to be speaking quickly, angrily, and the expression on his face was perfectly clear to Wallace. The unexpected had happened. It was the Prince.

Sir Leonard did not wait to see anything more, but made his way down the hill to the spot where the skiff awaited him. Once aboard the launch, he instructed the coxswain in charge to find a place where she could lie hidden. To avoid the noise which the engine would have made, one of the other sailors got into the skiff and towed her. Before long they reached a great cave where the water was quite deep enough. A ledge of rock made an excellent landing stage, and to this the launch was tied up after some difficulty in finding a place capable of holding the rope.

Whilst Batty prepared tea, his master lay down on the cushioned seat in the small cabin, which the night before had been his bed, and commenced to make his plans. The Prince's whereabouts had been discovered, but not the least difficult part of the undertaking remained. The tall Moor, who was apparently His Highness's captor, had twelve men with him – Wallace had counted that number – there were probably others. The house, like all Moorish buildings, was difficult of ingress, and Sir Leonard only had three men to help him; one would have to remain in charge of the launch. Three British sailors might well prove a match for twelve Moors, but the odds were too great to take such a risk when so much was at stake. Their only chance of rescuing the Prince and his companions seemed to be to attempt to enter the house by stealth, but even then, if they succeeded in getting in, how were they to find where the prisoners were kept? It was a pretty problem. Eventually Wallace determined to enter the house alone, keeping the three men in hiding close by ready to come to his aid if required. He chose midnight for the attempt, feeling certain that by then everybody would be asleep.

It was almost as light as day, when the four men set off on their desperate enterprise, the moon making Sir Leonard's flashlight unnecessary. Each of his followers carried a revolver, but had been instructed not to fire except in a case of emergency. They toiled up the hill cautiously for fear that a watch was being kept from the top, but, on reaching the summit, discovered that their apprehensions were baseless. Even so, their care was redoubled in descending the other side. Both the house and the dhow were in darkness, and not a sound disturbed the silence of the night. At last they stood on the margin of the open space before the house, and Wallace took a whistle from his pocket.

'Keep in among the trees here,' he instructed them, 'and don't make a sound. If you hear this whistle, come to my aid, but otherwise wait here until I come back.'

The two sailors murmured their assent, but Batty was dissatisfied.

'Seems to me, sir,' he muttered, 'that you want a consort in this 'ere cuttin' out expedition. 'Adn't I better come with you?'

'You'll stay here, Batty.'

'Aye, aye, sir,' returned that one-time mariner with a deep sigh.

Wallace crossed the lawn almost like a shadow, or at least that is what he appeared like to the three watchers. He reached the archway without raising the alarm, and stood for a moment in the shadows. Halfway along was a gate, which looked as though it would take a good deal of effort to open, but out came that bunch of steel instruments without which he never went on an expedition of that nature. Ten minutes' hard but silent work followed, after which he gave a low grunt of satisfaction. The gate was unlocked. But when he pushed it gently it refused to budge. It was barred. For a second or two he stood staring at it, a frown on his forehead then, as silently as he had come, he returned to the three waiting men.

'I shall want help after all,' he whispered. 'Perhaps it would be as well if you all came with me, but, for Heaven's sake, don't make a noise.'

Batty and his companions gave vent to sounds expressive of their satisfaction, and followed him with cumbersome attempts at silence back to the gate. When under the archway:

'I'm going to knock,' he murmured. 'I hope someone will come and open it. If not, I shall have to think of something else. At any rate, if it is opened, I want you to go for the fellow, and lay him out without a disturbance. Do you think you can manage it?'

In hoarse whispers they assured him that they could. He knocked sharply and, soon afterwards, they heard footsteps coming towards them on the other side of the door. The man made a lot of noise removing the bars, but presently the gate swung open, and a tall Moor wrapped up in his burnous looked out. Immediately a brawny arm encircled his neck, the hand clapped hard against his mouth, two others clasped him round the middle and drew him forward, while Batty, scientifically wielding a heavy revolver, tapped the fellow into a state of unconsciousness. Wallace watched his three assistants place the body of the Moor gently on the ground, and smiled approvingly.

'Give me his burnous,' he whispered.

''Is wot, sir?' queried Batty.

Wallace indicated what he meant. There was some difficulty in removing the voluminous garment, but at last Batty handed it to his master.

'There's a lot o' top 'amper on this nightgown, sir,' he muttered disparagingly.

Sir Leonard cloaked himself in it, drawing the hood well over his head.

'Stay here, you three,' he said, 'and if that fellow wakes up put him to sleep again. I'll close the gate, but won't lock it, and come to me at oncc if you hear my whistle.'

He entered and, pushing the massive door to, walked on to the end of the archway, emerging presently into the courtyard with the inevitable fountain playing in the centre. Above him, running round four sides of the building, was a veranda, and he wondered where the prisoners were lodged, but a feeling of exultation filled him when he caught sight of the dim outlines of a Moor, armed with a rifle, squatting before a door at the far end. Casually he walked up the steps of the veranda, and strolled along towards the man, his fingers gripping the barrel of his revolver, the hood of his burnous drawn still closer round his face. The fellow took no notice of him until he was a yard or so away, then looked up, indulging in a prodigious yawn as he did so. But the yawn was cut short, and ended in a queer grunt, as the weapon in Wallace's hand caught him hard on the temple. He sagged over sideways, and his rifle clattered to the floor before his assailant could catch it. Expecting an alarm, Wallace looked anxiously round, remaining perfectly still for nearly a minute. To his relief, nothing happened. He bent and searched the clothing of his victim, presently, to his joy, finding a large ring containing two keys. Stepping over the sprawling Moor, he inserted one in the keyhole of the door the fellow had apparently been guarding. It turned at once, and he found himself in a room lighted only by a small aperture high up, through which the moonlight only showed faintly.

Not daring to speak for fear that perhaps, after all, the prisoners were not there, he closed the door, took a flashlight from his pocket, and switched it on. The only furniture the room contained was a divan, though several costly-looking rugs covered the floor. Two men, fully dressed, sat up and blinked, and a great sigh of relief broke from him. One was Cousins, the other a stranger, whom he guessed to be the equerry of the Prince of Emilia. Of the Prince himself there was no sign. Wondering why they showed no enthusiasm at his appearance, he suddenly realised that, being behind the light, they could only see a shadowy figure in a burnous.

'You're a nice sort of a chap,' growled Cousins. 'Is it part of your beastly game to keep us awake all night?'

'I think you'll have to keep awake tonight, Cousins,' replied Sir Leonard quietly, 'if you want to get away from here.'

There came a startled gasp, then Cousins was on his feet, hauling up the other man.

'Jehoshaphat!' he exclaimed. 'It's Sir Leonard Wallace himself.' He began an appropriate quotation, stopped in the middle of it, and asked: 'How did you get here, sir?'

'There's no time to answer questions now. Where's the Prince?'

'In a room close to El Arish's apartments.'

'Who's El Arish?'

'The owner of this den of thieves, sir.'

'Well, show me the way, and watch your step.'

He opened the door, and stepped out. The unconscious form of the guard reminded him that it would not do to leave the man where he was lying. With the help of his companions, he carried the fellow into the room, where he was tied up and gagged with strips torn from his own clothing. Then Cousins led the way along the veranda, and stopped before a door at which he pointed silently. Guessing that the other key would open this, Wallace tried it, and found he was right.

The three of them stepped into a room which they saw by the light of Sir Leonard's torch, was far more sumptuously furnished than the other, but was just as much a prison, for it contained no windows. A bed stood in an alcove, and on it was lying the Prince, fast asleep, wearing gaudy pyjamas. Wallace stole across the room, and gently shook him. The young man started up, and was about to cry out, when Sir Leonard's hand on his mouth prevented him.

'Silence,' he warned in a low voice. 'We are here to rescue you, and—'

A door suddenly swung open behind a heavy arabesque curtain, which was drawn aside, revealing in the light, thrown from the lamp which he carried, a tall man with a revolver in his other hand. Wallace recognised him as the Moor he had seen with the Prince on the lawn.

'Surely my guests do not propose to leave me?' he remarked coolly in excellent French, and stared hard at Sir Leonard, who, when waking the Prince, had thrown back his hood. 'Who are you, sir?' he demanded.

'My name is Wallace,' replied Sir Leonard as coolly as he, 'and, if it is of any interest to you, I am attached to the British diplomatic service.'

'Indeed? I find it most interesting. I should like to know how you got in, but that can wait. It appears that I am to have another prisoner on my hands.'

Wallace was amused at his calm manner. Here, he thought, was an opponent worthy of his steel.

'You've made a slight mistake,' he observed. 'I have come to take the Prince away from you. Do you realise that you have committed the crime of *lèse-majesté*?'

The Moor shrugged his shoulders.

'That means nothing to me,' he returned contemptuously.

'I am afraid it will mean a great deal.' He turned to the Prince. 'Will your Highness be good enough to dress?' he requested.

The Moor's manner changed slightly, as the Prince obeyed

with alacrity, assisted by his equerry. He placed the lamp on a convenient table.

'I have no objection to that,' he said, his eyes glittering evilly, 'but, as none of you will leave this place, it is a waste of time. In two minutes I will call my men, and you will be helpless.'

'And I will call mine,' returned Sir Leonard. 'What then?'

'Your men! Where are they?'

'You will soon know.'

He looked towards the door, and the Moor's eyes followed his. Thus was he tricked for, as he looked away, like lightning Wallace's torch had disappeared and, in his hand, pointed steadily at the Moor, was a revolver.

'Drop that gun!' commanded the Englishman sternly. 'I shall not have the slightest compunction in shooting you after what you have done, if you give me the chance.'

A look of baffled fury showed for an instant on the Moor's face, then he smiled.

'You will be very clever, if you get away from here,' he observed, and placed his revolver on the table.

'Not a bit of it,' retorted Sir Leonard. 'It is easy. All I want you to remember is that the slightest attempt on your part to sound an alarm will mean your sad demise. I hope you understand me. And if you think that, as soon as we have left this house, you will be able to rouse your men, and attack us before we can get clear, let me remove that impression from your mind at once. You are coming with us!'

With what sounded very much like an oath, El Arish's hand shot out to grab his revolver, but Wallace stepped quickly across the room, and placed the muzzle of his weapon within a few inches of the other man's eyes.

'We'll have no nonsense, if you please,' he said sternly.

El Arish broke into voluble protests, half in French, half in Arabic. All his coolness had vanished, and he looked terrified, but Wallace paid little attention to him. As soon as the Prince was dressed, Sir Leonard ordered Cousins to lead the way.

'Go as quietly as you can, all of you,' he warned. 'I will bring up the rear with this gentleman. You will find my three men awaiting us in the archway; they will lead you to the boat.'

Cousins, followed closely by the Prince and his equerry, walked silently along the veranda, and down the steps to the courtyard. El Arish once again began to protest, but the touch of Sir Leonard's revolver in his back cut him short and, with a shrug, which typified the fatalism of his race, he went after the others, his captor close to his heels. Once, going down the steps, he pretended to stumble, but a low-voiced threat from Wallace showed him the necessity of being more circumspect. After that he gave no further trouble. The shadowy figures of Batty and the two sailors rose from the ground, where they had been sitting, when the others arrived.

'Here, Batty,' called Sir Leonard, 'keep your gun pointed at this fellow while I remove the burnous.'

The disrobing process was quickly accomplished, and he gave a sigh expressive of relief as he threw the voluminous garment down beside its owner.

'It was a trifle smelly,' he muttered. 'Thanks, Batty. I've got him covered. Lead on as silently as you can.'

'Wot about this 'ere bloke?' questioned the ex-sailor in a hoarse whisper. ''E's beginning to come round, sir.'

'Tie him up and gag him; then put him inside and shut the gate.'

With naval thoroughness it was done, after which Batty and

the sailors led the way back to the launch. No alarm was raised behind them, and nothing untoward happened during the hour it took them to reach the boat. Every now and then Wallace prodded his prisoner in the back, as a warning that he was still there, but El Arish had accepted his fate apparently, and made no more protests.

Once in the cave, Sir Leonard set two men to keep watch on him, and drew the Prince aside.

'I don't think any good purpose will be served by taking El Arish with us, your Highness,' he observed. 'This, I believe to be a matter for settlement between your country and another. El Arish has been merely the tool.'

He proceeded in a whisper to enlarge on his suspicions to the astonished Prince.

'If you agree,' he concluded, 'I'll tell him he can go if he confesses.'

The Prince nodded, and Wallace confronted the Moor.

'You can go,' he declared, 'if, to use an Americanism, you come clean.'

'How do you mean?' queried the Moor.

Sir Leonard explained and, once he understood how much the Englishman knew or suspected, El Arish gave away the whole plot. It had, as Wallace had guessed, been engineered by a nation jealous of Great Britain and antagonistic to Italy. By the light of a lamp brought from the launch, he agreed to write down his part in the affair, and sign it. When that was done he was told he could depart.

'If I were you,' advised Sir Leonard, 'I should take a long holiday in the interior of Morocco until this affair blows over.'

The Moor who, at the prospect of release, had recovered his insouciance, bowed mockingly.

'Your anxiety on my behalf,' he observed, 'touches me deeply.'

He watched his late prisoners climb aboard the launch; then bowed again, and walked away. With three additional passengers the boat was somewhat crowded, but nobody minded the crush. The Prince was in high good humour, and repeated again and again the great debt of gratitude he owed to Wallace, until the latter became rather embarrassed and sought the company of Cousins. To the latter he handed the morocco-bound notebook, and the little man's wrinkled face creased in its extraordinary way into a smile.

'So you saw through my design, sir,' he chuckled. 'I thought you'd be sooner or later on the trail, and nobody else but you would have guessed what I wanted to inform you. It was very clever of you, if I may say so, sir.'

'Not so clever as your idea to leave such a clue.'

'It was a lucky thing I had the book with me, and in my hip pocket. I wouldn't have been able to get at it, if it had been elsewhere. My hands were tied behind me, you see.'

'But you always carry the book in your hip pocket, don't you?'

'Generally. How did you know, sir?'

'Just observation, that's all. You can get at it more surreptitiously there, when you can't think of an appropriate quotation, can't you?'

Cousins actually blushed, but it was too dark for his smiling chief to see his face distinctly.

'How did you trace us, sir?' he asked hastily. 'The book only told you we were in Morocco, but it's a biggish country in which to search for anybody.'

Wallace told him the whole story; then inquired how they had been kidnapped. It appeared that after they had been walking up and down the lawn of Government House for ten minutes or thereabouts, and at the moment were at the far end close to the shrubs and trees, they were suddenly pounced upon by several men, who threw some sort of thick material over their heads, and tied their arms and legs. Then they were thrown on the ground, while a whispered conversation took place in Arabic, a language which Cousins knew well. By straining his ears he heard a man telling others to climb over the wall, and get back to the dhow as soon as the Prince and his companions had been placed in the car. He added that it was necessary that the boat should sail for Morocco as soon as possible. Cousins, straining at his bonds and wondering what to do to leave some sort of clue behind, suddenly remembered that his notebook was bound in morocco leather. It was a slender hope that anyone would grasp the significance of the little volume, but there was nothing else he could do. He managed to get his fingers into his hip pocket, pull out the book, and leave it on the ground. A few minutes later they were picked up, carried a few yards and bundled into a car, which immediately started. It seemed a long time to Cousins before it stopped again and, when at last it did, they were thrown into a boat and rowed some distance, before being transferred to the larger vessel.

'We only reached the house of El Arish,' he concluded, 'about thirty hours before you came along, sir, and, do you know, we were tied up all the time we were on that blessed boat. El Arish pretends to have manners, but he's no gentleman. "What is he but a brute whose flesh has soul to suit" – Browning, sir!'

'Thanks,' returned Wallace sarcastically. 'Did you look in the book for that one?'

Cousins became silent.

The relief of the Governor of Gibraltar was tremendous when his royal guest was brought back to him, as was that of the British Foreign Office. The revelations of Sir Leonard Wallace caused a tremendous sensation in diplomatic circles, with the result that the nation which had hoped for so much from the abduction of the Prince of Emilia was forced by Italy, backed by Great Britain, to eat very humble pie indeed.

'The old country came out of the affair with flying colours,' observed Wallace to his wife, as a week or so later they sat together once again on the terrace of their New Forest home.

'Thanks to you, dear,' she murmured.

'No; thanks to Cousins' passion for quotations and the little book in which he writes them.'

CHAPTER THREE

Sentiment and Suicide

'The whole gas question is in the air,' observed Major Brien with great profundity.

Sir Leonard Wallace, who was busily engaged in signing documents, glanced up at his friend and smiled.

'Where did you expect it to be?' he queried. 'Buried in the ground?'

Brien looked at him suspiciously; then he, too, smiled.

'Rather a *bon mot* that,' he said in self-congratulatory tones. 'But what are you going to do about this Mason affair?'

Wallace did not answer. Instead he went on reading through the reports, and appending his signature. The last one appeared to give him a good deal of thought, but at length he signed it.

'Is that all, Stephenson?' he asked the man standing respectfully at his side.

'Yes, sir,' was the reply.

'Very well. Take them away. As soon as Mr Cousins returns tell him I am waiting here for him.'

The clerk gathered up the papers and quietly left the room.

'Now, Bill,' urged Sir Leonard, 'tell me what's worrying you.'

Brien rose from the chair in which he had been lounging.

'It's that message from Brookfield,' he asserted walking across to the bookshelves, and running his finger along the titles as though in search of a particular volume. 'It seems fairly evident from what he says that Professor Mason's secret is out – in fact that it is a secret no longer, and that the poor old chap not only lost his life, but all he has worked for since the War.'

Wallace nodded.

'Looks like it,' he agreed, 'but the formula may not have been in the safe at all. What are you looking for?'

'That book of yours on Lewisite.'

'Third shelf down, seventh book along from the right-hand side,' was the prompt direction.

Brien turned, and looked admiringly at his chief.

'How do you do it?' he asked.

Wallace laughed.

'I was glancing through it myself half an hour ago,' he confessed, 'and that's where I put it.'

Brien uttered a sound expressive of disgust, removed the book from its shelf; then returned, and sank into the chair he had vacated. He quickly found the chapter he wanted, and began to read carefully. Sir Leonard rested his head in his hands – one natural, the other artificial – and gazed unseeingly at his desk. Although he had spoken so lightly to his friend, he was feeling anything but elated.

Professor Mason who, practically since the cessation of hostilities, had been seeking a poison gas that would be supreme, that would destroy all life against which it was directed, and stifle any attempt at resistance, had at last succeeded. Working with care and patience on the principles of Lewisite, he had gradually evolved a gas so malignant that, according to him, no mask could be invented that would be proof against it. He had been actuated all the time by the belief that such a gas would make war impossible. In the hands of a nation, as honourable as Great Britain, he declared that it would prove far more efficacious for peace than the League of Nations could ever be. At the same time he was forced to admit that, if the formula fell into the hands of an unscrupulous country, the result might well mean that all other nations would become subject races to that country. Despite themselves, high officials at the War Office had been impressed, with the result that during the final stages of the professor's work the Secret Service had been asked to supply a man to guard him and his discovery from possible curiosity on the part of agents of other powers. Sir Leonard Wallace had sent Brookfield, a very clever member of his staff, who, after proving himself one of the successes of the Special Branch at Scotland Yard, had been transferred to the Secret Service.

For six weeks Brookfield had lived with the scientist in his rambling old house at East Minster on the Isle of Sheppey, keeping constant vigilance, but nothing untoward had happened. Even he had not been permitted to enter the large laboratory where the professor conducted his experiments. It was a chamber that possessed double doors, the inner one being constructed of steel, both of which were locked when Mason was inside. There were no windows, air being supplied in plentiful quantities through three ventilators. As soon as he was satisfied that his five years of careful experiment had proved successful, the professor informed the War Office and arranged a date for final demonstration of the efficacy of the gas, which he had named Veronite. Major Brien had been present with the experts on the day appointed and, like his companions, had been amazed and shocked by the manifestation.

'It was devastating, catastrophic,' he had told Sir Leonard Wallace on his return to the office. 'I had never even imagined anything so dreadful, and I hope I never see the infernal stuff in action again.'

The War Office specialists had been enthusiastic, and had desired to take possession of the formula there and then, but Professor Mason had told them there was still one little experiment he wished to carry out before announcing that his work was complete. That morning he had failed to appear at breakfast, and repeated and loud knocking on the door of the laboratory had met with no response. Thoroughly alarmed Brookfield rang up Sir Leonard Wallace, who promptly sent down Cousins to help in the investigation. Two hours later Brookfield telephoned with the information that he and Cousins had broken in the first door and opened the second by means of a steel cutter to find the professor lying dead, shot through the brain. Cousins was then on his way to Town to make his report, whilst Brookfield remained awaiting orders.

'Has it struck you,' asked Brien suddenly looking up from his book, 'that the most terrible consequences may result from this tragedy?'

'Naturally,' was the reply. 'There would be something wrong with my mentality if the thought had not occurred to me.' He glanced keenly at his friend. 'What kind of a man was Mason, Billy? I never met him, you know.'

'A genial little chap with a mop of white hair and the face of a schoolboy,' returned Brien. 'I was rather struck with the youthfulness of his complexion. It was as smooth as a woman's, and hadn't a line or wrinkle in it. It made me think of that big poster of a schoolgirl which advertises Palm Olive soap.'

'Would you think he was the type of man to commit suicide?'

Brien shook his head emphatically.

'Absolutely not,' he declared. 'Why? Do you think—'

'I can hardly think anything until I've heard what Cousins has to say,' interrupted Wallace. 'It occurred to me, however, that the appalling nature of the force he was handing over to others may have suddenly caused him misgiving; a dread that he had no right to put such power into the hands even of Great Britain. You know what these savants are. Their minds are not normal like yours and mine.' Brien smiled to himself. Nobody would ever have described Wallace's mind as normal, a mind that had been on several occasions, spoken of as one of the most brilliant in England. 'There is just a chance, therefore,' went on Wallace, 'that a sudden revulsion of feeling came to him, whereupon he destroyed his formula and shot himself.'

'But,' objected Billy, 'Brookfield spoke as though he was certain of murder. If it had been suicide, a weapon would have been found, and he made no mention of one. I hope,' he added reflectively, 'that it does turn out to be suicide. The idea of the gas being in the hands of a nation that does not hesitate to employ agents, who commit murder to attain their object, does not bear thinking about.'

There was a knock on the door and, in response to Wallace's call, one of the most remarkable and popular figures at Secret Service headquarters entered. Cousins, with his slim boyish figure and wrinkled face, was generally a source of amusement to his colleagues. But on this occasion neither Wallace nor Brien smiled a greeting at him. His sharp brown eyes had a look of solemnity in them; the humorous curves of his face had, in some extraordinary manner, changed into lines of grim solicitude. Without a word he sank into the chair his chief indicated, and accepted a cigarette from the silver box that was pushed across to him. Both his superior officers were watching him anxiously. He took two or three quick puffs at his cigarette before he spoke, then:

'It's murder without a doubt,' he proclaimed, 'and I'm just as certain that the formula has been stolen.'

A sharp intake of breath came from Brien. Sir Leonard gave no sign, but his steel-grey eyes were boring into the little man's face as though he expected to read the solution of the mystery there.

'You found no weapon, I suppose?' he asked quietly.

'No, sir. Apart from that there is no sign of singeing as there would have been if the bullet had been fired from very close range.'

'Well, being certain that the professor was murdered, how did his assailant get into the laboratory?'

Cousins raised his hands in a helpless sort of gesture.

'That's what Brookfield and I have been trying to puzzle out all morning,' he observed ruefully. 'He not only got in, but he got out again, and left both doors *locked from the inside*.'

'I suppose they are self-locking,' put in Brien, 'and all the murderer had to do was to pull them to after he was out.'

Cousins looked at him, the glimmer of a pitying smile on his face.

'We happen to have noticed that neither latch was self-locking,' he remarked with the slightest trace of sarcasm. 'Also I found both keys lying on one of the tables in the laboratory. Not only that but

Brookfield sat on an armchair close to the outer door all night, only leaving his post when the housekeeper told him breakfast was ready at eight this morning.'

'There are no windows in the laboratory, are there?'

'No sir. It is lit by half a dozen powerful electric lights. There's not even a chimney.'

'Then,' declared Brien with conviction, 'the professor must have killed himself, unless—' he stopped as a sudden thought struck him. 'Would it have been possible for the man, whoever he was, to have hidden in the room and made his escape when you and Brookfield were bending over the professor? You see there is a chance that Mason took the fellow in with him.'

'Nobody went in with him,' replied Cousins. 'Both Brookfield and a maid saw him go in alone, and bade him good night; and it is out of the question that the murderer could have been hiding there. When we finally succeeded in opening the steel door we both stood at the entrance for some time while I bound up Brookfield's hand which had been cut during the process. If anybody had been in there we would have been bound to have seen him. There's nowhere a man could hide effectually. Besides, Mrs Holdsworth, the housekeeper, was standing outside in the passage.'

Brien, looking thoroughly mystified, sat back in his chair. 'It beats me,' he confessed. 'He must have shot himself, but how?'

Wallace who had remained silent since his first question, and appeared to be deep in thought now looked up.

'Any theory, Cousins?' he demanded.

'I'm afraid I haven't,' was the reply. 'The whole thing is impossible on the face of it, and yet it has happened. Take the bare facts as they stand, sir: nobody could get into that room, yet somebody did; nobody could get out without going through the double doors, yet somebody did.'

'Perhaps the murderer had duplicate keys!'

'I have gone into that possibility, sir. But I ascertained that the locks were specially made with only one key for each door, which never under any circumstances left the professor's possession.'

'Why are you so sure that the laboratory was entered?' asked Sir Leonard quietly.

'How else could the professor have been murdered, sir, and the safe ransacked?'

'Ah! The safe was ransacked, was it? Brookfield only told us on the telephone that you found the door open. How do you know it had been ransacked?'

'It was full of papers mixed together in hopeless confusion, as though someone had conducted a hasty search. While the doctor was examining the body, I went through them. There was no sign of the formula for Veronite either there, in Professor Mason's pockets, or in fact anywhere in the laboratory.'

'How do you know?' demanded Brien.

Cousins smiled.

'I happen to have a fairly extensive knowledge of chemistry,' he replied, as though he were confessing a weakness, 'and there was certainly no formula concerning poison gas.'

'Is there anything you don't know, Cousins?' asked Wallace.

The little man sighed.

'A lot more than I should care to confess,' he said. 'What I do know can only be classed as extraneous knowledge, sir. I browse in the suburbs so to speak.'

'They must be singularly well-informed suburbs,' observed Brien.

'"Give me ae spark o' Nature's fire, that's a' the learning I desire",' murmured Cousins.

'Were the lights on when you entered the laboratory?' asked Wallace.

'All of them, sir.'

'Did you inform the Sheerness police?'

Cousins shook his head.

'I thought you'd want to have a look round first,' he pointed out.

'Quite right. We'll let Scotland Yard know. If they want to send a man down they can, but they'll probably leave a matter like this to us entirely. Who is the doctor you called in?'

'A man called Cummings, with a practice at Minster, sir. He wanted to call in the police, and was altogether an officious sort of person. I told him to stay in the house, and gave Brookfield the tip not to let him out. He's the sort that would have blabbed the news to the whole countryside, if we had let him go. He made a bit of a fuss; imagines Brooky and I are criminals of the deepest dye, I think.'

'The usual type of country practitioner, I suppose.'

'Worse than the usual, sir. Simply oozed importance when he knew what we wanted him for, and talked an awful lot. Still he knew enough to be able to declare life extinct, which was clever of him considering poor old Professor Mason was shot right through the centre of his forehead.'

Wallace rose.

'I'll go along at once. Perhaps you'd better come with me, Billy, and you too, of course, Cousins. Is the sewing machine here, Bill?'

The sewing machine was his disrespectful name for Major Brien's car and, after many protests against such a title, the latter had accepted the inevitable, and even used the designation himself. He nodded.

'The car with the finest engine in London is below,' he said firmly.

Wallace grinned.

'Well, you shall have the privilege of driving Cousins and me to East Minster,' he declared.

'Thanks for nothing,' retorted Brien.

Wallace rang up his wife to inform her that he would not be home for luncheon, then the three of them started in Brien's somewhat ancient but thoroughly efficient car. They halted for some minutes outside New Scotland Yard where a startled Commissioner listened in amazed and angry silence to Sir Leonard's story.

'What a dastardly crime!' he exclaimed when the Chief of the Secret Service had finished.

'The theft of the formula,' commented Wallace grimly, 'and there is little doubt that it has been stolen, is even more dastardly. Can you imagine what the loss of that may signify?'

'My God!' ejaculated the Commissioner, and he spoke in little more than a whisper, while the blood drained slowly from his face. 'That aspect did not strike me before. It may result in an appalling calamity.'

'Of course it may. Even in the possession of a weak nation it would mean world domination until some sort of defence against it could be invented.'

They sat looking at each other for some seconds, the faces of them both indicating the grave nature of their thoughts. At last the Commissioner spoke.

'You won't want us to take a hand,' he surmised. 'A case of this nature comes under your purview, not mine. Besides, it asks for the unrestricted methods of your department, not the restrained red-tapism to which we have to submit in our investigations.'

'Exactly,' agreed Sir Leonard; 'but once I obtain a line leading me to the formula and thus to the murderer, you'd better take up the affair, and treat it as a common case of murder. The motive for the crime, in fact everything respecting the discovery of Veronite, must be hushed up.'

The grey-haired Chief of Police nodded.

'We shall simply declare robbery to have been the motive,' he said. 'God grant you are able to recover the formula,' he added earnestly as Wallace rose to go.

An hour's rapid run took the car to Professor Mason's house at East Minster. The building stood on a cliff overlooking the sea in grounds that had been badly neglected, and was half a mile from any other dwelling. It was a peculiar place having originally been a cottage of five rooms to which had been added others, from time to time, eventually to give it a strange appearance as though it was endeavouring to face in three directions at once. Only the front remained unaltered probably because it would have been impossible to extend in that direction.

Brookfield met them, and conducted them to the drawing room, where a sharp-featured woman was waiting with a stout, undersized man of about fifty-five. The latter, his little eyes gleaming angrily through his pince nez, greeted them with a snort of indignation.

'I demand an explanation for my reasonless detention in this house,' he commenced, looking from Brien to Wallace and back again. 'It is scandalous that a man of my position and calling should have been treated in such a manner. During my thirty years' experience I have never—'

'Is this the doctor?' asked Wallace turning to Brookfield.

'Yes, sir,' was the reply. 'Cousins and I thought it would be as well if he stayed here until you arrived. He didn't approve, and I've had a great deal of difficulty in persuading him to remain.'

'Approve!' barked the doctor. 'Of course I did not approve. I have been in this house for three and a half hours, and it is now past my luncheon hour. I want to know the meaning of it, sir. It is—'

'All right, doctor,' interrupted Wallace soothingly, 'you'll be paid for the time you have spent here. It was important that you remained on the premises.' The little man was mollified to a great extent.

'Well,' he conceded, 'that alters the complexion of the business somewhat. I did not understand that I was to be remunerated for the hours I have – er – wasted here. My time is valuable, and I have many patients – many patients. All the same I am mystified. Are you from Scotland Yard, sir?'

'Not exactly from Scotland Yard,' replied Sir Leonard, 'but somewhere close by.'

The doctor blinked at him, and was about to ask further questions, but he turned away and, taking Brookfield by the arm, led him to a corner of the room.

'Is everything as you found it?' he asked.

'Yes, sir, except the contents of the safe,' replied the fair-haired, well-built man who had acted as the professor's guardian and watch-dog. 'Cousins sorted the mass of documents we found there in the hope that the formula for Veronite would be amongst them.'

'I know that. The body has not been moved?'

'No, sir.'

'Good. It was your habit to sit outside there in the passage when the professor was in here?'

'Yes, sir.'

'You were there last night?'

'Yes, sir.'

'Did you hear anything – a noise of any kind?'

'No, sir. I can't understand why I didn't hear the shot. Of course the walls are thick and there are double doors, but even so, I should have expected to hear a muffled sort of sound.'

'Perhaps the murderer used a silencer. Was the professor in the habit of working at night?'

'Not quite in the habit, but he did pretty frequently.'

'I see. Have you searched anywhere else besides the laboratory for the papers?'

'Yes; I have examined all Professor Mason's clothing, drawers and cupboards. I have even looked inside his books.'

'No result I suppose?'

Brookfield shook his head.

'I can't tell you how I feel about this, sir,' he confided dismally. 'I would give five years' pension if it could be undone.'

Wallace nodded.

'I can understand your feelings,' he observed, 'but it can't be helped. You weren't to blame as far as I can see. Take me to the laboratory.'

It was a large apartment built onto the rear of the house, the walls and floor of which were lined with slabs of white marble. Two long tables of the same material stood parallel to each other in the centre of the room. On these were various appliances of modern chemistry. Three of the walls contained shelves covered with bottles, most of them nearly full of powder or liquid, retorts, burettes and other articles. The other side of the room was bare except for a solitary chair and a large safe, the door of which was wide open. The laboratory was lit by six powerful electric bulbs so placed that no shadows could be thrown by anything, no matter where its position might be.

Wallace stood looking round appreciatively for a few moments; then walked to the silent form lying in the centre of the room between the two tables. Kneeling down, he examined the tiny hole in the forehead, and took note of the position in which the body was lying. Someone had closed the eyes, but Wallace raised the lids, and gazed long and earnestly into the glazed depths. Suddenly a puzzled frown wrinkled his brow. He raised the head, and carefully felt the back of it; then once more gazed into the eyes.

'Ask Major Brien and the doctor to come here,' he instructed Brookfield.

The two were soon standing by his side, and he looked up at the medical man.

'How long do you think the professor had been dead, doctor, when you saw him?' he asked.

'Between six and eight hours without a doubt,' replied the little man fussily. 'There is no—'

'What time was it when you saw him?'

'Precisely at ten.'

'That means that he died between two and four.'

'Most decidedly.'

'I suppose you have examined the body thoroughly?'

'I have,' returned the doctor – his tone was almost indignant.

'Did you find anything unusual about it?'

'Unusual! My dear sir, a violent death can never be considered anything but unusual.'

Sir Leonard rose to his feet, and looked straight into the other's eyes.

'I'm sorry to have to say it,' he observed coldly, 'but I have come to the conclusion that you are no ornament to your profession.'

'How dare you, sir!' cried the doctor angrily. 'How dare—'

'Not so loud,' commanded Wallace. 'May I remind you that a certain amount of respect is due to the dead.'

He turned his back on the angry little man, and spoke to Brien.

'Ring up Scotland Yard, Billy,' he instructed, 'and ask the Commissioner to send down his most competent police surgeon. Brookfield, I want you and Cousins to comb the neighbourhood, and find out if any strangers have been seen about recently. If so, get descriptions of them, names if possible and, in fact, all the information you can. Before starting out, ask the housekeeper if she can give you a meal of some sort. I could do with a snack myself.'

He was left alone with the doctor and the dead body of the professor.

'I hate to show my contempt for any man,' he remarked, addressing the still fuming medico, 'but you call yourself a doctor, and apparently fail to notice what even I saw, and my knowledge of the science of medicine is remarkably vague.'

'What did you see?' demanded the doctor, interested in spite of himself.

'Did you examine the professor's eyes?' counter-questioned Wallace.

'Of course I did. I closed the lids.'

'And you saw nothing peculiar about them?'

'No; I can't say I did. They were no different to any other dead eyes.'

Wallace gave an exclamation of impatience.

'You can go home, doctor,' he said. 'But please remember to keep absolutely silent regarding this affair for the present. Send your bill to Room 12 at the Foreign Office, and you will receive payment.'

The doctor looked at him curiously; then bowed slightly and went out.

'Of course, the little fool *will* blab,' muttered Sir Leonard to himself, and added philosophically, 'but he can't do any harm, simply because he is such a fool.'

He was examining the doors of the room, when Brien came back and announced that Scotland Yard's most competent surgeon was engaged at the moment, but would be down before four o'clock.

'That will do,' commented Wallace. 'Get hold of Brookfield and Cousins before they go off on their little jaunt, and tell them to carry the body to the bedroom, will you?'

Brien nodded.

'Have you any theories?' he asked.

'I'm afraid not. Two peculiar things have struck me. One I will keep for the police surgeon, the other is that after murdering the professor the criminal probably took the keys of the safe from his pocket, opened it, then put them back. Now why did he bother to do that? Any ordinary individual would have left them in the door.'

'Ask me another?' remarked Brien. 'I'll bite. Why did he?'

'That's what I want to know.'

'I don't see that it matters very much. Perhaps the safe was opened by the professor.'

'He'd be no more likely to return the keys to his pocket until he had locked it again than anyone else.'

'No; I suppose not. Let us go and eat. I believe a meal is awaiting our attention in the dining room. At any rate, Cousins and Brookfield are tucking in already, and I'm famished.'

While they were eating Wallace's mind was busy, and he hardly spoke a word. Directly the meal was finished he went back to the laboratory, and once more examined the doors. The lock of the first, the common type, had been smashed in by Cousins and Brookfield; the second was impossible to break open, and the two Secret Service men had been constrained to send to the dockyard at Sheerness for a steel cutter, with which they had cut out the lock and thus opened the door. The keys still lay on the table where they had been found. One was a powerful affair with a double flange. Sir Leonard inspected it carefully; then put it down and took up the other. That also he subjected to the same careful scrutiny. Brien sat on the solitary chair, smoking a pipe, and watching his colleague. As the latter placed the smaller key by the side of the other, Billy took the pipe from his mouth, and gazed wide-eyed at him.

'What's the matter, Leonard?' he queried. 'I don't think I've ever seen you look quite so grim. Have you discovered anything?'

'I'm getting on.' The speaker smiled mirthlessly. His grey eyes were as cold in their expression as the steel door by which he stood. 'What is the name of the maker on that safe?'

Brien rose and looked; then told him.

'Go and ring them up, and ask – no; wait a minute!' He walked out into the passage, and called to the housekeeper. She came quickly, and entered the room timidly in his wake. 'Can you tell me, Mrs Holdsworth,' he asked, 'if the professor ever mislaid the keys of the safe?'

'Yes, sir,' she replied promptly. 'It was about a fortnight ago. There was a great fuss, and we ransacked the house for them. The maids and I had a bad time. You see, sir, the professor couldn't get at some papers he wanted very badly, and he stormed and raved until Mr Brookfield advised him to communicate with the makers. They sent duplicate keys down. Then two days afterwards the others were found.'

'Oh! Where were they?'

'The professor had left them in the pocket of a pyjama jacket which had been thrown into the soiled linen bag. I found them when I was getting the laundry ready.'

'Was he usually absent-minded?'

'No, sir, very rarely.'

'When they were found, what did he do with the duplicates?'

'That I can't tell you, sir.'

'Never mind. Perhaps Mr Brookfield may be able to tell me. Would you mind showing me to the professor's bedroom?'

She led the way, and left him and Brien alone in the pleasant chamber which had been the professor's sleeping apartment. The body of the old scientist now lay on the bed covered by a sheet, having been carried upstairs by Cousins and Brookfield.

Wallace walked round the room apparently taking a very perfunctory interest in it. A medicine cupboard was the first object to rivet his attention. It was locked, but the key was in the keyhole, and he opened the door and examined the orderly rows of bottles arrayed within. Presently, with a low whistle, he took down a phial which was labelled differently from the others, pulled out the stopper, and sniffed the contents. Then he closed it tightly again, and put it in his pocket. After that he went downstairs, and once more called Mrs Holdsworth.

'Have you ever had reason to suspect that Professor Mason was addicted to drugs?' he asked.

'Good gracious, no, sir,' she returned in astonishment. 'Why do you ask?'

He smiled.

'Great chemists often are,' he observed in non-committal tones. 'And, as far as I can make out, the professor usually worked all night. It is quite likely, therefore, that he may have taken drugs to ward off fatigue or strain on his nerves.'

'I don't think he was given to that sort of thing, sir. He was always so bright and cheerful; not at all the sort of man I should imagine a drug taker would be.'

Sir Leonard stood in thought for a few seconds; then 'Did he have any refreshment on the nights he worked in his laboratory?' he asked.

'Yes, sir. I always prepared a tray with a plate of sandwiches and a coffee boiler with, of course, milk and sugar.'

'When did you take it to him?'

'He used to carry the tray in when he went to the laboratory, sir. None of us were ever allowed inside.'

'What became of the tray that he took with him last night?'

'I removed it during the morning.'

'Have the coffee boiler and other articles been washed?'

'Yes, sir.'

Wallace abruptly took the small bottle from his pocket, and held it up before her eyes.

'Ever seen this before?' he asked sharply.

Her face paled, and she gazed at the bottle as though fascinated.

'Yes, sir,' she murmured. 'Where did you find it?'

He ignored the question.

'Is it yours?' he demanded.

She damped her lips; then nodded as though too overcome to speak.

'Will you kindly tell me what it was doing in the professor's medicine cupboard, if it belongs to you?'

'I-I don't know,' she stammered after a moment's hesitation. 'I lost it two days ago, and wondered what could have happened to it.'

'How could you lose it?' he queried sarcastically. 'It is hardly the kind of thing one leaves about, is it? And in any case it couldn't have walked from your room to the professor's.'

'Perhaps he borrowed it, sir.'

'I presume he would have asked you if he wanted to do that. He wasn't in the habit of walking into your room and helping himself to your belongings, was he?' She shook her head dumbly. 'There's another thing, Mrs Holdsworth,' he went on. 'Professor Mason had quite enough drugs in the laboratory to stock a chemist's store. Why should he take one which you had in your possession?'

'I don't know,' she murmured again.

'What did you have it for?'

'I have suffered from toothache for several weeks, and the only way I could get any rest was by using it.'

'Whereabouts in your room did you keep this bottle?'

'On the washstand, sir.'

'Not even locked up? That was extremely careless of you. It's dangerous stuff to leave about, you know, Mrs Holdsworth.'

He asked a few more questions; then took aside Brien, who had listened to the catechising with interest.

'Keep an eye on her, Bill,' he whispered, 'and don't let anybody come upstairs until I return.'

'What's all this got to do with the murder?' asked Brien.

'Quite a lot.'

'What's in the bottle?'

'Smell!' He uncorked the phial, and held it up to his friend's nose. 'Recognise it?'

'Ye gods!' exclaimed Brien. 'I should think I do.' He watched Wallace run up the stairs. 'Things are getting curiouser and curiouser, as Alice would say,' he murmured to himself.

It seemed to him that Mrs Holdsworth had an air more of perplexity than of guilt. That she should be in any way connected with the murder seemed absurd, and he wondered what was at the back of Wallace's mind. He had made no attempt himself to solve the mystery, knowing well enough that if his chief's astute mind failed, his had little chance of succeeding. Yet he thought deeply enough about the extraordinary circumstances of the murder, and was puzzled by the line Sir Leonard was taking. To him it seemed rather aimless wandering about rooms looking for clues when probably the assassin, if indeed the professor had been murdered, had long before crossed to the Continent. There had, in all likelihood, been a boat of some kind waiting for him below the cliff and, as soon as his foul work was completed, he had set sail in her, and was by that time well out of reach of Great Britain's Secret Service. Brien began to think, as he waited at the foot of the stairs, that this case would prove to be one of Sir Leonard Wallace's rare failures.

'It seems to me,' he soliloquised, 'that he is not showing his usual skill. This worrying about trivialities will, as far as I can see, lead us nowhere.'

It was quite half an hour before Wallace appeared again;

then he came slowly down the stairs, his face set in an expression which Brien thought almost suggested dismay. He went straight to the laboratory and, standing by the table on which the keys rested, looked upwards. High up in the adjacent wall was a large ventilator and, for some minutes, he stood gazing at it as though it fascinated him. Eventually he left the laboratory, and walked out of the house. He calculated where the exterior of the ventilator should be and, having found it, went in search of a ladder. He was not long in discovering one lying in an outhouse, and carried it back with him. As he placed it against the wall of the laboratory, he noticed a stain on one of the rungs, similar smears were to be seen elsewhere as he ascended, while a large one was on the embrasure into which the ventilator was set.

Standing at the top of the ladder he examined the appliance. It possessed three iron slats between two of which, when open, there was plenty of room to insert an arm and, at the samc time, look down into the room. Within his field of vision was the end of the marble table where lay the keys. The door and the place where the body of the professor had been were also visible. Having satisfied himself on that point, Wallace turned his attention to the slats of the ventilator, inspecting them carefully; then slowly he descended the ladder, and replaced it in the outhouse. Two or three minutes later he was back in the hall of the house, where Brien stood talking to Mrs Holdsworth.

'Have you communicated with the professor's relations?' he asked the woman.

'As far as I know there is only a brother living at Gloucester, sir,' she replied. 'I sent a telegram to him as soon as I knew of the – the tragedy. His reply came just before you reached here. He said he was coming at once.'

'Good. Then there is no reason why we should stay down here after the surgeon from Scotland Yard has arrived and made his examination. The local police will take charge this evening.'

Brien followed him into the drawing room, where he wearily threw himself into a chair, and subjected him to a string of questions.

'For the Lord's sake, leave me alone for a little while, Bill,' he pleaded. 'I want to think.'

He filled and lit his pipe, and lay back in the chair with his eyes half-closed. His whole attitude appeared to denote lassitude and, feeling decidedly intrigued, Brien left the room and took a turn in the neglected garden. He had become by now convinced that Wallace felt himself unable to unravel the mystery. To his mind there could only be one solution, and that was that the professor had committed suicide. What had become of the revolver was, of course, a puzzle, but there was a possibility that Mason, being an inventor, had shot himself in a manner not at once apparent to those who looked only for the weapon. With that idea in his mind Brien started to investigate on his own, eager to prove that suicide was the only feasible solution, and thus to succeed where Wallace, who had completely ignored such a contingency, had failed.

He commenced his search by crawling under the marble slabs, thinking that perhaps the revolver had been fixed beneath one of them and the trigger manipulated in some ingenious manner. But neither had anything underneath to which the weapon could have been fastened. There was not even a ledge. He was sitting on the floor between the tables, feeling rather disappointed, when Wallace entered and stared at him.

'Hullo, Billy,' he observed, 'reconstructing the crime?'

'I don't believe there has been a crime at all,' declared Brien obstinately; 'at least not the crime of murder. I suppose suicide is a crime, as it is forbidden by law.'

'You still think the professor committed suicide?'

'I thought that he might have fastened the revolver under the table, sat down on the floor and pulled the trigger by means of a string, or something.'

Sir Leonard laughed.

'Why should he do that?' he asked.

'He may not have had the courage to hold a revolver to his head and fire. Pulling a string is, after all, not so cold-blooded. Perhaps he didn't want it to be known that he had killed himself.'

'But, my dear fellow, such a contrivance would have been discovered sooner or later. In fact it would have been found immediately, for the string would have given it away. No; he didn't commit suicide I can assure you. I wish he had,' he added with deep feeling.

'Then you have discovered something?'

Wallace nodded.

'As far as I am concerned,' he replied, 'the case is practically finished.'

Brien looked at him admiringly; then hastily rose to his feet. Now that Wallace was with him he began to feel that his efforts at investigation were astonishingly absurd. He decided in his own mind that he had made himself appear ridiculous.

'I feel an ass,' he confessed, 'I actually thought I was going to steal a march on you, and triumph where you had failed.'

'I wish you had, Billy,' returned Wallace seriously. 'Knowing what I know now, nothing would have given me greater pleasure.'

'What do you mean?'

Sir Leonard was about to answer, when a car was heard to drive up, and he hurried out to meet the doctor from Scotland Yard.

'Hullo, Sir Leonard,' greeted the latter, an alert, good-looking man of early middle-age. 'You have work for me I believe?'

'I have, Hastings,' was the reply, 'but it won't take you more than a few minutes.'

He told him of the tragedy, took him into the laboratory, and described the position in which the body had been lying. The doctor listened attentively, asked a few pertinent questions; then glanced round him with an air of appreciation.

'Fine laboratory,' he commented. 'So this is where Veronite was created? The Commissioner told me some of the facts before I left,' he added by way of explanation of his knowledge. 'Have you discovered yet how the murder was committed?'

'The professor was shot through the head,' put in Brien.

'Yes; I know that,' smiled the doctor. 'I meant to say: have you discovered how the assassin got in here?'

Wallace nodded.

'That and more,' he observed grimly.

'Do you think you'll be able to recover the formula?' asked Brien eagerly.

'I hope so. Do you want to see the body right away, Hastings?'

'Please. Where is it?'

Sir Leonard led the way up the stairs and, entering the professor's bedroom, removed the sheet that covered all that remained of a famous scientist. Deftly, quickly, the police surgeon conducted his examination, while Wallace and Brien stood by watching him. Five minutes passed; then he straightened himself, and looked at Sir Leonard.

'He was drugged before he was shot,' he announced sharply,

'Exactly what I thought,' returned Wallace. 'That is why I brought you down. The local doctor quite failed to notice that the pupils of the eyes were dilated.'

'He must be a fool,' commented Dr Hastings.

'He is,' agreed Wallace with feeling. 'What drug do you think was used?'

'Some preparation of opium,' was the prompt reply.

'Laudanum?'

'Yes; very likely laudanum.'

Wallace produced the small bottle from his pocket, and held it out to the doctor.

'This is where it was taken from,' he said quietly. 'A few drops were poured from this bottle into either the coffee pot or milk jug that Mason took into the laboratory with him last night.'

'Good Lord!' blurted out Brien. 'Do you mean to say that Mrs Holdsworth was the murderess?'

'S'sh!' warned Wallace.

He had caught the sound of footsteps on the stairs, and presently the housekeeper passed by the open door. He went out to the corridor, and looked after her. She entered her own room farther along, and shut herself in.

'Well, I'm damned!' swore Billy softly, as his colleague came back to the bed. 'She is about the last person one would have suspected. I suppose the agent of some foreign power got at her. But still I don't understand how she got in and out of the laboratory.'

'What is more puzzling to my mind,' observed the doctor, 'is why Professor Mason was drugged.'

'That is easily explained,' asserted Sir Leonard. 'In the first place there was no intention of murdering him, but the dose of laudanum was not of sufficient strength, and he was probably beginning to regain consciousness while the criminal was searching for the formula. The latter then shot him while he lay on the floor to which he had slipped under the effects of the drug. If you examine the back of his head, Hastings, you will find no bruise of any kind there. He was lying flat on his back and, if he had been standing when shot, he would have fallen with such force that his head would have struck the hard floor violently, and certainly been bruised. Am I not right?'

After an examination of the back of the dead man's head, the police surgeon nodded.

'There's not a doubt of it,' he agreed. 'In slipping to the floor under the effects of the laudanum he went down too gently to hurt himself. Probably he first sank to his knees, all the time making an effort to fight against the drug; then rolled over onto his back as it overcame him.'

'What a dastardly crime!' ejaculated Brien. 'Great Scott!' he added. 'I see now why you were puzzled by the fact that the keys had not been left in the open door of the safe. It wasn't opened by the professor's keys at all, but by the duplicate set which the Holdsworth woman must have obtained somehow or other. Probably—' He stopped suddenly. 'I am going a bit too far,' he said in rather a sheepish voice.

'You were going to say,' interposed Sir Leonard, 'that probably the loss of the original keys was contrived in the hope that a duplicate set would be sent for. You are quite right. That is exactly what happened. Then, in order to still any suspicion that may have been roused, the originals were found in the pyjama jacket in the soiled linen bag. Of course they had been put there first.'

'Good Heavens, what a woman!' exclaimed Doctor Hastings

in a tone of horror. 'How were the duplicates obtained do you think?'

'The professor was watched. He had apparently locked them away in this drawer.' He walked across to the dressing-table, and indicated a drawer half pulled out. 'You see the lock has been forced. I discovered that on my second visit to this room. Anybody looking through the keyhole of the door would have had a view of this drawer, and seen the professor locking away the keys.'

'It's a wonder she didn't contrive that the keys of the laboratory door were lost also, so that duplicates of those would have been available,' commented Billy. 'But I suppose that would have caused too much suspicion.'

'It would have been impossible,' Sir Leonard informed him. 'Mason carried the keys of the safe in his pocket, but the keys of the doors were on a chain round his neck and only detached when he wanted them. Look!' He undid the clothing at the dead man's neck, and disclosed a silver chain to view.

'Besides,' declared Brien, 'it would have been out of the question to have entered that way, as Brookfield always sat there when the professor was in the laboratory, unless—' He paused suddenly, and a gleam came into his eyes. 'Of course,' he exulted; 'I see it all now. She did have duplicate keys and, like Professor Mason, *Brookfield was drugged*.'

'By Jove!' exclaimed Dr Hastings. 'She seems to be a woman who stops at nothing to gain her ends.'

'The sooner she is arrested the better,' suggested Billy. 'She must surely know that you suspect her, since you questioned her about that bottle.'

'She's in her room,' returned Sir Leonard, 'and there's no need to trouble her for the present.'

'But, man alive, she may escape through a window. It's not far to the ground and—'

'She won't do anything like that,' Wallace replied with quiet confidence.

Brien smiled.

'It was damn cheek on my part to make suggestions,' he chuckled. 'I might have known that you had prepared for all eventualities.'

A trim little maid with frightened eyes knocked at the door.

'Please, sir,' she said. 'Mr Brookfield told me to tell you that him and the other gentleman have returned.'

'Thank you,' acknowledged Wallace. 'Coming down, doctor? I may ask you to find that bullet in the professor's head later on, but I don't think it will be necessary.'

He suddenly looked older, and Billy wondered if he were feeling unwell. He was about to ask, but Wallace passed him abruptly, and ran down the stairs. The other two followed more leisurely. He took Cousins and Brookfield into the laboratory and, as Brien and the doctor followed, he told the former to close the doors.

'I don't want the servants listening to us,' he added by way of explanation. 'Discover anything?' he demanded of his two agents.

'Nothing, sir,' replied Cousins. 'The only strangers seen in these parts during the last three weeks were a clergyman, his wife and two children, and we were able to establish beyond doubt that they were quite innocent. This is the wrong time of the year for visitors, and that made our job easier. As Henry Vaughan so beautifully expresses it, "They are all gone into—"'

'Be quiet!' snapped Wallace angrily.

His three colleagues looked at him in dismay. Seldom before

had he displayed such irritation, never at Cousins' everlasting quotations. Abruptly he swept the little man aside, and confronted Brookfield.

'*Hand over that formula*!' he commanded harshly.

A hiss of indrawn breath from the three men behind him was the only sound for a dramatic moment. Brookfield's eyes glared into his unbelievingly, and gradually every vestige of colour drained from the man's face.

'What – what do you mean, sir?' he gasped.

'I mean what I say – hand over the papers which you stole from that safe after murdering Professor Mason!'

The ensuing silence lasted upwards of twenty seconds, during which every man in that room stood rigid, three overcome by sheer amazement, one by stark horror and fear, the fifth watching with strained concentration the man he had accused. Then, with almost an animal-like cry, his face now distorted with hatred, Brookfield threw himself forward at his chief, quite forgetting that by his action he was confessing his crime. With his usual rapidity, Sir Leonard drew his revolver, pointing it at his would-be assailant.

'Back!' he snapped in the tone he might have used to a mad dog.

Brookfield hesitated before the grim muzzle aimed at his head, but not for long. Possibly he welcomed death in such a manner now that he had been unmasked; possibly he was too overcome with rage to care whether he lived or died, his only desire being to get at Sir Leonard Wallace. Whatever was in his mind he launched himself with passionate ferocity at his chief, to be brought up with a cry of pain as the revolver was dashed into his face with all the power of Wallace's arm behind it. With hands clasped to his bleeding countenance he stood swaying before the other, then reeled against one of the tables half-stunned. Sir Leonard turned to Cousins.

'Search him!' he ordered sharply. 'Take everything from his pockets, and put it on the table.'

Brookfield made no resistance; he was too badly injured. Cousins went about his job thoroughly, and brought to light several articles of no interest to anyone but their owner. Then came a pocket-book in which were two sheets of paper folded together – *the formula for Veronite!* Cousins' features creased into an expression of pain as he announced his discovery. Up to that moment he had been hoping against hope that Sir Leonard had made a mistake, that Brookfield would prove to be innocent. Brien had felt the same. The honour of a great service was at stake, a service that, as far as they knew, had never before been discredited. Suddenly Billy realised why his friend had appeared to look old, understood the distress he had seen in the steel-grey eyes. The discovery of Brookfield's treachery and recreancy must have been a terrible shock to the man who was so proud of the honour of the British Secret Service and the devotion and altruism of the men and women under his authority.

'That is all, sir,' announced Cousins quietly.

'Bathe his face,' ordered Wallace. 'There's a tap and towels over there.'

Not another word was spoken until Cousins led his one-time colleague back to Sir Leonard; then:

'You have committed the worst crime it is possible for man to commit,' declared the latter in harsh tones to the subordinate in whom he had trusted. 'You have prostituted the trust placed in you, and brought shame and dishonour on a service that prides itself on its glory and integrity. You have murdered a man in cold blood and stolen something of the utmost importance to the country which gave you birth, with a view to enriching yourself and betraying that country. You came to us with the highest reputation from Scotland Yard, and have been entrusted with secret commissions of importance. I suppose most of them have been sold to other nations and—'

'Stop!' cried Brookfield in an anguished voice. He had been standing with bowed head leaning against a table, now he stood upright, and tried hard to meet his accuser's eyes. 'I have never before betrayed my trust,' he declared, 'and wouldn't have done so now only – only I had been for a long time in the hands of money-lenders, and the temptation was too great.'

'And you actually intended selling Great Britain; perhaps cause the world to suffer the greatest calamity that has ever befallen it, to get yourself out of personal difficulties, which a man with your responsibilities should have avoided like a plague!' Sir Leonard's voice vibrated with the utter loathing and repugnance that filled him. 'Upstairs,' he went on, 'lies the victim of your perfidy, murdered by the man who was sent to guard him and his secret, murdered in cold blood while he was lying under the effect of a drug administered to him by you.'

'I didn't mean to kill him – I swear it!' cried the distracted scoundrel, endeavouring desperately to find excuses where no excuses could be. 'He began to recover his senses when I was in the room – I lost my head and shot him. It was the—'

'It was I who sent you here,' went on Sir Leonard coldly, mercilessly, and as if Brookfield had not spoken. 'And all my life I will feel that I was partially responsible for Professor Mason's death, because I trusted and believed in the fiend I sent to protect him. May God forgive you – no man ever can!'

'It's done now,' muttered Brookfield sullenly, 'and I shall expiate it. There's no reason for you to—'

'You can never expiate such a crime,' snapped Wallace. 'No blacker transgressions have ever been perpetrated in history than yours. Execution to a thing like you is no expiation, it is far too merciful.'

Brookfield, shaking like a leaf, looked hungrily at the three faces beyond that of Sir Leonard, possibly hoping to find in one, at least, a certain measure of pity. But each was a replica, in its intense abhorrence, of the chief's. Each was pale with the cold fury engendered by feelings of utter repugnance. Whatever he might forgive, no true member of the Secret Service could ever pardon a betrayal of trust, and such a betrayal of trust, in one who had been a comrade. Brookfield read in those faces nothing but pitiless aversion, and his base soul revolted.

'Damn you!' he snarled at Wallace. 'Who are you to judge a man? You have never had the experience of being screwed and twisted and bled by ghouls under the names of money-lenders. You have never known what it is to be tempted – you might have been the first to fall if you had.'

'Enough of this!' returned Sir Leonard sternly. 'It nauseates me to talk to you. You cannot even meet disclosure like a man. Such a thought as the possibility of being found out never occurred to you, did it? Your greatest mistake was in taking it for granted that you would not be suspected.'

'I should like to know how you found out, you devil,' jerked out the fellow, his curiosity getting the better of him.

'You shall know. I first suspected you because of two things, both connected with that steel door there. Cousins, when he reported to me in Whitehall this morning, said that, when you and he had succeeded in cutting out the lock of that door, you both stood at the entrance, while he bound up your hand, which had been badly cut in the process. Now when I was examining the lock I remembered what Cousins had said, and, in a detached sort of way, wondered why there was no sign of blood on the jagged edges round the lock or on the floor, as there should have been if you had in reality cut your hand there. You thought that by declaring the accident to have happened there and then, you would save a lot of questions, while Cousins no doubt was too engrossed in other things to wonder at the lack of blood.'

'I never saw the cut, sir,' put in Cousins. 'He had already started to bind up his hand, when he asked me to complete it for him.'

'Just so. I guessed something like that had happened. The second thing that roused my suspicions was that on both keys were several marks, which at first puzzled me. Then I recognised them as having been made by steel tweezers. Obviously somebody had attempted to turn the keys from the outside. The first lock must have responded, as the key of the second also shows the marks, but the second lock proved obstinate, otherwise there would have been no necessity to attempt other methods. You, Brookfield, were in the habit of sitting outside the laboratory door when the professor was working inside. Naturally, therefore, I was forced against my own inclinations to suspect you. How could anyone have passed you, and attempted to turn the keys of the door with tweezers, without your being aware of the fact? You may have been drugged, but that was hardly possible to anyone outside the house, while inside were only three women, Mrs Holdsworth and the two maids. Now only expert criminals or people like ourselves, who have made a study of opening doors when the keys are in the inside of the locks, would have thought of using tweezers. Mrs Holdsworth has been in the professor's service for twelve years, the maids three and five. None of them could have been expert crooks.

'From that time I worked on the theory that you were the criminal, and I proved correct. I had noticed that the professor had been drugged, and came to the conclusion that it was with some preparation of opium. I went upstairs to look, knowing very well that he would hardly have been likely to drug himself in the laboratory. Before going into your room, Brookfield, I looked round the professor's. In the medicine cupboard was a small bottle of laudanum, but it had Mrs Holdsworth's name on it, and was not labelled by the professor, but by a firm of chemists in Sittingbourne. I wondered what it was doing there – it is certain the professor would not have borrowed it. I learnt from Mrs Holdsworth that she had purchased the stuff for toothache, and that the bottle disappeared from her room two days ago. I also found out that the professor was in the habit of taking a tray containing sandwiches or coffee into the laboratory when he worked at night. I might have thought that Mrs Holdsworth was working in collusion with you, but inquiries showed that last night she was out when the tray was prepared for the professor. It was left on the dining-room table while he smoked a pipe after dinner in the garden. I've no doubt the coffee was then doped by you with a few drops of laudanum from the bottle taken from Mrs Holdsworth's bedroom. Afterwards you were unable to return the bottle to the place from where you had taken it, for the simple reason that Mrs Holdsworth was in her room. You, therefore, put it in the professor's medicine cupboard, which you had already probably searched for the drug you wanted, convinced that it would never be noticed there.'

'All this is very interesting,' sneered Brookfield. 'It is only supposition though, and doesn't convict me.'

'When connected with facts it does,' retorted Wallace sternly. 'After interviewing Mrs Holdsworth I returned upstairs, went into your bedroom, and opened the locked suitcase under your bed. It was an easy enough task. Hidden under various articles of clothing I found this, this, and this.'

He took from his pocket a small revolver, a pair of fine steel tweezers, and a ball of string. 'The revolver is fully loaded *except for one cartridge*,' he said significantly 'the tweezers you used on the keys of the laboratory door; the ball of string puzzled me for a time until I remembered that I had noticed a small but powerful magnet in the professor's medicine cupboard. I went back and examined it. There was a smear of blood on it. The string also, I might add, was in several places smudged with blood.

'I began to get a glimmering of how the murder and robbery had been accomplished, and hurried downstairs to put my theory into practice. As I looked again at the keys lying on the laboratory table, I wondered why they had been taken out of the doors. Obviously the professor must have taken them out when he first entered, rather a curious thing to do, considering that on previous occasions he had left them in the doors. Perhaps he suspected that an attempt had been made on them; he may even have heard you when you tried, for I presume that it was not last night but on some other occasion that you made the endeavour. Whatever the cause, you knew that they were taken out, and that helped you to evolve the plan which succeeded.

'The sight of that large ventilator up there told me the use to which you had put the string and magnet. I found a ladder in an outhouse, the one you had used, for several rungs had smears of blood on them which you knew nothing about, as it was too dark for you to see that you were leaving such marks. I climbed the ladder; then found how you had damaged yourself. In opening the iron slats you had been a trifle careless, with the result that they had snapped back, jamming your hand. There was enough blood up there to give you away completely. In order to keep the slats apart, you stuck your fountain pen between them, and afterwards forgot about it. I have it here.' He laid it on the table next to the other articles.

Brookfield was ghastly now, beads of perspiration showed on his forehead, while his hands were trembling convulsively. The reconstruction of every step of his crime, and the cold, incisive manner in which Sir Leonard Wallace spoke, affected him even more than the knowledge that he had been unmasked had done.

'You must have used that ventilator as an observation-post more than once,' continued the Chief of the Intelligence Department, 'and laid your infernal plans accordingly. Last night, or rather early this morning, when you climbed up the ladder, you found, to your satisfaction, that Professor Mason was lying on the floor drugged. The magnet was let down on the end of the string; you swung it to and fro until it was in juxtaposition with one of the keys which immediately adhered to it; then you drew it up, taking care that it was not jerked off by coming in contact with the wall. The same process was repeated with the other key. After that you had no difficulty in entering the laboratory. You opened the safe with the duplicate keys taken from the drawer in the professor's bedroom, obtained the formula, and shot the poor old man dead as he lay there.

Whether or not you committed the deed because he began to regain his senses makes no difference. It was as foul a crime as any I have ever heard of. I believe you did it wantonly – for, if you had succeeded in getting into the room on the occasion you had used the tweezers, I presume you would have shot the professor dead as soon as you were in. Brookfield, you must be a devil incarnate.'

'How did he put the keys back in the room after locking the doors?' asked Brien in a hushed voice.

'By the simple process of letting them down on a loop of doubled string, swinging them backwards and forwards until they rested on the table; then letting go one end of the string and pulling it through the ring.'

Brookfield had nothing to say for himself now. He stood and looked dumbly at the man who had found him out. His thoughts just then must have been terrible, for his soul had been unveiled in all its naked hideousness and, if he had not already done so, he must have realised himself for the thing he was.

Wallace paced the laboratory, his chin sunk on his breast, for several minutes. Suddenly he stopped close to the man who had so dishonoured an honourable service. He spoke quietly.

'I am going to do a thing, or rather countenance a thing, which under no other circumstances would I be a party to. Perhaps it is sentiment, but I am resolved to protect the honour of the department as far as it is possible. Understand, Brookfield, there is no desire on my part to make things easier for you. Thank God, you are not married. Major Brien and Mr Cousins will conduct you to headquarters. You will be handed this revolver,' he picked it up from the table, and gave it to Cousins, 'and will then enter a vacant room, and shut yourself in. Need I say more? The only alternative to that, as you well know, is a felon's death on the scaffold. Do you accept?'

For some seconds Brookfield was unable to speak, and stood clasping and unclasping his hands; then suddenly he found his voice.

'Yes, damn you!' he ground out. 'I accept.'

Wallace turned away.

'See to things, Billy,' he murmured to his friend. 'Take his belongings up in the car with you.'

Brien nodded. His face was white, but his lips were drawn tightly together in one grim, unrelenting line. Ten minutes later the car left for London, Brookfield sitting tightly wedged between Major Brien and Cousins. Wallace and Dr Hastings watched it out of sight then the former turned to the police surgeon.

'I can rely on you, doctor?' he queried.

'Most certainly,' was the reply. 'It was the only way.'

'I suppose you think I have let sentiment get the better of me?'

'Not at all. A department like yours must be protected from any vestige of scandal. I suppose you will acquaint the Commissioner with the facts to enable him to hush up the murder.'

Wallace nodded.

'We'll leave for Scotland Yard as soon as the professor's brother arrives here and takes charge.'

Mrs Holdsworth passed by at that moment, and he called her, taking the phial of laudanum from his pocket as she stopped and looked at him inquiringly.

'Here is your little bottle, Mrs Holdsworth,' he remarked. 'Take it and keep it in a place of safety for the future. If I were you, I shouldn't use such dangerous stuff.'

It was late evening, when eventually Sir Leonard reached his office. Late as it was, however, he found Major Brien patiently awaiting his arrival. The latter's face was pale and drawn. Wallace merely looked his inquiry, and the other nodded slowly.

'His sister is coming tonight to take away the body for burial,' he murmured. 'It's hell, isn't it?'

'It's worse than hell, Bill. Let us go home!'

CHAPTER FOUR

Russian Hospitality

Most people have read in their newspapers of the attempts made by the Russian Soviet to undermine rule in Great Britain, and cause disaffection in the Army and Navy. Few, however, know of the extent of the efforts in that direction, the lengths to which the agents went, and the measures they adopted. Fewer still have any knowledge of the manner in which the British Secret Service, assisted by the Special Branch of New Scotland Yard, combated the insidious venture. It is my privilege now to make public for the first time how Sir Leonard Wallace checkmated the Soviet, and rendered innocuous the power which that communistic body was beginning to obtain in England.

Ever since the War, agents of the Bolsheviki had done their utmost to persuade and encourage other countries to follow in the footsteps of the Soviet, throw aside their constitutions, and adopt the system of government prevailing in Russia. Great Britain was more a target for these endeavours than most nations, chiefly owing to the fact that it is an easy matter for aliens to enter the country, and also because British freedom of speech allows far more latitude than that of the majority of great powers. At first there was no great harm done, although a body of British communists began to make itself felt in the politics of the country; but when a Labour party, with distinct leanings towards friendship with Russia, was returned to power, matters looked serious. The Soviet took full advantage of this fortuitous circumstance, and deluged Great Britain with communistic propaganda. It became evident before very long that a big movement was on foot to cause dissatisfaction and perhaps revolution. Pamphlets, inspired by Russia, were mysteriously circulated among the troops at Aldershot, Shorncliffe, and other big military depots, and also among seamen of the Royal Navy and the Merchant Marine. In addition, miners and workers in all other branches of industry were 'got at' until an ominous situation arose. The level-headed members of the Government made an effort to prevent matters coming to a head, but they were badly handicapped by the rabid Socialist backbenchers, who were Bolshevik in all but name. Luckily for the country, a proposal to advance a loan to Russia raised the opposition of the Conservatives and Liberals, with the result that the Government was defeated, and the Conservatives returned to power with an overwhelming majority.

During the regime of the Socialists, Sir Leonard Wallace did his best, under difficult circumstances, to cope with the growing menace of Bolshevism, but on every side he met with obstacles, which made success impossible. Directly the new party came into power, however, he was given *carte blanche*, and immediately set to work to undo the mischief that had been done. Interviews with several ministers of State and the Chief of the War Office resulted in certain quiet-faced men taking up duties in various parts of the country as soldiers, railway-men, miners, dock workers and, in fact, in almost every class of labour at which the Soviet had aimed its shafts of unrest. Thereafter, reports reached Secret Service headquarters daily, but several weeks went by, and yet no information came to hand which would enable Sir Leonard to trace the Bolshevik activity to its source. Agents, who were distributing leaflets and pamphlets and delivering inflammatory speeches, were run to earth and arrested, but when questioned they either refused to speak or disclaimed all knowledge of the organisation under whose orders they were working. Despite the arrests, however, the propaganda still continued, and became more virulent than ever. A determined attempt was being made to corrupt the Army, with Aldershot as the centre of the undertaking.

'We seem to be up against it,' declared Sir Leonard one day to his friend, Major Brien. 'Not one of the reports received so far is of any great assistance. Scotland Yard has gone through London with a fine comb, and not a blessed thing has come to light. Yet I wouldn't mind betting that the organisation has its headquarters in this hub of the universe.'

'Couldn't the business be worked from somewhere on the Continent, or even direct from Leningrad?' queried Brien.

'It could, but I'm pretty sure it isn't. Such an arrangement would mean continual telegraphing or a constant succession of couriers from Russia with orders. You know as well as I that every person entering England from the Continent is being subjected to rigid scrutiny and, as for telegraph and wireless communications, you are better informed of their contents than I. Has the decoding department examined one message that has not turned out to be entirely innocent?'

Brien shook his head moodily.

'Well, there you are,' went on Wallace. 'Whoever is at the back of this Russian menace is in England, with full power to act as circumstances dictate. I am convinced that he is hidden away somewhere in London, and that all the pamphlets circulated among the troops and sailors have been printed in this city.'

'How about sending a man disguised as a Tommy to Aldershot,' suggested Brien suddenly, 'with instructions to appear influenced by the propaganda, and to talk Bolshy among the other troops? His supposed tendencies might reach the ears of the johnny behind the scenes, who would think he was a man likely to be valuable to the cause, and send for him.'

'A bright idea, Billy,' commented Sir Leonard, 'but we've already tried it. Carter is in the Cambridge Hospital at Aldershot now on account of it.'

'In hospital!' exclaimed Brien. 'What on earth is he doing there?'

'Recovering from the rough treatment he received at the hands of the men to whom he preached revolution.'

Billy stared at his chief for a moment; then collapsed into a chair and roared with laughter.

'Good old Tommy Atkins!' he chuckled. 'That's the spirit. I'm sorry for Carter, though.'

'I don't suppose he minds much,' smiled Wallace, 'except that all he has obtained from his efforts to attract the attention of the man we want so badly are a collection of bruises, a black eye, and a split lip. No attempt whatever has been made to get in touch with him, and I didn't expect there would be. A man who can run this Bolshevik organisation as cleverly as our unknown adversary, is not going to take unnecessary risks. He probably suspects Carter.'

'Perhaps he won't,' hazarded Brien, 'now that poor old Carter has been so roughly handled.'

'I don't think that will make any difference. It was a forlorn hope anyhow. I don't think many of the agents know the man with whom they are dealing.'

'But there must be an intermediary.'

'Exactly. He is the fellow we must find first and, as the present centre of operations appears to be Aldershot, I have placed two men of the Special Branch in the post office there, and want you to send down Hill, Cartright and Manning to take a hand. Let two of them go as commercial travellers, and the other as an artisan of some sort. Understand they must not arrive in Aldershot from London.'

Billy nodded.

'Do you want to see them before they go?' he asked.

'No; they know exactly what their job is. If they've any questions to ask, you can put them wise.'

Left to himself, Sir Leonard sat at his desk, and spent an hour pondering over the problem which was causing him so much difficulty. As a result of his deliberations, he sent for Maddison. That smart, keen-eyed individual appeared at once, and was given certain instructions to which he listened carefully, afterwards hurrying from the room. Ten minutes later Wallace sauntered out of the building and, without looking either to the right or left, entered his car, which was drawn up to the kerb awaiting him.

'Drive me to Aldershot!' he instructed the chauffeur laconically, as though it were not lunch time and a trip to Aldershot was a daily occurrence.

Without the flicker of an eyelid the man climbed into his seat, and a few seconds later the big car was threading its way through the traffic. Once away from the crowded streets of London, Sir Leonard pulled a mirror from one of the pockets in the tonneau, and held it before him in such a manner that he was able to see if he were being followed without turning his head and looking through the rear window. There were several cars close behind, however, and it would have been impossible to decide that any one of them was trailing his Vauxhall. He picked up the speaking-tube.

'Make for Esher,' he directed; 'cut across country from there to Byfleet; then continue to Aldershot by way of Woking.'

An almost imperceptible movement of the driver's head showed that he understood, and Wallace leant back in his seat, a faint smile on his lips. He had chosen a peculiarly zig-zag route, but it had the great advantage that it meant traversing several unfrequented country roads with the consequent certainty of being able to discover whether or not he was being followed. Before the car reached Byfleet he was able to assure himself that such was the case. A cheeky-looking sports model of some foreign make, which he did not recognise, was hanging to his heels. Its low and narrow build suggested great speed, and Wallace knew his car could never have shaken it off, if that had been his intention. Two men sat in the front, both wearing large goggles and hats pulled well over their foreheads.

'Now we're beginning to get on,' murmured Sir Leonard to himself in a tone of satisfaction.

He put away the mirror, and took no further notice of the car behind. He knew very well that the trackers were being tracked by Maddison, and that wherever they went, from that time on, there would be someone from headquarters on their trail, until they had led Sir Leonard to the man he was so keen to find, or had proved their uselessness.

As soon as Aldershot was reached, he spoke rapidly through the tube to the chauffeur; then instructed him to drive to the Cambridge Hospital. There he had an interview with Carter who, despite his bruises, was very cheerful. A muttered remark by Wallace, however, appeared to chase away all his light-heartedness, and he became morose and sullen. Treating his subordinate as though he were, in very truth, a military malcontent, Sir Leonard questioned him sharply, but elicited very little in reply apart from seditious utterances. The meeting was held in a small room on the ground floor and, though the two men were alone, orderlies, nurses, and doctors were continually passing the half-open door. At last, with a shrug of his shoulders, Wallace rose from the chair in which he had been sitting, and strolled across to the door, which he closed. All the time he spoke in a rapid undertone to Carter, who listened without making the slightest sign that he heard. Then, almost like a sleight of hand trick, a revolver passed from Sir Leonard's possession into a pocket of Carter's tunic.

A moment later the former rang a bell on the desk. His summons was answered immediately by an orderly.

'Ask Colonel Grace if he will be good enough to come here,' directed Wallace.

Two or three minutes went by, and a short, grey-haired man in the uniform of a Royal Army Medical Corps Colonel entered the room. He looked questioningly at the angry features of the visitor, transferred his gaze to the sullen face of the supposed soldier; then glanced back again at the other.

'Have you finished your inquiry, Sir Leonard?' he asked.

'I have,' snapped Wallace, 'and this man has appeared more obdurate than I expected. Is he fit enough to be discharged from hospital?'

'Oh, yes; quite.'

'Then the sooner he is under lock and key the better. Will you be good enough to see that he is returned to his unit under escort at once?'

'Well, of course, I—'

'I'll take full responsibility. How many men are on duty watching him?'

'Two.'

'They will be sufficient. I don't suppose he'll attempt to escape, especially after the rough handling he received the other day.' He turned to the scowling Carter, whose black eye gave him quite a villainous aspect. 'It means court martial and a long stretch for you, my lad,' he added. 'If you had only told me who are behind you, you would have got off lightly.'

'Damn you!' snarled Carter. 'I've already told you there ain't nobody behind me.'

Wallace shrugged his shoulders.

All right,' he observed, 'have it your own way. Will you please call the escort, Colonel?'

The grey-haired doctor, a look of regret on his face, hastened from the room, returning a moment later with two military policemen, who took charge of their prisoner, and marched him away. Sir Leonard and the colonel followed behind.

'I can't understand the man,' remarked the latter. 'He appeared to be quite a cheerful young fellow until you came, Sir Leonard. I suppose people of his type are generally irresponsible.'

'Exceedingly so,' returned Wallace, a faint smile lurking at the corners of his lips.

His car stood awaiting him with the engine running, while the chauffeur was walking round examining the tyres. Carter and his escort had just marched a little beyond it, when the former suddenly sprang back, and there was a revolver in his hand.

'Move a step, any mother's son of you,' he snarled, 'and you'll get a lump of lead in you.'

Backing to the driver's seat, he climbed in, and put the car into gear.

'Blast you!' he yelled at Wallace. 'You thought you were clever, didn't you? Take that and that!'

He fired three times at the Chief of the Secret Service; then, as the escort made a frantic dash for the car, it shot forward, tearing headlong for the gates. Men, attracted by the noise, came running from every direction. Two, close to the gates, made an attempt to jump on the swiftly-moving machine, but were swept aside, and left sprawling on the road and, gathering speed every moment, the motor disappeared. A few seconds passed; then a long grey car tore by the gates in the wake of the other; a moment later another, a racing Bentley, rushed past. Sir Leonard sighed softly, and turned to the white-faced colonel, who had been urgently demanding to know if he were hurt.

'Hurt?' repeated Wallace. 'No; I'm quite all right, thank you. Rather a clever piece of work that, don't you think?'

'Good Lord!' exclaimed the stupefied medical man. 'You seem to take the matter pretty coolly.'

'There's no use taking it any other way,' was the retort. He instructed his chauffeur to go back to London by train; then turned to the two depressed-looking military policemen. 'You men can return to barracks,' he said. 'I'll explain matters to your CO.'

'But, sir—' commenced one.

'It is all right. I am Colonel Wallace of the Intelligence Department.'

The men saluted and departed.

'Is there anything I can do?' queried the anxious doctor.

'You can put me near a telephone, and give me luncheon, if you will,' replied Wallace cheerfully. 'But perhaps it's too late to get food now?'

'Not a bit of it. Come along with me, Sir Leonard. You are sure you are not hurt? That scoundrel fired straight at you.'

'No; I'm not hurt,' declared Wallace, then added *sotto voce*: 'Blank cartridges don't do any damage – as a rule!'

Carter drove away from Aldershot at headlong speed, choosing bye-roads and lanes in preference to the more frequented main roads. He was enjoying himself thoroughly, and meandered across country almost joyfully. Carter had passed out of Sandhurst into the Army in 1917. His peculiar talents had made him an asset to the Intelligence Department and, after the Armistice, he had been given a billet at Scotland Yard where, in a short time, he had won quite a lot of fame and notoriety. Eventually, when Sir Leonard Wallace had asked for a man of ability and parts, he had been selected. The Assistant Commissioner's remarks, after conveying the news to Carter, are enlightening; 'I have chosen you,' he had said, 'partially because of your record, partially because I wish to save myself the sleepless nights your unconventional methods cause me. Good luck!' He had proved a great success in his new sphere, and his happy-go-lucky disposition, allied to his undoubted talents and efficiency, had made him extremely popular with all his colleagues from the chief down.

As he tore along, he alternately whistled and sang to himself, smiling every now and again, as he cocked an eye at the mirror jutting out by his side, and satisfied himself that he was being followed.

'Oh, for the life of a vagabond,' he sang; then swore as the speed of the car began to abate, and sundry spluttering sounds came from the engine. 'Running out of petrol,' he decided; 'but there must be a reserve tap somewhere. Now where the deuce is it?'

The engine gave a final splutter, and ceased functioning. Carter sat still, and frowned thoughtfully. He was in a quiet country lane apparently miles from anywhere.

'That's the worst of not knowing the car you're driving,' he soliloquised. 'Still, as well here as anywhere else. Heigho! For the Bolshie.'

A long grey car came gliding alongside, and Carter's manner changed immediately. He looked furtively at the men sitting in it.

'All right,' he growled. 'It's a cop. This blooming bus has run out of petrol, otherwise you wouldn't have pinched me.'

'My dear fellow,' protested one of the men in suave tones, 'what can possibly have given you the idea that we wanted to – er – pinch you? We have followed you in the hope that we might be of assistance to you.'

'Come off it!' jeered Carter. 'You tell that story to a bloke in a madhouse. He might believe you.'

'I quite appreciate your disinclination to believe that anybody would be anxious to help you after what has happened. Nevertheless we have followed you for that purpose. We have been interested in your recent adventures, and were lucky enough to witness your escape from custody.'

The look of suspicion on Carter's face was replaced by one of surprise.

'Who the hell are you?' he demanded bluntly.

'Never mind that now,' returned the other impatiently. 'There is no time to lose. By now there is a hue and cry after you and, if you want to escape, you'd better do what I tell you. My friend here will lend you his coat. That will hide your tunic, and you'd better throw your cap away. Come on – jump in quickly!'

Again the look of suspicion returned to Carter's face.

'Nothing doing,' he remarked. 'How do I know that this ain't a trick?'

'Don't be foolish!' snapped the man. 'Why should we desire to trick you? If we were helping the police, should we not have said so when you were so willing to surrender a few moments ago?'

'Tell me who you are then,' persisted Carter obstinately, 'and why you're so blooming interested in me.'

'Oh, very well,' was the irritable reply. 'We are agents of the Russian Soviet Republic, and our concern for your safety is prompted by the knowledge that you are in trouble through expressing sentiments coincident with ours. Now are you satisfied?'

'Struth!' exclaimed Carter. 'This looks like a bit of all right.'

He got out of Sir Leonard's car, and put on the overcoat handed to him by the second man, throwing his uniform cap over an adjoining hedge.

'What about this bus?' he asked.

'We'll have to leave it here, of course. You did not think we were going to take it in tow, did you?'

'No,' returned the young man in regretful tones, 'but it's a damn pity. I didn't want to lose it.'

'How far do you think you would have gone without being stopped?' sneered the other. 'A description of that car is being circulated all over the country by this time. Get in!' he added with an oath. 'We can't expect to be alone here much longer.'

Carter hesitated no more, and climbed into the tonneau. A moment later they were heading for London at breakneck speed. The Secret Service man glanced back anxiously, but a tiny object, merely a speck in the midst of a cloud of dust, reassured him, and he smiled to himself. When speaking to the Russian he had looked searchingly at the faces of him and his companion, but the huge goggles they wore were a most effective disguise. He had thus learnt nothing from his scrutiny. Not that it mattered very much, he reflected. During the journey he leant forward on several occasions, and asked questions, but the men in front were in no mood for conversation, perhaps because the speed of the car rendered any attempt at speech well-nigh impossible.

On reaching Kingston, pace was greatly reduced, and they turned northward running through Richmond and Kew and on to Willesden, after which they headed east skirting north London by way of Highgate and Stamford Hill, eventually pulling up outside a hotel at Leyton.

'I think you will be glad of a meal,' observed the man, who had spoken before, turning and smiling at Carter.

'I could certainly do with a bite, guv'nor,' replied the latter.

'Stay where you are, and we'll send you out something. You mustn't get out of the car or your khaki trousers will be seen.'

Carter nodded, and the two Russians entered the hotel. They spent nearly an hour inside, and the Secret Service man concluded that they were wasting time on purpose, in order to arrive at their destination after dark. They did him well, pressing enough beer and sandwiches on him to satisfy a platoon, as he put it. It was rapidly becoming dusk when the car left Leyton and ran south to West Ham, and it was quite dark when the Whitechapel Road was reached. Carter almost lost his bearings, as they twisted and turned their way through a labyrinth of dirty, ill-lit streets, eventually stopping before a building, the facade of which was grimy with the accumulated soot of decades. The ground floor was devoted to a second-hand clothes shop. Carter was hurried through this by the man who had done all the talking, up a narrow flight of stairs, dimly lighted by a smelly oil lamp halfway up, on to a spacious landing which, to his surprise, was softly carpeted, and also furnished with two well-upholstered easy chairs, a table on which were a few magazines, and a small bookcase crammed with the cheap editions of various novels. A tastefully shaded lamp threw a subdued light all round, enabling Carter to notice that three rooms opened on to the landing, and that the stairs ascending to the upper regions of the house were, unlike the flight he had just mounted, covered with a thick carpet. His guide removed his goggles, disclosing a fair, clean-shaven, somewhat fleshy face to view. His eyes were of such a pale blue that they looked almost colourless. He was a big, burly fellow, whose bulk suggested a liking for the good things of the table.

'You are about to enjoy Russian hospitality,' he said. 'Please sit here for a few minutes. I will return shortly.'

'Here!' checked Carter; 'half a minute, old cock. I'm getting a bit out of my depth. What have you brought me to this place for, and where's your mate?'

'My companion is putting away the car,' replied the Russian readily enough. 'As for the reason I have brought you here, is it not evident? Nobody will look for you in this building. Even if the whole of London is searched, you will be perfectly safe. And there will be a very thorough search for you, believe me.'

'I suppose there will,' agreed Carter. 'Did I kill that fellow I fired at?'

The other shook his head.

'Apparently not,' he returned. 'I do not think you even wounded him, which is a very great pity.'

'Why? What is he to you?'

'He is the inveterate enemy of freedom. Have patience, and you will know all in due course.'

He strode to a door, opened it, and disappeared, leaving Carter to sink into one of the easy chairs. Nearly a quarter of an hour went by before he emerged again; then he beckoned to the young man, who rose quickly and followed him into a brilliantly illumined room furnished most luxuriously as an office. A tall, dark man, whose features were decidedly Semitic, stood awaiting him with his back to a glowing fire. Dark piercing eyes, above a large hooked nose, gave him the appearance of a hawk. Instinctively Carter recognised that he was in the presence of a personality.

'This is the man of whom I have been speaking,' announced the guide by way of introduction.

The dark man bowed coldly to Carter.

'You seem to have got yourself into a lot of trouble,' he remarked. 'I understand that there are probably three charges against you: sedition, attempted murder, and desertion.'

'Looks like it,' admitted Carter ruefully.

'Thanks to Monsieur Dorin here, you are safe, at least for the time being.'

'What do you mean?'

'I mean that your subsequent safety depends very much on your future behaviour.'

'Blimy!' exploded Carter. 'That sounds like a blooming threat.'

'Not at all. It is necessary, however, for my colleagues and me to safeguard ourselves. If we use you, we must be certain that you will not betray us.'

'I can't say I like this,' muttered the young man. He turned to the other Russian. 'You said you wanted to help me to escape. You didn't say nothing about using me.'

'Quite so. But since you expressed yourself at Aldershot quite openly as a republican, and one who desired to see the Russian form of government in Great Britain, surely you can have no objection to assisting us.'

'I'm out to help you all I can,' retorted Carter, 'but there ain't no sense in threatening me.'

'We must be sure that you will not betray us.'

'Is it likely that I'd betray you, when my sentiments are the same as yours, and when the blasted police are all out to clap me into choky?'

'No; perhaps not,' acknowledged the dark man. 'There is a good deal of sense in what you say. Still we hardly know you, do we? The manner in which you upheld our doctrines to your comrades at Aldershot was reported to us, as was also the rough treatment you suffered. We decided then that you might prove useful to us. Unfortunately I'm afraid your escape and the attempt to shoot Sir Leonard Wallace has—'

'Sir Leonard Wallace! Who's he?'

'The man at whom you fired. Did you not know him?'

Carter shook his head.

'I didn't know his name,' he said. 'He's a bloke from the War Office or Scotland Yard, ain't he?'

Dorin smiled.

'He's even more important than that,' he stated. 'He is the head of the most efficient secret service in the world, which Great Britain pretends does not exist.'

'Secret Service!' exclaimed Carter. 'Struth!'

'Now perhaps you understand why I expressed the regret that you did not kill him. You must be a very bad shot.'

'Could you shoot straight, if you was putting a car into gear at the same time?' snarled Carter. 'Try it and see!'

'Well, well,' observed the Jewish-looking man in conciliatory tones, 'as you say in your language, there is no use in crying over spilt milk. We must see if we can make use of you, even though you will be a marked man. Sit down, and tell me exactly what that devil Wallace had to say to you.'

He crossed to the large desk, sat down behind it, and motioned Carter to a chair opposite him. Dorin took a seat close by. The two of them questioned the Englishman very closely, and he replied unhesitatingly and with apparent frankness. To his mind a lot of their questions were irrelevant, but their very irrelevancy kept him on his guard, as he felt that they were actually testing him. He began to entertain a great deal of respect for their shrewdness and keen intelligence, particularly with regard to the dark man, whose name it transpired was Levinsky. At last the latter rose, and stood, for a moment, looking down at Carter. There was a smile on his face, and a glint in his eyes, which the latter did not like.

'Your replies have been singularly open and convincing,' he observed. 'I congratulate you. At the same time, your bearing seems to me to be hardly that of a man desperate enough to attempt murder.'

'Here,' protested Carter, purposely misunderstanding him, 'you don't mean to say you are going to order me to croak someone?'

'Not at all. At least not at the moment. What I intended to convey was that your bearing now is hardly that of a man who, a few hours ago, did his best to murder another.'

'What do you expect me to be like?' asked Carter sarcastically.

'All wind up and goosey, I suppose? Well, let me tell you something; I'm not made like that, see? Besides, I didn't kill the bloke.'

'I am glad you have given us an insight into your character,' murmured Levinsky. 'We shall be able to judge you all the better, when you are put to the test.'

'What the hell do you mean by that?'

'Merely what I say.'

He turned to Dorin, and said something in a very low voice in Russian but, low as it was, Carter heard and understood. The Russian language was by no means strange to him. Dorin went quietly from the room, and Levinsky's piercing eyes rested on the young Englishman again.

'It may be of interest to you,' he remarked, 'to know that we have captured a spy. He will be brought here and questioned in an endeavour to discover certain things. Whether he answers satisfactorily or not, it is necessary that he should die. I said a few minutes ago that I had no intention of asking you to kill anybody; at least not just yet. I have changed my mind. You shall have the privilege of removing this man from the world, as soon as I give you the signal. Such an act will at once prove your loyalty to the cause, and give you an opportunity to satisfy your craving to commit murder.'

The cold-blooded manner in which he spoke sent a shiver down Carter's spine, but he gave no outward sign of the horror which filled him. Instead he winked an eye and laughed.

'Bit of a joker, ain't you?' he commented.

Levinsky leant on the desk, and his eyes held the other's, 'On the contrary,' he purred rather than spoke, 'I never joke.'

Carter's frown of amazed and incredulous wonder was well done.

'Let's get this straight,' he suggested. 'Are you really proposing that I should kill a bloke?'

'I certainly am.'

'Well, there's nothing doing, so get that into your nut.'

'Will you tell me what objection you have?' inquired Levinsky still in those sinister purring tones. 'You seemed to feel no compunction at firing point-blank at Sir Leonard Wallace this afternoon. Why then this sudden repugnance?'

'There are several reasons,' retorted Carter, 'all good 'uns. First of all I ain't a murderer by desire, although you seem to have got it into your head that I am. Second, I've got no hankering to feel a rope round my neck – I'm in bad enough as it is. Third, why the devil should I put myself into your blooming power by killing a bloke so that you could always hold the murder over my head? I ain't quite so green as I look, mister. There are other reasons, but I've given you enough to go on with.'

'You seem to forget,' observed Levinsky, 'that you are already in my power. It would be easy enough to hand you over to the police, if I so desired.'

Carter laughed with genuine amusement.

'I'll lay you a hundred to one that you wouldn't dare,' he chuckled. 'I know too much about you now, see?'

For a moment Levinsky's eyes glittered evilly then he smiled. He crossed the room to a side table, helped himself to a cigar, which he lit carefully, returned to the desk and resumed his seat.

'That proves to me,' he declared, 'that you are not to be trusted.'

'Tit for tat,' retorted Carter coolly. 'You play the dirty on me, and I do ditto with you. You play straight with me, and I play straight with you. That's fair enough, ain't it?'

'I do not make terms with underlings,' snapped Levinsky,

suddenly throwing all smoothness aside, 'and if I command you to kill this spy, you will do so. Do you understand?'

'I understand all right, but that isn't to say that I'm going to do your dirty work for you.'

There was the sound of a door opening behind him, and the tramp of several men entering the room, but Carter did not look round until Levinsky ordered him to stand up and move back. He rose to his feet nonchalantly then, and surveyed the newcomers. Dorin strode up to the desk, and threw himself into a chair close to Levinsky. Two foreign-looking men, one short and stout, the other of medium height but broad-shouldered, stood by the door closely guarding Maddison who, with pinioned hands, stood between them. No sign of recognition passed between the two Secret Service men. They looked curiously at each other as though each was wondering who the other was. Levinsky sat eyeing Maddison, a sneering smile on his face.

'So,' he remarked, 'I meet a member of the great British Secret Service; or is it that you are merely an interfering busybody? Approach closer that I may get a better view of you.'

His guards hustled Maddison up to the desk, and Levinsky sat looking at him, the jeering smile still on his face, his fingers tapping lightly on the blotting pad before him. Several seconds went by before he spoke again; then suddenly his light manner changed and he bent forward, his features distorted with fury.

'You fool,' he snarled, 'did you really think that you could follow my friend Dorin here without its being known? Oh, it was a very clever plot, no doubt, but you failed to give us credit for the intelligence we happen to possess. Your Sir Leonard Wallace goes off to Aldershot, and is careful to travel by way of lanes and byroads in order that he may ascertain that he is being followed – he probably knew that he had been trailed everywhere he went during the last few weeks. You have your instructions to drive along some distance in the rear and, of course, you quickly become aware that Monsieur Dorin is on the track of the so-clever Sir Leonard. You were directed not to lose touch once you ascertained that you were after your quarry until you discovered the destination and headquarters of Monsieur Dorin. Well, you have succeeded; you have done your job. You are satisfied I hope?'

'Perfectly, thanks,' replied Maddison quietly and, despite himself, Carter was unable to repress a grin.

'Ah, bah!' snapped Levinsky. 'You are fools, you and Sir Leonard Wallace, and all the rest of you. You perhaps think we are children to be taken in so easily? My friend Dorin knew you were after him before he reached – where is it?' He turned to his companion.

'Byfleet,' supplied the fair-haired Russian.

'Yes, Byfleet. What did he do? Did he endeavour to shake you off? No, Monsieur, he did not. When this poor soldier,' he indicated Carter, 'ran away, he followed him, and picked him up, but he knew all the time that you were behind. At Leyton, where Monsieur Dorin stopped for refreshment, he telephoned to me, and waited till the dark came so that it would be easier to capture you. As the result of our telephone conversation, I made preparations, and you entered the trap like the little fly going to the spider. Confess, Monsieur, you were very astonished when several men suddenly swarmed onto your car and rendered you helpless, were you not?'

'It was rather unexpected,' admitted Maddison sadly.

Levinsky laughed almost joyously.

'Why do you think you were allowed to follow my friend?' he asked.

'Because he couldn't shake me off,' retorted Maddison.

'Not so. It was because we could learn from you something of the plans of Sir Leonard Wallace.'

'And do you really think I should betray them, if I knew anything about them?' asked Maddison contemptuously.

'If you do not, you will die.'

'And if I do?'

Levinsky shrugged his shoulders.

'We shall have to keep you a prisoner until we can change our address so that you cannot again find us.'

'Don't talk such rot!' snapped Maddison. 'I know perfectly well that you'll kill me whether I talk or not, so why pretend?'

Again Levinsky shrugged his shoulders.

'Since you know so much, it is useless for me to talk. In seeing the car in which sat Monsieur Dorin, you learnt too much to start with. It is also a great triumph for us to be able to dispose of two of Sir Leonard's men at the same time.'

'Two?'

'But of course.' He turned sharply to Carter. 'Come here, you!' he commanded.

Carter stepped up to the desk, and found himself confronted by two revolvers, one held by Levinsky, the other by Dorin.

'Search him, and tie his hands together,' commanded the former, and the two satellites made a very thorough job of it.

'Here,' exclaimed Carter; 'what's the meaning of this?'

'It means that both strings to Sir Leonard Wallace's bow have come untied,' laughed Levinsky unpleasantly. 'We knew all along that you were not what you pretended to be. I know far more about you than this other gentleman. Your name is Carter, you were until a few months ago an inspector at New Scotland Yard. You see, I have my own espionage system. When you were discovered at Aldershot as a soldier delivering inflammatory messages, we watched events with interest. I must congratulate you on some very clever play-acting. You would have made a fortune on the stage. I confess that we would have been taken in completely, if we had not known who you were. Luck was on our side, Mr Carter, for you were the only member of your so-called Intelligence Department whom we knew by name and sight apart, of course, from Sir Leonard himself and Major Brien.'

Carter laughed. He decided that it was no use keeping up the pretence any longer.

'I suppose I must consider myself honoured,' he observed. 'Well, it's a relief, in a sense, to find myself unmasked. I can now give my well-known impersonation of a gentleman endeavouring to speak the King's English. It's a pity,' he added regretfully, 'that the little melodrama on the steps of the Cambridge Hospital went adrift. I rather fancied it was distinctly fruity.'

Levinsky banged his fist angrily on the desk.

'You appear to regard your capture as a joke,' he roared.

'Isn't it?' asked Carter, in tones of surprise.

The Russian's face was contorted with fury for a few moments; then abruptly he calmed down.

'You will quickly find that it is no joke,' he remarked quietly. 'I suppose Sir Leonard Wallace thought that one of you was bound to succeed. The gentleman in the car might have been shaken off, but, like veritable innocents, we would be sure to take you, Mr Carter, to our bosoms. We have done what was expected of us, but the joke is with us, and Sir Leonard loses two of his men.'

'There,' put in the irrepressible Carter; 'you admit yourself there is a joke. Gor' blimy!' he added, lapsing into his previous phraseology. 'Ain't you blooming inconsistent-like?'

Dorin shot an angry glance at him, but Levinsky now had himself more under command.

'Which of you is most *au fait* with Sir Leonard Wallace's plans?' he asked.

'Neither of us,' returned Maddison.

'What have you to say?' Levinsky demanded sharply of Carter.

'Quite a lot,' was the reply. 'I was always a good speaker. Now, what subject would you like me to discourse upon? I'm very good at horse racing or—'

'Be quiet!' shouted the angry Russian, unable to control his temper in the face of such facetiousness. 'If I have any more of that kind of thing from you, I will order you to be gagged.'

'Don't be unkind, uncle dear,' murmured the young man.

'Let him carry on, Tommy,' advised Maddison, 'or we'll be here all night, and I don't like his face well enough to view such an event with composure.'

'You've said a mouthful,' agreed Carter. 'He has a mug like the things on Notre Dame Cathedral in Paris. Go it, Beelzebub! What ho, for the inquisition!'

Suddenly Levinsky rose from his chair and, leaning forward, brought the flat of his hand down with resounding force on Carter's mouth.

'Perhaps that will help you to realise the seriousness of your position,' he ground out through clenched teeth.

But Carter still continued to grin, though a trickle of blood ran down from the corner of his lips.

'Naughty, naughty,' he chided, 'uncle mustn't lose his temper like that.'

'It is useless to hope to bring a man of such childish temperament to a sense of gravity,' interposed Dorin. 'We may perhaps learn something of interest from the other.'

'He will sober down quickly enough presently,' growled Levinsky.

He picked up the revolver, which had been taken from Carter.

'Loaded with blanks, I suppose,' he said, breaking the weapon, and shaking the cartridges out onto the desk. 'As I thought. A very pretty little comedy indeed. It is almost a pity that such a display of histrionic ability was not more successful.'

For nearly an hour he and Dorin tried by every means in their power to get the two Englishmen to divulge secrets of the Intelligence Department, but they might as well have been speaking to a blank wall. Maddison merely shook his head in reply to their questions, or answered in monosyllables. Carter continued to treat the whole affair as a species of entertainment in which he was cast for the comedy role. On more than one occasion Levinsky was on the verge of repeating his previous cowardly blow, but restrained himself, the unholy gleam in his eye causing Maddison to reflect that he was nursing some diabolical scheme.

Eventually the two Russians discontinued their cross-examination, and Levinsky stood up.

'I told you,' he observed, addressing Carter, 'that you would have the privilege of removing this man from the world. The time has come for you to do so. Afterwards my friends here will suggest a manner in which we can kill you amusingly, in order that you may enjoy the joke to the full.'

'Thank you very much,' said Carter politely. 'I hope it won't put you to any inconvenience?'

'Not at all,' returned the Russian, bowing ironically; 'it will be a pleasure.' He turned to Dorin. 'Will you call Dr Prilukoff, my dear Paul.'

The fair-haired Russian smiled grimly, and nodded. As soon as he had left the room, Levinsky resumed speaking in a politely conversational voice, but there was a deadly menace behind his words.

'Dr Prilukoff is, I think I may safely say, the finest hypnotist in the world. He has been exceedingly useful to the Soviet on several occasions, and enjoys a marvellous reputation in Russia. You have already declared, Mr Carter, that you will not kill your friend here; I as confidently assert that you will. If you will not do it of your own volition, Dr Prilukoff will hypnotise you into doing it.'

The fiendish ingenuity of the man robbed Carter of speech for a few moments. He stared wide-eyed at the cruel face before him; then began to laugh, though a trifle shakily.

'Of course you can't possibly mean it,' he muttered.

'I certainly do mean it,' was the reply, delivered in a merciless voice there was no mistaking.

There was no longer any thought of persiflage in Carter's mind. The inhuman barbarity of the Russian made it impossible to continue to treat him as a human being.

'You fiend!' he cried hoarsely; 'you damnable fiend! But if you think I can be hypnotised into committing such a devilish crime, you've made a jolly big mistake.'

'We shall see,' returned Levinsky confidently.

Except that his face had gone a trifle pale, Maddison showed no sign of concern. Carter looked at him questioningly, and received a shrug of the shoulders by way of reply. The door opened and Dorin reappeared, followed by the strangest-looking man Carter had ever seen. He was tall and thin almost to the point of emaciation. There was not a vestige of hair on his head, which was as smooth as a billiards ball, but a pair of the shaggiest eyebrows possible overhung deep-set eyes, magnified to a ludicrous extent by the rimless glasses he wore. His nose was long and pointed, and his mouth a slit without lips. The young Secret Service man gazed at this curious creature in wonder, and was only brought back to the realisation of his surroundings by the sound of Levinsky's voice telling the newcomer the purpose for which he was required. Dr Prilukoff gave a croaking sort of chuckle and, walking up to Carter, gazed at him long and earnestly. After a few moments his unkempt eyebrows met together in a frown, while he shook his head, and muttered to himself.

'He apparently doesn't think you're a good subject, Tommy,' observed Maddison cheerfully.

'He'll jolly soon find I am not,' replied Carter, 'if he tries any of his beastly tricks on me.'

'It will be necessary,' came the cruel voice of Levinsky, 'for this gentleman to be gagged as well as bound, I think. A sudden shout, as the – er – executioner approaches him, might seriously interfere with the satisfactory termination of the entertainment.'

Dr Prilukoff turned aside, and spoke earnestly to Dorin and Levinsky. Afterwards, Maddison was pushed into a chair and bound to it, while a gag was thrust into his mouth and fastened tightly. From a drawer in the desk Dorin took a long slender knife, and held it up for Carter's inspection.

'This is the knife you will use,' he announced, as though he were merely describing an object of casual interest. 'As soon as the doctor has brought you under influence, your hands will be untied, and this weapon handed to you.'

'It will be interesting to view your dismay when you come out of your trance, and realise what you have done,' observed Levinsky.

'If you think this old scarecrow is going to hypnotise me, you've made a bloomer,' snapped Carter.

Suddenly the doctor was standing before him, moving his talon-like fingers to and fro in front of his face. Behind them glittered those ludicrously distorted eyes, and they seemed to be boring into Carter's very brain. He had not realised before what power there was in them, and gradually it began to dawn on him that he would have to fight with all the strength of his mind to retain his senses. For the first time the real hideousness of the plot became apparent to him. He shouted his execrations, his defiance, but still those unholy, detestable eyes glared at him, the fingers continued their undulating movements, while not a sound issued from the ugly mouth of the scoundrel, who was doing his utmost to obtain an abominable control over his senses. The eyes were growing larger, more evil, until the whole world seemed to be eyes, merciless, hard, devouring. With a shock, Carter realised that a feeling of numbness was stealing over him; he was no longer able to cry out. Desperately he strove to turn his head, shut his eyes, anything rather than face that gimlet gaze any longer, but, like a rabbit stupefied by a hovering bird of prey, he was held in thrall. His brain was still working; thank God for that! He must concentrate with all his might against that sinister thing that was threatening his reason. Though he did not know it, the perspiration was running down his face in streams, as he fought that terrific fight with the hypnotist. But the agony was not all on his side. The doctor himself was feeling the strain. Never had he dealt with a subject so difficult. The onlookers stood fascinated, not daring to move, hardly venturing to breathe. With a mighty, supreme effort the mesmerist exerted all his power. Carter felt his senses reeling, he was beginning to lose hold on himself, his brain seemed to be enveloped in a cloud, and he was falling through space. In a great despair he became aware that he was praying, praying that this awful thing would release him from its miasmatic grip. Then, from what appeared to be miles away, came a voice:

'This has gone on long enough. Hands up, all of you!'

The spell was broken. Carter recovered full possession of his senses with a rush, but he was weak, unnerved, and was compelled to lean on the desk for support. At the sound of the voice, the Russians had turned with one accord towards the door. Sir Leonard Wallace stood on the threshold, a revolver in his hand. Behind him, and a little to one side, was Major Brien similarly armed, and farther back still could be seen the dim forms of several other men.

Dr Prilukoff took one glance at the newcomers; then, with an animal-like scream of fury, turned back to the man who had defied his hypnotic powers for so long, picked up the knife from the desk, and attempted to stab him. But the weapon never reached its object, a shot rang out, the doctor, for a moment, stood poised like a statue; then crashed to the floor.

'I think that's the best thing that could happen to him,' observed Sir Leonard coolly.

He stepped into the room, his companions crowding after him. Maddison was quickly released, and the four remaining Russians disarmed and shepherded into a corner. Someone found a jug of water, and gave Carter a drink, which he accepted gratefully. Levinsky and Dorin had been too overcome by astonishment and dismay to attempt any resistance. They stood now gazing at their captors, as though unable to believe the evidence of their eyes. Maddison pointed out Levinsky.

'That is the man you want, sir,' he explained. 'The other is number two, I believe.'

Wallace surveyed them with a smile.

'Our little plot seems to have worked quite well,' he observed.

Levinsky found his voice.

'What do you mean?' he snarled. 'We saw through the trick you tried to play on us when that man Carter made himself conspicuous by talking sedition, afterwards pretending to murder you and escape. We also captured the other, whom you set to track our car, and—'

'That's exactly what we wanted you to do,' interrupted Sir Leonard.

'How? Was it not your object that the man Carter should work his way into our confidence, and thus discover our secrets? Also that the other man should track the car, and find out our headquarters?'

'Yes,' admitted Wallace, 'but I anticipated that you would be too clever to be taken in. On the other hand the capture of these two gentlemen, and the belief that you had outwitted us, would lull you into a false sense of security, while I was making preparations to raid you.'

Both Levinsky and Dorin swore horribly. Despite himself, however, the former's curiosity got the better of him.

'How could you have known where to come?' he demanded.

'For the simple reason that below the steering wheel of Mr Maddison's car is a miniature wireless set, an aerial is concealed in the hood, which has double folds. All the time he was following you he was in touch with my headquarters. Thus he told us where Mr Carter had left my car, described your destination, even was able to send out the information that he was being surrounded and about to be captured.'

The chagrin depicted on the Russians' faces was almost comical. Levinsky turned on one of his subordinates with a cry of rage, and flung a rapid stream of Russian at him.

'If you are asking him why he did not discover the wireless outfit,' interposed Sir Leonard, 'let me answer for him. It has a secret hiding place, and the mere pressure of a button causes it to slide into position flush with the instrument board. Unless you happen to know it is there, the chances are against your finding it. Well, your game is up. We have found the printing press in the basement, captured the printers and compositors, and searched the whole building. The documents that have fallen into our hands are almost priceless from our point of view, and will put an end, once and for all, to Russian Soviet influence in this country. There is only one thing that puzzles me. What was the idea of attempting to hypnotise Mr Carter? We watched the performance for some minutes, but you were all too engrossed to notice that we had opened the door.'

Maddison recounted the diabolical scheme that had emanated from Levinsky's brain, and the expression on Sir Leonard's face, when he understood the significance of the scene he had witnessed, caused the Russians to shrink back in fear. For some moments his steel-grey eyes held theirs, and there was such a look of loathing in them that Dorin shivered convulsively.

'So that's the depth to which modern Russia has sunk, is it?' he snapped. 'You infernal brutes, you're nothing but cowardly scum, unfit for anything but the utter contempt and abhorrence of decent nations. You'll suffer a long term of imprisonment for this.' He turned to Carter. 'I am sorry I delayed our coming for so long,' he said.

'It's all right, sir,' returned the young man cheerfully. 'I did think something had come unstuck, though.'

Sir Leonard directed his men to remove the Russians, and send for an ambulance to take away the body of the hypnotist. He had hardly finished speaking, when Dorin gave a cry and sagged to the floor, his hand on his heart. Two or three men went to his assistance. He was lifted up, and placed in a chair close to the desk, while Brien sprinkled water in his face.

'Is he subject to that sort of thing?' Wallace asked Levinsky suspiciously.

'Yes,' nodded the latter sullenly, 'it's his heart.'

Suddenly there was a click and a grating sound, and the room was plunged in darkness. Wallace shouted for somebody to find the switch and, for some moments, there was the sound of scuffling and the deep breathing of men. Then came another sharp click, and the lights were on again. The Englishmen gazed round them in astonishment. The Russian subordinates were still present, but neither Levinsky nor Dorin were to be seen.

'Some disappearing trick!' murmured Carter.

Wallace gave vent to a full-blooded exclamation. Dashing across to the place where Dorin had been sitting he gave the desk a push. Immediately it began to move, as though it were on a swivel, and the lights went out. Continuing to push, he put out his foot cautiously *into space*.

'Strike a match, somebody,' he cried.

Several were lit, and the discovery made that underneath where the desk had been was an opening with steps leading down to the regions below.

'Ingenious,' he commented ruefully. 'The movement of the desk put out the lights, the two Russians then pushed until they could creep through the hole, shot the desk back into place, and on went the lights again. They're well away by now, but come on, Brien and Maddison, after them. The rest of you, guard the prisoners!'

The steps at first went straight down then meandered to the right, after which they walked along a narrow passage with a door at the end. This was ajar. They pushed it wide open, clambered over a pile of disused petrol tins, and found themselves in a garage – empty!

'Dash it!' exclaimed Wallace. 'As I thought, they've escaped.'

The whole of London was combed during the following days, and every port watched for the escaped Russians, but no trace of them was found. But to quote Sir Leonard's words:

'It doesn't matter much. We've smashed the Soviet plot against Britain once and for all. The information that has fallen into our hands is priceless, and will keep Russia toeing the line very carefully for the future, at least as far as this country is concerned. Still I'm damn sorry we can't make those two blighters suffer for the hideous scheme they concocted against Maddison and Carter.'

CHAPTER FIVE

A Soviet Dinner Party

'I thought we had heard the last of the Russians for some little time to come, but this latest development will badly need looking into.'

The speaker was Sir Leonard Wallace, and he was closeted with the Secretary of State for Foreign Affairs.

'I suppose your agent is quite sure of his facts?' queried the Cabinet Minister. 'I mean to say, he couldn't have been misinformed by any chance?'

Sir Leonard eyed his *vis-à-vis* rather scornfully.

'Every report that reaches my department,' he observed quietly, 'is authentic. If our agents were allowed to swamp us with rumours, it would mean chaos. Not a man or woman would dream of making a statement before he or she had verified it. After all that is what a secret service exists for, isn't it?'

The grey-haired Statesman smiled.

'I suppose it was foolish of me to make such a remark,' he said, 'but why on earth should the Soviet invite delegates from the countries you have mentioned to a secret conference?'

'That is what we must find out,' was the reply. 'I shall travel to Moscow myself and, if possible, attend the conference.'

The Secretary of State stared at him, as though he had not heard aright.

'Good Lord!' he exclaimed. 'You don't really mean that do you?'

'Why not?'

'My dear man, how can you possibly attend?'

'I don't know yet and, if I did, you could hardly expect me to give away my plans, even to you, could you?'

'But think of the risk you will run in entering the country. You'll never see England again, if you are discovered.'

'No; perhaps not. I should certainly not be declared a first-class life by an insurance company. But I don't see any reason why I should be detected.'

The Minister frowned at him thoughtfully.

'I don't like it,' he declared. 'After the way you smashed the Russian plot in England a few weeks ago, I should imagine you are regarded, by the Soviet Government, as the most dangerous enemy Russia possesses. It is possible there is an official collection of photographs of you in Moscow.'

'Quite likely I should think,' agreed Wallace coolly.

'Then what chance can you possibly have of successfully entering the country, let alone being present at this secret conclave?'

'My greatest chance will lie in the fact that it will never occur to the Soviet that I will attempt to enter Russia.'

'Couldn't you send someone else?'

'It has never been my practice to send a man where I would not go myself. In the present case I feel that it is very necessary that I should pay a personal visit to Moscow, and that's all there is to it.'

'What about Lady Wallace?' queried the Statesman.

'She will not know why I am going to Russia,' replied Wallace, 'and to quote an old proverb, "where innocence is bliss, 'tis folly to be wise." I presume you will not be foolish enough to inform her of my real object.'

'Certainly not. Surely you don't—'

'That applies also to your colleagues of the Cabinet,' went on Sir Leonard. 'Not a whisper of my intentions must leave this room, sir.' He smiled. 'Perhaps I have been foolish to confide in *you*.'

The Minister looked sharply at him, and a frown of annoyance creased his brow, but he caught the smile on the other's face, and allowed his indignation to fade.

'It is very difficult sometimes,' he complained, 'to know whether you are pulling one's leg or not. Well, since you are bent on entering this den of lions – I suppose I should say bears – I have no further comments to make. After all you're the chief of your department, and I've no right to interfere with your plans and arrangements, I suppose.'

'Has that only just occurred to you?' asked Wallace ironically.

This time the Foreign Secretary laughed.

'Thanks, Wallace,' he chuckled. 'I suppose that is a polite way of saying it's time I learnt to mind my own business.'

'More or less,' was the frank reply. He rose to his feet. 'Is there anything else you want to say before I go?'

'No; except to wish you luck. When is the conference to take place?'

'On the twenty-fifth.'

The Statesman looked at the calendar.

'Three weeks from today,' he commented. 'And the nations invited to send delegates are Austria, Germany, Turkey, and China you say?'

Wallace nodded.

'It looks like a plot,' remarked His Majesty's Minister.

'It *is* a plot,' retorted the Chief of the Secret Service.

'When will you leave?'

Sir Leonard smiled broadly.

'I shan't even tell myself until the last minute,' he said, 'and I certainly shall not cross to the continent by any of the known routes. Brien will be left in charge of course and, if anything occurs while I am away, you have only to get in touch with him.'

A little later, when walking up Whitehall, a grim look crossed his face.

'I wonder where they dig up these cabinet ministers,' he muttered. 'He thinks it *looks* like a plot. My God! What vast intelligence.'

The next day Wallace ran down to his estate in the New Forest where his wife and son were already established. He said very little to Lady Wallace about his proposed visit to Russia, and shut himself up in his study, where he did some very hard thinking. Early the following morning he was joined by Cousins, who spent a couple of hours playing golf with him, during which they acted as their own caddies, then returned to London.

A week later a dapper little man descended from the *rapide* at Strasbourg, and was driven to the Hotel Lorraine. His carefully trimmed imperial, his garments, above all his mannerisms, proclaimed him the Parisian. His cards declared him to be Monsieur Anatole Lalére, and he was well known at Strasbourg, as it was his custom, two or three times a year, to meet his agents from Berlin, Vienna, Rome and various other big continental cities at the Hotel Lorraine, and discuss business matters with them. Who has not heard of the famous Lalére perfumes? *Lalére et Cie* is known throughout Europe, America, and in fact the whole civilised world. No wonder, therefore, that Monsieur Anatole Lalére's coming to the Hotel Lorraine is always marked by a hearty and respectful welcome from the management. He is usually given the best suite of rooms, and his every wish gratified almost before it is expressed. Monsieur Lalére, it is well known, is a millionaire; in addition he is a charming gentleman, and distributes largesse with an unfailingly generous hand. His popularity, it will be seen, was a matter of the combination of the heart and the purse.

On this particular occasion he had arranged to meet three agents; one from Vienna, where, despite the sad decline of Austria, women are still beautiful, and love the scents of Lalére; one from Berlin, where women are not so beautiful but love expensive perfumes nevertheless; and the other from London, which boasts of the most beautiful women in the world, women whose beauty is enhanced by the delicately scented powders and creams of *Lalére et Cie*. It was unusual for the London agent to travel to Strasbourg, but it had become necessary for him to meet his confrères from Berlin and Vienna.

As was usual, the conference was inaugurated by a special luncheon at which the conversation, I am afraid, was almost entirely 'shop'. It was natural, however, considering that the affairs of the company were in such a flourishing condition and, at that time, were evoking a good deal of enthusiasm from those lucky enough to be employed by the amiable Monsieur Lalére.

A stranger glancing into the room, and taking stock of the four men, sitting round the convivial board, would have been struck by the manner in which each typified his nationality. Monsieur Lalére was so obviously French; big, burly Herr Gottfried, with his bullet head and fair hair, looked as though he might have been in the Prussian Guards; Herr Beust revived memories of those gallant and handsome young men who thronged Vienna before the Great War; and the fourth, tall, well-knit, with curly brown hair, fine features, and the bronzed complexion of the athlete, was as British as any man could well be. Yet, though Lalére had spent most of his life in France, Gottfried had been born and bred in Germany, Beust had lived in Austria since he was three years old, they were all as British in nationality as their companion, Tommy Carter, and all prominent members of the Secret Service directed by Sir Leonard Wallace.

The firm of *Lalére et Cie* is no myth. Its actual name is slightly different it is true, but it is as existent and as prosperous as I have stated, and Lalére directs it from Paris; while Gottfried, Beust and Carter are its agents in their various capitals, have their offices, and draw their salaries. It was founded with money supplied by Sir Leonard Wallace, and the gentlemen and ladies, who represent it in the big capitals of the world, are members of the British Secret Service.

As soon as luncheon was finished, the four men retired to Monsieur Lalére's private sitting room. Facts and figures regarding business were scrutinised with meticulous care, and plans for the future drawn up. Then Carter rose from his chair, and walked through the suite to make sure there were no possible eavesdroppers about. The advantage of holding a meeting in the sitting room was obvious. On one side was an anteroom, on the other a bedroom; it was quite impossible, therefore, for the discussion to be heard in adjoining suites. The only danger was the corridor outside the sitting room, but Lalére's manservant, also a member of the rank and file of the Secret Service, was posted on duty there. Carter locked all the doors, and returned to his companions.

'What have been the results of your investigations?' he asked looking from Gottfried to Beust.

The former was the first to answer.

'I had a great deal of difficulty in obtaining the necessary information,' he confessed, 'and even now I am not certain that what I have discovered has any connection with this Russian affair. But Paulus is leaving Berlin for Moscow on the twenty-second. His mission is supposed to be in connection with the agricultural inquiry, but I think it is fairly obvious to us what his real intentions are.'

'Paulus!' commented Carter. 'He won't be any help. He's a bullet-headed, beefy blighter like you, Gottfried, isn't he?'

'Yes,' nodded the other; 'though the comparison might have been expressed in more polite terms.'

Carter grinned cheerfully.

'But what,' inquired Lalére, 'has his build to do with the matter?'

'I'll tell you presently,' replied Carter. 'What about you, Beust? Don't say you haven't succeeded in discovering anything at all.'

'On the contrary,' replied the good-looking pseudo Austrian, 'I have actually seen the secret file relating to the conference in Moscow.'

'That's the stuff to give the troops,' interjected Carter. 'How did you manage that?'

'I heard that Otto Kahn had been delegated to attend the agricultural inquiry by the government, and put two and two together. It occurred to me that he would be the very man to be selected for a secret conference with Russia, so I did a little bit of house-breaking, and was lucky enough to find the file in his safe. I suppose he had taken it home to study it.'

'What's Otto Kahn like? Of course we've heard of him vaguely, but he's such a new star in the political firmament that very little is known about him. Have you the photographs?'

Beust nodded and, taking a pocket-case from the inside of his jacket, extracted three photographs, which he laid on the table in front of Carter. The latter examined them carefully, then whistled as though delighted.

'What's his height?' he asked eagerly.

'Somewhere in the neighbourhood of five feet eight, I should think.'

'Splendid! He's the man for our money. That's a bit of luck.'

'You're talking in riddles,' complained Lalére. 'What's the notion?'

'Listen!' Carter leant impressively towards his three colleagues. 'It is the chief's idea, if possible, to impersonate one of the delegates, and attend the conference in his place.'

Lalére whistled long and softly; Beust and Gottfried exchanged looks of surprise not unmixed with admiration.

'He was hoping that either the German or Austrian delegate would prove to be somewhere about his own build. This man Kahn is absolutely the goods; he's slim, same height, there's even a similarity in the features. He'll be as pleased as punch when he hears about Kahn and sees these photographs.'

'*Mon Dieu*! It's daring,' observed Lalére. 'It means, of coursc, that Otto Kahn will have to be kidnapped. How does Sir Leonard propose to do that?'

'Nothing has been arranged yet,' replied Carter. 'There was no use deciding upon any plan of campaign until he knew whom he intended to impersonate.'

'What would he have done,' asked Gottfried, 'if the Austrian delegate had turned out to be a bullet-headed, beefy blighter, as you so elegantly delineated Paulus?'

'In that case Shannon would have been the impersonator, and the chief would have gone with him in the capacity of secretary. Which reminds me,' he added, turning to Beust; 'have you any idea how many people are travelling with Kahn?'

'Two,' was the prompt reply; 'a secretary and his confidential manservant.'

'You're positive of that?'

'Certain.'

'That makes things easier.'

'If you are sure Sir Leonard will choose Kahn for this impersonation business,' put in Gottfried, 'you won't need these photographs of Paulus.'

'I'd better take them with me,' said Carter. 'No doubt the chief would like to gaze upon the features of a fellow delegate.'

He took the two photographs which Gottfried handed to him, and examined them critically.

'What a hog he looks,' he commented. 'There is certainly something of you about him, Gottfried.'

'Thanks very much,' murmured the latter drily, and the others laughed.

Carter rose to his feet.

'Well, I don't think there is anything else,' he remarked, 'and the sooner I get back to HQ the better. You'd better be on the *qui vive*, Beust. I daresay a mass of detailed instructions will be unloaded on you in a day or two.'

'Are you accompanying the chief to Russia?' asked Lalére.

Carter shook his head.

'No; worse luck. Those Levinsky and Dorin blokes made it pretty evident that the Soviet has me taped, and you can bet your bottom dollar Sir Leonard won't take any unnecessary risks of busting the whole caboodle.'

'The lad deals in very refined and polished English, I must say,' murmured Gottfried with a twinkle in his eye.

'What's the matter with you, Beefy?' retorted Carter.

The meeting broke up in a spirit of facetiousness typical of the men, who daily risked liberty, life, and honour for the country which meant everything to them.

Herr Otto Kahn, with his private secretary and confidential servant, left Vienna very quietly ten days later. The Austrian statesman had had a busy few days before his departure, and he stretched himself out in his comfortable coupé, and sighed his relief. He looked forward to a restful train journey. It is doubtful if his anticipation would have been so pleasant, had he known that in the next compartment to his were two men of the British Secret Service, and farther along two others. At Brunn, which was reached shortly before midnight, a fifth, a slight man of medium height, carrying only a small attaché case, entered the train, and occupied a coupé to himself.

There was no stop between Brunn and Prerau, and the Austrian, bidding his secretary, who shared the compartment with him, good night, settled himself for sleep. Half an hour went by; then the handle of the door was softly turned, and a tall, broad-shouldered man entered, followed immediately by a short, boyish figure. Without hesitation each bent over one of the sleeping Austrians, remained in that position for some minutes; then nodded to each other. The odour of chloroform began to permeate the atmosphere of the coupé, and the powerful-looking man gently opened the window. The other produced two long lengths of thin, strong cord, and five minutes afterwards Herr Kahn and his secretary, their pockets rifled, lay gagged and bound, and entirely oblivious to the world. Ten minutes ticked by, and again the door was opened to admit two more men.

'Everything all right?' whispered one.

The small individual nodded.

'Get the servant?' he asked tersely.

'Yes,' was the reply, 'we've deposited him in the next compartment.'

'It would be better to bring him in here.'

That was done, after which the little man and his companion returned to their coupé, and left the newcomers shut up with the unconscious Austrians.

'So far, so good, Cousins,' observed the broad-shouldered man genially. 'What's the next move?'

He stretched himself to his full height, and smiled down at his friend. Captain Hugh Shannon was the most powerful man in the service. Six feet in height, he looked shorter owing to his great breadth of shoulder. Even his clean-shaven face, with its clear-cut features, grey eyes and determined chin, gave an impression of strength both mental and physical. He had graduated to the Secret Service by way of the Indian Army and Foreign Office. Cousins presented a ludicrous contrast. Barely five feet in height, and with the figure of a boy of fourteen, he looked almost as though Shannon could have put him into one of his pockets. His extraordinary, wrinkled face corrugated into a mass of little puckers and creases as he smiled up at his big companion.

'We dump the bodies just beyond Prerau before the train gets up speed again,' he said. 'Beust has arranged for a car to be waiting, and he and Manning will drive to a lonely old farmhouse in the mountains ten miles beyond the town, and keep the goods there for a week.'

'But won't Kahn recognise Beust when they're both back in Vienna,' asked Shannon, 'and Beust is with his beloved scents and powders again?'

Cousins shook his head.

'You needn't worry about that,' he confided. 'Beust knows how to take care of himself, and you can be pretty sure he won't let himself be seen. He's got a platoon of brigands or something up in the hills. They'll look after the prisoners.'

Shannon threw himself into a seat, and lit a cigarette. The train tore on through the night until, at last, came a jarring of brakes, and it began to slacken speed.

'This must be Prerau,' observed Shannon; then added anxiously: 'I say, Jerry, we've forgotten the conductor. He saw us into this coupé, and was also fussing round Kahn and company. What's he going to say or do, when he finds us officiating tomorrow and the original duo missing?'

Cousins yawned.

'Now, look here, Hugh,' he murmured reprovingly, 'have you ever known the chief trip up on a little thing like that? He ascertained days ago that the attendants from Vienna are relieved at Prerau. There will be a new train gang on board from there. A bunch of wild and woolly Moravians, I expect.'

'I beg the chief's pardon,' grinned Shannon. 'But what about the other passengers?'

'I doubt if one of them noticed Kahn, secretary, and servant. Their departure was too secret. Besides, we aren't going to form convivial parties. Sir Leonard, you, and I will remain in the coupé next door until we reach Warsaw, when we change trains.'

'I am answered,' returned Shannon.

'Good. Well, the time for talk is o'er. Now we become men of action, at least, you do. May I request you not to dump the bodies too hard. We don't want to break any limbs; besides, Manning and Beust will be underneath remember.'

The train ran slowly into the station, and stopped. There was very little bustle owing to the fact that they had arrived in the early hours of the morning and, after a wait of ten minutes, it drew out again. Immediately Cousins and Shannon entered the next coupé. Beust and Manning slipped out into the corridor, opened the carriage door and, as the lights of the station were left behind, dropped to the permanent way. Shannon picked up the unconscious Kahn, as though he were a baby, and lowered him to the two men, who were now running by the side of the train. They put him down, and caught the secretary in the same manner. By the time Shannon had carried the valet from the coupé, speed was rapidly increasing, and Beust and Manning were compelled to sprint. The servant was a fairly heavy man, and his body reached the two Englishmen with such force that it bowled them over, but nobody was hurt. Cousins, who had been holding the door open for Shannon, strained his eyes into the darkness, and had the satisfaction of seeing them rise to their feet.

'That's that,' observed Shannon in tones of satisfaction. 'I hope nobody has spotted us depositing bodies at intervals along the permanent way.'

'It's most unlikely,' replied Cousins, closing the door. 'For one thing it's far too dark, and another, only the train attendants are likely to be awake at this hour, and they wouldn't be hanging gaily out of windows.'

They removed their meagre belongings from the compartment they had occupied, and carried them into the coupé engaged in the name of Herr Otto Kahn. There they sat down to await the coming of Sir Leonard Wallace. It was half an hour before he put in an appearance, and Shannon began to speculate on what was keeping him.

'Have patience,' recommended Cousins. 'He'll be along presently. "Patience! Why, 'tis the soul of peace; Of all the virtues, 'tis nearest kin to Heaven: It makes men—"'

'Have a heart,' interrupted his companion. 'Don't you think it's bad enough for me to be shut up alone with you in this cubby hole, without having to listen to your infernal quotations?'

'The trouble with you, Hugh,' said Cousins, shaking his head sadly, 'is that you have no soul. As Ruskin says—'

'I don't want to hear what Ruskin says.'

'No? That's a pity. An hour or so with him would improve your mind.'

Shannon was about to make a sarcastic retort, when the door gently opened, and a man, the very image of Herr Otto Kahn, entered carrying a small attaché case and a neatly folded overcoat.

'My hat!' ejaculated Shannon, as he and Cousins rose respectfully to their feet.

'You'll have to do the finishing touches, Cousins,' said the voice of Sir Leonard Wallace. 'I never regret the loss of my left arm more than when I am forced to make-up. Everything go off all right?'

'Without a hitch, sir,' replied Cousins. '"Our band is few but true and tried, Our Leader frank and bold—"'

'Oh, he's off again,' groaned Shannon.

The little man eyed him defiantly.

'"Then help us to love one another, For this we most earnestly pray",' he quoted.

Sir Leonard laughed.

'Probably,' he commented, 'Shannon would love you more, Cousins, if you quoted a few athletic records by way of a change.'

On the morning of the twenty-fifth, the pseudo Herr Otto Kahn with his tall secretary and little manservant emerged from the Kursky Voksal, accompanied by the commissary and escort that had met them. He had been received with every mark of respect, and was now driven to a hotel near the Krasnaya Plotzad, where everything possible had been arranged for his comfort. From the time that Sir Leonard Wallace had taken on the personality of Otto Kahn, he had acted in every way as he imagined the Austrian would have done. He and his companions had spoken German, and neither by word, sign, nor action had they shown that they were Englishmen engaged in ferreting out the reason for the secret conference in Moscow. Sir Leonard had carefully studied all the documents in the baggage of the Austrian delegate and, long before the capital of the Soviet Republic had been reached, had made himself *au fait* with Otto Kahn's standing, his instructions from the Austrian Government, had even managed in some subtle manner to lose his own personality in that of the man he was impersonating. There was little in the reports, records, and statements, through which he waded with such painstaking care, to give an inkling of the reason for this mysterious *pour-parler*, but he noted with a great deal of gratification that Herr Otto Kahn had been given full power to accept or decline on behalf of the Austrian nation whatever proposals Russia intended to place before the delegates. His only doubt of the success of his mission lay in his ignorance as to whether Otto Kahn had been previously acquainted with any member of the Soviet Government or Herr Paulus, the German representative. It was not that he feared his disguise might be penetrated, but was uncertain whether to approach them as strangers or acquaintances. However, that worried him very little; he would be compelled to rely on his quickness of perception.

His first act after he had bathed and partaken of breakfast, was to proceed to the government buildings where he presented his credentials and was received by Lenin. The latter greeted him with a courtesy that surprised Sir Leonard. He had expected to meet a man with rough and uncouth manners, instead of which the Russian showed a degree of refinement and culture quite out of keeping with his reputation. He discussed Austria with the assurance of a man who had made an intimate study of the vicissitudes of that country, and Sir Leonard began to feel very glad that he himself had always made a point of studying the political and economic questions of all European countries. Looking at Lenin, it was not difficult to understand why he had become such a power. There was strength in his face as well as the more obvious brutality and looseness, his piercing eyes were those of a fanatic, and the shape of his head suggested a capacity for deep thought. Wallace left him with the knowledge that he was trying conclusions with the most dangerous adversary he could possibly have chosen, a man who, if he discovered the trick that was being played upon him and his government, would act without mercy or the slightest impulse towards clemency.

The conference was inaugurated at three o'clock in the afternoon, and went on without interruption until six, when the delegates left in order to snatch a brief rest before attending the private dinner, which Lenin was giving in their honour at his residence. As Sir Leonard Wallace, attended by Captain Shannon, entered the gloomy portals of the one-time palace, a grim smile showed for an instant on his face. Soldiers, most of them in faded and untidy uniforms with red armlets, thronged round the doorways and crowded the corridors, making room for them to pass, but closing in again directly they had gone by. Escorted by an officer of high rank, they ascended the great staircase, passed through an anteroom, also full of soldiers, into a comparatively small chamber in the centre of which was a long table with five chairs placed on each side and one at the head for Lenin. The latter stood with a group of his colleagues at the far end of the room and, on recognising the supposed Herr Otto Kahn, immediately advanced to meet him, and presented him to the six Russians, who had followed him. To Wallace's relief none of them claimed acquaintance, neither did Herr Paulus, the German, who was announced shortly afterwards. A tall, dignified Chinaman, and a handsome Turk, completed the gathering. Sir Leonard had expected Leon Trotsky to be present, but was informed that he was away inspecting troops. The foreign delegates were seated with a Russian on each side of them, their secretaries accommodated at a smaller table between the great double windows, and proceedings commenced, the language used being French.

Lenin spoke at great length, first of the success which had

attended the efforts of the Soviet to found and maintain an ideal republic. He contended that the federation of free nations, which included Russia proper, White Russia, the Ukraine, the Transcaucasian Soviet Republic, and the Far Eastern Republic of Siberia, had brought to the country greater happiness and prosperity than it had ever before known. The complete social and economic revolution had given control of land, factories, business, and the general government of the country to the labouring classes, and thus had eliminated all possibility of power being restored to the exploiters. The nationalisation and distribution of land among the farmers according to their ability to till it, the transference of railways, mines, factories and mills from private ownership to the Soviet Republic, the administration of banks and all financial operations by the workers' and peasants' government had conduced in the mind of every Russian a pride in his country and in himself, and entirely eradicated the old inferiority complex of the days of Czardom and serfdom.

'All this was not done without opposition,' he declared, 'and at times we have been compelled to resort to severe measures to suppress obstruction and bitter antagonism. But those measures were only temporary, and were absolutely necessary to carry out the revolution despite the hindrance of our many enemies both within and without. Russia is the inveterate enemy of capitalistic industry and trade. It has been our object to fight for the victory of socialism in all lands. We have done our utmost to introduce the soviet control of manufacture and trade in other countries, but alas! The short-sighted people of those countries have failed to see what was for their great benefit, and allowed their governments to suppress such altruistic endeavours. My colleagues and I have decided that the time has come to make a further and greater attempt.'

He then went on to speak of the losses sustained by Germany, Austria, and Turkey, and gradually worked up to the proposals which he had to submit to the delegates. Briefly they amounted to the seizure of the lands of which those nations had been deprived as a result of the Great War, with the assistance of the Russian army and with the aid of all the resources which Russia was able to throw into the scale. China would act as decoy by drawing the eyes of the world to the Far East by activities in Manchuria, round the settlement at Shanghai, and on the borders of Korea. Immediately Germany would seize Posen and the East Prussian territory that had gone to Poland; Austria would invade Czecho-Slovakia and Hungary, and Turkey seize Bulgaria and Roumania. At the same time Russia would aid her allies by throwing armies into Poland, Roumania and anywhere else where they were wanted. By the time France, Italy and England were ready to fight, there would be a German and Austrian army waiting for them, with a solid phalanx of Russians behind, spread from one end of Europe to the other and prepared to act at any point rendered necessary by attack. As both Germany and Austria would be on the defensive, and England, France, and Italy forced into the role of invaders, everything was in favour of the two former from the start. This is merely a brief outline of Lenin's proposals. He went very deeply into the matter, displaying a knowledge of conditions and military exigencies that surprised Sir Leonard.

'Such an action is not a matter of a few months,' he concluded. 'It may take a year, two years, before you are prepared, but when the time comes, the blow must be struck suddenly and simultaneously. Your preparations must be absolutely secret, and the risk of detection nullified by leaving the bulk of munitions and instruments of war to be manufactured in this country. The endeavour is bound to end in success, after which further concessions will be arranged, such as the return of Alsace and Lorraine and her old colonies to Germany; the Trentino, Croatia and Bosnia to Austria; Greece and Albania to Turkey. China will be rewarded for her share by the granting of any demands within reason that she may make. It will be possible later on, no doubt, to win back Korea for her, but, in our opinion, it would be injudicious to antagonise Japan until the affair in the west is settled. I hope I have made the proposals of my government clear, gentlemen.'

Three of his colleagues followed, and spoke in the same strain; then commenced a general discussion. None of the foreign delegates had had any previous inkling of the scheme that was to be put before them, and thus were unprepared with any pronouncements inspired by their governments.

After the first surprise, however, they proceeded to examine the proposition, and Lenin and his confrères were subjected to a regular battery of questions and counter-questions, to all of which they replied easily and convincingly. As the discussion went on, it became evident to Sir Leonard that both Herr Paulus and the Turkish delegate were waxing very enthusiastic, but the Chinaman, although apparently inclined to favour the scheme, was more cautious.

'I understand, of course,' he observed once, 'that your scheme involves my country only in a minor sense, and thus we cannot expect to obtain a reward on the same scale as those awaiting Germany, Austria, and Turkey. At the same time it must be remembered that by keeping the eyes of the world on the Far East, and possibly occupying the anxious attentions of France, Italy, and Great Britain, we shall be doing a great deal to ensure the ultimate success of operations in the west.'

'That is quite true,' agreed Lenin.

'It, therefore, occurs to me,' went on the delegate, 'that I should be able to take back to my government something more definite than the promise of a *possible* return of Korea to China at some future date.'

'I have mentioned,' Lenin reminded him, 'that we shall be prepared to grant any demands within reason that China may make. Are you ready to put those demands before us now?'

The Chinaman shook his head.

'I must have time to think,' he said. 'Will you give me until the discussion is informally resumed, as I presume it will be, after dinner?'

'Most certainly,' agreed Lenin, and the Chinaman gravely bowed his acknowledgments. The Russian dictator turned his eyes on Sir Leonard. 'You, who represent the country which has most to gain, have said the least, Herr Kahn. Is there anything in our proposals to which you feel your government would not agree? You understand, of course, that we have only put the bare outline of the scheme before you. It will take many subsequent meetings to arrange all details, once the nations interested agree.'

'Naturally,' admitted Sir Leonard. 'The whole matter is so vast, however, that it would be foolish to allow one's enthusiasm to blind one to common-sense arguments against success.'

'What are they?' demanded Lenin with a frown.

'Are they not obvious? Germany and Austria are on the verge

of bankruptcy; the terrible terms of the Treaty of Versailles have crippled the two countries almost beyond recovery, as far as their status as military powers is concerned. Again in a war of the type you have depicted which, from our point of view, will be defence against invasion, neither Germany nor Austria have the economic resources to hold out, even if they could do so in a military sense by equalling their enemies man for man and gun for gun.'

'I have said,' replied Lenin with the air of one humouring a child, 'that it may take a year, or two years, perhaps even longer, to make your preparations.'

'Quite so,' agreed Sir Leonard, 'but remember we shall be compelled somehow to circumvent the clauses in the Treaty of Versailles, which only permit us armies of a hundred thousand men each, and forbid compulsory military service. It is easy enough to defy those clauses, but not so easy to defy them without the world becoming aware of the fact.'

'Herr Kahn has spoken with great wisdom there,' rumbled the deep voice of Paulus. 'How are we to raise great armies in such secrecy that no one learns what is being done?'

'It is a matter which will require very careful consideration I admit,' said Lenin. 'But it can be done, and I presume, with such rich fruit awaiting the gathering, will be done. As for the rest economically and financially Russia will stand behind you. There can be no danger of lack of supplies, for both Germany and Austria will be stocked by my country. You run short of food, Russia will supply the deficiency; munitions are required, trains loaded to the brim will be rushed to you; reinforcements are necessary, army corps will speed rapidly to the scene. Is it not the opportunity for which you have been longing and praying since 1918, my friends?'

'What does Russia get out of all this?' asked Sir Leonard quietly.

Lenin smiled.

'It is a question I expected,' he confessed. 'As far as possessions are concerned we regain Finland, Esthonia, Latvia, Lithuania and Poland; perhaps Georgia as well. For our help to your countries, we shall expect repayment naturally, and also that *you will adopt the soviet form of government.*'

'Ah!' exclaimed Wallace. 'That indeed will require much consideration.'

'No; I think not,' retorted Lenin. 'The plums are too many and too great to throw aside through what would amount to sheer obstinacy.' He rose. 'That concludes the official conference, gentlemen. We shall discuss matters informally after dinner, if it is your desire.'

Sir Leonard returned to his hotel in a very thoughtful frame of mind. His mission had been a great success. He had found out why the secret meeting had been called. The thought of what it might have led to appalled him, and he made a mental note to reward his agent in Moscow, a man holding a clerical post under the government, who had sent through the news. He wished he could have returned immediately to London instead of waiting until the following day, but such a move would have brought suspicion on him, and very little gained by it. He felt, however, that the sooner he was out of Russia the better, now that he had learnt what he had gone there for.

The same eleven people, who had attended the conference, were present at the dinner, which was not marked by any particular jollity. There was an air of suppressed excitement in the demeanour of most of the guests, though the phlegmatic Chinaman and Sir Leonard Wallace were notable exceptions.

Lenin was at times exuberant; at times thoughtful but, on the whole, he played the part of host to perfection. Nothing was said anent the proceedings of the afternoon owing to the presence of the waiters, but it was generally understood that the discussion would be continued informally later in the drawing room.

The meal was drawing to an end, when a waiter approached Sir Leonard, and informed him that his secretary desired to speak to him.

'Where is he?' asked the pseudo-Austrian.

'Outside in the lobby, comrade,' was the reply.

Making his excuses, Wallace left the room, and found Shannon impatiently awaiting him. The latter's face looked white and strained. Taking care that there was no one within hearing, Sir Leonard sharply asked why he had come.

'A code wire has just arrived from Beust, sir,' whispered Shannon. 'Kahn's secretary has escaped!'

'What?' It was only a mutter, but it was full of intense feeling.

'We'll have to get away at once, sir. There's almost sure to be a message through to Lenin very soon. Of course the secretary fellow won't know that his master has been impersonated.'

'In any case he's bound to wire and explain the reason for Kahn's non-arrival. You're right, Shannon, we must lose no time. Dash it! I wonder how it happened.'

'Cousins is waiting below with a few things in your attaché case, our coats, and two rugs, sir,' Shannon informed him. 'We shall have to leave the rest of the luggage I'm afraid.'

Sir Leonard nodded.

'Wait here,' he ordered. 'I'll be back in a minute.'

He re-entered the dining room almost jauntily, as though he

had not a care in the world, Smilingly he approached Lenin, who looked up at him curiously.

'I'm afraid I must claim your indulgence,' he said. 'My government are anxious, and I must return to my hotel and write a telegraphic despatch.'

'Why not do it here?' asked Lenin.

'It must be in code, you understand, and—' he shrugged his shoulders.

Lenin nodded.

'You will return when you have sent the wire?' he stated rather than asked.

'Certainly,' returned Wallace.

'I wonder if that telegram will be favourable to Russia?' murmured Lenin slyly.

Sir Leonard smiled.

'Among other things,' he declared, 'it will state that I am returning with excellent news.'

Lenin returned the smile.

'Hurry back, Herr Kahn,' he urged; 'our party will be very incomplete without you.'

Wallace was turning away when a secretary hurriedly entered the room, and went up to Lenin, to whom he handed an opened telegram. Fearing that it might refer to him, Sir Leonard hastened his steps, had reached the door, and was about to pass out, when there was a shout behind him.

'Stop that man!' bellowed Lenin.

It would have been useless to have endeavoured to continue his progress in the face of such an order. Turning and regarding the Soviet leader coolly:

'Were you referring to me?' asked Sir Leonard.

Lenin had risen to his feet, and stood glowering at him. The guests were regarding the Russian with a mixture of surprise and curiosity.

'What is the meaning of this?' he demanded, waving the telegram in the air.

'How can I tell you when I have not read it?' asked Wallace.

Lenin turned to the others.

'Listen, comrades,' he said in quieter but still menacing tones. 'That man is an impostor!' His announcement caused a sensation, and all, except the Chinaman, were immediately on their feet, subjecting Sir Leonard to a battery of hostile glances. 'I have a telegram here from the Austrian Government which states that Herr Kahn was kidnapped on his way to Moscow, and warning me to beware, as they suspect an attempt at impersonation.'

This was worse than Wallace had anticipated. He began to feel that the chances of escape were not worth considering. But he resolved to play his part to the end. A frown of anger wrinkled his brow, and he walked firmly back to the table.

'What nonsense are you talking?' he demanded. 'Show me that telegram!'

Lenin eyed him with cold fury.

'Who are you?' he snapped.

'You know very well who I am,' retorted Sir Leonard. 'Is this a plot? Will you presently be accusing Herr Paulus, Mr Feng Ho, and Karim Pasha of being impostors?'

His coolness, and the manner in which he was apparently turning the tables on Lenin, impressed the foreign delegates. One by one they turned and looked at the Russian, as though awaiting his answer. It came with the sudden fury of a volcanic eruption.

'You think to defy me?' he roared. 'You stand there expecting to continue the deception in the face of this message from Vienna? Do you think we, my comrades and I are likely to disbelieve our own eyes, and declare the words here to be a myth, or do you think we are fools enough to allow you to persuade us that the telegram is a practical joke? It definitely states that Herr Kahn was kidnapped between Brunn and Prerau, with his secretary, and locked up in a deserted farmhouse. But the secretary escaped. I suppose you are a Czecho-Slovakian spy. Well, you shall very quickly learn what the Russian Soviet Government does with spies.' He swung round to the man who had brought the telegram to him. 'Call a file of soldiers, comrade,' he ordered. 'Then see that the companions of this man are apprehended and brought here. We shall conclude our dinner party with a little entertainment.'

'You think so, do you?' retorted Sir Leonard.

A desperate idea had come to him. The chances of its success were not one in a hundred, but there happened to be no alternative. He stepped in front of the departing secretary, and ordered him to stop; then, before anybody thought of preventing him, had run to the door and called in Shannon.

'Lock that door,' he ordered. 'Have you a revolver?'

'Yes, sir.'

'Draw it, and keep these people covered. If anyone moves, shoot him.'

He held a revolver in his own hand now and, standing in such a position that he could command the whole room, told a waiter to close and lock the service door, and bring him the key. The startled man obeyed.

'Now, gentlemen,' he invited, 'kindly resume your seats.'

After a little hesitation, all except Lenin obeyed. The Russian Dictator remained standing, his hands clenching and unclenching, his eyes glaring hatred and death. It was obvious that once Sir Leonard's resistance had been overcome, he would meet with very short shrift.

'Did you hear me?' observed the latter coldly. 'Perhaps, as I used the word "gentlemen", you did not think you were included. Sit down!'

Lenin still continued to stand, but the sight of the revolver slowly being raised, until it pointed at a spot between his eyes, broke his resolution. He threw himself into his chair, his face livid not so much with fear as with fury.

'Thank you,' acknowledged Wallace politely. 'Now we can talk.'

'What good do you think this is going to do you?' stormed Lenin. 'You cannot hold us up like this for long.'

'You and I are about to make a bargain,' Sir Leonard informed him.

'Bargain!' exclaimed Lenin, and again, 'bargain!' He laughed cruelly. 'You amuse me,' he sneered. 'Do you really think I will stoop to bargain with you?'

'I do,' nodded Wallace. 'You have accused me of being an impostor, and it is obvious that, no matter what I say, you will continue to regard me in that light. That being so, you are determined that, with the information I possess, you will never allow me to leave this country alive. Am I not right?'

'You are perfectly correct,' agreed Lenin now in quiet, sarcastic tones. 'I will go further,' he added. 'You and the man with you will be shot in this very room. It will be a spectacle which will at once rid us of a danger and amuse my guests.'

Herr Paulus turned pale, and lifted a protesting hand.

'As the representative of Germany,' he said hastily, 'I could not possibly countenance an – an atrocity.'

Lenin regarded him coldly.

'It is necessary to deal with spies severely,' he remarked, 'and we, who have great issues dependent on us, must take steps to see that our secrets are not betrayed. If, as we sit here, we witness, with our own eyes, the execution of this man and his companions, we will be assured that we need not fear betrayal.'

'Are you quite certain that this – this gentleman is a spy? What evidence have you?'

'Is this not sufficient evidence?' returned Lenin impatiently, tapping the telegram he still held. 'There is only one fitting punishment for the crime of espionage – that is death! But we speak too much. Their bodies should, by this time, be lying lifeless before us.'

'You mean,' cried Paulus in horrified accents, 'you would shoot them without a trial?'

'Trial!' laughed Lenin harshly. 'What need is there for a trial?'

'No; there won't be a trial,' put in Sir Leonard quietly. 'You and I, Monsieur Lenin, are about to strike a bargain. There has, as you have remarked yourself, been too much talk. Listen to me!'

'I will not listen to you,' snarled the Russian. 'I do not talk with men of your type.'

'Nevertheless you will listen to what I have to say.'

Lenin started to speak again, but a sinister movement of the revolver silenced him. He was obviously not a brave man, and Sir Leonard began to hope that his scheme would succeed after all.

'You, who have sent so many people to their deaths,' went on the latter, 'will be sent to yours very promptly, if you do not agree to my terms.'

'What are they?' snapped Lenin, probably thinking that, if he were compelled to promise anything, he could easily break his promise, when the revolver was no longer there to intimidate him.

'My secretary and I will leave this room,' declared Sir Leonard, 'without interference. We shall depart from Moscow, and travel to the frontier in the car which is awaiting us below. There must be no attempt to detain us whatever. If there is any interference, you will be shot.'

'Oh,' sneered Lenin, 'and who will shoot me?'

'I will. You see, you are going to accompany us to the frontier as a hostage.'

This cool statement drove the Russian Dictator into a terrible passion. His countenance went from white to crimson and back again, while he struggled to find words.

Then a torrent of wild denunciations broke from his lips. Sir Leonard waited patiently until he apparently became exhausted.

'You are simply wasting time by behaving like this,' he observed. 'The sooner you realise that I mean what I say, the better. If you refuse to accompany us, I will shoot you dead where you are, and take Monsieur Vassiloff with me as hostage.'

One long look of hatred Lenin gave him; then he and Vassiloff, the Commissary of Police, spoke eagerly together in whispers. Wallace ordered Shannon to go round and search everyone in the room to ascertain if they had weapons concealed on them. The young man met with a certain amount of opposition, but his methods were not too gentle, and those who resisted became like children in his hands. Not a weapon of any kind was found.

'Now,' commanded Sir Leonard, 'we will depart, if you please. Stand up, Lenin, and you, too, Vassiloff!'

From the looks exchanged between the two Russians, it became evident that they had been plotting a counter-move. An expression of dismay spread over Vassiloff's face.

'Why am I included in that order?' he asked.

'Because I have decided to take you with me in any case,' was the reply. 'You're not an expert dissembler, Vassiloff, and it is evident that you and Lenin had hatched some plot or other. Get up, both of you; I am in a hurry!'

'Never,' ground out Lenin.

Sir Leonard walked slowly towards him until the revolver was only a few inches from his head.

'I'll count to three,' he threatened, 'if, by the time I finish, you are still sitting there, I'll fire. One – two—'

The Russian's face once again went livid, and he rose hastily to his feet.

'Good,' commented Wallace. 'You, too, Vassiloff.' He had no difficulty with the Commissary. 'Now, gentlemen,' he said, turning to the other Russians at the table, 'the best thing you can do is to return to your homes. I give you my word that, if any attempt is made to arrest or in any way interfere with my companions and myself, Messieurs Lenin and Vassiloff will be shot. It would be easy enough, for instance, to telephone through to some town or village en route, and order us to be stopped by soldiers armed with rifles and so on, but directly such an attempt is made, you can prepare to go into mourning for these hostages. I hope I am quite understood.' He turned his eyes on the foreign delegates. 'If I may presume to advise you gentlemen,' he said, 'I suggest that you return to your own countries as soon as possible, and entirely forget why you came to Moscow. Believe me, it would be the wisest thing you could do.'

'Who are you?' asked Herr Paulus in a hoarse voice.

'Does that matter?' smiled Wallace.

He told Shannon to unlock the service door and, as soon as that was done, ordered Lenin and Vassiloff to move. They made a last attempt at resistance, urging, among other things, the necessity for warm coats and hats, but the revolvers, held so firmly by Shannon and his chief, proved effective silencers to all objections, and complete answers to every argument. Led by Shannon, and with Sir Leonard in the rear, the quartet passed out of the room followed by the dismayed looks of the men remaining at the table. The door was locked behind them, and they descended the stairs, walked along several passages, and emerged into a side street. In their progress they had been fortunate enough to avoid meeting a soul, which was the reason why Sir Leonard had chosen the back way. It was a dark night, and there were very few people about. Sending Shannon round to the front entrance to fetch the car, he stood guard over his prisoners. It was chilly and a slight rain was falling, a fact which did not conduce to a better frame of mind in the Russians. Presently a huge car turned the corner, and pulled up close to them. Wallace sighed his relief when he saw that it was a limousine.

'You won't want coats after all,' he observed cheerfully.

Assisted by Shannon and Cousins, he shepherded the hostages in, and got in after them. The little man's face was a mass of delighted wrinkles.

'Shall we keep the driver, sir?' he asked.

Wallace pondered the question for a moment.

'No,' he decided at last; 'it will be safer to leave him behind. Not knowing the country, we may be driven into a trap, if we trust to him. You and Shannon will have to take turns. Get us out of Moscow; then we'll study the map in my case, and—'

'I've already taken the liberty of doing that, sir,' interrupted Cousins. 'Where do you intend to make for?'

'Smolensk, Minsk and the Polish border,' promptly replied Sir Leonard. 'I don't want you to go through those towns, if it is possible to avoid them, but that's the general direction. How about petrol?'

'We've enough to take us a hundred and fifty miles. I daresay we can get some more long before that runs out.' He turned to the chauffeur, who was sitting in his seat looking rather puzzled. 'Come on, little brother,' he said in Russian, 'out you get.'

The man commenced to protest, whereupon Wallace stuck the muzzle of his revolver into Vassiloff's ribs.

'Tell him it is your command,' he said.

Reluctantly he was obeyed, and the driver, looking more puzzled than ever, climbed out of the car. Cousins promptly took his place, Shannon jumped inside and sat next to Sir Leonard, and they were off. They were a long time getting out of Moscow, as Cousins chose a circuitous route in order to avoid the main streets, but eventually they were through the suburbs heading west. Vassiloff and Lenin sat like graven images, their faces eloquently expressive of baffled rage. Opposite them, revolvers handy, were Wallace and Shannon. Hour after hour went by, scarcely a word was uttered, but neither of the Russians made any attempt to sleep. It was long after midnight when the car stopped by a petrol pump in the outskirts of Viazena. Cousins' face appeared at the window.

'If I can wake up these people, sir,' he remarked, 'I think we'd better take in ten gallons, and a couple of tins of oil.'

Wallace nodded. Assisted by Shannon, the little man succeeded in rousing the fellow in charge of the petrol station, and obtained the necessary supplies. Shannon drove, when the journey was resumed, and Cousins took his place inside. Sixty miles from Smolensk, a tyre burst. Luckily there were two spare wheels, and the exchange was quickly made. Sir Leonard decided to rest where they were, and he and his two companions took turns in guarding the Russians. At seven they continued on their way, stopping at a small village for breakfast. Lenin and Vassiloff were not permitted to leave the car for fear that the sight of the Russian Dictator would excite comment. At first he and the Commissary refused food, but apparently the sight of it was too much for their appetites, for after some time they fell to almost eagerly.

All day long they travelled fast, stopping only for meals, petrol, and occasionally, in deserted places, to enable the Russians to stretch their legs. A way was found along the north bank of the Dnieper which enabled them to avoid going through Smolensk. At nightfall they were almost two hundred miles beyond that city and very close to Minsk. There had been no further punctures, and not a vestige of engine trouble.

'We'll be over the border by eight in the morning, if we start early,' exulted Shannon, when they drew up for the night. 'By Jove! It'll be good to be in Poland.'

In his enthusiasm he spoke in English. Sir Leonard's warning look was too late to stop him, and Lenin and Vassiloff exchanged significant glances.

'We are dealing with Englishmen, it seems,' observed the latter.

'You are,' admitted Wallace. 'You will realise, therefore, what is likely to be the result of your latest effort to break the peace of the world and force your system of government on other nations.'

'I realise,' growled Lenin, 'that it is necessary you three should be prevented from leaving Russia. Your deaths will be more acceptable than ever now I know you are English.'

Wallace laughed.

'Considering the position in which you are placed at present,' he remarked, 'I must confess that I find your optimism most refreshing – and amusing.'

The night passed off quietly, each of the Englishmen in turn keeping watch as before. At daybreak the journey was resumed. Minsk was reached in half an hour, but, in endeavouring to make a wide circuit, Cousins, who was driving, lost his way, and it was over an hour before he struck the main road running to the frontier. After that, however, he went all out in an effort to make up for lost time. Then abruptly he drew up. Wondering what had happened, Wallace and Shannon looked out, and the sight that met their eyes caused them both to utter exclamations of astonishment and dismay. They were in the midst of a great military encampment. Ahead, and on both sides, as far as the eye could reach, were troops, guns, tanks and ammunition trains. There must have been thousands of men in the vicinity. Wallace looked hard at Lenin.

'Of course you knew of this,' he observed. 'It explains a lot. I have been wondering all along why no attempt whatever has been made to capture us and rescue you.'

A sneering smile appeared on Lenin's dark face.

'As you see,' he said, 'there was no need. Naturally, it was known that manoeuvres were being held here and, as soon as it was ascertained which direction you had taken, matters would be left in the capable hands of my colleague, Leon Trotsky, who would, of course, be informed by telegraph.'

'So Trotsky is here?' murmured Wallace. 'This is very

interesting.' He studied the expression of smug satisfaction on the other's face. 'I suppose you expect the tables to be turned now?'

Lenin shrugged his shoulders.

'Did you really think such a plan as yours would succeed?' he jeered.

'I certainly did – and do,' was the sharp reply.

Cousins opened the door and looked in.

'There is a company of men marching towards us along the road, sir,' he reported, 'and others are closing in on both sides.'

Sir Leonard sat deeply thoughtful for several seconds. Then he made up his mind.

'We are at a disadvantage inside,' he observed.

Although he spoke in English, Lenin understood. 'That is very true,' he chuckled, 'and so, my friend, I—'

Wallace ignored him.

'There's only one thing for it,' he said to Shannon. 'Lenin and I will travel on the roof until we are safely through. Bundle him up, will you? There's no time for ceremony.'

Grinning all over his face, Shannon grabbed the Russian Dictator, and hauled him struggling from the car. Vassiloff made an attempt to go to his leader's assistance, but the cold muzzle of Sir Leonard's revolver at his temple caused him to change his mind, and sink back into his seat. Shannon lifted Lenin over his head at the full stretch of his arms, stepped on the running-board, and deposited his burden on the roof as though he had been a sack of potatoes. Shouting execrations the Russian attempted to jump down, but Cousins was covering him with a revolver, and he desisted.

'Get inside, Shannon, and look after Vassiloff,' ordered Sir Leonard. 'Hold this for me, Cousins, while I climb on top.'

He handed his revolver to the little man and, with amazing celerity, considering that he had only one hand, drew himself on to the roof of the car, and sat down beside Lenin. Cousins handed him the revolver, and was directed to drive slowly on.

By this time the Russian troops had approached quite close and, seeing the car advancing, the officer in charge of those in front halted his men and entirely blocked the road. He held up his hand and, when within ten yards of him, Cousins, at a word from his chief, stopped the vehicle.

'You are my prisoners,' stated the officer in loud, ringing tones. 'It will be to your advantage to surrender quietly.'

'As you observe,' replied Sir Leonard in French, a language which he spoke much better than Russian, 'I have Monsieur Lenin up here with me. Any attempt to fire at me, or in any way interfere with us, will end in his death. I ask you, therefore, to draw your men aside, and let us pass.'

The young man looked astounded.

'You – you do not mean that it is your intention to – to murder Monsieur Lenin,' he stammered.

'Not murder,' protested Wallace; 'that is hardly a nice word, is it? It is my intention, however, to leave this country safely and, until we are across the border into Poland, Messieurs Lenin and Vassiloff remain with us as hostages. It would be easy enough for you to order us to be shot where we are, but before any of your bullets could reach me, mine will blow out Monsieur Lenin's brains. I hope that is quite clear.'

The officer stood indecisively swinging a revolver in his hand. He found the situation beyond him. His orders had been to take these men dead or alive, and rescue the Dictator and the Commissary. It was perfectly obvious, however, that a situation of stalemate prevailed. He dare not risk the life of the head of Soviet Russia; yet it was impossible either to kill or capture the man, who sat there defying him, without doing so. Impatiently he clicked his tongue.

'This is a ridiculous situation, sir,' he exclaimed. 'I advise you, for your own good, to surrender Messieurs Lenin and Vassiloff to me.'

Sir Leonard laughed.

'Don't be foolish,' he remonstrated. 'They will be returned to you undamaged and none the worse for their brief captivity directly we cross the frontier, not before. Of course it is in your power to kill us at once, if you are prepared to face Russia afterwards with the knowledge that you were also responsible for the deaths of my two prisoners. You may have an army behind you, but I hold the whip-hand. What do you propose to do?'

Probably very much to his relief, the officer was saved from the necessity of making a decision. The deep and impatient note of a motor car horn could be heard from the rear of his company, a message was passed along to him, and promptly he drew his men on one side. It was done so smartly that Wallace nodded approval. A military car appeared, and drove up to within a few yards. Two men emerged from the interior, one in the uniform of a general, the other in plain clothes. It was upon the latter that Wallace fixed his gaze.

'Have I the honour of addressing Monsieur Trotsky?' he asked.

'You have,' came the reply in harsh, staccato tones. 'How is it my orders have not been obeyed? Who are you, and why are you and my colleague Lenin sitting up there?'

Sir Leonard explained, taking care to keep his revolver within an inch or two of Lenin's head. When he had finished Trotsky's eyes narrowed, he drew his companion aside, and they spoke excitedly together. At length apparently they had decided what course to pursue. Trotsky turned and looked up at Wallace.

'Let Comrades Lenin and Vassiloff go,' he said, 'and you will receive safe-conduct to the border.'

Sir Leonard smilingly shook his head.

'I am sorry,' he replied, 'I cannot agree. I will not free either of my hostages until my companions and I are in Poland.'

'You will not accept my word that you will be allowed to pass?'

'I regret I cannot.'

Trotsky flushed with anger. For some moments he paced the road biting his nether lip; at length he shrugged his shoulders.

'Very well,' he snapped, 'you will be allowed to proceed.'

Lenin muttered something under his breath; then addressed Trotsky loudly:

'You know what the result will be?'

The War Minister of the Soviet Government once again shrugged his shoulders.

'Exactly, my friend Lenin,' he returned, 'but it cannot be helped, unless you are willing to give your life to prevent such vital information from reaching our enemies. If such a noble act is your intention,' he added, 'I will promise you that your assassins will be hanged immediately afterwards from the highest trees in the neighbourhood.'

Lenin's face went absolutely bloodless, and he shrank back. Trotsky smiled sarcastically, and gave orders to the officer in charge of the troops.

'I shall be obliged if you will go ahead, Monsieur Trotsky,' said Sir Leonard, 'in order that there can be no danger of our being molested.'

Trotsky and his companion entered their car, which was turned and driven back the way it had come. Cousins slipped in his gears, and followed close behind. As they passed through the ranks, the men looked curiously up at the two figures on the roof, Lenin clinging to his undignified perch as though afraid of falling, Wallace holding his revolver close to the head of the man who ruled Russia's millions. It was an unforgettable scene, and did irreparable damage to Lenin's prestige. From that time his authority began to wane. The encampment extended for five miles, and Sir Leonard whistled under his breath as he made a rough calculation of the probable number of men there under arms.

The car ahead stopped as soon as the boundary of the military lines was reached, and Cousins was waved on. Wallace saluted Trotsky as he passed, and received, in return, a perfunctory nod. Three miles farther on he and his prisoner descended from the roof of the car, and got inside. They had almost reached the frontier when an idea occurred to Sir Leonard, and he ordered Cousins to stop. Leaving Shannon to watch the Russians, he took the little man aside.

'It is almost certain,' he remarked, 'that the Polish authorities will have been notified of our coming, and asked to detain us as escaped political prisoners. Such an eventuality may possibly lead to our being handed over, and we must not risk a misfortune of that nature. We'll send Lenin and Vassiloff back in the car from here, hide until nightfall, then sneak over the frontier. Understand?'

'Yes, sir,' replied Cousins, 'but supposing neither Lenin nor Vassiloff can drive?'

'We'll have to get rid of them some other way, that's all.'

'I hope we do get rid of them,' murmured the little Secret

Service man. 'Personally I'd rather be hail fellow well met with a pack of hungry wolves than exist in the same country as these two. Why, the shape of Lenin's head is enough to—'

'What's the matter with his head?' demanded Wallace.

Cousins smiled and quoted:

'"For burglars, thieves and co., Indeed I'm no apologist, But I some years ago, Assisted a phrenologist".'

It turned out that both men could drive, and were only too relieved to get away. The Englishmen watched the car out of sight, after which they turned their steps southward for a few miles, until they found an ideal hiding place less than a hundred yards from the frontier. All the rest of the day they lay hidden, suffering the pangs of hunger and thirst rather than risk discovery. Wallace removed his disguise. The manoeuvres of two Russian aeroplanes interested them; it was obvious they had been sent to discover what had happened to the fugitives, possibly in response to a notification from the Polish authorities that they had not been seen. However, despite the fact that they flew very low and spent hours in the neighbourhood, Wallace and his companions escaped discovery. Late at night they crept across the border, and made their way to the railway line, where they were lucky enough to clamber onto a slowly moving goods train, and hide themselves under the tarpaulin of an empty wagon. The train reached Brest Litovsk early in the morning, and was shunted to a siding. Making certain that all was clear, the fugitives climbed out, and separately and cautiously walked to the station. Thence they travelled by different routes to Berlin where they again met and, without further precautions, continued their journey to England together.

Manning was the first man to meet them in London. He

explained that unluckily one of the men whom Beust had employed to keep watch and ward over Otto Kahn and his two companions had, at one time, been the recipient of a great favour at the hands of the secretary, and had thus been persuaded to help him to escape.

'Extraordinary!' exclaimed Sir Leonard. 'This is a very small world after all. Never mind; we've come through all right. The only man who really has a grouse is Lenin, and I shall not be surprised if he nurses it for the rest of his life. The information we have obtained will cause a sensation.'

It did.

CHAPTER SIX

A Greek Tragedy

Sir Leonard Wallace descended from the Orient Express at Constantinople, and looked round him as though he were expecting to be met but, before he had a chance of examining the crowd properly, he found himself surrounded by a shouting, importunate horde of baggage porters. The short, stout figure of Batty, his eyes registering horror, his snub nose looking more pugilistic than usual, fought its way through the throng, showering nautical maledictions on the heads of the men who dared to press round his employer.

'I think one porter will be sufficient, Batty,' observed Sir Leonard, as the round, red face of his confidential servant appeared at his side. 'We hardly want a hundred.'

'I'll fix the swabs, sir,' promised the ex-naval man. ''Ere, you,' he crooked his finger at a fellow, who looked somewhat less villainous than the rest, 'come with me, and get ready to take luggage aboard. The rest o' you up anchor. Now then, look smart about it.'

They may not have understood his language, but there was no mistaking his meaning, especially when he had knocked a few heads together. Never was a traveller arriving in the *Sublime Porte* so quickly rid of the unwelcome attentions of the railway 'bandits', as Sir Leonard Wallace. Batty, having satisfied himself, as he picturesquely put it, that decks were cleared, went off to find the luggage, taking the selected porter with him, and Wallace continued his scrutiny of the travellers, loungers, and people who had come to meet friends. Presently a tall, spare man, with pale face and dark eyes, threaded his way towards him, and raised his hat.

'Hallo, Winslow,' greeted Sir Leonard, 'I was beginning to think that you were allowing me to arrive unheralded and unsung. How is Sir George?'

'Desperately ill, sir,' was the solemn reply. 'He is not expected to live.'

Wallace stared at the attaché.

'Not expected to live?' he repeated. 'I had no idea it was as bad as that.'

'None of us had, sir, until a few hours ago. He seems to be in terrible agony now, and all the science of Dr Von Bernhardt fails to give him any relief.'

'This is terrible. We had better drive straight to the embassy.'

'I have a car waiting, if you'll follow me, sir.'

Batty arrived with the luggage, and was given his instructions; then Sir Leonard, accompanied by Captain Winslow, drove to the house of the British Minister. Without delay he was shown into the sick room, where he found the famous Viennese doctor, a nurse, and Lady Paterson standing silently by the bed, anxiously watching the patient. Although the door was opened and shut very quietly, it was heard, and the tall woman, whose husband lay dying, turned sharply, and looked questioningly at the newcomer. Recognising him she crossed the room towards him, and shook hands. Despite her fifty years Lady Paterson was still a beautiful woman, but now her face was lined and ravaged by sorrow. Wallace was shocked to note her pallor and the tragedy that showed in her eyes. Quietly and simply he expressed his sympathy.

'Is there no hope at all?' he asked.

She shook her head, and tears began to course down her cheeks. Stifling a sob, she sank into a chair, and covered her face with her hands. He looked at her compassionately; then turned to the doctor.

'We met once before,' he whispered. 'My name is Wallace.'

'I remember you, of course, Sir Leonard,' acknowledged the celebrated medical man in excellent English. 'This is a very bad business. He is sleeping now, but the end cannot be long delayed.'

'What is he suffering from?'

Dr Von Bernhardt looked cautiously round.

'I am not sure,' he murmured, 'but I suspect – powdered glass!'

'What?' In his astonishment and horror, Sir Leonard spoke rather louder than he had intended. 'Do you mean that?'

The doctor nodded.

'I am afraid there is but little doubt,' he remarked.

'Then he is the victim of foul play?'

'It certainly looks very much like it.'

'But who—?'

Von Bernhardt shrugged his shoulders.

'It is impossible for me to make a guess at the identity of the assassin,' he observed. 'But the peritoneum is perforated, and I am very nearly prepared to swear that powdered glass has caused the damage.'

'My God!' exclaimed Wallace. 'How perfectly ghastly! Poor beggar, what a death to die! Have you made any investigations, doctor?'

Von Bernhardt nodded.

'I arrived from Vienna, in response to an urgent message, yesterday morning. The doctor, who was in charge, described the symptoms, and powdered glass at once flashed into my mind. In the afternoon we together examined the food, cooking utensils, and in fact everywhere in the kitchen, but there was not one little trace of what we were looking for anywhere.'

Sir Leonard looked down at the deadly pale face of the dying Minister, and his heart was torn with pity. He had always known Sir George Paterson as a fine, healthy, robust man, who boasted of the fact that he had never had a day's illness in his life. It was a terrible tragedy to see him lying there dying, and to be unable to raise a hand to help him.

'Can nothing be done at all, doctor?' he asked. 'Would not an operation save him?'

'Impossible now,' replied the medical man. 'It might have been possible, if he had been operated upon within a few hours of swallowing the glass. Unfortunately it transpires that he was in pain for three days before he uttered a complaint; then two days more went by before I was sent for. I came at once, but what can I do after a week in such a case as this? The X-ray photographs show a badly punctured peritoneum – no operation could put that right.'

'Poor old Paterson,' muttered Wallace to himself, and there was an unaccustomed lump in his throat.

A telegram had arrived at Secret Service headquarters from the Minister stating that he was ill, and asking the Chief of the Intelligence Department to travel to Constantinople, as he had information to give, which he could not impart to anyone of lesser authority. The request had been so unusual that Sir Leonard had left for the *Sublime Porte* at once. The idea that Sir George Paterson was dying had never entered his head, and the knowledge had come as a great shock. In his mind he was already beginning to connect the two things. It looked very much as though Sir George was being murdered to prevent the information he possessed from being handed over to his government. Possibly the murderer had expected him to die before he could communicate with Great Britain. Sir Leonard looked anxiously at the sufferer, and it seemed to him that there was a change coming over his face. Was he too late? Would Sir George pass away before he could divulge the secret?

Dr Von Bernhardt bent over and said something to the nurse. She left the room and, after some minutes, returned with the embassy doctor, who had been snatching a brief rest. The two medical men held a brief consultation; then Von Bernhardt crossed the room to the door, beckoning to Wallace as he did so. Outside he took the Englishman by the arm, and they walked along the corridor together.

'I have asked Dr Lansbury to watch Sir George,' he remarked, 'while I have a chat with you. First of all I will ask you a question, which you will answer or not according to your discretion. Is there any trouble between Britain and Turkey?'

'None at all,' replied Sir Leonard promptly. 'Why?'

'Sir George sent for you obviously to impart something of importance to you. It is not unreasonable to suppose that he is dying because of the information he possesses. This is Turkey where a man's life is not weighed in the balance if, by living, he is likely to be dangerous. Thus my question.'

'How did you know Sir George had sent for me?' demanded Wallace.

Dr Von Bernhardt smiled.

'He told me so,' he confided. 'In fact he has several times asked for news of you today.'

Wallace frowned. If there were anything very important behind the Ambassador's request for his presence in Constantinople, it seemed rather injudicious to speak so openly of his expected arrival. Still one must not judge a sick man too harshly.

'You will naturally desire to get to the bottom of this crime,' went on the famous physician. 'Your difficulties will be immense if, as I suspect, it has been engineered by Turkey. I brought you out here to tell you of certain suspicions, which have formulated in my mind. Before Sir George was taken ill, his wife was suffering from a bad attack of malaria fever. The doctor, who attended her, is a well-known Turk, Hamid Bey by name. The nurse was the girl who is now looking after Sir George, and it was from her that I obtained the information which roused my suspicions. She told me that Hamid Bey was continually holding whispered conversations with Lady Paterson's Turkish maid, and that once she saw them both emerging from Sir George's private study as though they desired to avoid being seen. This may mean nothing, of course, but I pass it on to you for what it is worth.'

'Thanks, doctor. There may be a great deal in it. I wonder why Lady Paterson had the Turk in attendance on her. Where was Lansbury?'

'Ah, that again is curious. Dr Lansbury had been invited to spend a holiday at the estate of Ibrahim Pasha in Brussa, which as you know is sixty miles away in Asia Minor.'

'Strange,' commented Wallace, 'but, if there was a plot to entice Lansbury away and get Hamid Bey into the house, how on earth could anybody know that Lady Paterson was about to be taken ill with malaria?'

Von Bernhardt shrugged his shoulders.

'Germs,' he murmured pithily.

The nurse suddenly appeared at the bedroom door, and beckoned to them.

'He is awake,' she said, when they had hurried up to her, 'and I'm afraid—'

The doctor pushed by, and entered the room, closely followed by Sir Leonard. The Ambassador, his eyes wide open, was breathing painfully, but nevertheless managing to smile at his wife, who sat on the other side of the bed holding his hand. An expression of relief crossed his face when he recognised Wallace.

'Thank God you've come.' He spoke in so low a voice that he could hardly be heard.

'I'm very sorry to see you in this state, Paterson,' murmured Sir Leonard, 'but you'll soon be fit again.'

The Minister smiled wanly.

'Not in this world,' he whispered. 'My number's up, Wallace, and you know it as well as I do.'

Lady Paterson failed to stifle the sob that broke from her lips and, very tenderly, he patted her hand, and uttered words of comfort to her. At his request he and Wallace were left alone, and he commenced to tell the latter why he had sent for him.

'There is a gigantic plot brewing in—' a spasm of intense pain shook him from head to foot, and for some moments he was unable to speak. 'I shall – have to hurry – it seems,' he gasped at last, and actually forced a smile.

But a further and more prolonged paroxysm gripped him, and Wallace rose to call the doctors. Somehow, though, Sir George managed to find strength enough to cling to his friend's hand. His lips were moving painfully, and the Chief of the Secret Service bent down until his ear was close to the dying man's lips. At first he heard nothing; then came:

'Secret drawer – my wife's escritoire – all information – notebook.'

Sir Leonard nodded to show that he had heard, and called back the medical attendants. The Minister soon afterwards drifted into a state of unconsciousness from which he never recovered. He died three hours later.

Lady Paterson, who had risen from her sick-bed to look after her husband before she had fully recovered from her attack of malaria, was prostrated with grief. Dr Von Bernhardt feared a complete breakdown, and ordered her absolute quiet. The result was that Sir Leonard was unable to ask her about the secret drawer in her escritoire until two days later, when, having returned from the funeral, he was given permission to see her for a few minutes. In the meantime he had not been idle. He had questioned everybody in the embassy carefully, and at length, but had been unable to elicit anything in the nature of a clue from which he could form a theory. A post-mortem examination was held, and proved that Dr Von Bernhardt had been correct. Sir George Paterson had been killed by powdered glass. The police were informed, and commenced their investigations, but

Wallace preferred to work on his own and, therefore, conducted his inquiries privately.

Mustapha Kemal Pasha called in person to express his deep sympathy and abhorrence at the nature of the tragedy. Sir Leonard was very much impressed by the personality of the Turkish President, his undoubted sincerity and strength of character. He felt that he had seldom before met a man of such honest and statesmanlike qualities, and the conversation they had together left him feeling that Turkey was indeed fortunate to possess such a man at the head of affairs.

'This terrible crime has shaken me to the core, Sir Leonard,' he observed, as he was taking his departure. 'No stone will be left unturned to bring the murderer to justice. I hope and pray that he will not prove to be a Turk, but I very much fear that it will be so. It will be a great blot on the honour of my country, if he is.'

When he had gone, Sir Leonard had a talk with the nurse. It had been impossible to interview her before on account of her duties. She was a beautiful Armenian girl with dark flashing eyes, and was anxious to tell him all she knew. It was very little, however, and added nothing to what Von Bernhardt had already told him. As a result of their conversation he sent for Lady Paterson's Turkish maid. A scrutiny of her face, when she entered the room where he was awaiting her, left him with no personal suspicions against her. She certainly had not the appearance of a girl endeavouring to hide a guilty secret. He questioned her thoroughly, attempted to trap her, but she answered him with apparent honesty, and emerged from her ordeal triumphant, leaving him a very puzzled man when, at last, he dismissed her.

A meticulous search of the kitchens and domestic quarters,

a thorough cross-examination of the cook and his mate, only succeeded in increasing his perplexity. There was not a single fact or thread to suggest a line of inquiry, the story of the nurse concerning the Turkish doctor and the maid being far too nebulous to be of any real help. There was nothing for it but to wait until he could obtain Lady Paterson's permission to go to her escritoire and open the secret drawer. When eventually he saw her, and was told how to find the hidden receptacle and open it, he hastened to the writing-desk in her boudoir, with a sense of great relief. At last he would be able to place his hands on something definite, perhaps even discover the identity of the assassin. Following the instructions given him he had no difficulty in locating the drawer. It was rather clever of old Paterson to think of hiding the precious notebook in his wife's escritoire. Nobody would think of searching there for it. He opened the drawer and looked in. An exclamation of baffled annoyance escaped him. It was empty!

He subjected the writing-table to a very thorough search, but it was of no use. The notebook had gone. He went out into the garden and, finding a secluded spot, sat down on a stone seat to think things over. This looked like being a problem beyond his powers to solve. If he had only had an inkling of the nature of the information Sir George had wished to impart to him, there would have been something to go upon. It should not have been very difficult to trace the murderer once he knew something of the story the Ambassador had been so anxious to relate to him. As it was he would be compelled to continue what seemed a hopeless search for the assassin and, if he were lucky enough to find the man, work on from that point in an effort to discover what had become of the notebook. He smiled grimly to himself, as he filled and lit his pipe.

'I certainly seem to have struck the very deuce of a riddle,' he murmured.

He had a further interview with Lady Paterson, and told her of his failure to find anything in the secret drawer. She was unable to help him, had not even known that Sir George had hidden a notebook in the escritoire.

'Somebody must have watched him put it there,' she said, 'and extracted it.'

'Obviously,' nodded Sir Leonard, 'but who? Did he ever mention to you, or hint in any way, that he possessed important intelligence which he intended passing on to the government?'

She shook her head and, noticing that any mention of her husband only distressed her, he forbore from questioning her further, and departed in search of Captain Winslow. The latter was engaged in his office, and looked up eagerly as Wallace entered.

'Any news, sir?' he asked.

'Not a thing,' was the reply. 'In fact the mystery deepens. I know I've put you through it pretty badly with my questions, but I've one more to ask. During the last two or three weeks did Sir George receive any letters or messages, apart from his private correspondence, which caused him any excitement or concern, the contents of which he kept secret from you?'

'Not that I know of,' returned Winslow, 'but of course, it would be difficult to say. Letters addressed to him personally were never handed to me or Wainwright unless they turned out to concern matters relating to the embassy.'

'If a letter, such as I have in my mind, did arrive, I should imagine it would be merely addressed to the British Ambassador or Minister.'

'In that case,' declared Winslow, 'Sir George would not have opened it – it would have been left to us.'

'That's natural of course,' nodded Wallace. 'Did he hold any private interviews during the period I have mentioned – I mean with people of whom you had no knowledge?'

The attaché thought deeply for several seconds; then:

'I can remember two,' he said. 'One was with a woman dressed in black and heavily veiled; the other was with a rather greasy-looking Greek.'

'How did they succeed in obtaining interviews?'

'I don't know. Wainwright and Gardener probably will.' He rang a bell and a clerk promptly entered the room. 'Ask Mr Wainwright to come into my office.'

A young man with the build of an athlete made his appearance.

'Do you remember that veiled woman and the Greek who had interviews with the chief about ten days ago?' asked Winslow.

'Yes,' returned Wainwright. 'They came on the same day.'

'Sir Leonard wants to know how they obtained interviews.'

'The woman sent in a cryptic message to the effect that she desired to throw herself on Sir George's mercy, because she understood all Englishmen were just and merciful. She would give no name, but Sir George was so interested that he saw her.'

'What nationality was she?' asked Wallace.

'I couldn't say, sir,' returned the young man. 'She spoke in French without any trace of accent, as far as I could judge, but she had such a thick veil over her face that it was impossible to see her features.'

'Do you think she was young?'

'Very, I should imagine.'

'And the man?'

'Oh, I can tell you more about him, sir. He was a Greek of the minor official class; tall, thin and oily. His name was Moropoulos, and he sent in a sealed letter to his Excellency, who saw him at once.'

'Ah! That sounds interesting.' He smiled at Winslow. 'So there was a letter after all,' he observed. 'Sir George said nothing to either of you concerning these people? You have no idea who they were, or what their business was?'

'None at all,' replied both men.

'Another cul-de-sac,' groaned Wallace. 'If we could only trace one or both, we might begin to obtain results. I wonder what became of that letter the Greek handed in? I've searched through all Sir George's correspondence very carefully, but nothing of any interest whatever was found, certainly nothing signed by a man calling himself Moropoulos. By Jove!' he exclaimed suddenly. 'Can either of you tell me what kind of clothing Sir George was wearing on that day?'

They stared at him curiously; then consulted each other.

'I believe he had on a brown suit,' said Winslow, 'but I couldn't be sure.'

'It wasn't a light suit that might have gone to the laundry?'

'No; it's been too cold lately for that sort of thing.'

'It *was* a brown suit,' broke in Wainwright. 'I remember now noticing that the Greek wore one of a similar shade.'

Sir Leonard left them, and ascended to the late Ambassador's dressing room. The valet was busy there packing away clothing and other articles. He had been devoted to his late master, and there was suspicious moisture in his eyes as he carefully folded the garments. He greeted Wallace respectfully, but without much interest.

'How many brown suits had Sir George?' asked the latter.

'Only one, sir,' was the reply. 'It was a colour Sir George didn't care for much.'

'May I see it?'

The valet went to a hanging-cupboard and, taking out the suit, placed it on the back of a chair. Sir Leonard picked up the jacket, and felt through the pockets.

'I'm afraid you won't find anything in the pockets, sir,' observed the man. 'It was my habit to remove everything when my master changed his clothing.'

'What did you do with the things you found?'

'Put them back, if I thought they were wanted, otherwise locked them up in that drawer over there. Sir George would look through it every now and then, and destroy any old letters or notes he didn't want.'

The mention of letters interested Sir Leonard. He had assured himself that there was nothing in the pockets of the brown suit, and now walked across to the drawer indicated.

'Is there anything in it?' he asked.

'Yes, sir; I haven't cleared it out yet.'

The valet unlocked it, and stood aside watching the Chief of the Secret Service as he searched through the conglomeration of articles within. There were several old letters, all of which he put on one side until he had finished examining the other things. Then he took them up one by one, and went through them. The first two were of no interest whatever, but the third drew from him a muttered exclamation of satisfaction. It was a note in French from a man signing himself Zeno Moropoulos, requesting an interview. The final paragraph caused Sir Leonard to emit a sigh of relief.

I have a most important communication to divulge to your Excellency. If you cannot see me now, will you let me know at what time I can call again. I am living temporarily at the Orient Hotel in the Grand Rue de Pera.

He put the note in his pocket and continued his inspection of the others, but none of them were of importance.

'How is it these were not destroyed?' he asked.

'I put them there only a day or two before Sir George was taken ill, sir. Is there anything else you wish to see?'

'No; I don't think so; at least, not just now.'

He sent for one of the embassy cars, and was driven to the Orient Hotel. There a partial disappointment awaited him. Moropoulos had left, but, although he had given no address for letters to be forwarded, the clerk was able to inform Sir Leonard that the Greek had gone to live with a compatriot, who kept a café in Galata. Writing down the address, Wallace thanked the man, and returned to the embassy. It was beginning to get dark by that time and, as he had had a certain amount of experience of the side streets of Constantinople at night, he determined to take Batty with him to Georgiadi's café. Two are a great deal safer than one. Most of the streets of Constantinople, with the exception of the Grand Rue de Pera, are very badly lighted and, after dark, are dangerous for wayfarers who look in any way affluent. Robbery, sometimes death, skulks in the shadows, and the watchmen with their long wooden staffs are often worse than useless. They are more picturesque than efficient. Under the wise and able guidance of Mustapha Kemal Pasha, conditions are daily improving, but it will be a long time before the inhabitants of the *Sublime Porte* are able to walk anywhere in the city without fear of molestation. Sir Leonard knew this and, though he had no fear of attack, saw no sense in taking needless risks.

Batty enjoyed the trip. He had never been to Constantinople before, though he had been close to it during the War, when he had been on the ill-fated *Irresistible* in the Dardanelles. Since his arrival in the Turkish city he had paid a visit to St Sophia, been rather awed by the magnificence of the distant views, but disgusted by the sordidness which disclosed itself on closer inspection.

They had no difficulty in finding Georgiadi's café. It was in a street which seemed devoted to cafés, pawnshops, and bars, where sailors of many nations congregated, and vendors of all kinds of wares crowded the sidewalks. The place itself possessed a kind of tawdry brilliance, and was redolent of cooking, garlic rising triumphant over the other odours. Sir Leonard sent for the proprietor, and a little fat man in a greasy travesty of full evening dress hurried up. His eyes glinted as they took in the spare, smartly-dressed figure. With a great effort he bowed almost double.

'Good night, sare,' he commenced in laboured English. 'I come at your service.'

Sir Leonard smiled.

'I wish to see Mr Moropoulos,' he announced.

An expression very much like fear appeared on the fat man's face, to be replaced, with an effort, by a forced look of surprise, which did not deceive Wallace.

'Who is it zis Moropoulos?' asked the Greek.

'Mr Georgiadi,' returned the Englishman in uncompromising tones, 'I am a busy man, and certainly have no time to waste in mummery. I understand Moropoulos is here. I am from the British Embassy, and I wish to see him – at once if possible.'

A change came over the little man's attitude. He looked round mysteriously.

'I think a private room, yes?' he inquired.

'A private room by all means,' responded Sir Leonard.

He and Batty were taken through the main restaurant, up a flight of stairs, and along a corridor which had numbered doors on either side. They were ushered into one of these, a small, barely furnished room, the chief articles it contained being a dining-table, a couple of cane chairs, and a couch. Batty looked at the couch and grinned.

'I will Moropoulos send,' announced the Greek.

He bowed again, went out, and closed the door behind him. Some minutes went by then a tall, thin man entered almost furtively. He stood looking at Sir Leonard, as though in a state of indecision, until beckoned forward and told to take a seat. He was an unpleasant-looking person with black shiny hair, small pig-like eyes, and several days' growth of beard on his jowl.

'Your name is Moropoulos?' began the Englishman.

The Greek looked uneasily round, but did not answer until Wallace told Batty to stand outside the door to prevent the possibility of eavesdroppers; then he nodded his head.

'I speak not the English well,' he remarked.

'We shall speak in French then,' decided Sir Leonard in that language. 'I have come from the British Embassy in order to find out what passed between you and Sir George Paterson. My name is Wallace, I am a high official of the English Foreign Office, and you can speak quite openly to me.'

A cunning gleam came into the fellow's eyes.

'How am I to know you are who you say you are?' he asked.

'If I were not,' retorted Sir Leonard, 'would I be here now? Sir George sent to England for me obviously to impart some very important information to me. I arrived to find him dying, and too late to receive that information. I am convinced that he was murdered to prevent him passing on a statement which you made to him privately.'

The Greek's face went a sickly yellow.

'No, no,' he protested vehemently; 'that cannot be. Nobody knew that – that I told the English Ambassador – what I told him. Nobody ever knew that I possessed the knowledge.'

'What was it?'

There was a long pause, during which Moropoulos sat twisting and untwisting his hands, obviously prey to a mixture of fear and irresolution. At length he shook his head.

'Monsieur,' he said, 'I cannot tell you – I dare not.'

'Come, come,' protested Wallace. 'If you can tell Sir George, you can tell me.'

'No,' he shook his head, as though he had definitely made up his mind. 'It is better that the secret should die with Sir George Paterson. I can tell you nothing.'

Sir Leonard regarded him thoughtfully.

'I presume from that,' he observed coldly, 'that you were paid by Sir George for your information, and that you expect another payment from me before you will open your lips.'

The Greek protested, but an avaricious gleam came into his eyes, which the Englishman did not fail to notice.

'How much?' he demanded.

But Moropoulos continued to express his intention not to speak.

'Look here,' persisted Sir Leonard, 'this attitude won't do, my man. It is obvious you told Sir George Paterson something which he considered important enough to pass on to his government. Will you come to the embassy and tell me there? That will convince you that I have a right to know what it is.'

'I do not doubt your right, Monsieur. But I made a mistake – I should not have told the Ambassador. It is well that the secret has gone to the grave with him.'

'The secret has not gone to the grave with him,' returned Wallace deliberately. 'He wrote it down in a notebook which he hid away. That notebook has been stolen from the embassy.'

The Greek received the news with stark, unadulterated terror, and commenced to babble unintelligible things. Sir Leonard took no notice of his consternation.

'It is quite likely,' he went on, 'that, after you had spoken to the Ambassador, you repented of doing so, and it was through you that the book was stolen. As far as I know, you may even have had a hand in his death. What is to prevent my handing you over to the authorities?'

Expecting that such a remark would complete the fellow's discomfiture, Wallace was surprised to observe a look almost of relief come into his face.

'I would at least be safe from vengeance then,' he murmured.

There came a sudden tumult at the door, which was flung violently open. Batty staggered backwards into the room fighting desperately to keep out three masked men, who were forcing him before them. At once Wallace was on his feet staring into the muzzle of a revolver pointed at him by the tallest of the three. Batty's efforts were brought to an end by the sight of another weapon held within an inch or so of his head by the second man to enter.

'It is a pity there was so much noise,' observed the tall man coolly, in perfect English, 'but we had no desire to kill your servant.'

He signed to one of his companions, who closed and locked the door.

'Who are you?' demanded Wallace.

'There would be no object in wearing masks,' was the rejoinder, 'if I were to tell you that. From our information we know that you are an official of the British Government who came out here at the request of the British Ambassador. He intended giving you certain information which he had received from that man there.' He nodded towards Moropoulos, who was cowering in abject fear in his chair, his face the colour of chalk. 'We have no quarrel with the British,' went on the masked man; 'nevertheless we are glad that Sir George Paterson died.'

'You then were responsible for his death?' accused Sir Leonard sternly.

'By no means,' was the reply. 'It was, from our point of view, a lucky event which prevented vital information from being made public. He was watched, however, from the time he interviewed this man, Zeno Moropoulos, until he went to his deathbed. We thus assured ourselves that he had not passed on the intelligence. He was seen to make notes in a book, which he hid away in a secret drawer. We procured that book, but it has nothing in it of the least interest to us.' He withdrew a small volume from a pocket, and threw it across the room to Wallace. 'Perhaps you will be good enough to return it to the British Embassy,' was his surprising request. 'It may be of use there.'

Sir Leonard, his pulse throbbing a little quicker than usual, picked up the book, and put it in his pocket.

'May I know,' he asked sarcastically, 'to what I owe the honour of this visit?'

The tall man nodded.

'We have come for the traitor Moropoulos,' he declared, and there was such a timbre of menace in his voice, that a shrill cry of terror broke from the bloodless lips of the Greek. 'At first, sir,' went on the masked stranger, taking no notice of the agitation of Moropoulos, 'we felt that Sir George Paterson must have told you everything before his death, and you have been under surveillance. The fact that you traced Zeno Moropoulos to this café proved, however, that the British Ambassador died before he was able to pass on his knowledge. There again we were lucky. You have learnt nothing here, for we have been listening in the next room. There is little doubt that Moropoulos would eventually have succumbed to temptation. He claimed one hundred thousand pounds from your Ambassador, to be paid in a fortnight, and if—'

The Greek broke into terror-stricken and vehement protestations, which died away to a whimper as the speaker's revolver was turned on him. A string of epithets in Greek was poured on his head, and he cowered in his chair more abjectly than before.

'If you had nothing to do with Sir George Paterson's death,' interposed Sir Leonard; 'then who is responsible for the dastardly crime?'

'I cannot say,' replied the man. 'It is a mystery to me.'

He turned again to Moropoulos, and ordered him to stand up. Shakily the latter did so; then suddenly threw himself on his knees before Wallace.

'Save me!' he pleaded, 'save me!'

At a word from the leader he was jerked to his feet by the third man, who had hitherto been regarding the proceedings with a kind of aloof interest.

'What are you going to do with that man?' demanded Sir Leonard.

There came another signal; then, before either of the Englishmen could make a movement or even cry out, so rapidly was it done, the third man had drawn a long knife, and stabbed Moropoulos between the shoulder blades. With a choking sob the Greek pitched headlong to the floor and lay still. Sir Leonard gave a cry of horror and, unmindful of the revolver which still threatened him, knelt down and turned the man over. He was quite dead and, stumbling to his feet, the Englishman gave vent to the shocked anger which filled him. Batty, his usually rubicund face white and drawn, was leaning against the wall staring down at the body of the man lying almost at his feet.

The leader of the masked men stood listening to Wallace's denunciations with his lips curved in a smile.

'You do not understand,' he remarked when his accuser paused. 'That carrion deserved death. He was worse than Judas, for he was betraying not one man but a whole people, and the result would have been unheard of misery, degradation and suffering for the country that gave him birth. Believe me, sir,' he added earnestly, 'we are not assassins. The deed we have committed was done for our country's good, and Moropoulos has died in a manner far too merciful for him.'

'Then you are Greeks?' said Sir Leonard quietly.

'Exactly,' acknowledged the tall man. 'Now that our work in Constantinople is finished, we return to our country at once. You will inform the Turkish police of this apparent crime, but it will be a waste of time. Neither my companions nor I will ever be traced, and no inquiries in Greece will bring to light anything of interest regarding us. The secret which I have saved from falling into the hands of your government can never be made public now. You may think that in the book I have returned to you it may still be found – perhaps was written in invisible ink – but I assure you it is not so. Every page has been submitted to a most careful test. As I have said before, I have the greatest respect for your country, but the secret in the hands of Great Britain, no matter how good British intentions may have been, would have meant ruin, utter and complete, to Greece. We will now relieve you of our company. I am sorry that circumstances compel us to lock you and your servant in this room with that body, but we must safeguard ourselves. If I may presume to advise you, I would suggest that you leave the disposal of the body to Georgiadi. Such a course will save you from unpleasantness, and from becoming mixed up in an unsavoury inquiry that will lead nowhere.'

'Then Georgiadi is an accessory?' observed Wallace sharply.

The masked man shook his head.

'By no means,' he replied, 'he is merely a Greek café proprietor who still retains enough love for country to know that his house has been the scene of an act of absolute justice. I bid you farewell, sir.'

The door was quietly opened and, one by one, the masked men slipped through, the leader going last, and keeping his revolver levelled at Sir Leonard until he was outside, when the door was slammed and locked. Batty gave a sigh of relief and looked at his employer.

'Swab my decks!' he exclaimed feelingly.

Instead of creating a din in order to bring someone to their rescue, Sir Leonard sat in a chair, and eyed the body of Moropoulos reflectively.

'I think he is right,' he murmured almost to himself. 'No good can come of getting mixed up in an inquiry by the Turkish police. It might place us in a damnably awkward position.'

He lapsed into silence, and Batty stood for some moments watching him before venturing to speak. At last:

'Shall I give an 'ail, sir?' he asked.

'No,' decided Wallace. 'I daresay we shall be released by the proprietor in a few minutes. It would be easy enough to smash open that door, if we wanted to start a hullaballoo, but we don't. You and I are not going to talk about this murder, Batty.'

'Aye, aye, sir,' returned the ex-seaman. He did not understand, but what his master said was law to him.

Sir Leonard knelt down, and searched the dead man's pockets. There was nothing of interest in them except a large roll of notes, and an official-looking letter written in Greek. He was thus engaged, when they heard the key turn in the lock and Georgiadi came slowly in. His face was ghastly, and he appeared to be in the grip of a bad attack of ague, for he was trembling violently. Wallace rose to his feet, and pointed to the corpse.

'You knew?' he asked.

'Yes, sare,' the Greek stuttered, 'I – I know.'

'Translate this for me.' He held the letter in front of the other's eyes.

Georgiadi read it almost eagerly; then:

'It say,' he explained, 'that him Zeno Moropoulos is discharge from him duties by government wiz no pension because of him doing bad tings.'

'What bad things?'

'Money stealing and information of secret giving.'

'As I thought,' nodded Wallace putting the letter in his pocket. 'Come on, Batty, we'll go.'

The fat little Greek stared at him unbelievingly, and gradually a look of hope dawned in his eyes.

'You not – you not p'leece telling?' he stammered.

Wallace shook his head.

'No,' he replied. 'You can hush the matter up if you like.'

'Oh, sare,' cried Georgiadi. 'I tank you wiz my 'eart.'

'How will you dispose of the body?'

'Oh, zat very easy,' declared the little man.

'I suppose it is – in Constantinople,' observed Sir Leonard drily. 'Are you disposed to tell me who were the three masked men?'

The Greek shrugged his shoulders.

'I not know,' he stated. 'Zey big mens my country, zat I know, for zey show me somet'ing I cannot – what is it you say?'

'Disregard?'

'Ah, yes, disregard. But who zey are I not know.'

Sir Leonard nodded and, with a sigh, passed out of the room with Batty. Georgiadi followed, carefully locking the door and putting the key in his pocket. He escorted the Englishmen down the stairs, through the restaurant, which was now nearly full of a heterogeneous collection of customers, and stood bowing low at the entrance until they drove away.

Back in the embassy Wallace went to his room, and, taking the notebook from his pocket, commenced to examine it with great care. It was half full of jottings on various matters relative to administration, with a few notes concerning certain affairs in which Sir George had taken a prominent part or been interested. One of these was in regard to a split in the Turkish Nationalist party in which he had been of assistance to Mustapha Kemal Pasha, the other a plot by Osmanians to replace the Sultan on the throne. Owing to certain information which he had received, Sir George had apparently been instrumental in placing facts before the President which had led to a great number of arrests. But concerning the business which had brought Wallace to Constantinople, and a memorandum of which the Ambassador, on the point of death, had whispered was in the notebook, there was not a sign. Every page was subjected to a searching test, but it was obvious that nothing had been written in invisible ink. Wallace was not disappointed. He knew very well that the masked man would never have returned the book, if he had imagined there was the slightest possibility of the information, he and his companions considered so vital to Greece, being contained therein. Yet the dying Ambassador had definitely stated that the intelligence was written in the notebook. It was a great problem, and Sir Leonard in perplexity ran his fingers through his hair until it stood almost on end.

Suddenly he whistled, and bent once more to examine the little volume. Sir George had *not* said the information was *written* in the book. He had merely stated that it was in it. In his eagerness he fumbled owing to the fact that he had only one hand to use, but he removed all the contents, and laid them on the desk before him. Like all diaries of the same type the book had pockets at each end. In these were a few stamps and half a dozen banknotes of small denomination. Wallace carefully slit open the covers, but nothing came to light. Then he examined the banknotes, subjecting them to the tests for invisible ink. He was rewarded almost at once, for a mass of tiny writing came to view. The Greek emissaries had, after all, blundered. Whoever had watched Sir George had not been near enough to see that he had been writing on the banknotes, and not in the book. In consequence they had not examined the former, and had come to the conclusion that whatever the Ambassador had written did not concern them.

Wallace locked all the doors of his apartments; then sitting again at the desk began to wade through the collection of miniature words on the notes. As he read a look of intense interest came into his face to be gradually replaced by a grim frown. When he had finished a long drawn whistle pursed his lips, and he sat gazing before him as though in his mind was the vision of terrible things. Once again he looked down and read the last few lines:

I have asked you to come out here specially in order that you and I can consider the whole thing together. What is wrong with me I don't know, but I feel I am going to die, and this is the only way I can think of to safeguard this terrible news. You will do what you think best, Wallace, but I consider it is not a matter in which Great Britain should meddle. In my opinion nothing must ever be known. Greece will cease to exist, if the slightest inkling of this ever goes beyond your lips and mine. Moropoulos should be handed over to his country.

'You are quite right, Paterson,' murmured Sir Leonard, as he folded up the banknotes, and put them away in his own pocket-book, 'nothing of this must be divulged. You are dead; Moropoulos is dead; I will never report it. But this isn't the reason for your death – of that I'll swear.'

Wallace went to bed very thoughtfully that night.

He was up early the next morning, and spent an hour pacing the garden before breakfast. Directly after that meal he went to his rooms, and again examined the notebook, reading through carefully everything that had been jotted down by Sir George Paterson. The result of his scrutiny was that he ordered a car, and was driven to the residence of the President. He was with Mustapha Kemal Pasha for a long time, during which he learnt the names of all the leaders concerned in the recent attempt to bring back the Sultan to Turkey, and also those of their families, relatives and, in a good many cases, their friends. On his return to the embassy, he once again locked himself in his rooms, and studied the list of names and addresses he had brought with him. One by one he eliminated all but those of three men, who had been executed, and their connections. Very little was known about one, but the other two had been men of high repute and good family. Having classified the list, he sent for the Chief of Police and asked him to cause investigations to be made concerning the antecedents of the various people whose names he had written on a slip of paper.

'I should like you, if you can,' he added, 'to trace their movements from the time their relatives were arrested.'

The dark-faced official glanced at him astutely, and nodded his head.

'You think then,' he observed, 'that Sir George Paterson's death was a matter of revenge.'

'It may have been,' admitted Wallace. 'In any case it is an eventuality that cannot be overlooked. Have your investigations given you a clue of any kind?'

'Not a thing,' replied the Turk. 'At first I thought that such a crime must have been committed by somebody living inside the house, but, despite a very rigid examination of everybody employed here, and a careful search of all the rooms, there was nothing to cause the vaguest suspicion of anyone. Sir George was very popular with all in this household, and nobody had any motive either of revenge or gain to murder him. There is one thing, however, and it is perhaps ridiculous, but I have neither questioned Lady Paterson nor searched her suite of rooms. Is it possible, do you think, Monsieur, that she can have been responsible for the death of her husband?'

'Absurd,' returned Sir Leonard at once. 'Such a theory is out of the question altogether.'

'I expected you to say that, but you must admit that it is not impossible, though it may be improbable. Wives have been known to kill their husbands before.'

'In this case it is not only improbable but impossible as well,' declared Wallace with decision. 'I have known both Sir George and Lady Paterson for several years and, I can assure you, they were an extremely devoted couple.'

Hakim Pasha shrugged his shoulders, and rose to his feet.

'I must thank you,' he remarked, 'for the suggestion of this new line of inquiry.' He tapped the list of names he held in his hand. 'It is very likely that from among these people will be found the murderer. I will let you know directly there is anything to report.'

When he had departed, Sir Leonard went down to Winslow's office, and endeavoured to learn something more concerning the mysterious veiled lady, but nobody was able to give him any further information. Afterwards he sought an interview with Lady Paterson, and was relieved when told that she was well enough to see him. He found her lying on a couch in her beautiful boudoir overlooking the Bosphorus. She looked very frail and ill, but greeted him warmly. Her maid and the nurse were in attendance on her, but were dismissed as soon as Sir Leonard was announced. The latter was not in uniform and, on inquiry, Wallace learnt that she was leaving that day as the doctor had decided there was no longer any need for a nurse.

'I don't think he is very wise,' opined Sir Leonard. 'You look as though a nurse is necessary.'

She smiled wanly.

'I have my maid,' she reminded him, 'and an English girl is on her way out with my sister to escort me home as soon as Dr Lansbury thinks I am fit enough to travel. Did you find George's notebook?'

'Yes,' he told her, 'but there was nothing written in it of any great importance.' The prevarication was necessary he considered and, to prevent her asking further questions, he changed the subject. 'Do you trust your Turkish maid?' he demanded.

'Of course, why?'

He told her what Dr Von Bernhardt had said, and questioned her closely concerning Hamid Bey. Lady Paterson was obviously interested in the disclosure, but refused to suspect the Turkish doctor or the maid.

'I am convinced they had nothing to do with George's death,' she declared.

'I am not so sure,' returned Wallace seriously. 'Your husband, I am inclined to believe, made some enemies when he passed on information to the Turkish Government concerning the royalist plot. It is quite likely that Hamid Bey was a member of the Osmanian party. At any rate I have caused investigations to be made concerning him.'

'They will prove fruitless,' she replied confidently. 'Dr Hamid is a man of absolute honour and integrity, I am sure.'

He shrugged his shoulders, and let the matter drop.

'Did Paterson tell you about the mysterious veiled lady who called to see him?' he asked.

'Yes,' she nodded, 'she wanted him to intercede on behalf of her brother, who had been condemned to five years' imprisonment for plotting against the government.'

'Ah! This is interesting. Who was she?'

'She had asked him not to divulge her name and, therefore, I did not press the matter.'

'Did Sir George tell you anything else about her?'

'No; except that he felt very sorry for her, and informed her that he could not interfere.'

'You don't know the brother's name?'

She shook her head.

'All I know,' she informed him, 'is that he was tried and sentenced to five years' imprisonment.'

Sir Leonard rose to his feet.

'It looks,' he observed, 'as though I shall have to reclassify my list. It should not be difficult to trace him and, once I know his name, I shall find the lady.'

'Then you think she had something to do with my husband's death?' asked Lady Paterson.

'It is quite likely,' nodded Wallace, and left her.

He met the nurse on the stairs, and had a short conversation with her. She looked more beautiful than ever dressed, as she was, in a simple voile frock. Even a somewhat ugly necklace of amber beads failed to detract from her loveliness, and he regarded her with the approval of a fastidious male. The Turkish maid walked quietly by as they were chatting, and it seemed to Sir Leonard that she glanced at him rather furtively.

'I do not like that girl,' announced the nurse, when the maid was out of ear-shot. 'I think she could tell quite a lot about the death of Sir George Paterson.'

Wallace nodded thoughtfully, and continued his descent of the stairs. In his sitting room he lit a pipe and, throwing himself into an armchair, gave himself up to thought. He remained as he was for some time; then rose and perused, once again, his list of names. Apparently none of them interested him much, for he quickly put down the paper, and began to pace the room. Suddenly he seemed to reach a decision. Knocking out the ashes of his pipe, he placed it on a table, and leaving the room, made his way quietly up the stairs. He paused outside Lady Paterson's apartments and, calculating where her bedroom was, walked to the door. He was about to bend down and look through the keyhole when he heard the sound of steps from within, and had only time to hide in a curtained alcove before the maid emerged from the room, and walked away along the corridor.

Directly she was out of sight he left his hiding place and, entering the bedroom, closed and locked the door behind him. There was another door communicating with the boudoir and, very quietly, he crept towards it and locked it without a sound. Then commenced a careful search. Having a pretty shrewd idea what it was he expected to find, Sir Leonard did not waste time in examining unlikely places. The result was that hardly ten minutes had passed before, climbing on a chair and exploring the top of a large hanging wardrobe; he found a small paper parcel. Lifting it down he opened it, drawing in his breath with a sharp hiss as his eyes took note of the contents. Rolling it up again, he pushed it under his jacket and, crossing to the boudoir door, silently unlocked it. A moment later he was gazing cautiously out into the corridor. There was nobody about, and he was able to return to his apartments without being seen. There he sat down to make a thorough examination of his find. A few minutes later he was talking on the telephone to the Chief of Police.

After tea Sir Leonard sat for a considerable time with Lady Paterson. She found his presence very comforting and, under the influence of his conversation, began to look much brighter. He was present at a pleasing little ceremony when she bade farewell to the nurse who had cared for her husband and herself so assiduously, and handed the girl a valuable present as a mark of her esteem. Sir Leonard opened the door of the boudoir for the beautiful Armenian to pass through, and she thanked him with a little smile. Then both of them received a surprise. Standing in the shadows of the corridor, and close to the door, was a tall, handsome Turk of early middle-age. He bowed to them.

'Oh!' cried the girl. 'It is Dr Hamid Bey.'

He smiled.

'I have come to pay my respects to Lady Paterson,' he announced. 'May I enter?'

Wallace stood aside, and allowed him to pass.

'I hope you succeed in finding the murderer, Monsieur,' murmured the nurse.

'I think I can safely say, Mademoiselle,' Sir Leonard assured her, 'that I am confident of doing so very shortly.'

'I am so glad,' she whispered. 'It will be some satisfaction for m'lady that her husband has been avenged.'

She nodded brightly and passed on. Wallace returned to Lady Paterson, who was engaged in quite animated conversation with

Dr Hamid Bey. He was introduced to the Turk who, after a short while, took his leave. He had been gone about five minutes when there came the sound of a sudden commotion from the bedroom. At once Sir Leonard was on his feet.

'Don't be alarmed!' he reassured Lady Paterson. 'It is nothing.'

Crossing the room quickly he passed into the bedroom, closing the door behind him. A dramatic sight met his eyes. The Chief of Police and two subordinates were dragging a struggling, white-faced woman from a chair, placed by the large wardrobe, on which she had been standing. *It was the Armenian nurse.*

'I have kept my word you see, Mademoiselle,' remarked Wallace quietly. 'I have found the murderer. The parcel for which you were searching is below.'

She suddenly became nerveless, and collapsed into her captors' arms.

'Take her down to my apartments,' directed Sir Leonard.

They half carried, half led her from the room. He rang the bell, and waited until the maid came in answer to his summons, when he told her to go to her mistress. Then he went below. The nurse, deathly pale, her eyes large with terror, was sitting in a chair, the policemen grouped round her. He walked up to her, and stood looking down at her for a few moments.

'Why did you do it?' he asked at last.

At first she found it difficult to speak, but presently the words came with a rush.

'He was instrumental in causing the execution of my beloved Philon,' she cried, 'whose only crime was that he took a leading part in the intrigue to place the Sultan on the throne. I knew Lady Paterson was ill and, when Dr Hamid Bey sent to the hospital for a nurse, I succeeded in getting myself selected. It was easy then.

Every morning it was the habit of Monsieur l'Ambassadeur to enter his study at eleven o'clock and partake of the stewed fruit placed there for him. One morning I crushed up some beads, and mixed them with the fruit. That is all.'

She bowed her head, and for a few seconds there was silence; then Wallace looked at the Chief of Police.

'This Philon,' he observed, 'was the third man to be executed, was he not?'

The chief nodded.

'Very little seems to have been known about him,' went on the Englishman, 'and although I included him in my classification, I had almost decided to rule him out as possessing no friend or friends who would desire to avenge him. Armenian, of course?'

Again the policeman nodded. Suddenly the girl looked up, and her great eyes bored into those of Sir Leonard.

'How did you know?' she whispered.

'Today, for the first time,' he replied, 'I saw you dressed in ordinary clothes, and you were wearing the necklace which you have on now.' Instinctively she put her hand to her neck. 'It was the first clue I have found in this case, Mademoiselle, and if you desired to save yourself from exposure, you made a great mistake in wearing it. I noticed that the beads were not real amber, but glass, and that the larger ones are unevenly matched, indicating that three or four were missing. From that slender clue, I worked on the supposition that you were the guilty person. I tried to put myself in your place, and imagine what you would have done. You knew that the whole house would be searched if the reason for Sir George's illness was discovered, and that, if you endeavoured to get rid of the remains of the beads and the implement you used to crush them, they would very likely be discovered and traced to you.

You, therefore, had to find a hiding place. At the time you were nursing Lady Paterson, and it occurred to you that no place could be safer than her bedroom, which it was most unlikely the police would search. As it happened, they did not, but I did an hour or so after noticing the beads round your neck today. On the top of the wardrobe was a parcel containing a small hammer, a little crushed glass, and half an imitation amber bead. There they are!' He pointed to a side table a little behind her. She looked round and shuddered. 'The rest is quickly told,' he went on. 'I knew you were leaving today, and it was fairly certain that you would take the parcel away with you. I telephoned to Hakim Pasha, and asked him to come and bring a couple of officers with him. I explained what I had discovered, and he and the two officers with him hid in Lady Paterson's bedroom until you entered, and they caught you climbing on the chair to obtain the parcel.'

'I do not care,' she muttered, 'I have avenged my Philon's death. You can send me to him if you wish.'

She took her handkerchief from a pocket of her neat coatee, and raised it to her face. But Sir Leonard's quick eyes noticed something else and, though he clenched his hand and gritted his teeth, he made no effort to prevent her from swallowing the pellet she had inserted in her mouth. Better that way than the misery and degradation of a sordid trial, followed by a felon's death. Suddenly she broke into hysterical laughter.

'Yes I killed Monsieur l'Ambassadeur d'Angleterre,' she cried, 'and I am glad, do you hear me? Glad! But I have cheated you – I am going to Philon without your aid.'

Her beautiful face became distorted with agony and with a groan she fell over sideways.

A little later, when they had removed her body, Sir Leonard

sank heavily into a chair, and wiped the perspiration from his forehead.

'What a hollow triumph!' he muttered. 'If only Paterson had not meddled in Turkish politics.'

A very deep sigh broke from his lips.

A few days later, when the new Ambassador had arrived, Wallace made his farewells to Lady Paterson, and left Constantinople. Once in the seclusion of his coupé, he drew forth his pocket-book and extracted the banknotes which contained so much information vital to Greece. He examined them with a quizzical smile on his face.

'If I had taken you to Athens,' he soliloquised, 'I could have claimed a king's ransom for you, been acclaimed a hero, the saviour of Greece – God knows what! On the other hand it might have been considered that I was too dangerous to live. The sooner I forget what is written here the better for Greece, in fact, the better for the world.' He sighed. 'One more secret to be relegated to the very depths of my mind.' Batty entered the coupé and looked at him inquiringly. 'Batty,' he observed, 'there's one thing I've never been rich enough, or fool enough, to do in my life yet.'

'Is that so, sir?' returned the ex-sailor, wondering what on earth his master was talking about.

'Do you know what it is?'

'No, sir.'

'Fill me a pipe, and I'll tell you.'

Batty performed the office, and handed the well-seasoned briar to Sir Leonard, who twisted the banknotes together, and asked for a match. From the latter he lit his improvised spill.

'I've heard of people lighting a pipe or cigarette with a banknote,' remarked Sir Leonard, as he watched the flame grow larger, 'but I've never done it myself until now, and I am using half a dozen at once. I may add that it is giving me more delight and satisfaction than I've felt for a very long time.'

He lit his pipe carefully, and continued to hold the burning flimsies until he was in danger of burning his fingers. Batty watched fascinated, his eyes almost popping out of his head. As the charred remnants of what had once been good money burnt themselves out in an ash-tray, and were ground to dust by Sir Leonard, the mariner heaved a deep sigh.

'Swab my decks!' he exclaimed in a low voice, but with intense feeling. 'If that ain't a sin, I don't know wot is!'

CHAPTER SEVEN

Brien Averts a War

The large touring car, grey with dust, tore through Ospedaletti and on along the sea-road towards Ventimiglia. It passed through the little straggling frontier town, up over the promontory, down the other side, and ascended the steep rocky road leading to the French Custom House. There it was detained for some time, while perfunctory search for contraband was made by the officials, and the passports of the two travellers examined. Then on again along the steep, winding, wind-swept road towards Mentone.

'Well, we're in France, thank the Lord,' observed Major Brien, turning and regarding his companion, a twinkle in his blue eyes.

'Yes,' returned the other, whose carefully trimmed moustache and imperial gave him the appearance of a typical Frenchman. 'We're across the frontier. Now what?'

'We'll draw up and have a smoke, I think. I don't seem to have had a pipe for hours.'

He brought the car to a standstill by the side of the road, the two of them lit up.

'It was a lucky thing you were at Genoa,' commented Brien, 'otherwise I don't think I should have got out of Italy.'

'What has actually happened?'

'As you know I have been travelling round Europe for the last fortnight receiving reports, and generally tightening things up. I concluded my itinerary at Rome and was ending to wander home by way of the Riviera – in fact my wife is meeting me at Monte for a spot of sunshine – when I saw that fellow Gibaldi outside the Palazzo Venezia. The sight of him made me wonder. Sir Leonard told me he had been dismissed from the Italian Secret Service and, from information supplied by Gottfried, had succeeded in getting taken on by Berlin. Yet there he was as large as life in Rome, apparently without fear of arrest. I guessed at once that there must be some dirty work on foot, and followed him. He was met by one of the understrappers of the Foreign Office, which made the affair look more mysterious than ever. Obviously he was expected and, therefore, it seemed to me, must be in possession of something worthwhile to Italy.'

He paused, and blew out a cloud of tobacco smoke, watching it curl away in wisps as the wind caught it.

'They went into a café in the Piazza di Spagna and sat at a secluded table in a corner. I rang up Tempest, told him where I was, and asked him to join me. Luckily he was at the office, or things would have panned out altogether differently. Great gift that lip-reading game; I've often envied Maddison and Tempest. He arrived promptly, and together we sat where he had an uninterrupted view of their faces. By Jove! I was jolly glad I had followed Gibaldi. It turned out that he had obtained possession of certain documents from the Quai d'Orsay, and was bargaining with the Foreign Office official for their sale to Italy, one of the conditions being his reinstatement in the Secret Service. Of course it wasn't our business, and we wouldn't have interfered, only Tempest caught one phrase which made us sit up and start taking interest in right earnest. The under-secretary fellow said: "But, if what you say is true, it means war most certainly." He arranged to take the Minister himself to meet Gibaldi that night in the spy's hotel, a little place quite close to the Hôtel de Russie where I was staying. To cut a long story short, Tempest and I crept into the hotel unseen before the hour appointed, found our way to Gibaldi's bedroom and, while I held him up, Tempest searched for and found the documents. Then we bound and gagged Gibaldi, and got away just as a closed car, which I presume contained the Minister and the under-secretary, drove up to the door of the hotel. Two hours later when I left Rome, the station was full of agents, no doubt looking for the men who had pinched the precious papers, and I caught a glimpse of Gibaldi. Thanks to the fact that I am not known, and look so innocent, nobody interfered with me; anyway I suppose they were searching for two men and Frenchmen at that.'

'But isn't it a wonder Gibaldi didn't recognise you?' asked the man with the imperial.

'Why should he?' returned Brien. 'Tempest and I, in true melodramatic style, wore caps drawn down low over our eyes, and handkerchiefs tied round the lower parts of our faces which we only put on before entering the bedroom, and removed as soon as we were outside again. It was lucky for us that Gibaldi stayed in such a rotten little place. If he had chosen one of the big hotels it would have been a much more difficult job.'

His companion laughed.

'I had begun to fear,' he remarked, 'that Tempest's usefulness as the Rome agent of *Lalére et Cie* had been badly impaired.'

He laughed again, and Brien grunted indignantly.

'What do you take us for, Lalére,' he protested. 'Do you think that either he or I would have been so dashed foolish as to meet Gibaldi face-to-face without a little bit of purdah. Fie on you!'

'This is a new rôle for you, sir,' chuckled Lalére.

'You bet it is,' returned Billy sucking at his pipe complacently, 'and I've enjoyed every minute of it. Do you know, Gibaldi travelled up in the same train. I'm jolly glad I remembered you were in Genoa on that Marchesa affair. If I had remained in the train I shouldn't have been able to cross the frontier without having to submit to an exhaustive search. There were two hawk-eyed johnnies scrutinising every person who descended from the train at Genoa. What would have happened at Ventimiglia, where Italian officials really get down to business and enjoy themselves, I shudder to think.'

'Where are the documents?'

Brien tapped his breast pocket.

'The safest place I could imagine,' he declared, 'because it is so thoroughly obvious.'

'Have you glanced at them yet, sir?'

'No; except for the cursory glimpse Tempest and I took in Gibaldi's bedroom to make sure we had the right ones. It wouldn't be a bad idea to have a look at them now. We could hardly be in a safer spot.'

He looked around him. Not a soul or a vehicle of any sort was in sight. In the distance could be seen Mentone; behind, the winding road that runs round the rugged coast towards the frontier; far below the deep blue of the Mediterranean sea washing the rocky shore. From his pocket he took a long, fat envelope, from which he extracted quite a dozen official-looking documents and, with his companion, perused them one by one. When the last had been returned to its cover, they turned and looked at each other, and a low whistle broke from Lalére's lips.

'I doubt if anything more compromising has ever been committed to paper in the world's history than what is written here,' he remarked. 'To think that two French statesmen could pen such letters to each other is well-nigh inconceivable. I certainly wouldn't have believed it possible, if I hadn't seen them with my own eyes.'

'They're astounding,' agreed Brien. 'Of course neither of them is in the present government.'

'It's lucky for France they're not,' returned Lalére drily. 'That doesn't alter the fact that the responsibility rests on the shoulders of whatever government is in power, and all the diplomacy and tact in the world would fail to explain away letters like these. In the hands of Italy they would have been bound to have caused tremendous trouble. You certainly have averted a war, sir. What do you intend to do with the packet?'

'Sir Leonard Wallace is in Monte, taking a short holiday with his wife. I'll hand them to him, and let him decide.' He knocked out the ashes in his pipe. 'We'll get on now, if you're ready. By the way, will your man know what's happened to you?'

'Yes,' nodded Lalére; 'I left a note telling him to return to Paris at once. He'll be awaiting me there.'

'That means that when you drop me you'll have to drive all the rest of the way yourself. I'm sorry we couldn't wait until he returned, but—'

'That's all right, sir. I don't mind driving; in fact I like it.' And the clever agent of the British Secret Service, who cloaked his real profession behind his position as managing director of the great Parisian firm of *Lalére et Cie*, leant back in his seat, and stretched himself comfortably as Major Brien let in the clutch, and drove onward towards Mentone.

The sun was setting as the car ran into Monte Carlo to draw up at last before the Hermitage Hotel, where Brien knew his wife, Sir Leonard, and Lady Wallace would be staying. As soon as his companion's baggage had been removed, Lalére shook hands, and drove on to the Gallia at Beausoleil, where friends of his had rooms.

'I shall remain there until tomorrow morning,' he remarked, 'and, if I hear nothing from you by ten, will leave for Paris.'

On inquiry Brien learnt that Sir Leonard Wallace, his wife, and Mrs Brien had gone to lunch with friends at the Reserve in Beaulieu, and had not yet returned. He, therefore, bathed and dressed leisurely in evening kit, afterwards sauntering to the wide terrace in front of the Casino where he sat down amid the palms, mimosa and geraniums and studied, with an interest he always felt in Monte, the cosmopolitan throng passing and repassing close by. He had hardly been there more than five minutes, when a medium-sized man with dark, saturnine face, a small black moustache, and little furtive eyes walked by in earnest conversation with two men not unlike himself. Brien sat up and stared, a soundless whistle pursing his lips. His eyes followed the three men until they were hidden from his view; then he rose to his feet staring thoughtfully down at the railway line below, the one blemish to what is probably the most picturesque scene in Europe. But he was not concerned with the picturesqueness of his surroundings just then. He was wondering why Gibaldi had left the train at Monte Carlo of all places.

'It looks to me,' he muttered under his breath, 'as though something has come unstuck. I wonder if he suspects me, and walked by in order that his companions could have a good look at me. But then, how the devil could he possibly know I was coming to Monte Carlo when I left the train at Genoa?'

He walked back to the Hermitage and, in the crowded entrance hall, impatiently awaited the coming of the party from Beaulieu. They arrived at last, greeting him cheerily as their car pulled up and they caught sight of him standing at the entrance. Phyllis Brien, quite unmindful of the people around them, kissed him affectionately.

'I expected you yesterday,' she said reproachfully; 'that's a whole day gone by out of our lives, when we might have been together, and weren't.'

He looked down at her sweet vivacious face and smiled.

'I was detained in Rome, old thing,' he explained. 'Awfully sorry and all that, but duty you know—'

He was greeted warmly by Lady Wallace and Sir Leonard, and the four of them strolled through the hall, and took a lift to the floor on which their various rooms were situated. Sir Leonard glanced keenly at his second in command as they were about to part.

'Why the portentous frown?' he asked. 'You look as though you have weighty matters on your mind.'

'I have,' returned Brien shortly.

Wallace raised his hand in protest.

'Well, for the Lord's sake don't spring them on me,' he expostulated; 'at least not in Monte. When we get back to London you can—'

'As soon as you have changed, Leonard,' interrupted Brien firmly. 'I'm coming along to your room. Molly will be ordered to join Phyllis, and wait for us, and I will proceed to unburden myself of certain grave matters.'

Lady Wallace made a grimace at Phyllis. Sir Leonard looked disgusted.

'The man's not nice to know,' he murmured.

'Come along, Phyllis,' said Billy, taking his wife's arm. 'You haven't kissed me yet!'

'Oh, you fibber,' she returned. 'I kissed you downstairs.'

'That was in front of the rude and scoffing multitude, and, therefore, doesn't count.'

He marched her off. Twenty minutes later he was admitted to Sir Leonard's dressing room, where Batty was engaged in putting the finishing touches to his master's evening wear. Taking the bulky envelope from his pocket, Brien extracted the contents, and handed them to his friend. Wallace took them casually enough, but he had hardly read one when his manner changed entirely, and he perused the rest with intense interest. After he had finished he glanced them through again; then laid them face downwards on the dressing-table.

'All right, Batty,' he said to the ex-sailor, 'that'll do. Help me on with my coat; then you can go. I shan't want you again until about midnight.'

'Aye, aye, sir.'

As soon as Batty had departed, Wallace looked sharply at Brien.

'Where did you get these?' he demanded.

Billy told him the whole story, and he listened intently, a smile of approval on his face.

'Good work,' he applauded as his assistant concluded. 'If

you hadn't acted in the way you did, the peace of Europe would have been shattered by now. You've read these letters, I suppose?' Brien nodded. 'The garrulous old fatheads!' went on Wallace. 'They must have been in their second childhood to sit down and write such stuff to each other. They've damned everything about Italy they could think of from her African policy down to internal finance. Nothing could have prevented a conflagration once these had reached the Italian Government. They're nothing but a collection of gratuitous insults written by a couple of fossils who ought to have known better. We have a few idiots among our statesmen, but none to equal these two. I should rather like to know what the letters were doing at the d'Orsay, and how Gibaldi got hold of them. By Jove! What a stew they must be in in Paris at losing them. Clement of the French Ministry of the Interior is staying in this hotel. I'd love to see his face if he knew the letters were here.'

'Do you think the whole thing may be a plot by Germany to cause a rupture between France and Italy?' asked Brien. 'Gibaldi, remember, had been taken on by the German Secret Service.'

Wallace considered the matter for some time.

'I don't think so,' he replied at length. 'It is possible of course, but Germany can have no object in stirring up strife between Italy and France just now, unless—' he stopped and frowned, then: 'The sooner these are back at the Quai d'Orsay the better,' he said. 'You're quite sure no suspicion attaches to you?'

'I should hardly have been allowed to leave Italy unmolested if there were,' returned Brien. 'And yet I'm beastly troubled about an incident that happened while I was waiting for you. I strolled over to the terrace in front of the Casino, and sat for a while watching the people. While I was there Gibaldi passed by with two fellows who might have been his brothers – they were so much like him. I wondered if by some chance suspicion had fallen on me, and he was pointing me out to them.'

'Gibaldi? Are you sure?' asked Sir Leonard sharply.

'Absolutely. What do you think?'

'It's difficult to know what to think. It is quite possible, of course, that he is on the track of somebody who left the train at Monte Carlo. You weren't subjected to anything in the nature of surveillance on the train or at the stations en route, were you?'

'No.'

'Naturally you would have been noticed. I suppose note was taken of everybody travelling from Rome.'

'But I left the train at Genoa, so it cannot be that Gibaldi is here after me.'

'Were your bags labelled?'

'Yes; to the Hermitage, Monte Carlo.'

Wallace smiled grimly.

'Then I'm afraid it is you, Billy, whom they suspect. The very fact that you left the train at Genoa with bags labelled Monte Carlo would raise their suspicions. You would have been wiser had you stayed on the train.'

Brien groaned.

'I hope you're wrong,' he said. 'Why didn't they hold me up at the frontier and search me, if I was suspected? A telephone call through from Genoa would have done the trick.'

'For the simple reason that they had nothing to go on but the fact that a traveller, who had booked through to Monte, left the train at Genoa; after all not an unheard of happening. You see they obtained your name and destination from the baggage. If, despite your apparent change of plans, you still arrived at the Hermitage they decided they would be able to go through your belongings at their leisure. At the same time all roads and routes out of Genoa would have been watched and, while you were congratulating yourself on getting across the frontier nicely, they were here waiting for you.'

Billy looked very crestfallen.

'Dash it!' he ejaculated. 'I thought I was being so clever, and all the time—'

Wallace smiled.

'Cheer up, old chap,' he consoled him, 'you've done some jolly good work. You have nothing to blame yourself for.'

But Brien refused to be consoled. He knew very well that the man who was congratulating him so generously would not have made such a slip. There came a knock on the door, and Lady Wallace looked in.

'Are you men ever coming to dinner?' she inquired plaintively. 'Phyllis and I are thinking seriously of eating the furniture.'

'Coming, Molly,' answered her husband cheerfully.

She disappeared, and he picked up the documents and put them back in their envelope.

'I'll take care of these for the time being,' he observed. 'Everything you possess will be gone through while you are away from your rooms. They'll be more certain than ever that you're the man they want, when they see you with me, for Gibaldi knows me well.'

'Your rooms will be searched also at that rate,' decided Brien.

Wallace nodded.

'Exactly,' he returned calmly, 'and, when the letters are not found, you and I will be held up and lots of nasty things will happen to us, if we're not careful. Lalére also, I'm afraid, will have quite an exciting night. We must warn him somehow. It's a pity this should happen when the ladies are with us.'

'Hang it all!' exploded Brien, 'you're taking it pretty coolly. What do you propose to do about it?'

'I don't know – yet. Look here, we mustn't keep the wives waiting any longer. Come on!'

He put the envelope in his pocket, and they joined their impatient womenfolk. Brien was rather moody during dinner, but Sir Leonard was full of joviality, and kept Molly and Phyllis from speculating too much on the cause of Billy's preoccupation. Even the latter fell under the influence of his friend's good spirits before the end of the meal, much to the relief of his wife who, from time to time, had been regarding him anxiously.

While they were drinking their coffee, Wallace left them to procure tickets for the opera. He was away nearly a quarter of an hour, and they had begun to wonder what was keeping him, when he returned. They strolled across to the Casino, presented their cards of admission, and walked through thc rooms before entering the theatre, which is in the same building. For a little while they watched the people playing roulette, but none of them were keen on gambling, and they were all rather glad to get away from the overheated atmosphere and feverish excitement, and take their seats for the performance of *Rigoletto*. As they sat together, Sir Leonard turned to Brien.

'It is as I thought,' he whispered, 'we have been followed all the way. Take this; you may want it before the evening is out.'

He pushed a small automatic into the other's hand.

'What about you?' asked Brien.

'I've another. I'd be looking forward to meeting Gibaldi and his pals if Molly and Phyllis were not with us. As it is, I'm afraid I'm not very keen.'

'Why not send them home after the show?' murmured Brien. 'We could then force a meeting on these fellows.'

'Not a bit of good. They'll wait until everything is in their favour. We must be prepared for anything. I rang up Lalére a few minutes ago, so he knows what to expect.'

'But shouldn't something be done about those letters? It seems to me that it is decidedly risky to carry them about.'

'Don't worry, Bill.' He turned his attention to the stage, curtain having just gone up. '*Rigoletto* is my favourite opera, and these people are said to be exceptional.'

Major Brien looked at him with a glint of admiration in is eyes. He wished he had the gift of being able to put aside anxieties as easily. To look at Wallace his whole attention now devoted to the opera, his attitude denoting enjoyment and approval, it was difficult to imagine that he had anything on his mind but Verdi's beautiful music.

Afterwards, as they walked back to the hotel, Brien continually glanced from left to right, momentarily expecting to be held up, even though he knew that such an attempt would be manifestly foolish when there were still so many people about. Still, strange things happened at Monte Carlo, and, as Wallace had said, it was as well to be prepared for anything. As they entered the foyer an obsequious attendant hastened across to them and bowing profoundly, held out a salver on which lay a letter.

'This was handed in for you, Monsieur,' he stated, 'at eleven o'clock precisely.'

Billy took the envelope and glanced at it curiously.

'Who the dickens?' he began; then stopped and sniffed. 'It's scented,' he proclaimed in disgusted tones.

Lady Wallace laughed merrily.

'Oh, Billy,' she bantered, 'what have you been doing during the last two weeks? Phyllis dear, I should inquire into this if I were you.'

Phyllis, who knew her husband far too well to misjudge him, was rather indignant.

'It's probably one of Monte's cocottes who has taken a fancy to you, Billy mine,' she decided. 'What awful cheek!'

'It wouldn't be a bad idea to open the thing and see what it's all about,' suggested Wallace quietly.

He walked on with his wife, but had hardly taken more than half a dozen paces when an exclamation behind him caused him to turn and look inquiringly at his colleague. The latter was standing gazing at the half-sheet of notepaper in his hand, looking anxious and bewildered. Sir Leonard retraced his steps.

'What's the trouble?' he asked.

Without a word Brien handed the letter to him. It was written in a quaint mixture of French and English:

Monsieur,

Excusez la liberté que je prends de m'addresser à vous without the introduction, but la gravité it compel me. Mon ami, Monsieur Anatole Lalére, has been hurt much by un coup de poignard. He ask for you, Monsieur. Je vous serais infiniment obligé if you can quickly come.

Mes salutations bien empressées.

Mireille Garreau.

Wallace handed the note back without a word.

'Poor old Lalére,' murmured Brien. 'I wonder how it happened?'

'What's the matter, Billy?' asked his wife.

He handed the letter to her, and she and Lady Wallace read it together, presently giving vent to various expressions of sympathy.

'Is it that nice man to whom you introduced me in Paris?' asked Mrs Brien.

Her husband nodded.

'What are we to do about it?' he asked Wallace.

'Ring up the manager of the Gallia,' returned the latter promptly, 'and find out all about it.'

They walked across to the office while the two ladies awaited them in the lounge.

'It looks to me like a very crude attempt to get hold of us,' observed Wallace. 'Who is Mireille Garreau?'

'She's a pukka friend of his all right,' was the reply. 'He mentioned that she was staying at the Gallia with her mother. What do you mean by a crude attempt to get hold of us?'

'If nothing has happened to Lalére,' declared Sir Leonard, 'and this is merely a blind, then Gibaldi and his friends have shown an absurd lack of common sense. I rather think, however, that he has probably been attacked in order to get you or me or both of us into their power. They know, at least, that he is a friend of yours, and guessed that you would be sent for. Somewhere between here and Beausoleil they are awaiting us.'

Inquiries by telephone quickly assured them that Lalére had been set upon in the grounds of the Gallia Hotel, and badly wounded. Only the cries of Mademoiselle Garreau, who had been with him, had prevented his assailants from murdering him. She, the manager informed them, had been brutally knocked down, when she had attempted to grapple with the scoundrels. Monsieur Lalére had certainly asked very urgently for Monsieur le Major Brien.

'There's nothing for it but to go,' remarked Wallace, as he and his colleague turned away from the instrument. 'It is quite likely that Lalére has something important to tell us. Ten to one though, we'll either be attacked going or coming back.'

They informed their wives of their intention to go to Beausoleil, and escorted them to their rooms, where they changed into lounge suits. As Sir Leonard bade good night to Lady Wallace, she regarded him a trifle anxiously.

'Monsieur Lalére is one of your men, isn't he?' she asked.

'Well, in a sense,' he replied jokingly. 'He is the managing director of a firm which pays me a nice fat dividend on the money I invested in it.'

'Don't be foolish, dear,' she pleaded; 'you know what I mean. He is actually a member of the Secret Service, isn't he?'

'Well, yes,' he admitted.

'Are you going into danger?' she asked in uneasy tones.

'Good gracious, no!' he laughed. 'At least not to my knowledge.'

'Do be careful, dear,' she returned. 'I have an uneasy presentiment.'

'Don't then,' he said kissing her. 'Go to bed. We'll be back in a couple of hours at the most.'

Before rejoining Brien he spent five minutes in his dressing room talking to Batty, the latter's contribution to the conversation being several repetitions of his usual: 'Aye, aye, sir.'

A car had been ordered, and Wallace ascertained that the chauffeur was a Frenchman well-known to the hotel authorities. The drive to Beausoleil was uneventful, and they found Lalére very ill indeed. He had been stabbed behind the right shoulder, the knife just missing the lung by a hair's breadth. The police had made their inquiries and had departed. A doctor and nurse were in attendance; the former assuring them that Lalére had had a very narrow escape but would recover.

'At present he cannot be moved,' he added, 'but in a day or two arrangements will be made to convey him to a nursing home. Madame and Mademoiselle Garreau have very kindly taken charge of everything.'

They were taken to the invalid, who smiled at them painfully.

'He would not sleep until you came, Monsieur,' observed the doctor to Brien, 'but please do not let him speak too much.'

He and the nurse left them, and they questioned Lalére about the attack. He could tell them very little, however, as he was sitting with Mademoiselle Garreau at the time, and the first intimation he had of any danger was when the knife entered his back.

'I don't think they meant to kill me,' he added, 'for they had ample opportunity to make certain of stabbing me in a fatal spot.'

'Exactly what I thought,' nodded Sir Leonard. 'But, by Jove! They were pretty desperate. Had they made a search of your rooms, do you think?'

'Yes. Mademoiselle tells me that the contents of my suitcases were strewn all over the bedroom floor when I was brought in. I daresay they intended to search me also, but she, plucky little soul, grappled with them and screamed.'

'I wonder who were with Gibaldi,' mused Wallace. 'They can't be genuine members of the Italian Secret Service. It's only renegades of Gibaldi's type who use methods like this to gain their ends.'

'That's what I wanted to tell you,' gasped the injured man. 'I wouldn't have brought you up here otherwise, although at first I thought I was booked for another world. As I lay on the ground, and before I lost consciousness, I saw them quite distinctly in the moonlight, when they were trying to silence Mireille. I'll swear that one of them was André Chalant.'

Sir Leonard whistled under his breath.

'Are you sure?' he asked in incredulous tones.

'As certain as it was possible to be under the circumstances.'

'Then we are up against it,' muttered the other. 'It's no wonder Gibaldi was dismissed from the Italian service, if he is an associate of a man like Chalant.'

The information caused him to become very thoughtful. André Chalant was one of the most notorious criminals in Europe, a man who stopped at nothing, and for whom the police of almost every European country had been on the watch for months. Wallace's expression was grave when he and Brien, having assured themselves that Lalére was in good hands, took their leave. Outside they found Mademoiselle Garreau waiting to speak to them. She could add little to what they already knew, however, and having complimented her on her pluck, they departed for Monte Carlo.

Careful precautions were taken during the run back, but no attempt was made to interfere with them, a fact that caused Sir Leonard's anxiety to increase. When he and his companion stepped from the car, his face looked white and stern, but Brien was smiling broadly.

'You were wrong, old soldier,' he observed. 'There wasn't the slightest sign of an attack.'

To his surprise Wallace took no notice of his remark, but hurried into the hotel, leaving him to follow more leisurely, wondering what had come over the chief. The night clerk and a porter were standing in the hall, and welcomed the two Englishmen with exclamations of surprise, but made no further comment until Wallace halted directly in front of them.

'What is it?' he demanded. 'I can see from your faces that you are surprised about something.'

'But no, Monsieur,' protested the clerk; 'it is not our business to be surprised if Monsieur alters his arrangements.'

'Ah! What arrangements?'

'On the telephone, Monsieur,' the man replied in a conciliatory voice, thinking perhaps it were best to humour this strange guest, 'you gave instructions that the mesdames were to be informed that you and Monsieur the Major were staying the night at Beausoleil; that you desired them to join you, and would send a car for them.'

Brien had come up, and was listening in perplexity. Wallace, his face now almost bloodless, still spoke calmly.

'And the mesdames?' he asked. 'Did they go?'

'But yes, Monsieur. Half an hour ago the car arrived, and they were driven away.'

'Did they depart alone?'

'Yes, Monsieur, but your valet went through the hall directly afterwards. I thought his manner strange.'

'Has he come back?'

'No, Monsieur; at least not this way. He may have entered through the servants' door.'

A glimmering of what had happened had begun to penetrate Brien's mind. He felt suddenly nerveless, and his face became as white as that of his colleague. The two Frenchmen, looking from one to the other, gathered that all was not well.

'Messieurs,' the clerk cried, 'I do not understand. Is it that—'

'Those ladies have been abducted,' interrupted Wallace sternly, 'and they must be found. Tell me quickly: what was the car like in which they were driven away?'

'I do not know, Monsieur. I did not see it.'

The porter was also unable to supply the information, having been engaged elsewhere at the time.

'Well, the driver – you must have seen him?'

The description was so good that both Wallace and Brien recognised it.

'Gibaldi himself,' cried the latter. 'In God's name, Leonard, what are we to do?'

Wallace drew him away, then turned back to the clerk.

'Keep by the telephone,' he instructed, 'and let me know directly if a call comes through for me. My friend and I will be waiting in the lounge. Look here, Billy,' he went on, as soon as they were well out of hearing, 'in a sense I almost thought something like this would happen.'

Brien's eyes stared at him out of a countenance rendered ghastly by its extreme pallor.

'What?' he cried.

'I don't mean to say that I thought they would be abducted. Actually, as you know, I expected that we would be attacked on the road. But all the same, I did not like leaving Molly and Phyllis alone. What I then considered a wild idea flashed through my mind that Gibaldi and his companions might attempt to get at us through them in some manner.'

'Then why on earth—?' began Brien wrathfully.

'Wait a minute. In case of accidents I warned Batty to keep watch in the corridor so that he could see the doors of both suites, and prevent anybody attempting to get in. I also told him that if Phyllis or Molly left their rooms, he was to follow them, and see that they came to no harm. I did not think that they would be abducted in this barefaced manner, but Batty has obviously followed them somehow, and all we can do is to wait until he rings up or comes back to tell us where they are.'

A glimmer of hope showed in Brien's eyes.

'God bless that head of yours, Leonard,' he murmured, 'I believe we'll soon be able to rescue them after all

'Don't be too sanguine yet, Bill,' remonstrated the chief. 'Batty may have failed to follow them, they may even have captured him, but that's most unlikely. He's not the sort to be caught napping. I wish to God I had let you go alone to Beausoleil, but what's the use of wishing now. I went because I expected that an attack would be made on the road, and two of us could have accomplished what one couldn't.'

The hope suddenly died out of Brien's eyes.

'Supposing the clerk is right,' he cried, 'and Batty re-entered by the servants' door. Why, he may be waiting upstairs now.'

'No; if the car had eluded him, he would have waited in the hall for us. But go and look, if you like.'

Brien hurried away. He returned in five minutes.

'There is no sign of him,' he announced.

'Good. Then we can be sure he's on the track somewhere.'

It was agonising waiting, and both felt the strain badly. Every few minutes either one or the other walked out into the large hall, gloomy now in its half-lighted emptiness, hoping to hear the telephone bell ring in the office; but an hour went by and still there came no news.

'I am convinced now that André Chalant is in this business,' observed Wallace when, for the twentieth time he returned to his companion, and found him sunk dejectedly in the depths of an armchair. 'It's the sort of scheme he would concoct. If we don't find Molly and Phyllis by breakfast time, we shall receive a note calling on us to hand over the package in some secluded spot, or harm will come to them. I should have been warned that a plot was brewing by the fact that as far as I know, no attempt has been made to search my belongings.'

'Mine haven't been touched either,' returned Brien. 'I made sure of that when we returned from the opera. It was clever of the fiend to anticipate that Lalére would send for us.'

'He couldn't have known that both of us would go. He must have had an alternative plan of some sort.'

They lapsed into silence again. Presently a clock struck.

'Damn it!' ejaculated Brien. 'Four o'clock. I can't stand this much longer.'

He stuck a cigarette in his mouth, lit it and began to puff furiously. Almost at once he took it out, and threw it away, for the porter came running into the lounge.

'Messieurs,' he cried, 'your valet – he is here.'

Batty appeared at the door, and both men made a dash towards him. His round, rubicund face was bright with excitement.

'Come on, sir,' he called to Wallace. 'I know where the swabs are – beggin' yer pardon, sir. I pinched their blinkin' car, and—'

'Right, Batty,' interrupted Sir Leonard sharply, 'tell us on the way. Do you know the address?'

The ex-sailor scratched his head.

'Can't say I do, sir,' he confessed. 'I know the way all right. It's a little 'ouse up the 'ill about two mile t'other side o' that place you told me about near Italy.'

'You mean Mentone?'

'That's the place, sir.'

'You're sure?'

'Take me oath, sir.'

'That's good enough.' He turned to the porter. 'Ring the *chef de la Sûreté*,' he instructed, 'explain to him that the mesdames have been kidnapped, and that we have gone to rescue them, and ask him to get in touch with the police at Mentone. I will send someone to guide them. There will not be time for us to stop and explain to the police at Mentone ourselves. Do you understand?'

'Yes, M'sieur.'

'Right. Come on, Bill.'

With Batty at the wheel, Sir Leonard by his side, and Brien in the back, the car was soon tearing on its way. As he drove, Batty described the manner in which he had managed to keep in touch with Lady Wallace and Mrs Brien.

'I saw her ladyship go across to Mrs Brien's rooms, sir, fully dressed as yer might say. Arter about ten minutes they both came out, Mrs Brien 'aving 'er 'at and coat on too. They was carryin' small suitcases, sir, and although I felt a bit surprised like, it wasn't my business to interfere. 'Er ladyship ses to me: "Batty", she ses, "we're goin' ter join Sir Leonard and the Major at—" I've forgotten wot place she said, sir. "'E didn't say nothin' about you comin', so I expect you'd better stay 'ere", she ses. Well, it didn't seem right ter me, arter wot you 'ad said, sir, so I ups anchor, and follers in their wake, meanin' no 'arm, but obeyin' orders, like, you see, sir?'

'Yes, yes, Batty. You did quite right. Go on!'

'You bet I did right, sir, now I knows the dirty work them swabs was up to. 'Er ladyship and Mrs Brien boarded car wot was waitin'. There wasn't no other in sight so, when it began to move, I ran out of me 'iding place, and climbed aboard the luggage carrier. I made 'eavy weather on that bloomin' seat – beggin' yer pardon, sir – but 'ung on all right. We went through Men – Men – the place wot you said sir – full speed a'ead, and at last dropped anchor on a lonely bit o' the road. I skipped off me seat quick, and I was glad I did, for three men came up sudden like and, opening the door, ordered the ladies to land. I felt inclined to sail into 'em, but thought it would be better to find out where they went, then give you the nod, sir. Two of 'em took the ladies up an 'ill, t'others pushed the craft closer inshore and follered. I follered them. They climbed to a small 'ouse all by itself about 'alf a mile up and went inside. I watched for a time through a winder. 'Er ladyship and Mrs Brien were lettin' 'em 'ave it good and proper, but the swabs only laughed at 'em – ugly looking blighters they are, too, sir. As soon as I had taken me bearings, I went back to the car, and turned it round. It was a bit of a job, sir, but I did it. Then I slipped me cables, and 'ere I am.'

'Splendid, Batty! You've done magnificently.'

'Wot I can't understand, sir,' complained the one-time mariner, 'is 'ow 'er ladyship ever got it into 'er 'ead that she was goin' ter you.'

Wallace explained, and Batty swore roundly and thoroughly, and so incensed was he that he even forgot to add: 'Beggin' yer pardon, sir.'

Very little more was said on the way, each being too full of his own thoughts and too grimly set on exacting retribution from the scoundrels for the manner in which they had abducted the ladies. The car tore through Mentone and, a few minutes later, pulled up on a particularly lonely part of the steep, rugged road. Brien uttered an exclamation.

'It was somewhere about here,' he observed, 'where Lalére and I had a smoke this afternoon. Good Lord! What a lot seems to have happened since then!'

'I hope to goodness,' remarked Sir Leonard, 'that they haven't discovered the car was missing, or they may have gone and taken the ladies with them. Perhaps they are even waiting in ambush for us. Which is the way, Batty?' The ex-sailor pointed it out. 'Well, you go up, and we'll follow about a hundred yards behind. If you're attacked, yell at the top of your voice, or fire, which ever you prefer.'

Batty set off, and they waited until they judged he was far enough ahead, then followed.

'I didn't know Batty carried a revolver,' muttered Brien.

'I gave him one this evening,' was the whispered reply.

Brien chuckled softly and almost happily to himself. It was impossible to think that anything could actually go wrong, he decided, when a man like Wallace, who never seemed to overlook or forget anything, was in charge.

Cautiously they crept up the hill. Wallace, who went first, seemed to be able to see in the dark, so sure-footed and silent was he. Brien, following close behind, was almost as noiseless. At last, a little distance away, they caught a glimmer of light, and the dim outline of a small cottage. At the same time the form of Batty loomed up in front of Sir Leonard.

'It's all right, sir,' he whispered. 'They're inside. I just 'ad a peep.'

An involuntary exclamation of relief broke from Brien.

'S'sh!' warned Wallace. 'Not a sound now. I'm going to have a look; then we can plan our attack accordingly. Hold yourselves in readiness and, if it comes to a fight, don't hesitate to shoot, but be careful of the ladies.'

He faded away in the darkness. Five minutes went by; then he was back, and his voice, when he spoke, was pregnant with fierce emotion.

'They are torturing Molly,' he whispered, 'apparently in an effort to force Phyllis to write a letter. There can only be two rooms in the cottage, one at the front and one at the back, with a door opening out from each. Both are locked, I think. At any rate, I tried them, and they wouldn't budge. There are three windows, two at the back on either side of the door, and one in front to the left. The front one's a ramshackle affair, though, with a couple of dilapidated shutters closed on it with the view, I suppose, of hiding the interior. The shutters are so full of holes, however, that one can see in quite easily. You swing them open, Bill, when I give the word. Batty, you stand by and smash in the window. Is that clear?'

They murmured their affirmatives.

'The chances are,' went on Sir Leonard, 'that as soon as the alarm comes one of them will blow out the lamp. If that happens, you run to the front door, Batty; and you to the back of the house, Bill, and be prepared to knock out anybody who attempts to get away. I'll enter by the window.'

'You would choose the most dangerous job for yourself,' grumbled Brien.

'Don't question orders, my lad. Are you both ready?'

Noiselessly they approached the cottage until the three of them were standing by the window looking through the numerous cracks into the room. Lady Wallace sat in a chair, an expression of indomitable courage on her white face. Two men stood by her side, one holding her right arm, which he was engaged in twisting mercilessly, while she bit her lip to prevent herself from crying out in her agony. At a table covered by an ancient cloth, also guarded by two men, sat Phyllis Brien, a pen in her hand, a pad of paper before her, her face as pale as death, obviously torn between her desire to write at the dictation of her captors and thus end Molly's torture, and a refusal to do something that possibly would bring catastrophe and tragedy upon her husband. Lady Wallace continually shook her head in an endeavour to prevent Phyllis Brien from writing, but it was obvious that the resolution of the latter would not long continue proof against the suffering she saw on her friend's face. Under his breath Sir Leonard gave vent to an expression that boded ill indeed for the inhuman ruffian who was twisting his wife's arm.

'Ready, Bill?' he muttered tensely; then: 'Right, carry on!'

Brien flung the shutters wide apart, and Batty, a revolver in one hand, the other wrapped in a large bandana handkerchief, crashed both into the window with such force that not only was the glass splintered but most of the woodwork as well. There came a chorus of startled cries, a suppressed scream, the sharp crack of an automatic followed by a groan; then the light went out. Wallace was through the remains of the window like a flash, tearing his clothes badly in the process, but not bothering about anything so long as he got in. Almost immediately he was tackled by someone, but slipped aside, a grim smile curving his lips as he heard the faint hum of a knife passing close to his ear. He realised that another man was coming towards him, and dashed his hand, revolver and all, into where he judged the face to be. It got home beautifully, a sharp cry of pain rewarding him.

It was all very confusing, this fighting in the dark. Avoiding the first man again more by instinct than anything else, he edged to the side of the room away from the window, and there came a lull. His opponents did not know where he was and stood still in an effort to trace him by the sound of movement. He did likewise, could hear the heavy breathing of somebody close by, an occasional groan farther away, and took care not to breathe loudly himself. He wondered if the ladies still remained where they had been when he had looked through the shutters, but when the alarm had come and the light been extinguished, Phyllis had risen quickly and darted to Molly's side. The two girls, their arms round each other, were now cowering in a remote corner of the room, hope rising in their breasts at this unlooked-for intervention, their eyes striving to pierce the pall of blackness round them.

Almost a minute must have passed before there was any further movement; then Wallace spoke.

'You had better surrender,' he said in French, the sound of his voice being greeted with a cry of joy from Molly. 'The house is surrounded.'

Immediately someone fired in his direction, but, anticipating it, he had dodged aside. He dared not return the shot for fear of hitting his wife, or Phyllis, but his movement had been heard; he knew there was a man groping for him close by. Edging silently in the direction where he knew the front door must be, he suddenly felt the breath of another man on his cheek. There was a shout of exultation, but he slipped rapidly to his knees, and felt a heavy body plunge over him. At once came the horrible sound of men at death grips, and he almost laughed as he realised that two of his adversaries were doing their utmost to kill each other. It was easy to reach the door now and, temporarily putting the revolver in the armpit of his artificial limb, he felt for the key, found it and unlocked the door. At the same time came a blood-curdling groan, accompanied by a cry of triumph.

'There is only one,' shouted a voice, 'and I have killed him. Quick! Escape by the window – the women must accompany us.'

'Stop where you are!' commanded the level voice of Sir Leonard. 'The first man to attempt to go through that window will get a bullet in him.'

A baffled curse answered him; then there was silence. Apparently the man who had killed his comrade by mistake was convinced now that, after all, more than one had entered by the window. Wallace pulled the door open suddenly, shouting at the same time to Batty to be careful. A figure loomed on the threshold for a moment, showing almost distinctly in the less opaque murkiness of the outer gloom; then disappeared as it went to the floor in response to Sir Leonard's warning. Two shots rang out, but Batty had acted too quickly, and neither touched him. The two survivors of the band of crooks appeared to realise at the same moment that the game was going against them. Wallace heard them dive for the inner door, but made no effort to stop them. Brien was at the back, probably fuming at being kept out of the fight for so long. It would be a pity to do him out of his share, Sir Leonard decided.

'Got a match, Batty?' he asked.

'Yes, sir.'

Almost immediately one sprang into flame, and the sailor was directed to relight the lamp. As soon as this was done, Lady Wallace was across the room and in her husband's arms.

'Did they hurt you very much, dear?' he asked solicitously.

'Then you knew?'

'I saw through the shutters,' he returned grimly. 'That was why that fellow was not given a chance.'

He nodded across the room to a man lying against the chair on which she had been sitting. As she recognised him she shuddered.

'Is he badly hurt?' she asked.

'I shot him through the right shoulder in a place, I hope, which will mean his being handicapped for the rest of his life. It will remind him that a woman's arm was not made to be almost twisted from its socket. Batty, stand by that door, and keep a watch for those other fellows. They may try to fight their way back, when they find Major Brien is guarding the door and windows.'

He turned his attention to the second man. The fellow was lying on his face in a pool of blood. Advising Molly not to look, he bent down and turned him over gingerly. It was Gibaldi. He had been stabbed through the throat and was quite dead. Wallace looked up to find his wife gazing down at the body in horrified fascination.

'How – how was he killed, Leonard?' she asked.

'He and one of the others fought, each thinking they had got hold of me. This is the result. Funny, isn't it?'

'Oh, Leonard,' she cried with a shudder. 'What a horrible thing to say. But – oh, I am so glad it was he and not you.'

He smiled and kissed her. Then a frown of perplexity puckered his brow. Not a sound came from the back of the house, which was very strange. If the crooks had attempted to leave either by windows or door, Brien would have been bound to see them. Could there possibly be another exit which he had overlooked? Taking care that Molly and Phyllis were in a part of the room where they were in no danger, and leaving Batty to keep guard, he crept quietly into the other room. A faint light heralding dawn was now showing through the windows, and enabled him to see that the apartment was devoid of furniture. Of the two men there was no sign, and neither the windows nor door were open. He was beginning to feel very puzzled, when a faint scraping sound was audible above his head. At once the solution burst upon him. There was a loft above, probably with a window through which the men would squeeze, slide down the roof and escape.

He raced back through the other room and out of the front door. Running quietly round to Brien, he told him to watch the roof on one side; then went to watch the other. Almost at once there was a cry, and dashing back to his colleague he found him rolling on the ground fighting desperately with a man; another lay still close by. In the advancing light he could just distinguish friend from foe, saw an arm of the latter raised to strike, the glint of an ugly looking knife in his hand and, without hesitation, and at point blank range, fired. The knife dropped to the ground and the fellow cursed horribly, but he still went on fighting frantically with his uninjured arm, legs, and teeth. It was not long, however, before the two Englishmen had knocked all the fight out of him. They strapped his arms to his side with his own belt, and tied his legs together with a scarf he had worn round his neck.

'Almost an anti-climax,' commented Wallace, rising to his feet.

'I had only just got here,' explained Brien, 'when that first bloke jumped from the roof. I dotted him one, and laid him out, but hadn't time to recover myself before the other tumbled on top of me. He would have finished me too, if you hadn't happened along.' He picked up the knife and examined it. 'A pretty nasty weapon,' he observed. 'Why, Leonard, there's blood on it.'

'I suppose he's the fellow who stabbed Gibaldi,' returned Wallace, and explained what had taken place in the cottage. 'Let us carry these two inside.'

They lifted the pinioned man, who was groaning and swearing at the same time, and conveyed him into the hut. Brien returned with Batty for the other. The latter was regaining his senses, and was tied up in the same manner as his companion.

'Kind of them to wear scarves and belts,' remarked Brien. 'One could almost imagine they anticipated our being short of the necessary materials with which to bind them. How about the groaning gentleman?'

He indicated the wounded man leaning against the chair.

'He's too sorry for himself,' replied Sir Leonard, 'to want to cause trouble. Batty, go down to the car, drive to Mentone, and fetch the police. You'll probably find them waiting for you.'

'I don't speak the lingo, sir,' objected Batty.

'That doesn't matter. They probably speak English of a sort.'

The ex-sailor departed, and Wallace looked down at the man who had so nearly done for Brien.

'So, André Chalant,' he remarked in French, 'your activities are at an end. I have never met you before, but I've seen enough photographs of you to recognise you anywhere. You've ended your nefarious career pretty badly. The kidnapping of these ladies and the murder of Gibaldi make a nice combination.'

The fellow stopped cursing, and glared balefully at him.

'What do you mean?' he demanded. 'Gibaldi is not dead.'

'He certainly is. You fought with him in mistake for me, and stabbed him. He lies over there.'

He indicated the still form, now covered by the dilapidated tablecloth which Brien had thoughtfully spread over it. André

Chalant was visibly disconcerted and, from then on, lay sullenly silent, occasionally staring up at his captor with very nearly a glint of respect in his eyes. His wound and that of the other injured man were roughly dressed.

Lady Wallace and Mrs Brien were not disposed to talk much, having been badly shaken by their experience, but they were eager to know how they had been traced, and expressed their great admiration for Batty's resource. Molly, who knew Monte Carlo and its environs well, told her husband that she quickly became suspicious that all was not well when in the car, but the driver went so fast that it was impossible to do anything but sit still and wait whatever fate was before them. Her arm was still painful, but Wallace assured himself that no permanent damage had been done to it. The look he turned on the man who had been twisting it caused that individual to shiver.

Before long they heard the sound of voices, and Sir Leonard went outside to meet Batty and the party of police the latter had brought with him. The *chef de la Sûreté* of Mentone himself had come with three other officers.

'What is this I hear, M'sieur?' he demanded, after Wallace had introduced himself. 'A case of abduction most terrible I was informed, but of details there were none.'

Wallace quickly related the whole story, making no mention of the reason why the ladies had been kidnapped.

'You will have a great haul, Monsieur,' he concluded. 'I think that apart from the abduction charge, you will probably find other crimes have been committed by the three prisoners. One, indeed, is André Chalant, who is wanted badly by the police of many countries.'

The little keen-eyed official gave a gasp of incredulous surprise.

'What is that you say, M'sieur? André Chalant here? You are sure?'

'Certain.'

Talking excitedly, the four officers of police hurried into the cottage. They made no secret of their exultation, when they found that the well-known criminal was in truth among those present. The *chef de la Sûreté* shook Wallace by the hand with great enthusiasm.

'It is marvellous this,' he cried. 'The gratitude of France is due to you, M'sieur, and to these other gentlemen. These others are also wanted men. That one,' he pointed to the shrouded form of Gibaldi, 'I do not know, but what matters it? He is dead.'

Ten minutes later, leaving the police with their prisoners and the body of the renegade Italian, Wallace and his party left for Monte Carlo. It was now quite light, and the early morning air was delightfully refreshing. Brien sat in front with Batty, and they had barely traversed a mile when, with a sudden exclamation, he turned and regarded the Chief of the British Secret Service.

'Do you know, Leonard,' he declared, 'what with the disappearance of Molly and Phyllis, and one thing and another, I had quite forgotten the documents that caused all the trouble until this moment. What have you done with them?'

Wallace laughed.

'That's the joke of the whole business,' he chuckled. 'All this bother has really been about nothing, because the package containing those delightfully incriminating letters left for Paris in the *rapide* at ten-fifteen last night.'

'What?' cried Brien. 'You old blighter, how on earth did you manage it?'

'I think I told you Monsieur Clement of the Department of the

Interior was staying at the Hermitage?' Brien nodded. 'Well,' went on Sir Leonard, still smiling, 'when I left you people after dinner I went to him, gave him the letters, and told him how they had come into my possession. I also gave him my opinion of politicians who put in black and white such dangerous statements. In return he told me that a severe inquiry concerning them was to have been held, and that they must have been stolen from the Quai d'Orsay, where they were kept pending the investigation. He was so agitated that he left for Paris with them by the first available train.'

'You men are talking in riddles,' murmured Phyllis sleepily.

'Billy's made history,' replied Wallace. 'Behold the man who prevented a war!'

CHAPTER EIGHT

East is East

The Statutory Commission appointed by the British Government to inquire into the working of the Indian Constitution wended its futile way through India, meeting at every turn opposition and obstruction, hindrance and hostility. Its members did their utmost to carry out their duties conscientiously, but their efforts, as history has since proved, were wasted. The Report, when published, was more or less still-born; it was condemned by almost every party in India. The gentlemen forming the Commission went from province to province, town to town, village to village, examining local conditions, making voluminous notes, listening carefully to the evidence, studying the mass of reports placed before them. The Congress boycotted them; they were told to go back to England by extremist volunteers the moderates only cooperated reluctantly, and after a great deal of hesitation. Despite all this they completed their task, and returned home full of information regarding India, which Indians had kindly manufactured for their benefit, but with remarkably little knowledge of the true state of affairs existent in that country.

Following them in their progress through India was a slim man of medium height. The somewhat lazy expression on his attractive, good-humoured face was belied by the keen grey eyes and indomitable jaw. With him was a lady, obviously his wife, a most beautiful woman, and a young man who acted as his secretary. The latter, tall and well knit, possessed excellent features and had the frame of an athlete. It was his first visit to India, and he was enjoying the experience immensely. To the ordinary observer these three would appear to be tourists, but while the Royal Commission was searching painfully for facts and figures, obtaining the latter but seldom the former, the slim man with the grey eyes was making investigations from a totally different angle. The information he thus acquired was not at all in accord with that obtained by the commissioners; it was absolutely reliable and authentic, while theirs, though they did not know it, was not.

Sir Leonard Wallace had had a good deal of experience of Indian mentality. Not only had he been stationed in India with his regiment before the Great War, but on two occasions since, as head of the Secret Service, he had carried out certain investigations. He knew the Indians well enough to realise that they would only allow the commission to see what it was to their benefit to let it see; that, as far as possible, everything of a detrimental nature to them would be hidden or glossed over. He travelled to India to find out exactly what power the extremists had in the country, and to investigate fully the very depths of political agitation. The result was that, in journeying from place to place in the wake of the Statutory Commission, he had obtained a wonderfully complete insight into the ramifications of the Congress party. His knowledge of the habits and customs of the people, and his mastery of Urdu, enabled him to disguise himself at will, and move among them as one of themselves.

'And this,' he observed to his secretary, who was no other than Carter of his own department, as they sat together in the lounge of Faletti's Hotel, Lahore, 'is the country that thinks it is able to rule itself.' He tapped with his finger a book lying open before him. 'Everything entered in this book is authentic. It has been culled from my own observation. When we return to London it will be placed before the Cabinet. It should show the government, once and for all, that India is not in a fit state for any further institutional reforms. Yet its only use will be to give our politicians a deeper insight into, and greater understanding of, the real India than they have ever had before, and make them wary in their future dealings with Indian politicians.'

'But surely, sir,' remarked Carter, 'that will show them the futility and danger of further reforms?'

'Not a bit of it,' declared Sir Leonard. 'Even with evidence like this before them, they will find it very difficult to do other than receive Indian demands sympathetically. London is a long way from India and, to our hard-headed statesmen, India is merely a part of the Empire like South Africa, Australia and Canada. Their argument is: if those three countries are fit to rank as dominions, why not India. You and I can put masses of proofs before them showing that India is too divided, with its various races, castes, religions and languages, to make a success of self-government. We can point out the low mentality of the majority of its inhabitants, its superstitions, its corruption, the shame of untouchability. We can prove that it is fatuous ever to expect that Hindus and Muslims will agree and that, if they cannot settle their differences under British rule, they certainly never will under home rule. There are a hundred cast-iron reasons in this book to show that it would be dangerous to go any further with constitutional reforms for many years at least, but I don't suppose, for a moment, they will have any effect, except to make the Cabinet act with a certain degree of caution. It doesn't matter to me – I am only out here on a job of work. If my pronouncements are ignored, or not taken proper account of, I cannot be responsible. One thing my report will do,' he added with a smile, 'and that is, render the report of the Statutory Commission useless. But, in any case, I don't anticipate that it will be accepted.'

'What do you think will eventually happen to India, sir?' asked Carter.

'Oh, in a few years' time, some sort of federal government will probably be instituted, the Indian statesmen will make a mess of it, the country will get into a state of chaos and there you are. Perhaps I'm wrong – I hope I am. But unless Indian mentality takes a sudden and miraculous change for the better, I don't see how I can be. I have not met an Indian yet who could hold a position of real responsibility without losing his head, or using his rank and influence to feather his own nest. They are all tarred with the same brush; the Muslims are perhaps a little bit more honest but not much. The Hindus see in self-government a wonderful opportunity of ruling the roost and forcing the Mohammedans under foot. All I can say is: God help the Mohammedans in an India with dominion status. Provincial autonomy might meet with a measure of success, but even that would be too full of communal and individual possibilities for our Indian friends to be able to resist the temptations arrayed before their designing eyes.'

'It seems to me,' said Carter rather diffidently for him, 'that this

Congress party is going to cause a heap of trouble before very long.'

'You're right there, Carter,' nodded his chief. 'It constitutes India's greatest danger, and before you and I return to England we must find out so much about the designs underlying its activities that whatever is attempted the course of the next few years will be nipped in the bud. The declaration by congressmen that independence is the goal of India will give rise to a lot of serious and unfortunate events, and Great Britain will be prepared for their coming. Gandhi is not worth worrying about; he is an idealist, and possibly the only honest man in his party, but the others are a lot of snakes in the grass ready to make any treacherous move that appeals to them. Their attempted boycott of the Commission has been a miserable failure, as anything they attempt will fail so long as the Indian Government is forewarned. That forewarning depends upon us.' He looked round to make sure that no one was within hearing. 'As soon as the Royal Commission has finished its inquiries, I will become a firebrand, and somehow or other insinuate into the inner circle of the Congress. You will be at hand wherever I go to render any assistance I may need, and act as liaison officer.' He closed the book and, putting it under his artificial arm, rose to his feet. 'I understand that Lady Wallace is taking me to renew acquaintances at Lorang's in the Mall in ten minutes,' he smiled. 'What are your plans?'

'I have none, sir.'

'Then come along with us, but be careful, Carter. Lahore is full of designing mothers with marriageable daughters.'

A few weeks later, when Lady Wallace was staying in Delhi as the guest of the Vicereine, a smartly dressed Mohammedan gentleman arrived in Lahore and, engaging a tonga, was driven to the Anarkali, where he engaged a room in a small native hotel. His arrival coincided with the visit of several Congress leaders, who intended delivering certain speeches in the Bradlaugh Hall. In his hotel he found, as he had expected, that the proprietor was a man with distinct pro-Congress sympathies, and he confided to him that he had travelled all the way from Kabul, where he was a man of substance, in order to study the Indian political problem.

'My sympathies,' he confessed, 'are on the side of Congress, and I have been wondering if it would be possible to help in any way.'

The landlord was greatly impressed. He had already put his guest down as a man from the north, owing to the fact that his skin was not very dark and his eyes were grey, a phenomenon that only occurred in northerners; he had even wondered if he were an Afghan. Rather pleased at his own astuteness, and delighted at his guest's sentiments, the proprietor of the dirty little hotel bowed low.

'Truly,' he remarked, 'you have come to Lahore at the right time. Tonight there will be many and great speeches at the hall which is called Bradlaugh. Your co-operation will be welcomed by those of our party. Our Muslim brethren have shown but little enthusiasm for the Congress. Tonight a big attempt will be made to enlist the sympathies of the Muslims of Lahore. If it please you, I take you to the meeting.'

The Afghan expressed his willingness to accompany his host, and together that evening they sat in a tonga, and were driven along Circular Road, past the District Courts and the Central Training College, until they reached the building which has such an unenviable reputation for seditious meetings. A great crowd chatted and laughed as it made its way into the hall. The Afghan and his companion were fortunate to find two seats near the front, a little way from the platform on which sat seven or eight men, all but two being Hindus. Close by were several well-known Lahore residents, including Dr Sir Mohammed Iqbal the poet, a man of enlightened mind and anti-Congress tendencies, who was probably present out of curiosity. He was invited to ascend the platform, but refused. Such an act, he knew, would have associated him with the speechmakers, and he looked as though he rather resented the invitation. One of the Muslims on the dais was a stout, smug-looking man, obviously one of the few Mohammedans who have sold their birthright for Hindu money. He was a barrister in Lahore, and was later to spend considerable periods in jail for sedition. The hotel-keeper, after fidgeting in his seat for some time rose and edged his way to the platform, where he got into conversation with this man. From the waving of arms in his direction, and the many glances, the Afghan concluded that they were discussing him. The barrister showed a great deal of interest, and presently descended from his perch. He was introduced to the Afghan, and expressed his great pleasure at seeing him there.

'My colleagues,' he asserted, 'will be delighted to meet you. May I take you to them?'

Thus was Sir Leonard Wallace received into the Congress camp. The refusal of the great bulk of Muslims to associate with the Congress was a very sore blow to the Hindu leaders, and they were prepared to go to almost any lengths to obtain volunteers from among the followers of the Prophet. It is a well-known fact that they were prepared to pay substantial sums of money to prominent Muslims to join them, but only a few fell to the temptation. The advent of an Afghan, who dressed and spoke like a man of education and importance, was an event. If public opinion in Afghanistan could be swayed to the side of Congress, there was no knowing what rosy prospects might be in store for India! At least that was what Sir Leonard's new acquaintances thought, and they gave him a warm welcome and a seat on the platform, even mentioned him in their speeches. Afterwards he was made much of, and had a long conversation with Lala Rajpat Rai, whose death from heart failure a year or so later was made an excuse for the cruel murder of the young police officer, Saunders. Rajpat Rai invited him to take up his abode in his house during the remainder of his stay in Lahore, but he declined. He preferred the liberty which the Anarkali hotel afforded him, even though there might be certain advantages in living in intimate contact with an important member of the Congress.

Having expressed his intention of travelling throughout India and studying Congress activities at first hand, he left Lahore a few days later armed with various letters of introduction. He arrived in Allahabad when Pandits Motilal Nehru and Jawarhalal Nehru were there, and had the satisfaction of meeting them and learning from them much of their intentions for the future. He found Jawarhalal a good-looking man with rather an ascetic type of face and mind that had been definitely sovietized. Nothing gave him more pleasure than to talk of modern Russia. He spoke well, and had a convincing manner, which Sir Leonard quickly decided would be very effective in moving the half-educated and easily swayed masses. The only item of real interest which came to his knowledge in Allahabad, however, was the fact that the two Nehrus, and other leaders of the Congress, were meeting Gandhi in Ahmedabad, where secret conference was to be held a week later. He resolved to be present if possible. He made no secret of his desire meet the Mahatma, and was promptly given a letter of introduction.

He took care not to arrive at Ahmedabad until the day before the conference was due to take place, hoping that, by that time, Congress circles would feel such confidence in him that he would be invited to the meeting itself. He went to Gandhi's Ashram at Sabarmati feeling that his work was nearing completion; that he was on the eve of making important discoveries. He was ushered into the presence of the Mahatma by Mirabai, the English girl who had given up everything to become a disciple of the man whom India idolised. He studied her covertly, but with a great deal of interest, and was surprised to notice how contented she looked. There was something suggestive of the fanatic in her face, but in her eyes shone a light as well which is usually only seen in the eyes of those who have found a great and abiding truth. Sir Leonard was impressed.

Gandhi received him courteously, but for some time he found it difficult to rid himself of a feeling of astonishment that such cultured accents could proceed from the wizened little object seated cross-legged on a mat, looking for all the world like a living gargoyle. He presented his letter of introduction, and was invited to squat near his host, who was engaged in his favourite occupation of spinning. Gandhi very quickly proved that he had an extensive knowledge of Afghanistan, and Wallace felt glad that he had taken the trouble to bring his acquaintance with affairs in the northern kingdom up to date. Afterwards the emaciated-looking Indian spoke earnestly and convincingly about the political problems that beset India, but there was more than a tinge of fanaticism in his observations, and a great deal of quite impossible idealism. One by one his disciples came up and squatted within hearing, hanging upon the Mahatma's words as though he were a prophet of old with all the assertion and authority which had enabled the numerous soothsayers of biblical times to impress and sway the impressionable multitude. Indeed, Sir Leonard Wallace had a sensation, as he sat there listening, that he had been conveyed back through the ages. His surroundings gave support to that feeling, for it was such a scene as must have been common enough in the old Israel of the Bible. The only modern note about it was his own Muslim dress, and even that was of the kind that has scarcely changed for centuries.

Gandhi added nothing to what Wallace had learnt since becoming identified with the Congress movement in Lahore. He more or less devoted himself to the painting of a highly imaginative picture of the India of the future, so Utopian in character that a faint smile even curled the lips of Mirabai, who had noiselessly approached and stood a few feet away. Eventually the Indian demagogue came to earth, and looked at the pseudo-Afghan, his eyes twinkling behind his large spectacles, as though he realised himself that he had been talking moonshine. Wallace, who had always felt that Gandhi was an idealist and nothing else, suddenly began to doubt the man's honesty of purpose. That half-smile on his face said quite plainly: 'It is wonderful how gullible Indians are. You see how easy it is to sway them with a lot of nonsense!' Sir Leonard became convinced at that moment that, though there might be a great deal of romanticism in the Mahatma's nature, he was, after all, a poseur; that his meagre dress, everything he did, everything he said, were merely part of a self-advertising stunt. It was the one thing most likely to impress his superstitious, semi-educated countrymen, and he had been clever enough to see it and act on it.

'After all,' he observed in a gentle voice to his visitor, 'we do not ask for much. The great object of the Congress is to attain for the people of India a system of government similar to that enjoyed by the self-governing members the British Empire. If you return to Afghanistan, and persuade your country-people that that is the motive behind Congress activities, I am certain that their sympathy will be with us. And if the whole world can be influenced to sympathise in the same manner, the British Government will not refuse to accede to our just demands. It dare not.'

'How do you think the whole world can be influenced?' asked Wallace.

'Ah! That I am not prepared to say – yet.'

He broke into a long Persian proverb, and Sir Leonard wondered if he had quoted it on purpose to test him and thus discover if he were really an Afghan. However Wallace's knowledge of Persian was as good as that of Urdu, and he replied by politely disputing the aptness of Gandhi's quotation, and citing another which, in his opinion, he declared, was more appropriate. Gandhi courteously conceded the point. Presently he dismissed Miss Slade and his other disciples. Wallace immediately thought that he was about to hear something of an important and secret nature, but was entirely unprepared for what actually came. Waiting until they were alone, Gandhi leant across and spoke quietly.

'Now, sir,' he said in English, 'perhaps you will be good enough to explain the meaning of this masquerade?'

If ever Wallace was taken by surprise during his career it was at that moment. For some seconds he merely sat and stared at his interlocutor, wondering what had given him away, feeling thoroughly foolish. The half-naked Indian before him gazed at him through his absurd glasses, a glint of amusement in his eyes. He seemed to be enjoying the situation. Sir Leonard recovered himself quickly. He saw that it was no use keeping up the pretence to the astute little man, who had, somehow or other, penetrated his disguise.

'How did you know?' he asked calmly.

Gandhi raised his hands in a gesture almost of apology.

'I knew that you and Lady Wallace were in India and—'

'Then,' interrupted Sir Leonard sharply, 'you also know who I am.'

'I do,' returned Gandhi. 'As I was saying, I knew you were in India, and being aware of your position as head of the British Intelligence Service, I naturally suspected your reasons for coming to this country. I have heard a lot about you, and some of your exploits have been related to me. In addition I have seen a photograph of you. When you came here today I must confess I was deceived, and really believed that I was entertaining an Afghan gentleman. It was only when I noticed the glove on your left hand that suspicions were roused – I knew of your artificial arm, you see. After that it was not very difficult to penetrate your very excellent disguise.'

'I see,' nodded Wallace. 'What are you going to do about it?'

The Mahatma raised his hands in another expressive gesture.

'What can I do about it?' he asked. 'You are here, and you will depart again. I have no wish to detain you. Even if I had, I don't suppose I could, as no doubt you possess a strong argument in favour of your being allowed to go unmolested in the shape of a pistol.'

'No,' returned Sir Leonard. 'I have no weapon of any sort on me.'

'Ah!' Gandhi smiled. 'That either shows that you had confidence in me, or in your disguise.'

'A little of both, I expect,' conceded Wallace. 'Then I take it you will make no attempt to hinder me?'

'None at all. Why should I? You have learnt absolutely nothing by coming here in this manner. I would have spoken to you as I have spoken, if you had come as your real self.'

'Perhaps you would have opened out a little bit, if you had not penetrated my disguise,' suggested Sir Leonard.

'There is nothing to open out about,' was the reply. 'You Britishers nowadays are full of suspicion. Believe me, the Congress has no ulterior motives. I will admit that there is an extreme left-wing, which is rather fond of making a noise, but really means no harm. Our object, as I said just now, is the attainment of a system of government similar to that of other dominions. Surely there is nothing harmful in such an ambition?'

Wallace smiled.

'I wonder if you really think I believe that?' he said. 'Personally I am convinced that it is a mere smoke-screen raised by you and your colleagues to conceal your real intentions.'

Gandhi shrugged his shoulders.

'You will, of course, think what you choose,' he murmured. 'I doubt if you have learnt any more in your spying expedition through India.'

Sir Leonard rose from his uncomfortable position on the floor.

'It seems that there is nothing more to be said,' he remarked.

'Nothing, except that I would have respected Sir Leonard Wallace more had he come to me undisguised. There was no necessity to come as a spy.'

'That is a matter of opinion,' returned the other calmly. 'The word spy has an unpleasant sound I admit but, at times, it can have a very noble meaning.'

'Not in my language,' retorted Gandhi.

He clapped his hands, and Miss Slade made her appearance. Continuing to speak in English he addressed her.

'Please see that this gentleman – Sir Leonard Wallace of the British Intelligence Service – is allowed to leave the premises without hindrance; then return to me.'

She gave a start of surprise, but made no further sign, and led Wallace to the gate, where she spoke for the first time.

'You came like this,' she stated rather than asked, 'to pry into his secrets? It was an incredibly mean thing to do.'

'I'm sorry you feel like that about it,' he replied gently. 'I do not agree with you, Miss Slade.'

'Don't call me that,' she cried almost angrily.

'Very well; Mirabai then.'

He bowed, and, turning, walked swiftly to the conveyance that awaited him. She stood looking after him for some moments; then returned slowly to Mr Gandhi.

Sir Leonard decided that he had come very badly out of his attempt to pry into the secrets of the Indian National Congress. He felt rather like a small boy who had been found out in some mischievous prank; nevertheless he had no intention of leaving the neighbourhood until he had discovered what he had come for, or proved that it was impossible to learn anything further. His mind was very busy during the ride to the small native hotel in which he had taken a room in Ahmedabad and, as he descended from the tonga, there was such a purposeful look on his face that it would have caused Mr Gandhi to ponder deeply could he have seen it.

That evening Wallace made several purchases in the bazaar, which he carried to his inn, afterwards going to the European hotel where Carter impatiently waited for word from him. Behind closed doors the young man was apprised of the disastrous ending to Sir Leonard's interview with Gandhi.

'By Jove, sir!' he commented. 'It was pretty cute of the old boy.'

'It was,' agreed Wallace, 'but his very cuteness in recognising that I had an artificial arm will possibly help to lead him into a little trap I am preparing for him. Tomorrow I am returning to the Ashram. He and his followers will probably be expecting me to make another attempt, and I will be on the look out. But when a sadhu turns up showing quite brazenly the naked stump of an arm, if I am not mistaken, they will be completely deceived. The last thing they would expect me to do would be to flaunt the very disability that gave me away. And I don't think they would ever dream that a fastidious Englishman would disguise himself as a sadhu.'

'What is a sadhu?' asked Carter curiously.

'One who follows a certain Hindu principle of asceticism. Tomorrow you will see what a member of the cult looks like. And as it won't do for you to be seen with one, I want you take careful note of what I am going to say. I think my plan to get into the Ashram will work all right, but in order to make certain, I want your help. About seven I shall make my way to Sabarmati, and you must hire a car and follow somewhere about ten. You will be the bearer of a message from me to Gandhi asking him for another interview in my proper capacity as Chief of the Intelligence Department. He may make an appointment; he may not – it doesn't matter one way or the other. But one thing does matter: you will be bothered by a horrible-looking fakir, naked except for a loin-cloth, bells round his neck and ankles, streaks of pigment on his body and face, hair matted with mud, and merely a stump instead of a left arm. Have you followed?'

'Yes, sir,' grinned Carter. 'Will that be you?'

'That will be me,' nodded Wallace. 'I'll solicit alms from you so earnestly and insistently that you'll lose your temper, and push me roughly aside. I'll fall, and be hurt and, I hope, will be carried into the Ashram. Do you get the idea?'

'Rather, sir. What do I do then?'

'Return to Ahmedabad. You'll probably be chased off the premises anyhow for daring to treat a holy man in such a manner.'

Carter looked disappointed.

'Pity you can't find me something else to do as well, sir,' he grumbled. 'My job seems tame.'

'It's very important,' returned Wallace. 'It will certainly help to establish my bona fides, and will probably be the only possible way of enabling me to get into the Ashram. But when you push me, push hard. It would look absurd and highly suspicious if I fell over for no apparent reason.'

Early next morning a figure was seen on the road to Sabarmati, which pedestrians and others regarded with reverence or disgust, according to their religious persuasions. His dark brown, almost black, skin was coated with dust, his only garment being a loin-cloth. His hair was matted with dried mud; his face and chest streaked with white paint. Round his neck and ankles were fastened bells, and he carried in his right hand a beggar's bowl, into which every now and again a pious passer-by would drop a coin. His left arm had been amputated between shoulder and elbow, and the stump, covered with dirt like the rest of his body, hung pathetically to his side. He took a considerable time to traverse the short distance between Ahmedabad and Sabarmati, as he walked very slowly most of the way, and visited every shrine he came to, but occasionally he would trot in order to make the bells ring, particularly when approaching people whom he thought charitably minded.

Sir Leonard Wallace had worn many disguises in his time, but nothing to equal this. In every way he looked the religious mendicant, one of the unclean, grotesque brotherhood so common in India. It was the only disguise that, in his opinion, would be effective in the Ashram of Mahatma Gandhi, after the detection of the previous day. But he hated the filth and indecency of it, loathed the necessity which compelled him to walk barefooted, abominated the unclean scent which, with many a shudder, he had sprinkled on his body in order to complete the effectiveness of the masquerade. A master of disguise, Sir Leonard always took care to assure himself that, in every particular, his make-up was perfect. The only amusement, however, his impersonation of a fakir afforded him was contained in the reflection that he would like his wife to see him and study her face when she knew it was he.

At last he arrived at the Ashram and found it a hive of industry. It no longer wore the placid appearance it had possessed when he made his first visit. Everybody moved about as though great events were about to take place, and he was surprised at the number of people assembled in the compound until he remembered that the two Nehrus were expected, and that the gathering was there to bid them welcome. He squatted at the gate, and watched. Several men approached, dropped coins in his bowl, and spoke reverently to him. Eventually Gandhi was apparently notified of his arrival, for he emerged from the building surrounded by a crowd of his disciples, and walked to the 'holy' visitor. Wallace prepared for the interview quite confidently. He had studied the religious mendicant business thoroughly, and felt no qualms that he would make a slip and give himself away. For several minutes the Mahatma spoke to him, asking questions and receiving appropriate replies, and it was obvious that despite his enlightenment, he possessed almost the same superstitious reverence for the ascetic squatting before him as his untutored companions. One of the first things he noticed was the stump of Wallace's left arm. It seemed to fascinate him and he asked questions concerning it, to receive a highly coloured recital of the imaginary accident which had led to the amputation.

'It is strange that thou should be in like state,' he remarked, 'to an Englishman who visited me yesterday. He also had lost his left arm, but in place of it was an instrument made by man.'

The fakir spat derisively, whether to show his contempt for the Englishman or the artificial limb was not clear, however. He was invited to enter the compound and partake of food, which Gandhi ordered to be brought to him, and rose and followed his host. As he did so a car arrived and turned in at the gate, pulling up close by. Carter descended, and walked up to the man he recognised as Gandhi.

'May I speak to you?' he asked politely.

The Mahatma bowed and led him a little aside.

'What can I have the pleasure of doing for you?' he asked.

'My name is Carter,' was the reply, 'and I am the secretary of Sir Leonard Wallace. He desires me to ask if you can give him an appointment. He would like to have an interview with you.'

Gandhi smiled.

'As himself, I presume?' he murmured.

'As himself,' assented Carter.

'Then please tell Sir Leonard from me that it will be a great pleasure to meet him – as himself. I will be free to receive him at seven this evening.'

Carter thanked him, and turned away. Suddenly he became

aware of the grotesque figure standing before him, and his eyes almost started from his head.

'My God!' he gasped below his breath, and for a moment still almost in a state of stupefaction.

He quickly recovered himself, however, when the bowl of the religious beggar was thrust before him. He pushed it aside, and started to walk to the car, but the fakir stepped in his way, asking for alms in a wheedling voice, and holding the bowl expectantly towards him.

'Out of my way,' snapped Carter.

The fakir was most insistent, however, and the Englishman at last appeared to lose his temper. He flung the man aside with such force that he staggered, lost his balance, and crashed to the ground on his left shoulder. Immediately there was a roar of rage from the spectators of the act of violence, some rushed to pick up the fakir, others advanced threateningly in the direction of Carter. A sharp word of command from Gandhi, and the latter hung back muttering angrily to each other. The Indian leader turned to the Englishman.

'You had better go,' he advised in a quiet voice.

'I'm beastly sorry,' said Carter. 'I didn't mean to throw the fellow down.'

He felt more than sorry when he noticed that Sir Leonard was bleeding badly from the stump of his left arm. The sight almost turned him sick, and he felt an insane desire to go down on his knees, and apologise to his chief. In that moment he realised what it must have cost Sir Leonard to adopt such a disguise. He was known to be terribly sensitive about his disfigurement, and only Batty, his manservant and, of course, Lady Wallace, had ever seen the stump, and here he was exposing it to the gaze of a crowd of

Indians for the sake of a cause. Carter knew that he would probably be complimented by Sir Leonard for the effectiveness and apparent genuineness of his shove, but that did not cause him to regret any the less that he had hurt the chief. He turned away regretfully, and entered his car, which left the compound followed by the hoots and catcalls of the enraged Indians.

Leonard was lifted up by willing hands and, at Gandhi's command, conveyed to a room close to his own quarters. Here he was attended to by Mirabai, but refused to allow the torn stump of an arm to be dressed. The reason he gave, a religious one invented on the spur of the moment, was respected; actually he was afraid that, if the wound had been washed, some of the stain would have been removed, and result in his being unmasked. Although the stump was exceedingly painful, he smiled inwardly at Carter's very realistic effort. The brutality of the Englishman would probably be the talk of the Ashram for some time. Wallace counted a great deal on his being made an object for compassion and pity, and being exhibited to the Nehrus and other visitors as a victim of the cruelty of a member of the governing race. Perhaps then he would be able to learn, from a chance remark dropped in his hearing, where the conference was to take place. But that did not worry him very much; it was bound to be nearby, for he was close to Gandhi's own apartments.

Mirabai and another woman tended him carefully. He was brought food, of which he took little, continuing to utter groans and call down curses on the head of the white man who had treated him so ill. Lying on a *charpai* in the little room, he presently pretended to fall into a sleep. A blanket was laid gently over him, and he was left alone.

The sound of cheering caused him to raise himself a little and listen eagerly. Several minutes went by, during which the cheering was renewed at short intervals. Then there was silence, after which he heard footsteps coming in the direction of his room. He lay down again, and resumed the pretence of slumber. In a few seconds the *chick* at the door was drawn aside, and several people appeared to enter, and group themselves by the bed. He recognised Gandhi's voice speaking quietly. He was relating what had happened, his description being punctuated by various remarks from the men with him expressive of sympathy for the victim and abuse for the assailant. A harsh voice which Sir Leonard had not heard before was more vituperative than the others. It obviously belonged to a firebrand.

'If I had my way,' it said, 'I would train young India not to a campaign of non-violent resistance, but to a properly organised reign of terror. Milk and water methods are too good for the English.'

Someone laughed softly.

'Gupta is feeling bloodthirsty again, it seems.' It was Pandit Jawarhalal Nehru speaking.

'My friend,' murmured Gandhi, 'your sentiments are repugnant to me. Bloodshed is horrible, and I would rather this country was wallowing in slavery than that my compatriots should endeavour to obtain their rights by assassination.'

An impatient exclamation broke from the lips of the man with the harsh voice. Another spoke in support of him and Jawarhalal again interposed.

'It is quite certain,' he observed mockingly, 'that we all have to name our friends from Calcutta the Bloodthirsty Bengal Brigade.'

His remark brought a heated reply from one of the others, and Gandhi hastened to change the subject.

'Do you remember the Afghan gentleman to whom you gave a letter of introduction for me?' he asked.

'Yes,' returned Pandit Jawarhalal. 'I found him a most charming man.'

'So did I,' went on the Mahatma with a little chuckle. 'I also discovered who he really was. My friends, you gave shelter to a man whose purpose it was to learn our secrets, and divulge them to the British Government.'

'A spy?' cried several voices.

'A spy indeed; perhaps the greatest spy in the world today. It was the famous Sir Leonard Wallace of whom you all must have heard.'

For a few moments there was a stupefied silence; then the harsh voice broke out in a more violent diatribe than before, even reviling the Nehrus for their carelessness.

'Where is that man now?' it concluded fiercely.

'He is in Ahmedabad with his secretary,' replied Gandhi.

'Then I will see that his activities are ended for ever. Tomorrow the British will be mourning the passing of Wallace Sahib.'

Several voices spoke sharply to the fellow, the Mahatma's predominating.

'If you dare take action which will, in any way, harm the Englishman,' it said, 'you will be cast from the Congress in ignominy. Remember my words, and subdue those violent tendencies of yours.'

He received a hot reply in which the speaker stated that there was a strong party in the Congress that felt as he felt, and would be ready, at a word, to split from the more pacific members.

'Think,' advised Gandhi; 'such a split would ruin all our aspirations. Separately we would be too weak to take any action.

Can you not see, my friend, that violence would ruin all, that desperate measures would be met with desperate measures, against which our people would be helpless and our cause destroyed?'

The voice of Pandit Motilal Nehru spoke for the first time.

'Are we then to commence our conference standing over this poor fakir?' he asked sarcastically. 'What arrangements have you made, Mahatma Sahib, in order that we may converse without fear of eavesdroppers or interruption?'

'This part of the Ashram,' replied Gandhi, 'will be entirely cut off from communication with the other part. I have instructed several of my young men to guard it, and allow no one to enter, not even Mirabai. I suggest also that we should speak in English in order that this holy beggar may not understand if, by any chance, he should hear.'

'Why not remove him elsewhere?' asked a voice.

'It is unnecessary,' came the answer, much to Sir Leonard's relief. 'Come, gentlemen!'

The men retreated from the room, and Wallace was left alone. He opened his eyes, and looked round; then sat up and smiled to himself. He appeared to be in luck's way. As nobody was to be allowed in that part of the building, he would be able to move about without much fear of detection. The thought that the Congressmen would speak in English, in case he overheard, amused him immensely. He felt that he would dearly like to share the joke with Gandhi later on.

'I'm afraid,' he muttered regretfully, 'that the old boy's sense of humour would not be proof against such a revelation.'

He looked down at his filthy body and shuddered; then got off the *charpai* and stepped quietly to the door. The bells round his ankles tinkled softly and, after a moment's hesitation, he bent down and removed them, leaving them on the floor. Pushing the *chick* slightly aside he looked along the veranda. There was not a soul in sight, but the murmur of voices reached him, seeming to come from a room a little way along. Treading carefully he approached it; then suddenly stopped dead. Like all the others, *chicks* hung before the window and door, and he knew very well that, though it was impossible to see into a room through a *chick*, those inside can see out. He returned to the little chamber which had been allotted to him, and sat down on the *charpai* to think things out. A closed door caught his eye. Obviously it communicated with the next room, and it was reasonable enough to suppose that in that room would be a door communicating with the apartment in which the Indians were holding their meeting. He walked across to it, but it was bolted. Nothing daunted, he went out onto the veranda, and was able to enter the adjoining chamber that way. As he had guessed, there was a door at the upper end opposite the one that was bolted and, putting his ear against it, he heard the voices now quite distinctly, proving that the conspirators were indeed in the next room. This door was also locked, but it did not matter much. With the exception of a few words he was able to hear everything that was said.

As he stood there, his ear pressed hard against a panel, he wondered what he would do if someone entered the apartment. Like all the rooms in the Ashram he had seen, it was barely furnished, and certainly possessed nothing that would suffice to hide him. However, as Gandhi had given instructions that nobody was to be allowed into that part of the establishment, there was not much danger unless it came from the conspirators themselves. It was quite possible, of course, that Gandhi or one of the others would enter the room or take it into his head to go and look at the fakir. In that case, Sir Leonard decided, he would have to act as the situation decreed; there was no use bothering about it now, when he was so occupied in listening to the discussion in the next apartment.

For a long time nothing was said of particular interest. The man with the harsh voice tried very hard to impress upon his colleagues that violent methods should be adopted in the coming campaign, but he was overruled, and thereafter his voice was seldom heard. A long and boring debate followed concerning the Statutory Commission, and an almost equally tiresome argument about the Hindu–Muslim problem. Wallace smiled grimly as he realised that the general inclination was to throw dust into the eycs of Muslims by pretending to agree to the majority of their demands, and thus get them to declare themselves on the side of Congress.

'Afterwards,' observed a voice which he did not know, 'we shall see!' There was a general laugh.

Then came the intelligence for which Wallace was waiting so eagerly. Gandhi was speaking.

'I have given matters very deep consideration,' he said in his excellent English. 'We are agreed, I take it, that although we have stated publicly that Dominion status would be acceptable to the people of India, actually we are determined upon a demand for complete independence.'

A chorus of assent greeted his remarks.

'To attain that,' he went on, 'I suggest that a campaign of civil disobedience be mapped out. It will probably take at least two years before it can be put into effect, but what matter two or three or four years, so long as everything is prepared properly, and so well organised that there can be no hitch or failure. Every move made by the British government, which has not as its ultimate object complete independence for India, must be systematically boycotted, not in the unprepared manner that the Commission has been boycotted, but in a way that will make success an absolute certainty. In every conceivable manner the government must be harried, subverted and checkmated, until in desperation it is forced to give in. The programme of civil disobedience I outline is this: every law that it is possible to break, apart from criminal laws such as murder, theft and that type of misdemeanour, must be broken. We must see that the income of the government is reduced by persuading the people not to pay excise and customs duties; we shall induce government servants to resign; we shall picket shops dealing in British goods and also liquor shops; and urge the masses not to pay land revenue, *chowkidari* tax and forest grazing fees.'

He paused, and a babble of excited and enthusiastic comment broke out.

'Our preparations must be so complete,' he went on after some time, 'that the movement will come as a complete shock to the British government, and cause credit and confidence to be shattered, and trade and commerce to be paralysed. Men, women and even children must be included in the campaign, all with their special duties. In a desperate attempt to cripple us the government will, no doubt, promulgate ordinances, but we will defy them. We shall be thrown into jail, but what will that matter? Let us fill the jails of the country, there will always be others to follow us and carry on our work, if our organisation is as complete and perfect as I hope it will be. That, my friends, is the outline of the civil disobedience I propose. If you accept the suggestion, all that remains to do is to set to work now, and organise quietly, carefully, efficiently. I only stipulate one thing, and that is: there must be no violence. The most effective way of gaining freedom is through non-violence. Thus shall we merit and receive the sympathy of the world. In each capital city in Europe and America we must place a small committee, the duties of which will be to circulate propaganda on our behalf. In India we shall choose a leader, call him the dictator if you will, and in each province there must be a deputy dictator presiding over a small committee of action. Only thus can the work go on successfully. If you are with me, let our watchword be *Satyagraha*!'

As his speech drew to a close his voice vibrated with feeling, and a united shout of *Satyagraha* greeted the conclusion. It was obvious that, among the leaders of the Congress gathered in the room with Mr Gandhi, there was not one dissentient. All were absolutely, enthusiastically in favour of the campaign of civil disobedience. A long discussion followed regarding details, but Sir Leonard only lingered until he was certain that the Mahatma's proposals were to be adopted, and that there was nothing else for him to learn. He crept quietly back to his little room, fastened the bells round his ankles again, and sat down to wait. He felt that he would have given anything for a smoke, but it would be several hours before he could satisfy his craving for tobacco. The stump of his arm ached abominably, and a large clot of blood had formed on it. He felt it ruefully, and grimaced at the thought that blood-poisoning might possibly set in.

Half an hour went by; then abruptly the *chick* over the door was drawn aside, and Gandhi entered. He inquired solicitously after the welfare of the injured fakir, and received by way of reply a stream of invective regarding white people in general and the man, in particular, who had caused the injuries. He again suggested that the wound be dressed, but the fakir would have none of it, and announced his intention of departing to join brethren of his, whom he had arranged to meet in Ahmedabad. Gandhi made no objection and, having assured himself that his queer guest was fit enough to go, took him to the Congress leaders, who expressed their sympathy for his injury and threw various coins into his bowl. Wallace rolled up the money with the other he had collected in a corner of his loin-cloth, salaamed deeply and departed, being escorted to the gate by the courteous Gandhi.

Wallace estimated that it must have been long after three in the afternoon when he left the Ashram. Although the cool season, it was very warm in the open. The sun beat down on his unprotected head, and caused him to speculate uncomfortably on the possibility of sunstroke afflicting him, while the hot, dusty road burnt the soles of his bare feet with every step he took. It was a very weary man who eventually arrived in the neighbourhood of the hotel where, as an Afghan, he had taken a room. But now a new problem beset him. It had been easy enough in the early hours of the morning to slip out without being seen. It was a much more difficult matter to get in. Two Mohammedans sat close to the door sharing a *hookah*, a vendor of sweetmeats had propped up his stall close by, and was lazily waving the flies away with a dried palm leaf, while the narrow little street was crowded with pedestrians. A thought struck him. He remembered that his room overlooked a lane at the back devoted to bullocks and goats. It was on the first storey, and it might be possible to climb in.

He found the lane after twice losing his way and almost his patience as well. The bullocks were away on their lawful occasions and, except for a few goats, and a woman engaged in removing unwelcome intruders from a child's head, the place was deserted. The woman and child, to his delight, moved hastily away at the sight of him, and he stood and gazed upwards calculating which was his room. He quickly found it, and muttered an exclamation of relief when he saw that the window was open as he had left it. An old bullock-cart wheel lay close by. This he raised with an effort and leant against the wall. Climbing up he found he could reach the window sill quite easily. Then with his one hand – a feat of strength he had often been called upon to perform before – drew himself up, and climbed into the room.

Once inside he looked out again to make sure that he had not been observed, but there was still nobody about. The sight of the beggar's bowl lying where he had left it, when raising the wheel, caused him to smile. It was a pity he could not have retained it; he would have liked to have kept it as a memento of the day when he became a fakir.

Like most native hotels the bathing arrangements were sadly inadequate, but he did not bother to do anything but remove the paint and stain from his face, which he lightly tinted afresh to resume the character of the Afghan. He bathed the stump of his arm carefully, and was relieved to find that, though it was badly gashed, it showed no signs of suppuration. Fixing on the artificial limb, however, was a painful ordeal, and he grimaced several times before it was in place and fairly comfortably arranged. A quarter of an hour later he had his meagre belongings carried to a tonga, paid his bill and drove to the hotel where Carter awaited him. He found an anxious young man pacing his sitting room who, at the sight of him, gave a great cry of relief, and started to ask questions and apologise for the incident of the morning in the same breath. Wallace held up his hand.

'Pay off the tonga like a good chap,' he requested, 'and tell the driver to bring my goods and chattels in here. Then order the biggest bath the hotel has ever known.'

Carter carried out instructions, and ten minutes later Sir Leonard was lying in his bath feeling a marvellous sense of relief and well-being.

'Thank God, I am beginning to feel clean again,' he murmured. He eyed the discarded loin-cloth and the heap of odd coins lying scattered on the table. 'Quite a profitable day,' he decided. 'If I ever get hard-up I shall have to adopt the profession of sadhu.'

Later, in spotless linen and European clothes, which Carter had been carrying round for him, he lay back in a long chair, and gratefully sipped the tea his assistant had thoughtfully ordered for him.

'It's been a beastly ordeal, Carter,' he admitted in reply to a remark from the other, 'but it has been worth it. And if you apologise again for toppling me over so beautifully, I'll – I'll send you back to Scotland Yard. Where's the book of doom?'

Carter opened a suitcase, took out a steel box, which he unlocked, and produced the volume in which Sir Leonard had written detailed information concerning his investigations in India. For half an hour the latter sat and wrote rapidly; then returned his fountain pen to a pocket and handed the book back to the young Secret Service man.

'Lock it away, Carter,' he directed; 'it's precious now.'

At seven o'clock exactly a large car drew up in the compound of Mr Gandhi's Ashram, and Sir Leonard Wallace descended. Carter remained with the bags for, after his interview with the Mahatma, it was Wallace's intention to depart for Delhi. He was received courteously, and spent over an hour talking to the

Indian demagogue. None of the other leaders were present, and Sir Leonard presumed that they had already departed for their various headquarters. At last he rose to go.

'I prefer you as an Englishman, Sir Leonard,' remarked Gandhi as they shook hands.

'I rather prefer myself in that capacity,' admitted Wallace. 'By the way, my secretary is very apologetic over an incident that happened this morning. He lost his temper with a beggar, he informs me, and knocked the poor fellow down.'

'Ah, yes,' replied Gandhi, 'it was an unfortunate accident. Strangely enough the sadhu had also lost his left arm. Now, if you could have brought yourself to adopt a disguise of that nature, even I might have been deceived.'

'God forbid!' returned Wallace fervently.

Gandhi laughed.

'You Englishmen are a lot too fastidious,' he declared. 'It would do you good to experience some of the wretchedness and poverty that is so prevalent in India. I could almost wish to see the immaculate Sir Leonard Wallace transformed into a religious mendicant, if only for a day.'

'I don't think that is very kind of you, Mr Gandhi. Well, goodbye. I am delighted to have made your acquaintance.'

'But not so delighted, I imagine,' returned the Mahatma with a sly smile, 'as you would have been had you succeeded in imposing on me, and perhaps discovering thereby rather more than it is good for you to know at present.'

Wallace shrugged his shoulders.

'That is a matter of opinion,' he said. 'I shall always treasure the remembrance that I have been a welcome guest your Ashram.'

On the way to the station he sat for most of the time deep in thought, but once or twice smiled quietly to himself.

'Our work is done, Carter,' he observed at length. 'Thanks to Gandhi's firm belief in the fastidiousness of an Englishman, we know exactly what the Congress will do. It may be a year, two years, even more before the campaign of civil disobedience commences, but government will know what to expect, and no matter how well organised it may be it will be a failure.'

History is proving the accuracy of Sir Leonard's forecast.

CHAPTER NINE

The Poisoned Plane

His Majesty's Secretary of State for Foreign Affairs stroked his greying moustache and frowned. He was confronted with a problem which he regarded as serious, and the well-dressed, slightly built man standing on the hearthrug with his back to the fire was not, according to the Minister, giving that attention to the matter which it required. In fact his manner was almost flippant, though it must be confessed that the look in the steel-grey eyes was anything but frivolous.

'Am I to understand that you are not interested in this affair?' asked the Foreign Secretary.

'On the contrary I am intensely interested,' was the reply; 'but as you have merely stated that there is a mission on its way to England from the King of Afghanistan, and that you are anxious about its safety, you haven't exactly caused me to tremble with excitement.'

'*You* tremble with excitement!' echoed the Secretary of State scoffingly. 'I should like to see such a phenomenon. It would be a relief to discover that you are subject to human emotions sometimes.'

Sir Leonard Wallace smiled.

'You libel me,' he protested. 'Few people are more demonstrative than I. But let us leave personalities alone, shall we? I'm a busy man, and I want to know what you're anxious about.'

'Sit down and listen.'

The Chief of the Secret Service obediently took a chair, and leant forward in an attitude of attention.

'I'll tell you all I know,' went on the Cabinet Minister. 'The King of Afghanistan, surrounded as he is by rebels and enemies of all kinds, decided to ask our help in safeguarding his throne. In return he offers us certain important rights and concessions. What they are I do not know, but his requests and proposals are embodied in official documents which are now on their way to this country care of a trusted emissary. This gentleman is travelling by a P&O mail boat and, as far as Port Said, had no reason to suspect that he was in danger. Since the steamer left that port, however, his cabin has been twice ransacked, and yesterday his life was attempted. By great good fortune he warded off the attack and with the help of a steward, succeeded in capturing his assailant, who is now in irons.'

'What nationality is the fellow?'

'I have no information about him at all. The ship reaches Marseilles early the day after tomorrow. Can you send someone to meet him there and accompany him to London?'

'I'll make arrangements,' nodded Sir Leonard. 'By way, is he travelling alone?'

'No; he has a secretary and a servant with him.'

'What is his name?'

The Minister looked through some papers.

'General Said Ullah,' he announced after a short delay.

'Have you any reason to suspect that there is a party in Afghanistan antagonistic to the Amir's designs?'

'No; but since his return from his European tour, he has, as you are aware, roused a great deal of resentment and opposition by his reforms. Afghanistan is an intensely conservative country, and some bitterness has been caused among certain sections of his people, by the sudden changes he has brought into operation.'

'Sudden,' commented Wallace drily. 'He has been altogether too drastic. He is endeavouring to change the whole structure of Afghan society. In a few weeks he has ordered women to emerge from seclusion and doff the veil, impose new codes and taxes, prescribed the co-education of boys and girls, forbidden officials to practise polygamy, and ordered European dress for the people of Kabul. Do you imagine that Afghans with their hatred for any sort of innovation can at a moment's notice adapt themselves to revolutionary changes of that nature? Naturally there is bitter opposition. Afghanistan is not Turkey, neither is the Amir Mustapha Kemal Pasha. There will be trouble before very long and, unless I am greatly mistaken, he will soon find himself without a throne. Personally I think it would be as well if Britain did not interfere. What use will rights and concessions, guaranteed by him, be to us when he is driven from his kingdom? And short of lending him a British army to maintain his power, and aid him in carrying out his reforms at the point of the bayonet, I don't see how you can help him safeguard his throne. To do such a thing would not only be impolitic, it would be gross and unwarranted interference in the internal affairs of a country over which we exercise no control.'

'You're right of course,' agreed the Statesman, 'but proposals must be put before the Cabinet and properly entertained. They may well be worthy of consideration, and perhaps it will be possible to render him assistance without, in any way, committing ourselves, or intervening in matters outside our purview.'

Wallace clicked his tongue impatiently.

'If I were a member of the Cabinet,' he remarked, 'I would have nothing to do with a ruler who has shown such utter lack of foresight, tact, and statecraft.'

'You mean you would refuse to negotiate with him?'

Sir Leonard inclined his head.

'I would refuse to negotiate with him,' he repeated firmly. 'It has been said that, during his visit to Russia, he was immensely impressed by the people, the country, and the government. Why didn't he seek help from the Soviet? The two countries are in an ideal position to make a friendly alliance. Of course we shouldn't have liked it, but it seems a reasonable enough proposition. I daresay the Soviet will hate the idea of an understanding being brought about between Great Britain and Afghanistan, when—by Jove!' he interrupted himself; then stopped.

'What's the matter?' demanded the Minister.

Wallace laughed.

'It suddenly occurred to me,' he observed, 'that the man who searched the envoy's cabin and attacked him may be an agent of the Soviet. Perhaps Russia has taken a hand, and is determined to prevent any negotiations taking place between the Amir and Britain.'

The Secretary of State looked thoughtful.

'I wonder if you are right,' he murmured. 'It may well be that Russia has an inkling of what the Amir's proposed concessions consist, and that they do not meet with the approval of the Soviet.'

'It is very likely indeed,' nodded Sir Leonard. He chuckled. 'Somehow I have a feeling,' he observed, 'that I am about to try conclusions once again with my old friends from Moscow.'

The Foreign Secretary made a grimace.

'The worst of you fellows of the Secret Service,' he grunted, 'is that you are always looking for trouble.'

'It happens to be our job,' was the calm rejoinder.

'Well, I suppose I can rely upon you to see that this Afghan envoy comes through safely with his despatches?'

Wallace nodded his head.

'Yes,' he asserted, 'I think you can rely upon that, provided, of course, that he gets off the boat at Marseilles without losing his life or his precious papers.'

Sir Leonard walked across to the building which housed Great Britain's Intelligence Service, in a decidedly thoughtful frame of mind. Instead of entering his own office he sauntered along the corridor to the room occupied by Major Brien. He found the latter sitting at his desk, a great pile of reports in front of him, an ash tray, full to the brim with cigarette ends, by his side. His fair hair, going a little thin on top these days, was ruffled as though he had been running his fingers through it. He looked up with a frown which changed to a smile when he recognised his visitor.

'Hullo,' he greeted. 'Have you come to invite me to lunch?'

'Not to my knowledge,' was the reply. 'Are you becoming polite?'

'What do you mean?'

'You don't generally wait for invitations.' The speaker threw himself into a chair, shook his head disdainfully at the box of cigarettes pushed across to him, and commenced to fill the pipe which he had drawn from his pocket. 'Would you like to go to Marseilles, Bill?' he asked.

'I should hate it,' was the prompt reply. 'Why?'

'Because you're going.'

'Oh, am I? When, why, and wherefore?'

Sir Leonard explained.

'I want you to go,' he concluded, 'because we're frightfully short-handed. Only Maddison and Cousins of the experts are at headquarters just now, and they may be wanted at any moment for that Irish business. I can't very well send an inexperienced man, because it seems to me that there may be trouble to meet. There remains only you.'

Brien grunted.

'Since when have I become a blessed nursemaid?' he grumbled. 'Who's interested in Afghanistan anyway?'

'We are at the moment. As a matter of fact I have an idea that our old friends of the Soviet are busy once more.'

'You think that the fellow they put in irons is an agent of the OGPU?'

Wallace nodded.

'If so,' he remarked, 'your job won't be so easy as it seems. You may have a pretty sticky passage getting the envoy safely to London.'

The good-looking man seated on the other side of the desk began to appear more cheerful.

'That sounds better,' he remarked. 'Life has not been very exciting lately. When do you want me to leave?'

'The boat docks in Marseilles early the day after tomorrow. You'll be in time if you fly to Paris tomorrow morning and catch the *rapide*. But perhaps you'd prefer to fly all the way?'

Brien shook his head.

'No,' he decided; 'I like to save the department's money when I can. An air liner to Paris and the *rapide* will be good enough for me.'

Wallace laughed.

'No wonder you're going bald, Billy,' he observed. 'Virtue is forming a halo and pushing the hairs out.'

Brien felt the top of his head ruefully.

'Can't understand why I've gone thin like this,' he uttered.

'Try a little olive oil,' advised Wallace still smiling.

'It's all very well for you to grin. What about your grey hairs?'

'I am honest enough to admit that age is creeping on me,' was the retort. 'I don't pretend to regard the grey hairs with wondering surprise as you do your bald patch.'

Preferring not to rush matters, Brien altered his arrangements somewhat, and flew to Paris that afternoon, catching the evening *rapide* for Marseilles. On arrival he put up at Hôtel de Louvre et Paix to await the arrival of the P&O mail boat. He had never been particularly fond of Marseilles, but he passed the time pleasantly enough and, after dining, went to the opera. Later he entered a crowded café in the Rue de Rome, and sat for an hour listening to the orchestra and watching the gay *habitués* seated round him. Afterwards he strolled down the Cannebière now almost deserted, and had nearly reached his hotel, when a burly man stepped from the shadows and accosted him.

'Pardon me, Monsieur,' he apologised. 'May I request the great favour of a light for my cigarette?'

Brien obligingly struck a match, and held it towards him. It seemed as though his action had been expected as a signal, for immediately a closed-in car drew in silently to the kerb, two men stepped out and, before the Englishman quite realised that treachery was afoot, a length of lead piping descended on his head with crushing force, his knees gave way, and he sagged to the ground unconscious. At once the three conspirators picked up and bundled his body into the car, which turned and swung rapidly up the Cannebière. The attack had been so well organised, and so quickly executed, that the few people in the vicinity had noticed nothing amiss. There had been nobody close enough to see distinctly what had happened. The vehicle sped along the Boulevard de la Liberté and stopped at the Gare St Charles, where one of the men got out and disappeared into the station. Thence with glaring headlights it tore out of Marseilles, taking the broad road that leads to Arles.

Prompt to time the great liner from Bombay glided alongside her wharf, gangways were erected, and passengers, most of them bronzed Englishmen on leave from India, with here and there a sprinkling of Hindus or Mussulmans visiting Europe, took their places in the P&O special train. A well-dressed man with a carefully trimmed moustache went on board, and asked for General Said Ullah. He was taken by a steward to the smoking room where the quiet-faced Afghan was waiting with his secretary and, handing a card to the envoy, introduced himself as Major Brien of the British Intelligence Department.

'I was expecting you, sir,' stated the general in excellent English. 'A telegram from your Foreign Office informed me that you would meet me and escort me to London. I am very glad to make your acquaintance.'

He seemed greatly relieved at the arrival of the supposed British officer, and talked merrily as they disembarked. He spoke about the manner in which he had been attacked on board ship almost as though it were a joke.

'My assailant,' he remarked, 'will be taken on to London and tried there. I am afraid he will not like the extra week at sea.'

'In order that there can be no fear of further molestation, General,' said the man impersonating Major Brien, 'I have arranged to take you by air to London. Your secretary and servant can follow with your luggage by train. Is that quite agreeable to you?'

'Quite, thank you,' was the reply. 'I shall enjoy the trip very much.'

It was thus arranged, and he entered a car that was waiting and, with his companion, was conveyed to the flying ground. There they climbed into a large black and white monoplane, which took off immediately and headed north. It was merely a speck in the sky when a motor car, furiously driven, arrived at the aerodrome. Brien and another man sprang out before it had quite pulled up, and immediately interrogated the authorities concerning the Afghan general and his escort. Their dismay was great when they learnt that they had arrived a few minutes too late. Brien, pale of face, and still wearing evening clothes, was almost in despair – he had not properly recovered from the blow he had received and felt very shaky. The man with him, a high official of the Sûreté, was inclined to shrug his shoulders and take no further interest in the affair, but the Englishman soon had him actively engaged again.

'An aeroplane,' he cried. 'I want the fastest machine you've got! You can use your authority to have one placed at my disposal, Monsieur, can't you?'

The police officer spoke rapidly to the man in charge,

who replied that there would be no machine available for at least half an hour. A young man, standing by, listened to the conversation with great interest; then stepped forward and bowed to Brien.

'You desire to catch that monoplane, I understand, Msieu,' he remarked. 'Perhaps you will do me the honour of permitting me to take you after it in my aeroplane. I am the Comte de Vérac at your service, and I keep my own machine here.'

'By Jove!' exclaimed Brien. 'Do you mean that?'

'Most certainly. You are in trouble, and it is so unusual to see an Englishman in trouble that I am sure something serious has happened.'

'You're quite right,' Brien informed him, speaking rapidly. 'I am from the British Foreign Office. I came to Marseilles to meet an Afghan envoy who is carrying despatches to London. He has been kidnapped, and only God knows what will happen to him.'

'*Mon Dieu*! That is bad. Come, M'sieu!'

He set off at a run towards a hangar. Brien and the police official followed him. A beautiful *Clermont* was wheeled out by several mechanics who had dashed up and, at a word from the Comte, busied themselves in getting the machine ready. Apparently the young man was very popular, to judge from the willingness with which every order he gave was obeyed. He had a pair of twinkling brown eyes and a most engaging smile.

'Do you think you can catch them?' asked Brien anxiously, as he donned the flying coat, helmet and goggles handed to him.

'Of course,' was the proud response. 'My *Gloire d'Avignon* is one of the fastest machines in France.'

'But we can't rescue the envoy in mid-air. How do you think we can get hold of him?'

'They must descend sometime, M'sieu,' smiled the Comte. 'We will follow until they do. Climb in!'

Brien turned to the agent of the Sûreté.

'Will you be good enough to see the manager of the Hôtel de Louvre et Paix, settle my bill,' he handed him some money, 'and ask him to despatch my belongings to the Foreign Office, London?'

'Most certainly, M'sieu,' promised the man courteously.

Brien thanked him, and climbed into the machine.

Rising to a great height, the *Gloire d' Avignon* flew northwards, two pairs of anxious eyes watching eagerly for the monoplane. A fear that, as soon as it was out of sight of Marseilles, it may have changed its course, and now be flying in a totally different direction, worried Brien. If so there was no hope of rescuing the Afghan general, or of getting hold of the despatches he carried. The tremendous pace at which they were travelling exhilarated him, however, and helped him to regain a certain measure of optimism. He had never flown at such a speed before, and he found it very thrilling. His head still ached abominably, but he forgot all about the pain in the excitement of the chase.

On the previous night, or rather during the early hours of the morning, his captors had taken him to an old ruined building on the outskirts of the small village of Lançon. There he had been gagged and bound, and left to his fate. It was unlikely that he would ever be discovered in such an out of the way spot and, for all the men who had left him there cared, he would eventually die of starvation and exposure. But they had been a little careless in their confidence. When Brien regained his senses and discovered his predicament, he immediately set to work to find a means of removing his bonds. It was daylight before he succeeded and then, quite close by, he saw that part of the old wall of the building had broken sharply away, leaving a jagged edge. Slowly and laboriously he had rubbed the cord confining his wrists against it until at last it had been sawn through. Very soon after that he was free. He had wandered about for some time before he had reached the village; then had been lucky enough to find a man who owned a ramshackle car and, for a consideration, had taken him back to Marseilles. He had gone straight to the Sûreté, told his story and, accompanied by the agent, had driven to the docks, only to find that the envoy had been taken to the flying ground.

Having twice missed the Afghan by such a small fraction of time, he was very troubled lest he should lose him altogether and, as the minutes sped by and there was still no sign of the monoplane, he almost began to lose hope. Suddenly a little chuckle of delight came to him through the speaking tube.

'See, M'sieu,' announced the Comte, 'our quarry is ahead.'

There was no doubt of it. Flying hundreds of feet below them, now shining in the sunlight, anon a mere dim outline wrapped in mist as it passed through the clouds, was the black and white monoplane. Brien's spirits rose with a bound. He felt certain now that he would be able to rescue the Afghan general. The Comte reduced his speed and, dropping a thousand feet, followed with the other machine at a slightly higher altitude. Hour after hour went by, and the chase still continued, the monoplane showing no sign of landing. Brien began to feel exceedingly hungry. He had had no breakfast, and it was past lunchtime.

The cheerful voice of the young Frenchman reached him. '*Mon*

Dieu!' it said, 'your friends do not desire refreshment apparently. Me, I am both thirsty and hungry.'

'So am I,' returned Brien. 'I'm awfully sorry to cause you to miss a meal in this manner.'

The Comte laughed.

'It is nothing to worry about,' he answered. 'I owe you an apology for not thinking to bring food with us.'

He had hardly finished speaking when the machine ahead began to descend.

'Ah!' cried de Vérac. 'We must land at the same time, so that he cannot take fright and rise again, or escape with your man before we can stop him.'

'Where are we?' asked Brien.

'Close to Melun,' replied the Frenchman.

He went into a steep nose-dive, and the Englishman experienced one of the greatest thrills of flying. Suddenly, when he began to feel certain they would crash, the machine flattened out, and a few moments later gently touched the ground, rose slightly; then ran along smoothly on a perfect piece of turf. The Comte had made a wonderful landing, but Brien had no time for thoughts concerning the Frenchman's skill. He quickly realised that the monoplane had reached a rendezvous. The field in which they had landed was surrounded by woods, and there was no sign of human habitation anywhere near by. In the distance was a gate, and two men with a motor car were waiting there. The black and white machine had stopped, and the Comte de Vérac brought his cleverly alongside. Thanking his stars that he had not been searched when taken to Lançon, Brien drew out his revolver, and climbed quickly to the ground. He found himself face-to-face with the burly man who had asked him for a match.

'Hands up!' he snapped.

The man was apparently too surprised to resist. His arms went above his head, while an expression of baffled fury distorted his face. The startled eyes of the Afghan gazed at the scene from the aeroplane; a snarl that had something horribly animal-like in it came from the pilot, who began to climb to the ground.

'Stop where you are!' commanded Brien.

The fellow took no notice and, without hesitation, the Englishman fired, the bullet passing within an inch or two of his head.

'Next time,' warned Brien, 'I won't be so kind.'

He almost allowed his surprise to take him off his guard, when his eyes fully embraced the grotesque figure now standing snarling by the monoplane. Not more than four feet in height, it had long arms reaching to its feet; a pair of great teeth protruding on either side of its mouth had the appearance of fangs. In its flying coat, helmet and goggles it looked repulsive enough, without them it must have been a disgusting sight. Brien wondered if it were human.

'What have we here?' murmured a voice by his side. '*Mon Dieu*! Is it animal or man?'

'It's a terrible-looking thing, whatever it is,' was the reply.

'The people who were with the car,' went on the Frenchman, 'are now running this way. Shall I take them in hand, my friend?'

'Have you a revolver?'

'No, but I can manage without, I think.'

'But they are sure to be armed. You have done so much for me; I cannot allow you to risk your life.'

The Comte laughed.

'You have no choice, because you—'

He did not finish the sentence. Brien had allowed his attention to wander from the pilot during his conversation, with the result that the creature suddenly and furiously launched itself at him. He fired but missed and, in a moment, was rolling on the ground, the hideous thing on top of him. The Comte acted with great promptitude, bringing down a heavy spanner, which he had carried from his aeroplane, with terrific force on the head of Brien's adversary. At the same moment the other man threw himself forward and endeavoured to grapple with him, but with a little laugh he stepped aside, neatly tripping the fellow.

'Stay where you are,' he commanded. 'If you attempt to rise I will be compelled to hit you on the head also.'

There was a sharp crack and a bullet hummed past his ear like an angry wasp. The two men from the car had arrived within shooting distance. Brien, in the act of rising from the ground, returned the shot to such good effect that one of the newcomers dropped his revolver and clasped his right arm. The Comte de Vérac laughed again.

'We seem now to have the advantage,' he observed coolly.

He jumped aside, to avoid another bullet, and again Brien returned the fire, this time without success. Quickly the Frenchman bent and dragged to his feet the man he had tripped.

'Resist, and you will realise what a steel spanner feels like,' he threatened. 'Now march!' He had placed himself behind the fellow and, using him as a shield, made him walk forward. 'Follow closely behind me, my friend,' he added to Brien. 'You will thus be able to shoot those others without much danger to us.'

The manoeuvre was successful. Their one remaining armed antagonist fired twice, but the small Frenchman and Brien, who took care to stoop, were too well protected by their burly captive.

'Throw your revolver down,' shouted the Secret Service man, 'or I will shoot.'

The fellow took no notice, and tried another shot which passed so close to the individual, who had been forced into the position of a human shield, that the latter shouted out in mingled rage and terror. At the same time, Brien took careful aim and knocked the revolver out of the man's hand. It was a beautiful shot, and the Comte de Vérac gave an exclamation of admiration. He stepped back a little, and he and his companion contemplated the three scowling faces before them.

'It is a police matter this,' he remarked. 'What say you, my friend?'

'We'll search them and let them go,' decided Brien. 'I don't want to be bothered with a court case now. I must get the Afghan envoy to London.'

'Ah, yes. I was forgetting. Keep them covered.'

He walked forward, picking up the two revolvers on the ground, and carefully searched the clothing of their adversaries. There were no other weapons, the burly man proving to be unarmed, which accounted for the fact that he made no great attempt at resistance.

'Now go,' ordered Brien, 'and take that thing with you.'

He pointed to the prone body of the queer pilot. The two uninjured fellows walked to the creature and, picking him up, were about to carry him away when the Comte stopped them and insisted on searching the unconscious dwarf. All he found in his clothing was a small tube, shaped something like a stylo pen, and after glancing at it curiously, he replaced it.

'Ugh!' he murmured in disgust, 'what a travesty of a human being this is. Take it away – it is indecent.'

'What about the aeroplane?' asked the wounded man sullenly.

The Comte shrugged his shoulders.

'Perhaps sometime you can come back and claim it,' he observed, 'but not when my friend and I are here. Go on; march!'

Holding a revolver in either hand, the large spanner showing from the pocket of his coat, where he had placed it, he drove the men before him, and did not leave them until they had driven away in the car. Then he returned to Brien, who was busily engaged explaining matters to the astounded Afghan general. It was some time before the latter was convinced of his bona fides; then he was all gratitude to the men who had rescued him.

'What would they have done with me?' he wondered, as he climbed out of the monoplane.

'They probably brought you to this lonely spot,' returned Brien drily, 'with the intention of murdering you and robbing you of your despatches.'

The envoy looked distinctly startled.

'And you have let them go!' he exclaimed reproachfully.

'My duty,' the Englishman informed him, 'is to get you to London as soon as possible. If I had handed the fellows over to the police, we should have been detained.'

The Afghan nodded.

'I understand,' he said. 'But who are these people?'

'Can't you guess?' asked Brien; then added as the other shook his head: 'Sir Leonard Wallace will, no doubt, inform you, when you see him in London.'

With a broad smile on his face the Comte joined them.

'This has been a morning of great enjoyment,' he asserted. 'Now what, M'sieu?'

Brien introduced him to the Afghan envoy, who apparently spoke French as well as he did English.

'This is the gentleman to whom you owe your rescue, General,' he added.

'Ah, no,' protested the Comte. 'I have not done much.' He walked across to the monoplane and busied himself with the engine for some time; then returned to the others. 'It will require two hours' work before she will be ready to fly again,' he informed them.

'You think of everything, Comte,' returned Brien.

'So do you, my friend, except in one particular.' The Frenchman smiled at him slyly.

'What is that?'

'You have a great advantage over me. You know my name, but I do not know yours.'

Brien apologised and hastened to repair the error.

'Now everything is OK, as you say in English,' cried the Frenchman gaily. 'I suggest we now go to Paris.'

'I hardly like trespassing on your kindness further,' said Brien. 'You must want to return to Marseilles.'

'No, no. If you wish I will take you to London.'

'I wouldn't think of such a thing. I am already in your debt to such an extent that—'

'*Mon Dieu*!' interrupted the Comte. 'I always thought Englishmen did not like the fuss. You, my friend Brien, are too much like a Frenchman. Perhaps you would like to walk to Paris with Monsieur the General?'

Brien laughed.

'Not quite,' he said, 'but you informed me that were near Melun, and—'

'Yes, but Melun is three miles away, and I do not think there is a house nearer than a mile and a half. I know because I once made a forced landing in this very field.'

'That accounts for the revolver shots not being heard.'

'As you say, that accounts for the revolver shots not being heard. Climb in, Messieurs; my hunger is so great that I shall presently feel cannibal propensities coming upon me.'

Humming cheerfully to himself, he threw the spanner and two revolvers into the cockpit, and followed them in. Twenty minutes later the *Gloire d' Avignon* landed gracefully at Le Bourget, the three travellers climbed out, and made a beeline for the restaurant. As he was still wearing evening dress, Brien kept on his flying coat, but that made no difference to his appetite. Hungry as he was himself, Comte de Vérac failed to equal his English friend as a trencherman, and expressed his admiration almost enviously.

Directly the meal was over Brien interviewed the manager of the Imperial Airways Company and, after explaining who he was and showing his credentials, was assured that one of the smaller air liners would be placed at his disposal as soon as he was ready to cross to England. He then despatched a long telegram to Sir Leonard Wallace, after which he took a cordial farewell of the young Frenchman who had rendered him such signal assistance. The latter eagerly accepted an invitation to visit his new friend in London, and they parted on that understanding, each having formed a sincere attachment for the other.

Piloted by a man who had been in the service of Imperial Airways since the inauguration of the company, and with its two passengers, the Handley Page machine rose smoothly, and commenced its journey to London. The Comte de Vérac watched its departure, and was turning away towards his own machine, when he became aware of a man, his right arm in a sling, standing some distance from him, also gazing up at the air liner. The Comte's eyes were good, and immediately he recognised the fellow whom Brien had wounded. At once he walked rapidly towards him, but the conspirator saw him coming and, jumping into a car standing close by, was swiftly driven away. The Comte de Vérac shrugged his shoulders, and lit a cigarette.

'I hope no further mischief has been attempted,' he murmured.

On the previous evening about the same time that Major Brien was dressing for dinner in his room at the Hôtel de Louvre et Paix in Marseilles, Sir Leonard Wallace left his office in Whitehall. It was not often he stayed quite so late; but he had had an exceedingly busy day and was, in consequence, feeling rather tired as he emerged from the building. His car was nowhere to be seen and, with a frown of annoyance, he signalled to a taxicab standing on a rank a little way down the road. The car drove up to him and, giving directions to the driver, he stepped inside, and closed the door. At once he became aware that the taxi was already occupied, and he made a quick movement to retreat, when a hand grasped his arm in a grip of steel.

'The slightest attempt to get out, or to attract any attention, and you will be a dead man,' said a low, sinister voice.

The car was already on the move, threading its way through the traffic. Wallace accepted the situation and, with a shrug of his shoulders, sat down, and turned to confront his captor. In the dim light he could see a powerful-looking individual in a suit of some dark material. Over his nose and mouth was what looked like a small gas mask; a bowler hat was drawn low on his forehead, but not low enough to shield a pair of glittering eyes which, in the half light, had an intense, piercing quality about them.

'What is the meaning of this outrage?' asked Sir Leonard quietly.

His companion laughed.

'I never thought,' he returned, 'that it would be so easy to trap the great Sir Leonard Wallace. Friends of mine have tried it before, only to fail – I think they must have been great fools.'

His voice was muffled by the mask he wore, but he spoke very good English with little trace of a foreign accent.

'You have trapped me certainly,' observed Wallace. 'The question is; can you keep me now you've got me?'

'I do not think there is much doubt about that. I am holding a little tube in my hand containing a new and very deadly poison gas. The slightest movement on your part will mean your sudden decease.'

'That is interesting,' commented Sir Leonard, 'but the – er – unhappy event of your being compelled to release that gas, how will you protect yourself?'

'I am prepared, as you see,' was the reply.

'But as yet you have not explained why you have found it necessary to kidnap me.'

'It is urgent that you should be out of the way for the next thirty-six hours. At the end of that time you will be released and, if you behave yourself, no harm will come to you.'

'I presume I am indebted to you for the fact that my car was not waiting to take me home?'

'Exactly. A messenger dressed in government uniform told your chauffeur that you would not be requiring him this evening, and he drove away. If he had not, it would have made no difference – we had other plans.'

'And where are you taking me?'

'To a very quiet spot outside London. You will be quite comfortable there.'

For a time there was silence. The taxicab made its way through Trafalgar Square, up Charing Cross Road, crossed Shaftesbury Avenue, and was approaching Camden Town before Sir Leonard spoke again; then:

'I am afraid you are having your journey for nothing,' he remarked quietly.

'What do you mean?' asked his captor suspiciously.

'You perhaps notice that my left hand is in my overcoat pocket? In that hand is a revolver which is pointed at you. I am quite able to shoot through a pocket, and a bullet is even quicker than gas. It will save a lot of trouble, if you stop the taxi and permit me to alight.'

The man leant back in his corner, and laughed sardonically.

'A very good bluff,' he retorted, 'but I happen to know that your left arm is artificial.'

'Nevertheless I have a revolver in that pocket, and it is pointed at you.'

'Then it would be safer for you if I relieved you of it.'

He leant across the car, his right hand searching for Wallace's left.

'You notice,' he threatened, 'that I am holding this tube close to your face. If you resist, I will press the nozzle, and then – God help you!'

The fellow's hand had reached Wallace's coat pocket, was searching for the way in when with a mighty blow of his right fist, the Englishman struck the deadly tube upwards and sent the other staggering back. At once a strong aromatic odour assailed his nostrils and, as he flung open the door, he felt his senses reeling. He sprang from the taxi, and rolled over in the gutter. Quickly he was surrounded by pedestrians. The taxicab went on and disappeared in the distance.

In a state of semi-consciousness Wallace was half-carried, half-led into a chemist's shop by the sympathetic onlookers who had raised him from the road. It was some time before he fully regained his senses. He was subjected to all kinds of questions, but avoided them adroitly, merely stating that he had fallen from the car. At last he was allowed to depart in another taxi, obtained for him by a very puzzled policeman, first assuring himself that it was quite innocent before entering it.

He was sick and dizzy that evening, and found it necessary to call in his doctor to whom he told the story. The latter prescribed for him, and, after a night's rest, he felt fit again. He went to his office at the usual time, and again had an exceptionally busy morning. He was surprised that no news had been received from Brien and, as time went on, began to feel anxious. It was not until half past four that the long expected telegram arrived; then, as he read it, he whistled. He immediately sent for Cousins.

'Major Brien has been having adventures,' he informed the little man, 'but everything seems all right now. Still one never knows. He is coming across with the envoy in a special air liner, and I think you and I had better meet it.'

'"From the clouds he came; His mantle—"' commenced Cousins.

'No time for that now,' smiled Wallace. 'They will arrive in Croydon before we can get there, if we don't hurry.'

Taking precautions to prevent a repetition of his unpleasant experience of the previous night, and making sure that the car was not followed, Sir Leonard, with the little Secret Service man, was driven rapidly to the Croydon Airport. They had barely arrived, when the machine, in which Brien and the Afghan were travelling, emerged from clouds and, circling round, glided down and came to a stop twenty yards away. The pilot climbed out of his seat, but there was no sign from the interior and with troubled countenances, Wallace and Cousins ran to the aeroplane. They opened the door, and at once staggered back, their hands covering the lower parts of their faces.

'Quick!' shouted Cousins to a mechanic standing by. 'Fetch a doctor and an ambulance. Hurry!'

Two men could be seen stretched out on the floor of the saloon, and Wallace recognised the same odour as that in the taxi, when he had so nearly lost his life the previous evening. People in the vicinity were beginning to cough, and were compelled to draw back to a safe distance.

Tying handkerchiefs round their noses and mouths, and holding their breath, the two Secret Service men dashed into the interior, and drew one of the prone figures into the air. Willing hands relieved them of their burden and they returned for the other, emerging the second time with their senses reeling, but with the unconscious envoy in their arms. By this time two doctors and an ambulance had arrived, and the medical men knelt down and conducted an examination. Then one stood up. He turned to Sir Leonard, whose face was drawn with horror and anxiety, and pointed to the body of the Afghan general.

'This gentleman is dead,' he stated. 'The other is still alive, but we'll have to get him to hospital at once.'

'Will he recover?' asked Wallace hoarsely.

'There is a good chance,' was the reply. 'They have been gassed with a solution of cacodyl isocyanide, one of the most deadly gases known to science.'

Brien was rushed to hospital, and a message sent to his wife. The body of the dead envoy was taken into a private room in the aerodrome. His clothes were searched, and Wallace took possession of all papers found upon him. As far as he could ascertain there was nothing of importance among them. It took a long time for the gas to disperse but, having obtained masks, Sir Leonard and his assistant entered the aeroplane and made a thorough examination. The first thing they discovered was an object, something like a stylo pen, lying on the floor. It was evident that it was from this the gas had been emitted. Nothing else was in the saloon. Apparently the envoy had brought nothing with him in the way of baggage. What had happened to Brien's was a puzzle, as was the fact, which Sir Leonard had noticed when going hastily through his friend's pockets before he was taken away, that he was in evening dress. Wallace had still to learn of the adventure that had befallen Brien in Marseilles.

The pilot was questioned, but no information of any importance was elicited from him. He had noticed nothing in the least unusual either at Le Bourget or en route. With his mind centred on the supposition that it might have been possible for the pilot to have sprayed the gas into the saloon, and then thrown in the tube, Wallace cross-questioned the man on all points in an endeavour to get him to give himself away, but his answers were unhesitating and clear, and it became obvious that he was telling the truth. He had been searched, but nothing incriminating had been found on him.

Sir Leonard left the waiting room a very puzzled man.

'How in the name of all that's wonderful can they have been gassed and robbed in mid-air?' he murmured to himself, as he returned to the aeroplane.

A mechanic who had been examining the machine, looked up as he approached.

'How many parachutes did this plane carry, sir?' he asked.

Sir Leonard looked at him vacantly, his thoughts elsewhere. Then suddenly the significance of the man's question struck him.

'What's that?' he demanded so sharply that the mechanic looked at him in surprise.

'I was asking about the parachutes, sir,' he muttered a trifle resentfully.

'Why?'

'Well, it seemed to me curious that the bus should only have one parachute. There are attachments for three.'

'By Jove!' exclaimed Wallace, and made his way back to the waiting room. 'How many parachutes did you have when you left Paris?' he demanded of the pilot.

'Two, sir.'

'You're sure of that?'

'I am certain,' was the reply.

'You did not see anybody drop from your plane?'

'No.'

'Can you remember feeling a jar of any sort?'

The man thought for a moment.

'None whatever, sir,' he said at last.

Sir Leonard hurriedly returned to the aeroplane, and found Cousins still inside. He looked round the interior and frowned.

'I've come to the conclusion,' he remarked almost to himself, 'that the fellow who committed this crime was hidden in here when the plane left Paris, but where the dickens could he have concealed himself? There's hardly room to hide a dog, let alone a man.'

Cousins looked reflectively at a locker under the couch. His face went into hundreds of creases indicative of deep thought.

'It couldn't have been there,' he murmured, 'and there's nowhere else. There isn't even a cubby hole for luggage. It's out of the question to think that he was standing here awaiting them, I suppose, sir?'

'Of course it is,' snapped Wallace. 'If they had found him here, they would have handed him over to the police at once; they wouldn't have taken him with them.'

'Unless Major Brien thought it best to bring him across, sir.'

'Oh, nonsense!' exclaimed Sir Leonard impatiently.

'Well, there's only that locker, sir, and that could only contain a child, or – or a dwarf.'

'Ah!' Wallace's eyes gleamed.

Cousins looked at his chief in astonishment.

'You don't mean to say that you think—' he commenced.

'I'm trying to think of all feasibilities. We've got to get those documents back, if it is humanly possible, and I dare not dismiss any theory, even if it does sound absurd.'

'Perhaps Major Brien has the documents on him,' hazarded Cousins.

'He hasn't. I searched his pockets before he was carried way. Did you examine that locker, Cousins?'

'Yes, sir,' replied the little man. 'There wasn't even a pin in it. But suppose there was someone in the aeroplane, could he have opened the door at that altitude, when the machine was probably going a hundred miles an hour?'

'Yes. It happened once before when a famous financier was killed.'

'Of course; I recollect.'

'And if I remember rightly the pilot noticed nothing unusual on that occasion?' murmured Sir Leonard.

He went outside, and sat on an overturned box, his pipe clenched between his teeth. As he sat there one of the doctors drove up in a car.

'I came to let you know that Major Brien will recover,' he announced.

'Thank God!' murmured Wallace fervently. 'It's decent of you to come, doctor,' he added gratefully. 'Is he conscious?'

'No. I'm afraid it'll be a long time before he comes round. However he's safe now.'

With a smile he drove away.

'It is certain I shall not be able to get any information out of Billy,' muttered Wallace, rising to his feet and knocking out his pipe. 'There is just one slender chance, and I'll have to take it.'

He crossed to the wireless station, and for ten minutes was engaged in sending out messages. It was some time before he received any answers, and he fumed with impatience when four unsatisfactory replies trickled back across the ether. At last came one that brought a smile to his lips, and a faint flush to his cheeks.

It was from a small coasting steamer, and informed him that a parachute had been seen to fall from an aeroplane in mid-channel. As far as the crew of the steamer could make out, a large motorboat had been standing by which later had set a course apparently for Holland.

Wallace waited only long enough to telephone to the Air Force Depot at Dover; then, commandeering the fastest aeroplane in the Croydon aerodrome, he and Cousins flew to the seaside town. Arrived there, he found a flying-boat awaiting him, and a somewhat worried squadron leader trying not to look anxious. He saluted Sir Leonard with great respect, however.

'Did you mean what you said about the machine gun, sir?'

'Of course I did,' was the reply. 'We may want more than a machine gun. Are the bombs on board?'

'Yes, sir. I hope that everything is in order, though.'

Wallace smiled.

'Of course it is. My boy, you are on special duty now and, if we are quick, you'll be rendering your country an inestimable service.'

The young airman smiled, and all his doubts seemed to vanish.

'Good enough,' he cried. 'I'm ready if you are, sir.'

'Who is piloting the boat?'

'I am, sir, and I have three men aboard; two for the machine gun, and one for the bombs.'

'That means six of us,' said Wallace. 'That'll do. Now my information is not very clear, but look out for a large motorboat probably making for the Dutch coast. The chances arc it will beat us, but we may do it. It must be well over a hundred miles to Holland from the place where it was seen, but it has nearly two hours' start.'

A few minutes later the flying-boat rose like a beautiful bird and flew at a high altitude towards the coast of Holland. As they travelled, the eyes of all aboard were glued upon the calm blue sea below them. Wallace had brought a powerful pair of glasses, and his eyes seldom left them. Boats of all descriptions were seen; large cargo steamers carrying the merchandise of the world, one or two pleasure yachts, a host of fishing smacks, occasional passenger liners, but not one motorboat.

Then, when all hope seemed gone, and the coast of Holland was looming almost at their feet, they sighted a motorboat apparently making for Walcheren.

'It must be our quarry,' said Sir Leonard.

'It's got to be,' shouted Cousins, and the grim look on his face made his wrinkles look more grotesque than ever.

The flying-boat glided down in a beautiful spiral, and presently was circling over the craft below, which was tearing through the water at an amazing pace. There were four men aboard her, and they were looking up with expressions of hatred not unmixed with fear. One was seen to raise a revolver, but another snatched it from his hand and appeared, from his attitude, to be overcome with anger.

Sir Leonard smiled softly.

'I don't think we want any further proof than that, Cousins,' he shouted in the little man's ear. 'They have wireless on board, and must have received messages and replies, and guessed I'd be after them somehow, but they reckoned without a flying-boat, otherwise they would have changed their course.'

'My God! Look!' gasped Cousins, and pointed below.

Emerging from the covered-in portion of the bows was a terrible-looking creature. Not more than four feet in height, it had arms that reached to its feet, a great hairy head that was so repulsive to look at that it gave one a feeling of nausea, and two great fangs which stuck out of its mouth like the tusks of a boar. It looked up, made a diabolical grimace, and shook a large, hairy fist.

'So that was what was concealed in the aeroplane, and used the gas,' muttered Wallace to himself, and shuddered.

The creature was thrust under cover by a man standing near

the bows. A minute later the flying-boat struck the water in front of the motor-craft and, swinging round, raced towards it. At Sir Leonard's direction the machine gun was discharged above the oncoming boat, which swerved just in time to avoid a collision.

Apparently recognising that they were in a hopeless position, the occupants brought their vessel to a stand, and the aeroplane floated alongside.

'Look out for treachery!' warned Wallace.

A big man stood up in the stern.

'What do you want with us?' he shouted.

'We are here on behalf of His Britannic Majesty's Government,' replied Sir Leonard. 'You have stolen some documents belonging to the King of Afghanistan which were on their way to Great Britain. In addition you have been the cause of the Afghan envoy being murdered. I am coming aboard.'

'You cannot interfere with us,' was the reply; 'we are in Dutch waters. Apart from that, I deny your charge.'

'As for your being in Dutch waters,' said Sir Leonard smiling quizzically at the fishing fleet almost surrounding them, 'I don't think His Majesty's Government will have much difficulty in settling that point with the representatives of the Queen of Holland. On the other count I have simply to remark that I am coming aboard to arrest you, and search your boat.'

Almost before he had finished speaking, a man standing behind the spokesman in the motor-launch, raised his hand as though to throw something. There was the crack of a revolver, the fellow staggered, clutched wildly at his companion, missed him and toppled into the water.

'Not a bad shot,' murmured Cousins, gazing at his still smoking revolver.

After that there was little opposition. The three remaining men seemed to be cowed, while the dwarf had made no further appearance from his hiding place in the bows. Wallace climbed aboard followed by Cousins and one of the machine-gunners. Each was armed with a revolver. They made a careful search of the sullen-looking trio, but the documents they were so anxious to procure were not forthcoming. They had started on the boat itself, and Sir Leonard was standing with his back to the bows, when suddenly Cousins uttered a warning cry, but it was too late. A terrible figure shot out of the decked-in space behind him, and launched itself upon his back. At once he went down with the horrible, snarling, biting, clawing thing upon him. It had the strength of three men, and Sir Leonard, with his one arm, was hopelessly handicapped. The other men in the boat took advantage of this interruption, and turned on Cousins and the machine-gunner, but here they more than met their match. One went down with a bullet in his kneecap, another with a blow on the skull from the butt-end of a revolver. The third, the leader of the party, gave up the struggle, and sat down by the steering wheel with an expression of sullen resignation on his face. Wallace and the dwarf were still fighting frantically in the bows, and Cousins waited anxiously for the chance to shoot, and save the chief's life. Presently it came; the horrible little creature rose on top of his intended victim. With a prayer in his heart, Cousins fired; there was a scream of agony and with incredible rapidity, the dwarf rose from Wallace, dived into the bows, reappeared almost immediately, and sprang overboard, but in its hand it clutched a large blue envelope.

Sir Leonard fired this time and, with an inhuman sob, the

loathsome creature, half animal, half man, fell lifeless on the water and began to sink. With great celerity Cousins picked up a boathook and dragged the body to the side of boat. Wallace took the large envelope from the stiffening fingers, and examined it. It was covered with sealing wax, upon which was stamped the Afghan royal arms, and was addressed to the British Secretary of State for Foreign Affairs. It obviously had not been tampered with and, with a sigh of deep relief, he thrust the sodden mass of paper into his pocket. At that moment a Dutch torpedo boat out of Flushing, attracted by the sound of firing, steamed busily up and came almost alongside. A dapper little officer stood on the conning-tower.

'What is this?' he shouted in passable English. 'Do you know you are doing a great breach of International Law?'

'I welcome you, Captain,' replied Sir Leonard with smile. 'We have been waiting for you.'

'What is that? Waiting?' asked the puzzled officer.

'Yes. These men murdered, or caused to be murdered, a foreign emissary on a visit to England. We chased them in a flying-boat, and were waiting for you to come up.'

'You want to arrest them – yes?'

'Unfortunately they reached Dutch waters, so I was compelled to wait until you arrived, in order that you could take charge of them until such time as His Majesty's Government asks for their extradition.'

The Dutch officer bowed courteously.

'I will see that they are kept for your policemen, sir,' he promised. 'And of the dead body?'

'Unfortunately he and another were killed in attempting to escape while I was acting on your behalf,' replied Sir Leonard.

'So. It is their own fault, therefore. This one will be taken ashore and buried. I thank you for your courtesy, sir.'

'Not at all,' murmured Wallace.

A few more compliments passed between the two; then Sir Leonard climbed back into the flying-boat, followed by the admiring Cousins and dumbfounded machine-gunner.

As the aeroplane rose in the air, Wallace raised his hat to the torpedo boat in solemn salute. Cousins smiled, and quoted to himself:

'"The sun upon the calmest sea,
appears not half so bright as thee".'

CHAPTER 10

It Happened in Capri

'Inspector Lawrence to see you, sir.'

'Show him in, Clarke.'

An alert, business-like man entered Sir Leonard Wallace's office and, accepting a chair and the cigarette offered him by the Chief of the Secret Service, wasted no time on preliminaries.

'I've called to see you about the theft of those plans, sir,' he announced.

Wallace nodded.

'I gathered that,' he admitted. 'Has anything further transpired?'

'We know the man who has them, sir,' was the quiet reply.

'The deuce you do.' Sir Leonard permitted himself the rare luxury of expressing surprise. 'That's jolly good work. Who is he?'

'He has so many aliases,' smiled the police officer, 'that it is difficult to know his real name. He is down on police records, however, as Luis de Correa.'

Wallace whistled.

'You're full of surprises this morning, Inspector,' he said. 'This is a new line of business for Correa, isn't it? I thought he generally devoted himself to the work of relieving fascinated ladies of their jewels.'

'He is usually known as a jewel thief, sir,' nodded the other, 'but he has brought off many coups in other directions. I think the only crimes we can safely say he hasn't committed are bigamy and murder.'

'And yet he has never received a conviction, has he?'

'Neither in this country nor in any other, as far as I know, sir. He's as cute as they make 'em. I understand that the police of Paris, Madrid and Berlin, to mention only a few, spend their days sighing for him. Yet he could walk into any police office in Europe, and they wouldn't have the power to detain him, although they have long lists of the crimes they know he has committed.'

'He must be very clever,' observed Wallace. 'Of course, I've heard about him, but I've never had any personal interest in him. What makes you think he has the plans?'

'We don't think, sir; we know. For once in a way Mr Luis de Correa has slipped up. We had cause to suspect an Admiralty clerk, who had access to the room where the plans were kept, of being concerned in the theft. He is a man with a passion for gambling, who is known to have lost enough money on the turf to make him and his family absolute paupers. Yet he bought a car yesterday that must have cost him five hundred quid, and took home a fur coat and God knows what else, as presents for his wife.'

'A fur coat in May!' exclaimed Sir Leonard.

Inspector Lawrence laughed.

'I suppose he wanted to make certain of obtaining one when he was in funds, or when they are reduced in price. As it was, he paid a hundred guineas for it.'

'A nice thought,' murmured Wallace. 'I like a man who thinks of his wife when he has money to spend. But all this doesn't explain much. It certainly causes one to suspect the clerk, but hardly supports your contention that Luis de Correa has the plans.'

'I'll explain, sir. We knew Correa was in London two weeks ago and, as is usual when a big crook is about, a watch was kept on his movements. He put up at the Metropole under the name of Don Almeida Suarrez, and behaved in a perfectly respectable manner. Four days ago, that is the day before the theft, the clerk, whose name is Shaw, dined with him. The following day he both lunched and dined with him, and after dinner went with him to his room, where they were shut up together for some time. The plans must have been handed over then. It was not until ten yesterday morning that their disappearance was discovered. Inspector Vining went to the Admiralty, but, as he had no knowledge at that time of Shaw's intimacy with de Correa, the clerk was given no cause to suspect that he was under suspicion. He had already obtained leave for the afternoon and, as I have told you, went and bought a car and the other things.'

'What a fool!' ejaculated Wallace. 'He must have been crazy.'

'No, sir,' returned the inspector. 'Men of his type are always like that when they go wrong. All their lives they live in an atmosphere of respectability, with no knowledge of police methods or reason to worry about the police. Then, when they go off the rails, it never occurs to them that their history is known, and they do the most absurd things, feeling quite convinced that they are as safe as houses. Shaw probably thinks he is very cunning. There is nothing at the Admiralty to connect him with the crime. If there were no professional crooks, and crime was only committed by hitherto respectable people in impulsive moments, a policeman's job would be money for jam.'

Sir Leonard laughed.

'The world would be a very nice place to live in in that case,' he remarked, 'though it might be somewhat boring at times. Go on!'

'Well, sir, while Vining was at the Admiralty, I was going through the reports concerning de Correa in a casual sort of manner, but suddenly the significance of his frequent meetings with Shaw struck me in the light of the theft at the Admiralty. I went at once to the Metropole, and found that the man known as Don Almeida Suarrez had vacated his rooms at seven that morning, and had gone, leaving no address. I searched the rooms, and found this.' He took a folded sheet of blotting paper from a pocket, and opened it out. 'It was in a blotting pad on a small writing table in the sitting room,' he explained. 'Have you a mirror, sir?'

'There's one over the wash basin in the lavatory,' replied Sir Leonard, and led the way into the small adjoining chamber.

The detective held the blotting paper a few inches from the glass and, except for a letter here and there, Wallace could read quite plainly the words dried thereon:

> *. . . for rec.ipt of c.rta.n docu.. nts. Bal.nce of £2,500 to be p.id today w.ek (24-5-19-8).*
>
> *Si. ned Almeida S.arrez*

'You see now, sir,' remarked Inspector Lawrence, 'that I have reason for my assertion that I know the man who has the plans. I think you will agree with me that for once in a way Luis de Correa has made a slip.'

'It looks like it,' nodded Wallace, 'if you are certain Suarrez and Correa are one and the same.'

'I am positive,' replied the detective with confidence. 'Apart from the fact that he is so well-known from numerous photographs in our possession, we have a specimen of his writing at the Yard, and it tallies with this.'

'Have you traced him?' asked Sir Leonard as they returned to the office.

'Unfortunately no, sir. London and the suburbs are being combed for him and all the ports watched, but up to now there has been no news. We are taking no steps against Shaw yet in the hope that he will lead us to Correa. The main thing at present is to get the plans of that gun back, afterwards will be time enough to make the arrests.'

'But, man alive,' exclaimed Wallace, 'if you're going to wait until Shaw meets Correa again, you'll do neither. Obviously the Spaniard has paid something on account to Shaw for the plans. On May the twenty-fourth he will pay the balance, but in the meantime he will have sold them to a foreign power, and it is very unlikely he will return to London to meet Shaw. Even if he is foolish enough to do so, and you arrest him, that will be mighty poor consolation for the loss of the plans.'

'You're right there, sir; that is why I have come to you. We have notified the police of every European country that de Correa is wanted. In the circumstances I think the plans will be safe enough for a while, for he will not dare to approach any foreign power when every policeman in Europe is eagerly looking for him, glad to have an excuse at last for laying hands on him. In spite of our precautions, I feel sure he has got away from England. The Commissioner sent me to put the facts before you, sir, and hand over the tracing of Correa and the plans to you. Of course, we continue our job in England and, if he's still in this country, I hope we land him before he can dispose of the things.'

'You should have come sooner, Lawrence,' remarked Wallace sternly. 'I had no idea you would want the Secret Service in a matter like this. From what the Commissioner told me yesterday morning, I understand the police had the matter pretty well in hand. Since that time nearly twenty-four precious hours have elapsed. Of course, as a precautionary measure, all our agents in Europe and America have been warned of the theft, and told to be on the *qui vive*; but, if you'd come yesterday, they would have known for whom to watch before he could have had a chance of getting anywhere.'

'I'm sorry sir, but—'

Sir Leonard ignored him. Then Inspector Lawrence, a member of a department that prided itself on its capability and competency, had his eyes opened by a display of sheer efficiency that almost caused him to gasp. Wallace sat for few moments writing rapidly; then pressed three of the numerous buttons under the ledge of his desk. Almost immediately three men appeared. He handed the sheet of paper on which he had been writing to one.

'Code to Lalére,' he said sharply, 'with instructions to relay to every agency and sub-agency in Europe.'

The man departed, and Wallace turned to another.

'The plans of the new Naval gun Maddison, are in the possession of Luis de Correa, the international crook. He was living at the Metropole under the name of Almeida Suarrez – left there hurriedly at seven yesterday morning. Send Shannon and Carter to all aerodromes, in or round London, private or otherwise, to find if he left by air and, if so, when, where bound for, name of pilot, and so on. Despatch experts in planes with complete description of Correa to Havre, Calais, Boulogne, Ostend, Antwerp, the Hague and Hamburg. If they succeed in tracing him they must follow him until they get the plans from him. Quite clear?'

'Yes, sir,' returned Maddison and was gone.

'Stephenson, you heard what I have just said to Maddison?' Sir Leonard turned to the third man, the wireless expert. The latter answered in the affirmative. 'Get in touch with every craft possessing wireless that has sailed from an English port between seven or eight yesterday morning and now. Give a description of de Correa and ask if he is on board.'

'Very well, sir.'

The man quickly left the room and Lawrence looked at Sir Leonard with ill-disguised admiration.

'We have already sent wireless messages to the ships, sir,' he stated.

'I daresay you have,' was the terse reply, 'but I like to have my own reports.'

The detective rose to his feet.

'I don't think de Correa stands any chance with your men after him, and all the foreign police looking for him,' he grinned.

'Don't be too sure of that, Lawrence,' retorted Wallace drily. 'I suppose you haven't informed the foreign police what he is wanted for?'

'No, sir. We only told them there is a warrant out for his arrest, and that as soon as they notify us they have him, we'll send the extradition papers.'

'Exactly. And do you think they'll inform you they have arrested him, if they discover what he is wanted for?'

'I don't see why they should find out,' objected Lawrence uneasily.

'They will when they search him. Luis de Correa has proved again and again that he is no fool. If he is arrested, he'll immediately send for a high official, and bargain with him; the bargain, of course, to include his release. In my opinion, our only hope is that he'll discover he is being hunted, and make no attempt to sell the plans at present for fear of losing them and his liberty as well without gaining any profit. If he thinks he is unsuspected, he'll just make for the country to which he intends to dispose of them, and promptly be arrested. Then, as far as we are concerned, the fat will be in the fire, unless my men get hold of him before the police do. Perhaps he has already been in negotiation with some foreign power. I have a great admiration for Scotland Yard, Lawrence, but twenty-four hours, man – twenty-four hours!'

Inspector Lawrence took his departure looking distinctly crestfallen. If the truth must be told, he was himself to blame for the delay. Professional jealousy had led him into an error committed by many better men. He had expected to make a clean-up himself, and had only passed on the details concerning the robbery, when he had reported his non-success to the Commissioner, and been promptly ordered to go at once to Sir Leonard Wallace. It is not often that the Secret Service and Scotland Yard overlap in their investigations and, when they do, they invariably work amicably together; but cases of individual resentment on the part of officers of the CID and Special Branch – at what they are apt to consider interference by outsiders – are not unknown.

As soon as Inspector Lawrence had gone, Sir Leonard sent for the man in charge of the photographic department. This branch of the Secret Service is as extensive and complete as that at New

Scotland Yard. Not only does it possess photographs of every important diplomatic and political personage in the world, every known secret agent of other powers and well-known agitators both British and foreign, but it also has a collection of pictures of international criminals. There is no knowing when the activities of men and women, who earn their living by travelling about the Continent committing crime, may require the attention of the Secret Service.

The expert entered briskly but quietly, and stood awaiting his chief's orders.

'I suppose there was no difficulty about photographs of Luis de Correa?' asked Wallace.

'No, sir,' was the reply; 'we had him in three positions, which we retook. We are now printing a dozen copies. The men you have detailed for the Continent will be given one of each.'

'When will they be ready?'

'In about five minutes, sir.'

'Excellent,' approved Sir Leonard. 'Send me up some copies, will you?'

'Very well, sir.'

When they were brought, Wallace studied them carefully, until he was certain he would know the man anywhere. Two were in profile, the other full-face, and he was impressed by the strength and beauty of the countenance. A high, intellectual forehead, wide frank eyes, a small straight nose, sensitive mouth, and firm, well-shaped chin were the very antithesis of what one would expect in the face of a criminal. Sir Leonard was still occupied in his inspection when the door opened, and his second-in-command, Major Brien, strolled into the room. He looked up and greeted the newcomer cheerily.

'I didn't expect you back so soon,' he added, 'Everything all right?'

Brien sank lazily into a chair, took a voluminous package from a pocket, and threw it across to the other.

'As right as rain,' he stated. 'At first I thought I was going to be three weeks over the job but, as you see, I've done it in seventeen days.'

Wallace put the report in a drawer, which he locked.

'I'll go through it this afternoon,' he promised; 'at present I'm busy.'

'What have you got there?' asked his friend, helping himself to a cigarette.

'Photos of a handsome man,' was the reply.

'Organising a male beauty contest?'

Sir Leonard laughed, and handed them across to the other.

'Recognise them?' he asked.

Major Brien studied them carefully; then handed them back.

'No,' he replied. 'He's a good-looker, whoever he is; intellectual and all that sort of thing. Who is he?'

'Luis de Correa, the international crook!'

'What? My hat! I'm a nice judge of faces, ain't I? If I'd been asked I should have said the fellow was as straight as a die; a regular stickler for the straight and narrow, in fact.'

'So should I,' admitted Wallace, 'which shows that faces are poor guides to character.'

'All the same,' insisted Brien, 'although he may be a crook, I bet he's a sportsman. What are you doing with the photographs? Has he been interfering in diplomatics?'

'More or less,' replied Wallace. 'Remember the new naval gun, which experts agree will revolutionise naval warfare?'

Brien nodded.

'You mean the beauty that fires a projectile clean through hard steel armour? Yes; I was present at the demonstration, if you remember.'

'Well, the plans have been stolen from the Admiralty, and de Correa has them.' He proceeded to tell the story of the theft. 'If Scotland Yard had only let us know details sooner, our chances would have been better,' he concluded. 'I shall have a word or two to say to the Commissioner when I see him next.'

'Things often get delayed when the Yard get their fingers in our pie,' complained Brien. 'The silly asses try to do without us, and get in a muddle; then we have to toddle along and extricate them. I've nothing to say against Scotland Yard, when it comes to hunting down criminals, but when those blokes start taking a hand in diplomatic intrigue and political crime, they're like a lot of nursery kids.'

Wallace laughed.

'You're in an uncomplimentary mood today, Billy,' he commented. 'Clear off! Your sorrowing spouse will be wanting to see her hubby again, and I'll get into trouble if I keep you.'

On his way home for luncheon, Sir Leonard's car was held up in a traffic jam in Piccadilly Circus for some time, and he was beginning to get impatient at the delay, when he looked idly into the interior of a taxicab standing alongside waiting, like his own car, for the traffic constable's white arm to go down. Abruptly he gave vent to an exclamation, sat back in his seat for a moment; then leant forward again, and took another and longer look at the occupant of the next vehicle. He felt certain now. Incredible though it appeared, the smartly dressed man in correct morning garb, sitting within a few feet of him, was Luis de Correa. Without hesitation he lifted the speaking-tube to his lips.

'Johnson,' he instructed his chauffeur, 'when we get clear, let the taxi on your right go ahead and follow it. There's a man in it I want. Understand?'

Johnson slightly nodded his head; then glanced carefully to his right. A few seconds later the clear signal was given and he obeyed instructions meticulously. They had not far to go. The taxi drew up outside the Ritz, and its occupant alighted, and hurried into the hotel, carrying a small black portfolio in his hand. Behind him went Sir Leonard Wallace. Luis de Correa spoke to a commissionaire, who nodded, called a boy, and gave the latter certain instructions. Watching from a chair conveniently close to a pillar, Wallace presently saw the boy reappear carrying a suitcase in either hand, which he carried out to the taxi. The Spaniard tipped the commissionaire, and was about to follow when Sir Leonard accosted him.

'May I have a few words with you?' he asked courteously.

The other stared at him in surprise, and the colour ebbed a little from his face.

'You have the advantage of me, sir,' he remarked in a well-modulated voice with just a trace of accent.

'I will soon explain who I am, if you will accompany me to a quiet spot where we can talk without being overheard.'

'But I regret much I am in a hurry. Is it important what you have to say to me?'

'Very. If you have no objection, we will drink a cocktail together in the lounge.'

With an impatient shrug of the shoulders, de Correa agreed, and accompanied Wallace to a secluded table at which they sat. With a word of apology the latter drew out a small pocket cheque book, and wrote rapidly on a form.

'I am afraid I have run short of cash,' he smiled. 'I find the management here most accommodating.' He called to a waiter, who evidently knew him. 'Take this to the office, Jules,' he directed, 'and ask them to cash it for me.'

The man hurried off, and handed it to a clerk.

'Sir Leonard Wallace wants cash,' he explained.

The clerk looked casually at the small slip of paper in his hand; then stiffened, and his eyes opened wide in surprise. On the form was written:

Ring up Scotland Yard. Tell them Sir Leonard Wallace Ritz with de Correa. Send flying squad van.

Quickly recovering from his astonishment, the young man, who, like most Londoners, was very quick-witted, turned to the telephone. In the meantime Wallace had ordered two cocktails, and was talking rapidly of anything that came into his mind in an effort to gain time. Before long, however, de Correa made an impatient gesture, and interrupted him.

'Yes, yes, señor,' he protested, 'but, as I have said, I am in a hurry. What is it you wish to say to me of importance?'

At that moment, a tall, lean man of cadaverous aspect walked up to the table, and looked straight at de Correa.

'Well,' he exclaimed, 'if it ain't José! Say, I guess I'm glad to see you.'

He held out his hand and, with a cry of delight, de Correa rose and grasped it.

'My friend,' he said, 'this is a pleasant surprise. From where have you come?'

The other, an obvious American, led him a little aside.

'Never mind that now,' he whispered. 'I don't know what lay

you're on; perhaps I'm butting in, but, in case you don't know it, that guy you're sitting with is the big noise of the British Secret Service.'

Luis de Correa showed no sign of agitation, instead he laughed heartily as at a joke, and clapped his friend on the back.

'It is funny that,' he chuckled. 'Well so long, my friend. I will see you again some other time; no?'

The American nodded and strolled away, while Luis de Correa resumed his seat. Sir Leonard had not liked the interruption, though it had assisted in passing the time, and, as far as he could see, nothing had happened of an inimical nature to him. The cocktails had arrived, and he raised his.

'To our better acquaintance, señor,' he said.

The next moment he had dropped the glass, and was lying back in his chair choking for breath and, for the time being, completely and painfully blinded. The Spaniard had produced a small water pistol, and discharged the contents, consisting of ammonia, full into the face of the Englishman. As the latter fell back gasping, Luis de Correa leapt from his seat and, before any of the people at the other tables had quite grasped what had happened, was out of the lounge, through the entrance hall, and in his taxi, which drove away at once.

It was a long time before Wallace was able to breathe freely, and longer still before he could open his eyes with any degree of comfort. Several guests of the hotel and attendants had gone to his rescue, and he had been taken into a small room where he was solicitously attended to. The flying squad van arrived while his eyes were being bathed, and the inspector in charge quickly apprised of events. In a low voice, Wallace gave him the number of the taxicab and a few other details, and before long the whole of the flying squad was scouring London for Luis de Correa.

Sir Leonard, his eyes still inclined to water at frequent intervals, eventually was able to escape from the kindly ministrations of the hotel staff. When he emerged into the noisy bustle of Piccadilly, his car was nowhere to be seen. He seemed in no way perturbed, however, and, refusing the offer of the door-keeper to call a taxi, walked to his house a hundred yards or so distant. Lady Wallace was lunching out, and he ate alone. Directly he had finished he rang up Maddison.

'Have any reports come in?' he asked.

Several had, but none of very great importance.

'Deal with the rest yourself, Maddison,' he instructed. 'I shall probably leave for Madrid this afternoon. Inform Major Brien when he arrives, and ask him to take charge for a few days.'

He rang off and, calling his manservant, told him to pack a bag. He then telephoned to his brother-in-law, Cecil Kendal, a wing commander in the Royal Air Force stationed at Farnborough. It took him some time to get the connection, but at last he heard the voice of Kendal.

'Can you get a couple of days' leave?' he asked.

'I daresay. Why?'

'I may want to go to Madrid this afternoon and, in preference to the usual official mode of asking for an RAF machine, I thought you might like to take me in your Puss Moth.'

'Sounds very mysterious and thrilling,' laughed Kendal. 'Righto; I'm on. Where shall I pick you up?'

'There is a chance that it may not be necessary for me to go after all. As soon as I know, I'll telephone. In the meantime get your leave fixed up. It won't do you any harm to have a spot of vacation.'

'That'll be all right. I tell you what I'll do. I'll fly up to Stag

Lane in half an hour or so. Ring me up there. If you don't want me, I'll mooch off on a little expedition of my own. Oh, by the way, how long do you expect to be in Madrid?'

'I haven't the vaguest idea. I may be a day, I may be a week. Perhaps I won't stay in Madrid for long – may have to rush off somewhere else – but all I shall want you to do will be to take me there. You can be back early the day after tomorrow.'

He rang off, and went to his study to wait. Half an hour went by; then the butler entered to inform him that the chauffeur was waiting to see him.

'Send him in at once, Sims,' he directed.

Johnson hardly waited until he was in the room before commencing to apologise for driving away from the Ritz without his master, but Wallace cut him short.

'That's all right,' he observed. 'You followed the taxi, didn't you?'

'Yes, sir. When I saw the gentleman you were after run out of the hotel, as though in a state of agitation, jump into the taxi and drive away, I guessed there was something wrong, sir, so I thought you would wish me to follow.'

'You were quite correct, Johnson. Where did he go?'

'To Croydon, sir. Embarked on an air liner for France.'

'He got away, did he?'

'Yes, sir. I saw the labels on his bags, sir, when they were carried from the Ritz Hotel. They had "Palace Hotel Madrid" on them.'

'Yes, Johnson, I saw that myself. You've done jolly well. Thanks very much. Go and have some food now; then be ready to drive me to Stag Lane Aerodrome.'

'Very well, sir.'

As soon as the chauffeur had left the study, Wallace again went to the telephone. This time he rang up Scotland Yard and asked to speak to the Commissioner.

'Is that you, Wallace?' came the voice of the police chief. 'We haven't traced de Correa yet. I'm damned sorry you let him get the better of you with that ammonia trick though.'

Sir Leonard laughed.

'Aren't you delighted you've found something to hold up against me?' he commented. 'Good old Scotland Yard. But it's nothing to what I have against you.'

'What do you mean?'

'Weren't your men supposed to be watching all the ports?'

'Yes; why?'

'Did that include the airports?'

'Naturally.'

'Then, if I were you, I'd order every detective at the Yard to have his eyes tested and take to glasses. Luis de Correa left Croydon in an air liner, as bold as brass, about an hour ago. My chauffeur tracked him there, and saw him go. Not being a policeman, he couldn't stop him. What are you going to do about it?'

A volley of words, sounding distinctly uncomplimentary, came from the other end of the line; then:

'Where was he bound for?'

'Paris and Madrid, but for the Lord's sake don't start telephoning to the police there. I'm off to Madrid myself presently.' He was turning away when an idea occurred to him. 'Send a wireless to the air liner, will you? Sign it Shaw, and address it to Almeida Suarrez, telling him to beware of the police at Le Bourget.'

'What on earth for?'

'Because the French police, at your instigation, will be watching for him, and their eyes are probably not dim like those of your men. We don't want Luis to be arrested by the French or any other police, since the English can't do it. For the future, I think your motto had better be, "Leave it to the Intelligence Department" – I said *intelligence*.'

'Oh, ring off!' cried the exasperated Commissioner.

'Exactly what I am about to do.' He replaced the receiver on its hook, smiling broadly as he did so. 'The ammonia trick, indeed,' he murmured. 'He's probably sorry he ever mentioned that now. And, if I'm not mistaken, there'll be other sorry people at Scotland Yard very shortly.'

He had still another telephone call to make, and that was to his own headquarters. He instructed Maddison to get a clear line through to *Lalére et Cie* in Paris, inform Lalére in code that Correa was crossing by air liner, and that he was to be met, but not interfered with, and followed wherever he went. In the event of his arrest by the police he was to be rescued, and under no consideration allowed to dispose of the plans. All communications were to be sent in code to Wallace in care of the agent in Madrid, who was to be informed that he would put up at the Palace Hotel there.

Having made sure that his orders were understood, Wallace rang off, feeling easier in his mind than he had done since his interview with Inspector Lawrence in the morning. He knew now that, unless something extraordinary happened, Luis de Correa would be under the constant surveillance of Secret Service agents until he himself was able to get in touch with the man. The fact that the Spaniard's suitcases were labelled for Madrid may have been a blind, but that did not matter very much. Whatever his ultimate destination was, he would not be lost sight of again. The most efficient service in the world was watching him.

After writing a note to his wife, which he left in the butler's care, Sir Leonard, his only luggage a small dress case, was driven to Stag Lane Aerodrome, arriving there shortly before four o'clock. Batty, his ex-sailor servant, who usually accompanied his master wherever he went, had been left behind, much to his disappointment, but there was only room for two in Wing Commander Kendal's small aeroplane. The latter was awaiting his brother-in-law, his face lighting up when he saw him.

'I began to think the trip was off,' he remarked, as they shook hands. 'I've been expecting a telephone call for ages.'

'Why should I bother to telephone since I was coming?' asked Wallace sapiently. 'And between you and me, Cecil, I'm sick of telephones. There was no difficulty about the leave, I suppose?'

'Good Lord, no! I took a fortnight.'

'A fortnight? In Heaven's name, why?'

'Oh, I thought you might want the old bus a little longer than you stipulated. Are you ready?'

'Quite,' laughed Sir Leonard.

Kendal led the way to the machine, Johnson following with his employer's bag.

'I say,' suggested the airman. 'How about staying in Paris tonight? We might have a look at the Folies, and do—'

'This is not a pleasure trip, although we'll tell the Spanish authorities that it is,' interrupted Wallace firmly. 'I want to reach Madrid as soon as possible. How far can you get tonight?'

'I've worked the whole thing out, my lad,' was the reply, 'so don't worry your head. We'll have enough daylight to take us to Tours. Tomorrow, if we leave Tours at seven, we can be in Madrid in nice time for pre-lunch cocktails. How will that suit you?'

'Admirably.'

'Atta boy!'

Kendal, who was still as irrepressible as he had been when he had won a reputation as one of Britain's finest airmen during the War, handed a flying coat and goggles to his brother-in-law, adjusted his own, and climbed into the aeroplane which was the pride of his heart. The propeller whirled, and they were just about to take off when he turned to his companion and grinned boyishly.

'Any pretty girls in Madrid?' he shouted down the speaking tube.

'Cecil,' admonished Sir Leonard, 'I'm ashamed of you. Think of Dolly!'

'She's OK, bless her,' was the reply. 'She always says she likes me to enjoy myself.'

Experiencing perfect weather all the way, they arrived in Madrid earlier than anticipated and, leaving Kendal to answer inquiries respecting their trip, and make arrangements about housing the plane, Wallace was driven to the hotel in the Plaza de Canovas, where he booked rooms for himself and his brother-in-law. He found the British Secret Service agent awaiting him, and was handed half a dozen telegrams. These he carried to his room and decoded, after a short conversation with the man. One told him that de Correa had been met at Le Bourget aerodrome, where, muffled in an overcoat and leaning heavily on a stick, he managed to escape the attentions of the police. Satisfaction at this news was short-lived, however, for further revelations showed that the Spaniard had either changed his mind about travelling to Madrid, or had never intended to go there. He had driven to the Gare de Lyon, where he had booked through to Naples by way of the Riviera. Lalére himself, with an assistant, had taken tickets for the same destination, and had succeeded in obtaining a compartment in the same *wagon-lit*. The last telegram, despatched from Nice that morning, stated that de Correa had left the train there, and had met a friend living in a small hotel in the Boulevard Gambetta. Apparently the break in his journey had nothing to do with the disposal of the plans, for he had been carefully watched, and Lalére had ascertained that he intended continuing on his way to Naples that afternoon.

Wallace decided that there was nothing for it but to wait, make certain that the Spaniard actually was en route for Naples, then fly to the Italian town. He was delighted now that Kendal had taken longer leave than had been suggested, and told that young man so when the latter arrived from the aerodrome, and unceremoniously entered the room, where Sir Leonard was dressing after a bath and shave.

'I knew you'd want me,' was the complacent reply. 'How about those cocktails? Don't let us have them here. Let us sally forth and find an American bar.'

'How about a wash and brush-up first?' retorted Sir Leonard.

'M'm,' nodded Kendal; 'I could do with something of that sort. Be with you in a jiffy.'

He emerged from his room ten minutes later looking fresh and cheery. At that moment he was remarkably like his sister, and Sir Leonard, who was very fond of him, declared that he had never noticed the resemblance quite so definitely before.

They walked along the busy Carrera de San Jeronimo until they came to the Puerta del Sol, where, not far from the Ministerio de la Gobernación, Kendal declared they had found the ideal place. Considering he had never been to Madrid before, he showed remarkable instinct in ferreting out the type of saloon for which he was in search.

Soon after four another telegram was brought to Wallace. It had been despatched from the station at Nice, and stated that de Correa was about to leave, that there was no doubt that it was his purpose to travel to Naples. Sir Leonard had a private conversation with his agent, instructed him to open all further telegrams, and wire any important news to the *poste restante* at Naples. He then informed Kendal of his intention to start at once for the Italian city, and they spent some time studying an up-to-date aviation map, which the airman had brought with him. That night they rested at Manresa in Catalonia, and left again at daybreak. Breakfasting at Marseilles, they flew along the Riviera, across the Gulf of Genoa to Leghorn, thence down the coast of Italy to Civitavecchia, where they descended for lunch. Naples was reached at three.

There were two telegrams at the *poste restante*, but neither contained very important news, merely telling Wallace that information despatched from Pisa and Rome showed that de Correa had remained on the train. Sir Leonard had told his brother-in-law the story of Luis de Correa's escape from England with the plans of the new naval gun in his possession, and the manner in which he was being trailed across Europe by the British Secret Service. As they emerged into the brilliant sunshine from the *poste restante*, the airman was looking puzzled.

'You know the blighter is here now, I suppose,' he remarked, 'but how the devil are you going to find him? Naples is a pretty big place.'

Wallace smiled.

'We shan't have to find him,' he replied. 'We'll be taken to him. One of the two men on his track will either be on the look-out for me here, or, if he's gone on further, a message will be sent revealing his ultimate destination.'

Almost before he had finished speaking, a dapper little man, looking every inch a Frenchman, from his laughing dark eyes and well-trimmed imperial, down to his shiny, pointed shoes, approached them quietly, and raised his hat with true Parisian politeness.

'Good afternoon, Sir Leonard,' he greeted the Chief of the Secret Service. 'You have been wonderfully quick.'

Wallace shook hands with him.

'Yes; thanks to my brother-in-law here,' he admitted. 'You don't know each other, do you?'

Cecil Kendal was introduced to Anatole Lalére, one of Sir Leonard's most famous agents, the man who so successfully ran the well-known firm of *Lalére et Cie* in Paris, and thus cloaked his other and more important profession. They walked on together.

'Well, Lalére,' observed Sir Leonard, 'where is our friend Luis de Correa?'

'In Capri,' was the quiet answer.

'In Capri!' echoed the chief. 'I wonder why he has gone there.'

'It's a very good place in which to hide, sir,' remarked Lalére, 'and I think that de Correa has come to the conclusion that it will be as well if he lies up for a bit. He had a very narrow escape at Le Bourget. I watched him alight from the air liner in a big coat the collar of which was turned well up, while his cap was pulled well down. He leant heavily on a stick like an invalid, but two gendarmes were closely scrutinising the passengers, and they stepped forward to examine his features, so I created a diversion and took their attention away.'

'What did you do?' asked Kendal, who had been listening with great interest.

'I had taken a little dog with me,' was the reply, 'and, as soon as

I saw that de Correa was likely to be found out, I let it loose, and sent the two gendarmes running after it. You see,' he added with a smile, 'I am rather well-known in Paris, and they were naturally anxious to be of use to me.'

'Have you any idea why de Correa stopped temporarily at Nice?' asked Wallace.

'I rather think he and the man he met are some sort of partners,' said Lalére, 'and that he simply left the train to tell him that he was wanted by the police, and intended lying low. I engaged the room next to the one in which they met. There was a communicating door and, although we were unable to hear their conversation, Digby and I took turns at looking through the keyhole.'

'You have Digby with you, have you?' commented Sir Leonard. 'He's a good man.'

'One of the best,' returned Lalére enthusiastically. 'He's gone across to Capri with de Correa. I had a wire from him an hour ago to say that the Spaniard was in the Villa Licata about half a mile above the town, and that he would await our arrival in an olive grove close by.'

'Then all we have to do,' smiled Wallace, 'is to go across and interview Señor Luis.'

'That's all, sir.'

Kendal was given the choice of accompanying them or awaiting their return in Naples, and decided to cross to Capri. It seemed to him there might be the chance of a little excitement on the island, and he had no intention of missing it, if he could help it. He was enchanted with the view as the little steamer crossed the famous bay. On the left towered the grey height of Vesuvius, its crater surmounted by a cloud rising above it like a plume. Ahead, seventeen miles away, could be seen the outline of the island for which they were bound.

A short stop at beautiful Sorrento; then on again past Massa with its fascinating caverns and ancient watch-towers, across the channel separating Capri from the mainland, until they were under the lee of that island of enchantment.

They were driven from the Grande Marina up to Capri's picturesque Piazza in a *carozze*, thence, inquiring their way, they proceeded on foot between white-walled gardens, plantations of lemon trees, olive groves, and vineyards until they reached the Villa Licata. They found it a house charmingly situated amidst a number of tall cedars, surrounded by an exquisite garden, which was beautifully laid out with white pergolas and terraced walks, and commanding a wonderful view of the island and the Gulf of Salerno. A mass of red poppies and other spring blossoms caused the garden to be brilliant in rich colouring, and they stood fascinated for some moments, admiring the beauty of it all.

'What a home!' exclaimed Wallace. 'But we haven't come here on a sightseeing expedition. I wonder where Digby is?'

Presently they caught sight of a man emerging from an olive grove close to the house. It was the Secret Service agent, a man who, in Paris, acted as foreign correspondent for the firm of *Lalére et Cie*. He greeted Sir Leonard respectfully, and lost no time in telling him that Luis de Correa was still in the Villa.

'I have ascertained that it belongs to him, sir,' he stated. 'He lives here under his own name.'

'Now we know why he came to Capri,' commented Sir Leonard. 'He must be a man of taste.'

'What are you going to do?' asked Kendal.

'I shall walk up to the door like any ordinary visitor,' replied Wallace, 'and ask to see him. You three must guard the exits from the house and, if he attempts to get away, stop him. I don't think he will somehow; he will probably consider his position fairly safe, and defy me. If I do not emerge at the end of half an hour, it will mean that I have been unable to persuade him to hand over the plans, and you must make your way into the house and help me to get them by force. Do you all possess revolvers?'

'I don't,' replied Kendal, while the others nodded.

'Oh, well, it doesn't matter, Cecil. I don't suppose they'll be needed. If a rough and tumble of any sort occurs, you have a pretty useful pair of fists.'

The airman grinned; then looked suddenly serious.

'I say, you know,' he observed, 'be careful. Do you think it wise to go alone?'

'I shall be all right,' Wallace assured him. 'Now spread out. I'll give you a couple of minutes to post yourselves; then walk in. Digby has studied the lay of the land, and will know the best positions to take up.'

The three consulted together, after which they moved away; Kendal and Lalére towards a lemon plantation, from which a view of the front of the house could be obtained; Digby to his previous station in the olive grove. Sir Leonard gave them ample time to get into place; then walked through the garden up to the front door. The melody of a waltz, played exquisitely on a piano, reached his ears, and he stood listening for a few seconds before pulling the old-fashioned bell rope. A dark-visaged servant came in answer to his ring.

'I wish to see Signor de Correa,' the Englishman told him in Italian.

'What name shall I give, signor?' asked the man, regarding him somewhat suspiciously.

'He would not know my name. Merely inform him that a gentleman wishes to see him.'

The fellow hesitated slightly; then, leaving the door open, went off on his errand. Wallace quietly followed, and entered a tastefully furnished salon behind him. A man was sitting at a grand piano and, at the sound of the servant's voice, stopped playing and swung round. He immediately caught sight of his visitor, and stared at him in dumbfounded surprise. The servant turned and glared at Sir Leonard resentfully, as though he considered the latter had shown a great lack of politeness.

'We meet once more, signor,' greeted Wallace, bowing courteously, and still speaking in Italian. 'Our last meeting, if you remember, was rather unfortunately interrupted.'

Luis de Correa recovered from his astonishment with a great effort and, rising from the stool, carefully closed the top of the piano.

'Am I to understand,' he asked in English, 'that you have come all the way from London to my little retreat here to – to continue the conversation you commenced in the Ritz Hotel?'

'More or less,' smiled Wallace, and looked significantly at the manservant, who still lingered.

Luis de Correa took the hint.

'Leave us, Guiseppe,' he ordered. 'Will you be seated, sir,' he added politely, reverting to English.

Sir Leonard accepted a chair, and the Spaniard sank into another.

'This time,' commenced the former briskly, 'there will no beating about the bush. Señor de Correa, I have come for the plans, stolen from the British Admiralty, which you have in your possession. You have probably discovered already that a warrant is out for your arrest in England. It would be easy enough for me to give information to the authorities here, and cause you to be apprehended to await extradition. However, I have no intention of doing that, if you will return the documents to me.'

The good-looking Spaniard smiled slightly. He had quite recovered from his surprise, and there was no trace of uneasiness noticeable in his face.

'That is very good of you,' he remarked, 'but what if I do not admit that the plans, of which you speak, are in my possession?'

'Such an attitude would be a useless waste of time,' Wallace assured him. 'I know you have them. They were handed to you by a man named Shaw in your room in the Metropole Hotel, London. You paid him a sum of money, and gave him a promissory note for £2,500, the balance of your agreement, to be paid on the twenty-fourth of May.'

For a few moments de Correa sat quite still.

'You seem to be well-informed,' he murmured at last. 'I will admit, therefore, that I had those plans. You cannot expect, though, that I still have them.'

'I do,' returned the other. 'Since you descended from the air liner at Le Bourget you have been under constant surveillance, and it is known that you did not part with them.'

'So. Now I understand how you discovered I was here. You are very clever, señor.'

'It would have been perfectly easy to have taken the plans from you,' went on Sir Leonard, 'long before you arrived in Naples.'

'Why did you not make the attempt?'

'Because I wished to interview you personally, and ask you to hand them over to me without trouble.'

'You mean,' retorted the Spaniard coolly, 'that you feared the police of France or Italy might interfere and obtain possession of them. I am not a fool, my friend. I very much regret the necessity that made me squirt ammonia into your face in London. It was very distasteful of me, but I obtained those plans at considerable expense, and I intended to leave London without giving them up. I succeeded, and I assure you my intentions remain the same. If you wish, you can call in the police of Capri; you can have me extradited to London, but you will not obtain those very precious documents.'

'And why not?'

'Because I intend to sell them, and enrich myself.'

'At the expense of my country?'

Luis de Correa shrugged his shoulders.

'Your country is nothing to me,' he remarked. 'If they were plans belonging to Spain it would be a different matter – perhaps.'

'Listen to me,' persisted Wallace earnestly. 'If you go to England under arrest, it will not only be the charge of having in your possession stolen property that will hang over you, as you are probably thinking. You are a man wanted by the police of almost every European nation. A long list of charges, which at present only lack certain links of evidence, might easily be substantiated once you were under restraint. Think of that, de Correa. The result might very well be that you would spend most of the remaining years of your life in penal servitude.'

There was no doubt that the Spaniard was affected. His face paled perceptibly, while those astonishingly frank eyes of his became troubled.

'That would be most unpleasant,' he said slowly. 'The humiliation, the bars, the animal existence – ugh! I could not stand that.' Then he laughed. 'Your threats sound dreadful, señor,' he went on, 'but, after all, they do not worry me. As you say, the police, for some strange reason, want me in their power, but they have never had me yet and, I assure you, I do not intend that they shall.'

'Then hand over the plans and, as far as I am concerned, no further steps will be taken against you.'

The Spanish crook shook his head.

'No,' he decided; 'I will not. And in case you really intend to carry out your threat, let me tell you that you can search the whole of this villa and garden, and you will not find them. I do not think having me under arrest would be sufficient to console you for their loss, so what are you going to do?'

'You are a very foolish man, de Correa. I should imagine that, with your apparently vast experience of breaking the law, you would understand when you have undertaken something that is too big for you.'

Luis de Correa took no notice of the observation, instead:

'I suppose it was the man Shaw who gave me away; am I not right? He is now in jail, no?'

'No, but he soon will be.'

'He is very foolish that one. Still he helped me by sending warning to me in the aeroplane by wireless. That was good of him. You know that?'

'Yes; I know a warning was sent, but it wasn't from Shaw. It was at my instigation, because I knew the French would be on the watch for you. Afterwards my agent saved you from being too closely scrutinised, otherwise you would even now be in a French prison.'

An unmistakable gleam of admiration showed in the Spaniard's eyes as he studied his visitor.

'Now I have again met you,' he remarked, 'and am beginning to know you better, I am more sorry than ever that I used means so violent to escape from you in London. It is not my nature to do that sort of thing, because I abhor force. But, alas! What else could I do after my friend so fortuitously informed me who you were?'

'Ah!' exclaimed Wallace. 'I guessed that the American had something to do with it. You are a very lucky man, de Correa.'

The Spaniard showed a perfect set of white teeth in a smile.

'I admit it, señor,' he nodded. 'All my life have I been lucky.' He leant forward. 'Since you want to take back to London the plans,' he suggested, 'let us make the bargain.'

'What kind of a bargain?' demanded Sir Leonard.

'I admit to you that the plans are yet in my possession. It would be useless to say otherwise, since you know so much. But they are hidden where neither you nor any other would find them. It was my intention to dispose of them to the nation which offered the best price. I will sell them to you, señor, for less than I would take from others, because you have been frank with me, and you are a man for whom I have conceived a deep respect.'

The Chief of the British Secret Service smiled.

'And what is your price?' he asked.

'My lowest price to other countries would be £100,000,' was the immediate answer; 'to you I will give them for £75,000. What do you say?'

'No,' declared Wallace. 'I will not even give you £100. They belong to England, and to England they will be returned for nothing.'

Luis de Correa shrugged his shoulders.

'It is ended then,' he remarked. 'I suppose you will call the police, and England will no more see the plans. It is a pity. Will you take some refreshment, señor?'

'No, thanks.'

At that moment there came the sound of a commotion outside. The crook looked a trifle startled, but Wallace merely smiled.

'It is my assistants,' he explained. 'I told them to come to me after half an hour. I suppose your servant is endeavouring to prevent their entrance.'

The handsome Spaniard sat as though speculating a moment; then rose from his chair.

'Since it is your wish that they should join you,' he said, 'I will bring them to you.'

Sir Leonard's eyes gleamed, and de Correa caught the look, promptly misunderstanding it.

'You think I will take the opportunity to escape?' he surmised. 'You are wrong, señor. You have my word that I will return and bring your men with me.'

Wallace slightly inclined his head.

'I accept your word,' he stated gravely.

Luis de Correa went out. He found Lalére and Kendal arguing with his manservant, and invited them to enter. They promptly accepted the invitation.

'Another has gone to the back,' said the Italian menial sullenly.

'Then he also shall be admitted,' was his master's reply.

Asking the newcomers to wait, he hurried to the rear of the house, and brought in Digby, who was becoming exasperated by the uncompromising refusal of a woman servant to let him enter. They joined Sir Leonard in the salon. He was still occupying his seat, but rose when they entered.

'We will return to Capri,' he announced. 'I am sorry, de Correa, that you refuse to listen to reason. Perhaps you will change your mind?'

'I will change my mind for £75,000, señor – no less,' was the reply.

Wallace turned to the others.

'Come on,' he said. 'We can do no good by staying here.'

Lalére and Digby looked at him inquiringly, Kendal began to ask a question, but thought better of it.

'And the police?' asked de Correa.

'I have come to the conclusion that I can do no good by calling in the police – yet,' replied Sir Leonard. 'It is a great pity that you have even caused me to think of such a step. You would be a very decent fellow to know, de Correa, if you were not a crook.'

'I am myself tired of the profession,' admitted the Spaniard. 'It was my intention to settle down here, if I were permitted.'

'There would be nothing to prevent you, if you had handed back the plans. It would also have been a gesture proving you really intended to live honestly in future.'

'It must remain my final coup as a crook,' laughed de Correa.

He accompanied his unwelcome guests to the door, and watched them walk down the path. There was a puzzled frown on his face.

'He has some scheme in his head,' he muttered in his own language, 'otherwise he would not have gone so easily. I wonder what it is!'

He returned to the salon deeply thoughtful; then, with true Southern gaiety, smiled and shrugged his shoulders.

'What does it matter?' he exclaimed. 'I have the plans. He little knew that, all the time he was sitting with me, they were right under his nose.'

Closing the door he walked across to the piano, lightly humming a tune, and lifted the lid. He then bent over the top, and stretched his arm inside. The next moment his face had paled, and his song changed to a string of startled oaths. Drawing out a small slip of paper, that looked as though it had been torn from a notebook, he gazed at it with incredulous eyes, and slowly and bitterly read:

> *You should not be over-confident. You thought the interior of the piano was the last place I would search. It was the first, because you took the unnecessary trouble of closing the lid when I entered the room. I thought I should have been compelled to use force. I am delighted you prevented that by going out to my friends, thus enabling me to help myself without opposition.*
>
> *Goodbye.*

NEXT IN THE SERIES

GET WALLACE

Sir Leonard Wallace, the famous chief of the Secret Service, finds that the peace of Europe is threatened by a gang engaged in the theft and sale of national secrets. Wallace gets busy, and is assisted by the gang-leader's own fear of him and his anxiety to get the Englishman into his power.

Wallace's investigations, his startling discoveries and his escapes from death make this one of the most exciting books in Alexander Wilson's espionage thriller series.